The Search for the Dice Man

The Search for the Dice Man

LUKE RHINEHART

HarperCollins*Publishers*

HarperCollins*Publishers*
77–85 Fulham Palace Road,
Hammersmith, London W6 8JB

Published by HarperCollins*Publishers* 1993
1 3 5 7 9 8 6 4 2

A catalogue record for this book
is available from the British Library

ISBN 0 00 223937 X

Typeset in Trump Mediaeval at The Spartan Press Ltd,
Lymington, Hants

Printed in Great Britain by
Hartnolls Ltd., Bodmin, Cornwall

Accident is the creator of life.

Charles Darwin

Life is at best a tenuous and hazardous enterprise, but mankind's puny efforts to protect himself from its instability and randomness seem worse than futile. It appears the best course is simply chancing it.

Emerson

It is necessary to resign from the human race – with a forged signature, of course.

Luke

Preface

You don't know about me unless you've read a book by the name of *The Dice Man*, but no matter. That book was made by me and I told the truth, mainly. There were things which I stretched, but mainly I told the truth.

In my fashion.

The book was all about how I came to make all my decisions by casting dice, to convert and pervert my psychiatric patients into the dicelife, and to blow my previous life to smithereens.

Now the way that book winds up is in the middle of a sentence, with me dangling on a vine over a cliff. That was in the seventies.

This book you're browsing through now doesn't pick up the story then. It skips a bit – about twenty years. It's mostly about my son Larry and his quest to locate me and give me a piece of his mind. He runs into a lot of my friends and followers and gets a little confused. He tells some of the story himself and I tell some, and to keep the intellectual reader awake, we've thrown in some excerpts from my journals. It's a good read.

Luke Rhinehart

Second Preface

The man is an incorrigible liar. He and his followers are utterly untrustworthy.

Larry Rhinehart

— *1* —

I might never have gone on a quest for my father if it hadn't been for an unexpectedly light rain in Iowa. I was long three hundred futures contracts of December wheat based on a forecast of torrential rains in the Midwest. I expected the heavy rains to ruin the harvest and raise the price of wheat. Unfortunately, the rains didn't fall mainly in the plain. They fell primarily on Cleveland, Chicago and Detroit, where very little wheat is grown. The price of wheat plummeted the next day and I lost about two million dollars for my clients. My employer called me in for a chat. My clients phoned me for chats. My employees and colleagues avoided me. The only people who phoned or dropped by were people who wanted to shoot me.

I'd lost big money for my clients a few other times, but somehow having to explain that 'I thought it was going to rain harder' was the sort of explanation that incites rather than soothes. And it didn't help matters that the rains that didn't fall mainly in the plains hadn't been my only recent miscalculation. For almost three months I'd been on what is charitably called a losing streak. If my indicators said corn and wheat were going up, corn and wheat immediately changed their minds and took a dive. If I took a long position in the stock market, some unexpected inflation report or mad Iraqi dictator would set stocks spiralling downwards.

For three years I'd been something of a trading hotshot – ever since at the tender age of twenty-five I'd accidentally made a name for myself. I happened to be short several stock market futures on that lovely day in October 1987 when the stock market dropped six hundred points. While all around me friends, colleagues and strangers stood shell-shocked at the monitors watching the value of their stock holdings nosedive, I stood beside them watching myself and my clients grow richer and trying desperately to repress giggles.

In the fickle ways of Wall Street, that day I made my name at Blair,

Battle and Pike (BB&P). At dawn I'd been a mere associate trader, given minimum leeway to dabble at my own ideas for trading. At dusk I was a Vice President and Senior Trader.

Mr Battle, the firm's esteemed leader, knew that he would feel more comfortable being able to tell people that his Senior Trader had been right on that infamous day rather than wrong, so he adroitly changed Senior Traders. In the morning the previous Chief Trader, Vic Lissome, had been king and I merely a peon. In the evening Vic was sitting blank-eyed in a local pub wondering how the market could have clobbered him so badly, and I was humbly thanking Mr Battle for his confidence – and trying desperately to remember why I'd decided to go short those futures.

And from then until the summer of 1990 I'd been a consistent winner, but in the last few months I'd begun to lose money. So when my father began to intrude again into my life after a fifteen-year absence, it came at a time when I was in a vulnerable position – financially, socially and emotionally.

My troubles began when I arrived back at the office after lunch. On a Friday afternoon in September, trading tended to be on the slow side, and this Friday was no exception. Jeff Cannister, a short, dynamic fireplug of a man who always greeted me with shades of nervousness ranging from nail-biting tension to total panic, announced that gold had gone down over a dollar and a half in the ninety minutes I'd been gone. Jeff always managed to report such market movements as if my personal absence had led to the fall in gold – or the fall in the yen, etc. – and that had I stayed in my office staring at my monitor I'd have held up the price and saved the firm money.

With Jeff tailing along behind, I continued to stride through the mass of open cubicles at which brokers and traders sat in various states of controlled frenzy. I was aware of how incongruous the two of us were, my tall and lanky frame towering over the squat Jeff so that backbiters, as I knew, sometimes referred to us as 'Mutt and Jeff'.

So gold had fallen slightly when I thought it was about to rise; at least it hadn't fallen through the floor, as wheat had done the week before.

'Any news to cause it?' I asked Jeff.

'Nothing I saw,' said Jeff. Despite his thick solidity, Jeff was totally unfit for the traumas involved in making and losing large sums of money in short periods of time. Still, he was good at what we did and I was happy having him as an associate trader – until he burned out, got hooked on coke, discovered religion or ceased to sleep. Then he'd have to be pensioned off – at the age of twenty-nine, probably.

'The grains are rallying now, especially beans,' announced Jeff gloomily – as if all over the country corn and wheat and soybeans were bursting upwards in a personal effort to thwart Jeff and his firm.

'Just maintain our stops and let me know if they get hit,' I said, flinging my suit jacket over the back of a computer monitor and throwing myself into my swivel desk chair.

As Jeff left I began examining my main monitor, which had quotes on all the stocks, bonds and futures I was actively trading. My phone line buzzed.

'Yes?' I said.

'Hi, darling, I miss you,' came the lovely voice of my fiancée, Honoria, who also happened to be the daughter of the head of the firm, Mr Battle. Oh, I was a winner in those days.

'Hi, sweetheart,' I said, leaning back in my chair and smiling.

'Daddy's house guests this week are two inscrutable Japanese bankers, one of them with a conspicuous interest in sex. When the tall one first met me he was masterful and flirtatious and eyeing all the more protuberant parts of my anatomy, but when he learned I was a VP at Salomon Brothers and engaged to you he lost interest and spent the day with an old issue of *Playboy*.'

'Say,' I interjected, 'what are two Japanese bankers doing as Mr Battle's guests, anyway?'

'I asked Daddy that and he was strangely secretive. I think he may want them to invest in the firm.'

'Not likely unless they actually buy him out. He's not thinking of selling, is he!?' I added with a brief flash of panic.

'Of course not, dear. He's grooming you to become head of the firm as soon as he retires at the age of ninety-nine.'

I frowned at the thought of Mr Battle's longevity. 'You know,' I said, 'I'd just as soon not see any more than I have to of your father and these Japanese this weekend. Maybe we can spend the day on my sailboat.'

'No, no sailing, dear. When I want to be bored and seasick at the same time I'll let you know.'

'Oh, yeah, right.' Honoria only liked water that was as flat and predictable as concrete.

'However, we can take a walk down to the river. When are you coming?'

'On the early train tomorrow morning. And I'm really looking forward to being with you this weekend.'

'Me too, darling. Oh, oh, big call coming in, have to say bye-bye. I miss your cock.'

And she hung up.

Her abruptness was typical. She enjoyed wealth and style, but liked to mask her enjoyment by sudden small eccentric acts of rebellion which made her seem detached and cynical. She was really a sexually conservative woman, and her saying that she missed my cock was one of her tiny acts to *épater les bourgeois*. When we were actually making love she somehow rarely seemed to notice my cock.

After I replaced the phone I let my gaze wander to the photograph of Honoria and myself on the bookshelf beyond my desk and complacently admired the handsome couple we made: me tall, dark and broodingly good-looking – a sort of gangly Richard Gere; she slender, blonde, nicely proportioned, exquisitely coiffed, flawlessly complected, and rich – an elegant Cybill Shepherd.

From the first time I met her, about a year earlier, I loved being with her, loved exchanging Wall Street gossip and admiring each other's trading coups, loved telling people we were going to get married, loved calculating our yearly income. A check of all the technical and fundamental indicators rated Honoria triple-A – a definite 'buy'. I knew that I, a poor orphaned nobody, was lucky to be where I was, if only I didn't blow it.

Another incoming call.

'Mr Potter on the line,' said Miss Claybell, my secretary. 'I believe he wants to talk to you about his investment in the BBP 21st Century Futures Fund.'

'I'll bet he does,' I said. 'Put him on.'

The BBP 21st Century Futures Fund was my personal brainchild, a mass of money – currently about eighteen million dollars – which we invested in various futures markets. The fund was unique in that we guaranteed a return of at least 2 per cent, even if the fund's value shrank and showed a loss. In effect, the company was promising to absorb any losses that the futures trading would show over a one-year period. This unique gimmick made the selling of a futures fund to conservative investors much easier. After all, how many investments – other than treasury bills and bonds – were guaranteed against loss? And the BBP Futures Fund promised it might return anywhere between 15 and 50 per cent per year. Since its inception two years earlier, money had come pouring into the fund, money from both speculators and more conservative investors like Mr Potter. And the fund's value had increased about 32 per cent a year. I had every right to be proud. Except for the last three months.

'Hello, Larry Rhinehart speaking,' I said in my dynamo trader voice.

'Ah, yes, Mr Rhinehart,' said the gravelly voice of the filthy-rich Mr Potter. 'Arthur Potter here. I see the net asset value of the fund fell for the third straight week.'

'That's right, sir.' I was tempted to say, 'I purposely let it fall again so we could have a chat,' but knew the irony would be either resented or lost.

'Markets tend to go both up and down,' I continued aloud, 'and our BBP Fund is no exception.'

'Since I put that million in eight weeks ago the value of the fund is down about 7 per cent,' Mr Potter went on. 'If the fund goes bust how do I know – '

'The fund it not going to go bust, Mr Potter. You've seen the record over the full two years. Does it look like the record of someone about to go bust?'

'Those figures could have been fabricated.'

I sighed. The trouble with Wall Street was that since so many people cheated it was hard for an honest man to be trusted.

'Then why haven't we fabricated the figures for the last eight weeks?' I asked. 'If we're cheating, why stop cheating?'

'I don't know,' said Mr Potter. 'Perhaps you're just being clever.'

'Mr Potter, sir,' I said, 'for you to lose your money the firm of Blair, Battle and Pike would have to go bust. You don't seri – '

'Like Drexel, Burnham, Lambert,' said Mr Potter.

With the phone gripped between my right shoulder and ear, I snapped a wooden pencil in two and resisted the urge to throw the fragments across the room.

'Normally, as you know,' I answered coldly, 'we ask clients to commit their funds for one full year. If you wish to withdraw your money I'll personally recommend we make an exception, but you'll have to take your 7 per cent loss. If you want your guaranteed 2 per cent profit you'll have to wait the full year.'

The silence on the other end of the line made me know I'd scored a direct hit.

'Mmmm,' said Mr Potter, and within thirty seconds he had hung up, having indicated he wanted to stay in the fund.

I finally smiled and dropped the two pieces of pencil into the metal waste-paper bin. The other thing that made the BBP Fund unique was that BBP, in return for guaranteeing the investors against losses, was taking one-third of the investors' profits, the highest profit percentage in the industry.

I tipped back in my swivel chair and felt a little angry at Potter and his ilk. No one seemed to appreciate what I'd accomplished since October 1987.

Up until that month – all through the 1980s – BB&P had made money the way most firms did – the old-fashioned way: by doing nothing. That is, they bought and sold stocks for other people and themselves, using all sorts of interesting theories or no theories at all, and despite all their efforts or lack thereof they made money.

For most of the eighties if you had money you made money. You bought a condominium – you were clever. You bought a stock, any stock, you were a genius. You bought a house, any house, you were sharp. It was an era when rich dumb guys finished first and richer dumb guys finished even firster.

Until October 1987, anyway. Then a funny thing happened. Almost everyone who for at least five years had been a genius was suddenly in one calamitous day a jerk. Seldom in human history have so many bright wealthy men awakened in just one day to discover such an unambiguous truth: that they were neither so bright nor so wealthy. Their clever condominiums became rather quickly empty and unsellable. Their genius junk bonds became ungenial junk bondage.

We humans don't take kindly to such awakenings. I suppose that when you lose several trillion dollars in one day you can be pardoned for not saying the obvious: all the wisdom of the previous five years had just been normal human stupidity. I'd happened to bet right on that horrible day but later I'd come to wonder whether if I'd been more mature and less cocky I might have examined 19 October 1987 a lot more carefully. Its most obvious lesson, I, like everyone else, never learned: what the market does on any given day may bear no resemblance to what it has ever done before.

Then my secretary marched into the room without buzzing. Miss Claybell was a chubby middle-aged woman who consistently wore clothing that looked as if it had been collected from church bazaars, applied too much make-up and never had an original thought. However, she was everything I wanted in a secretary – reasonable, unemotional, efficient, obedient and totally dedicated. Her very unemotional efficiency meant, however, that her slipping into my inner office unannounced must mean something was up.

'There are two gentlemen to see you,' she announced. 'They say they're FBI agents.'

2

At first I felt nothing; I just stared back at her, tipped forward in my chair and lowered my arms from behind my head.

'FBI agents?' I echoed vaguely.

'They won't say why they want to question you.'

I looked up at Miss Claybell neutrally, but with my heart now pumping panic and my mind desperately searching for the crime I must have committed. But since I was compulsively honest in all Wall Street financial dealings, my mind was filled with unpaid parking tickets, with a nineteen-year-old Goldman Sachs broker trainee I had seduced and abandoned, a 1987 income tax return that contained several creative deductions.

'Should I show them in?' Miss Claybell asked, watching me with that bland composure that made everyone else at Blair, Battle and Pike seem slightly panicky.

I came slowly to my feet, still staring at her uncertainly. I had an urge to pace, but managed to hold my feet to the floor, although my upper body rocked back and forth and my right hand was wrestling with pocket change.

'Yes,' I managed. But as Miss Claybell turned to leave I realized a futures trader being questioned by federal agents was bound to arouse a lot of not totally favourable conjecture.

'And I want you to be present,' I added.

She hesitated, nodded, and then, leaving the door open, disappeared.

The two men who soon entered looked like slightly unsuccessful businessmen who'd come to try to sell me some penny stocks or a supplemental health insurance policy. They introduced themselves as Hayes and Macavoy. They sat down stiffly in the two extra chairs while Miss Claybell, memo pad in hand, stood unobtrusively – or as unobtrusively as someone who dressed like Queen Victoria could – near the door, which she gently closed.

The one called Hayes, a hollow-cheeked man in need of a shave, glanced briefly back at her.

'We're here to question just you, Mr Rhinehart,' he said. 'Your secretary can go.'

'She's staying,' I countered quickly. 'I want a written record of our conversation.'

Hayes looked so expressionlessly at me that it was like looking at a computer screen whose language I didn't know.

'Have it your way,' Hayes said. After the briefest of glances at Macavoy he cleared his throat and continued. 'Is Luke Rhinehart your father?'

That stopped me cold. Parking tickets, male chauvinism and creative IRS deductions all disappeared, and I was left with the image of the big smiling father I'd barely known.

'*Was* my father,' I said.

Hayes stared hard.

'You believe your father is dead?' he asked.

'No, I mean Luke Rhinehart was my father until he deserted his family over fifteen years ago.'

'I see,' said Hayes. 'And do you know where he is now?'

'No.'

'When did you last speak to him?' Macavoy suddenly interjected. He was a slender man too, but taller, gangling, younger than Hayes. He looked like a prematurely aged teenage hoopster.

'Ten years ago,' I answered.

'What was the occasion?'

'My mother . . . had been killed in a car accident a week earlier,' I said as calmly as I could. 'He called to ask if my sister and I wanted to come live with him.'

Hayes and Macavoy waited for me to go on.

'Well?' Hayes finally asked.

'It was the first and only contact I'd had with him since he'd disappeared five years before. I told him to go to hell.'

Hayes blinked once and then nodded.

'And you've had no contact with him since?' he asked.

'None.'

'But you've had contact with his followers.'

'They've occasionally harassed me, if that's what you mean,' I said irritably.

'How have they harassed you?'

'By showing up. By telling me how my father has transformed their lives. Or ruined their lives. By being assholes.'

Macavoy coughed.

'Didn't any of them ever bring you a message from your father?'

'No.'

'Or told you some of the marvellous things your father is doing?' There was a sarcastic bite in the question.

'Look,' I snapped, abruptly standing. 'I really don't want to talk about this. How can you possibly be interested in pursuing my father for the stupid things he did fifteen or twenty years ago?'

Hayes looked at me a moment and then exchanged glances with Macavoy.

'We're not interested in what your father did twenty years ago,' he finally said. 'We're interested in what he's doing right now.'

I hesitated.

'Right . . . now!?' I managed.

'Yes.'

'And . . . what do you think he's doing . . . right now?' I asked, sinking slowly back down into my chair.

'We can't go into that,' said Macavoy. 'Let me ask you this: has anyone been acting strangely around you lately?'

I stared at him a moment and then laughed.

'Everyone. All the time. What else is new?'

'I mean has anyone new come into your life that struck you as odd?' the gangly hoopster persisted.

'No,' I said irritably. 'What are you driving at?'

'We have reason to believe that your father may try to get in touch with you,' said Hayes.

'I don't know what you're talking about.'

'Good,' said Hayes. He stood. 'But when you do, we want you to get in touch with us. Immediately.' He reached across the desk and handed me a card.

'May I ask why my father, after all these years, might now want to get in touch with me?'

Macavoy too now rose.

'He's your dice daddy,' Hayes said. 'Maybe the dice will tell him to.'

3

His father – his father was still alive somewhere.

After everyone had left the office, Larry sat frozen in his chair, trying to control the trembling in his hands, his lips, even his gut. The man whose betrayal had poisoned his life was now injecting some new infection into its present flow.

A successful psychiatrist, in the late sixties Luke had thought he'd discovered the cure for human misery: injecting chance systematically into one's life. He thought he could break down the normal stuck-in-the-mud personality and thus expand human experience, role-playing, and creativity. He embarked on the mad enterprise of trying to explore the malleability and multiplicity of the human soul. He introduced himself and his patients to diceliving – the making of life decisions by casting dice. His theory was that humans tended to get stuck in trying to live with one set of beliefs, attitudes and behaviour – one self – when the healthy human would be better off feeling free to be many selves, with many inconsistent attitudes and behaviours.

In dice therapy he encouraged his patients to create a variety of optional actions or roles, and let the dice choose their behaviour for a given hour, day or week. The goal was to break down the usual single stuck self and discover new habits, loves and lives.

Of course in successfully attacking his own personality, Luke broke up his family, ruined his professional standing, alienated friends, and broke enough laws to attract numerous law-enforcement agencies.

He also became somewhat famous – or notorious, dice therapy and diceliving becoming something of a fad in the early seventies. Luke became a minor cult figure like Timothy Leary or Ram Dass, seeming to symbolize the rejection of society's traditional values in favour of individual creativity and multiplicity. By jumping bail after his trial and disappearing from sight, he gave his life a certain romantic aura lacking in other counterculture figures who were raking in dollars on the lecture circuit, but the aura faded as his disappearance seemed increasingly final. Total absence is a difficult state to keep exciting.

As he sat in the office that day trying to steady his hand on the flat desktop, Larry remembered bitterly that as an eight-year-old child he had liked his father's dice games, both for their own sake and for Luke's playing them with him. He'd once cast a fat red die and seen it choose the option that he go fight a bully who'd been hassling him for months. He remembered knocking the snotnose down, and never having any trouble with him again. For a week, anyway, the event had made him a believer in the dice.

Another afternoon he'd let the dice continually choose in which direction he walk and, giggling, he kept ending up with his nose against some building's walls.

But his father had become increasingly erratic. He remembered one morning Luke's eating his eggs with his fingers and grunting like some animal, the eggs mostly not making it into his mouth, he and his sister giggling, Larry's mother in the background silently glaring. And he remembered his father, who never bought a Christmas present for anyone, unexpectedly bringing home half a dozen presents to both him and his sister, including a gigantic five-foot-high bear that he'd loved for years. And of Luke's striding around their apartment all one weekend, declaring in stentorian tones, like some Shakespearean actor, lines which were probably muddled quotations from plays somehow appropriate to what was happening.

But most of his memories of that time were less pleasant – of the tense parental silences, of his mother always shouting at his father and her fury when she caught Larry using the dice, shouting that if she ever caught him doing that again she'd send him to a foster home.

And when Luke finally disappeared without a word, Larry came to feel it was the dice themselves that had made him leave and ruined Larry's life – hence his bitterness against not only his father but against everything his father had stood for.

Nevertheless, there were times when he wished he'd accepted Luke's offer to take him in after his mother's death, since from that moment on he'd been on his own and broke. He'd had to work full-time every summer and part-time during all his college years, while most of his classmates were apparently free to loaf. In reaction against his father he'd come to believe passionately in the value of control, order and reason. His psychiatrists pointed out that making a religion of order was a dramatic rejection of his father's interest in irrationality and chance, and that he'd even chosen his profession in reaction against his father. One of the more notorious features of Luke's diceliving had been his followers' remarkable success at picking profitable stocks and bonds using the dice. At Wharton Business School Larry had determined to prove the value of reason and research over his father's bastard deity, Chance.

But in the last five years of conquering chance with his trend lines, resistance areas, momentum figures, stochastics, point and figure charts and Eliot Waves, how often some chance event would send a market reeling in a direction contrary to that predicted by all his indicators! And how annoying that, even without any measurable chance event, markets somehow refused to perform as all his technical indicators forecast they would.

Despite Larry trying to picture his father before he'd taken up his quixotic quest for the cure to human misery, he had absolutely no memories of him before the age of eight. That was a sure sign of repression, Dr Bickers had assured him. He groaned at the thought of having to talk to Dr Bickers about this FBI visit: how the man would smirk at this archetypal return of the father. And he grimaced too at realizing that despite his dislike of Dr Bickers he seemed to be consulting psychotherapists almost as often as his father used to consult the dice. He ought to bill his father.

Over the years he'd think he was making progress, announce to friends that he'd finally made a key breakthrough, and then a few weeks later tell these same friends that his therapist was a charlatan – and possibly a secret diceperson.

His reveries were abruptly interrupted by an official buzz from Miss Claybell: Mr Battle wanted to see him in his office immediately.

Ah, yes. Nothing like a visit from the FBI to make a trader's boss want to have a chat.

4

Mr Battle's being both the head of the firm as well as Honoria's father meant that his every word, sigh and stare had significance for me far beyond its merit. Every time I had a losing trade it not only meant a few fewer digits in the asset column, but also that my son-in-law rating went down several points. Rains failing to fall mainly in the plains constituted not merely a small financial disaster, but also a threat to my marriage, a marriage I devoutly and greedily desired. And there'd been far too many rains not in the plains recently.

When I neared the old man's cavernous office I veered off into the executives' men's room to do a bit of grooming. Mr Battle was a stickler for appearances. A trader with shirt unbuttoned, tie and hair askew was a man communicating not concentration and busy-ness, but rather a state of being overwhelmed. Since most traders *were* overwhelmed, such normal grooming was elsewhere the norm, but not at BB&P. Mr Battle wanted *his* traders all to look as if they'd just emerged from a men's fashion ad in the Sunday *New York Times* magazine section – cool, elegant and unflustered – million-dollar profits something they pulled off between aperitifs.

'A tie is a symbol,' he'd explained to me once when he'd caught me alone in my office with my tie off. 'A symbol of caring about power. If it doesn't always represent actual membership in the successful levels of society, it at least represents the wish to do so. Failure to wear a tie represents either rebellion against or indifference to everything that counts.'

'But I'm alone in here, sir,' I'd protested.

'*God* sees,' he said.

Mr Battle had been one of the three founding members of the firm back in 1977, Blair having the money, Pike being the brainy trader, and Mr Battle contributing a little money, his high social standing and extensive social and financial connections. Blair and Pike had

had the goodness to die over the next decade, leaving Mr Battle as majority owner and de facto boss. He was legendary for his ability to charm the rich into sharing their wealth with BB&P ('investing'), but hopelessly out of his depth in any intricate financial dealings. As long as I made money for BB&P and seemed a socially acceptable and presentable young man, I'd be in his favour. If ever I began to lose money for the firm or, even worse, turned out to be black or Jewish or the son of mongoloids, I'd be dropped with peremptory swiftness.

As I stared into the mirror to straighten my tie and brush my hair, I knew that I was not cool, would never be elegant and was as flustered as I ever got, since the thing that really flustered me was my damn father.

'Seeing the chief honcho, huh?' a voice said from behind me.

Changing the angle of my vision I spotted in the mirror the lugubrious face of Vic Lissome, the onetime Chief Trader I'd replaced three years earlier. Vic was seated in an open cubicle, fully clothed, reading the *National Inquirer*, a periodical much favoured by traders. Reading it kept them in touch 'with the pulse of the nation', said Vic, although I felt it kept them in touch primarily with three-headed dogs and childbearing men.

'Yeah,' I replied. Many people at BB&P assumed that I was a suck artist who'd somehow managed to wrap Mr Battle around my little finger, when in fact I usually lived in mortal terror of Mr Battle. I felt that everything I'd achieved had been achieved *despite* Mr Battle's preferences rather than because of them.

'You look like shit,' said Vic helpfully from his cubicle hideaway. 'You look like you just got hit with a Saddam Hussein.'

Ever since that August day two months earlier when Saddam Hussein had unexpectedly sent his troops into Kuwait to conquer six infantrymen and a mentally ill housewife (the only documented resisters) and thus sent various futures markets reeling off in new directions, any unexpected news development had been called, generically, a Saddam Hussein. This 'in' argot would last until the next notable Saddam Hussein.

'Actually it's more a minor domestic problem,' I said, not wanting to have to talk to Vic about the failure of the rains.

'Domestic?' said Vic. 'You mean the old fart is not too happy with your porking his daughter?'

'I got to go, Vic,' I said, moving quickly to the door. 'A man who is late is a man who is not there.'

This last line was not my own but a famous quotation from Mr Battle, a man noted for pithy sayings of questionable value.

'Ah, Rhinehart!' he said from behind his desk, a gigantic monstrosity of glass and metal tubing that closely resembled a glass pingpong table without the net. He was a large, good-looking man with beefsteak jowls and he dressed with immaculately tailored dignity. With his magnificent sweep of bushy hair nicely streaked with grey, he usually looked as if he was posing for an ad for some exotic liqueur.

'What's this about the FBI raiding your office?' he went on.

'Raiding my office?' I echoed uneasily. 'It wasn't anything like that.'

'One FBI agent talking to someone is an inquiry,' countered Mr Battle, spouting one of his aphorisms. 'Two agents is a raid.'

'Yes, sir,' I said, stopping to stand in front of the desk like a pupil before his principal.

'Exactly. Now tell me all about it. I believe in confronting unpleasantness immediately and wrestling it to the ground.'

'There, uh, was no, *is* no unpleasantness. The FBI was making an inquiry about someone I haven't seen in more than fifteen years. I couldn't help them and they left.'

'Really!?' exclaimed Mr Battle, scrutinizing me as if wondering if I'd really thought he'd swallow that one. 'Fifteen years . . . It must have been a pretty horrendous crime. Who was it, some serial killer?'

'They didn't say why they were seeking the man,' I said. 'They were vague and ambiguous. But I can assure you the whole thing has nothing to do with me or my work here at BB&P.'

Mr Battle continued to gaze at me as if wondering why I was telling all these lies.

'And who is this man the FBI is so curious about that they seek out people who haven't seen him in fifteen years?'

Oh, Jesus. Here it comes. Everything I'd been trying to hide.

'Uh, a relative, sir. A man who disappeared a long ti – fifteen years ago.'

'A relative!' said Mr Battle. 'That could be distressing. Not a close relative, I hope.'

Oh, Jesus.

'I . . . uh . . . was never close to him.'

'Who is it, an uncle?'

I stared back at Mr Battle numbly.

'My father,' I said.

Mr Battle looked not surprised but confused.

'But your father is dead.'

'Uh, not necessarily.'

'Not necessarily! I distinctly remember when reviewing your personnel file a few months ago that both your parents were deceased!'

'Uh, yes, sir. My mother was killed in an auto accident and my father hasn't been seen or heard from in – more than a decade. I, uh, assumed that he was dead.'

'And now you discover he is a serial killer!?'

'No, no, I'm sure he's not – the FBI didn't say why they wanted to contact him.'

'Contact him!' Mr Battle exclaimed, now sitting ramrod-straight in his chair and glaring at me. 'Arrest him, you mean! My God, man, you must have some idea why they're looking for him!?'

'I really don't!' I answered, feeling myself squirming. 'Years ago – almost twenty years ago – he got in some trouble with the FCC for disrupting a television programme and the unauthorized release of mental patients, and, uh, a few other matters. But the FBI indicated they wished to see him now about something else.'

Mr Battle, still eyeing me, rose from his chair and moved slowly forward with the soft tread of a predator about to pounce on its prey before the hypnotic spell was broken.

'This is a serious business, my boy,' he said.

'Yes – I mean no. I'm sure my father hasn't done anything serious. I think they just wanted to talk to him about something.'

'Nonsense,' said Mr Battle, coming to a halt three feet away and gazing at me again with that sceptical-physician stare that implied he was still seeking the exact nature of my fatal illness. 'The FBI doesn't send two men to question a son who hasn't seen his father in fifteen years because they only want to talk to the man.'

Mr Battle stared on another moment and then turned away with a sigh.

'This won't do, Larry, won't do,' he said as he slowly returned around the pingpong table to his seat behind it. 'I can't have my daughter marrying the son of someone on the FBI's "most wanted" list.' With another sigh he sat down and swung around to face me.

'I want her to marry the son of a man who is respectably deceased. I think you may tell people that this FBI visit was to ask you about a former employee. Do you understand?'

'I think I do.'

'It's safe to say it's in your interest to see that your father stays boringly buried.'

'I agree, but suppose – '

'Your personnel file states that your father is no longer alive,' Mr Battle said, beginning to shuffle some papers on his desk. 'Let us be content with the official truth.'

He then rang for his secretary and turned to gaze at the monitor on his desk – the interview was over. Until I could prove otherwise, my father would probably remain, in Mr Battle's mind, a corpse and a mass murderer.

5

Larry's session later that day with Dr Bickers began with Larry's claiming that when he began to lose money in his trading it made him feel as if his whole life was getting out of control, and he wanted to be able to control this anxiety with something other than tranquillizers.

Dr Bickers, ignoring Larry's usual complaint, asked why he was so upset this afternoon. Only then did Larry briefly mention the FBI visit to his office that morning.

Dr Bickers, scrunched in his chair like a shrivelled potato, rarely made more than two or three explicit comments during an entire hour and was content now to revert to his traditional commentary.

'Mmmmm,' he said.

'No, no,' Larry said irritably. 'After these months now with you I don't think my problems have anything to do with my father.'

As Dr Bickers reverted to his usual silence, Larry leaned back against the back of the deep leather chair he was sitting in, and with the memory of the damned FBI visit, felt his irritation rise.

'Not that it's been easy,' he said, trying to give his voice a soft confidence he wasn't exactly feeling.

'After all, he deserted me when I was barely twelve, disappeared to go off and lead his own mad life with no thoughts for me or my mother or sister. As you know, for a while I let that act poison me just a bit, made me resent traits he had, mentions of him, every aspect of him that I noticed in myself . . . But thanks to these sessions together, I really don't think that he's my problem any more. It's the trading losses.'

Larry straightened himself in his sitting position and glanced at Dr Bickers, who was peering up at him expressionlessly, a wrinkled turtle peering at a passer-by.

'Hey, it's not easy. I have to endure constant reminders of his life and what it stood for – not only the physical garbage of the book he wrote and articles about him, but human garbage too – people showing up and telling me how much they adored him or hated him . . . Me throwing them out after the first faint words of praise.'

Larry sighed.

'It's been hard,' he went on, 'but I've been toughened by it. By committing myself to order and reason I think I've managed to pretty much erase his presence from my life. Sitting here today I can say with some confidence that . . . that he's not an important factor in my life.'

'Mmmmmm,' said Dr Bickers' voice from off to one side. It was his third major contribution to the day's session. Agreement? Question? Larry was so used to rambling on he barely paused to wonder.

'I suppose some sons might have succumbed to the temptation to follow in their father's footsteps,' he went on. 'But not me. I've gone the opposite way. And hey, look, I'm rich, successful, well adjusted – except for these recent nightmares about being caught naked, too many calls and going bankrupt – and in five months I'll be marrying Honoria! A beautiful woman who shares all my interests and – so I really can't complain, despite my recent losses and having a father who betrayed and deserted me and will always stand as a symbol of irresponsibility.'

'Mmmmmmm,' said Dr Bickers firmly.

Larry stood up and began to pace.

'. . . A man who stands for all that's perverse in human nature, a man who was willing to destroy everything to pursue his hare-brained theory, a theory that defies all that is sacred, dignified, restrained and decent in life, a man who was mad, besotted with sick sexual salaciousness, a slave to inconsistency, a man who couldn't bother to bring up a son, a poor helpless child who worshipped him, but who this madman tempted into adoration and then abandoned for fifteen years, fifteen terrible, hateful monstrous abandoned years that I had to live through until this moment when I am . . . uh . . . at last . . . at last . . . uh . . . cured.'

White-faced, breathing heavily and with fists clenched, Larry stopped pacing and turned to face Dr Bickers.

Dr Bickers, his chin lowered toward his chest, glanced up over his rimless glasses.

'Mmmmmm,' he suggested.

'Hubie's Tavern' was the local hangout for futures traders, and I headed there automatically after fleeing my unsatisfactory session with Bickers. Bond traders had a more elegant hangout (their 'drinking establishment') a few blocks down; stock brokers had a half dozen local pubs they indulged in; the clerks had their watering hole; presumably, the custodians had theirs too.

Since Hubie's was home to two or three dozen young men (futures traders were mostly young men – there being no such thing as an old futures trader), all of whom considered themselves brilliant and daring, the tavern was considered lively and trendy. Actually it was noisy, crowded, smelly, dark and undistinguished, but since none of us ever looked at anything or anyone except each other and the occasional beautiful woman who made an appearance (a professional in every sense of the word), we thought it was terrific.

When I arrived I was immediately hailed by Brad Burner from a corner table and unthinkingly traipsed over. I didn't usually join the daily after-hours parade to Hubie's and had forgotten that I'd be forced to talk to people. Only as I was lowering myself into a chair did I notice that the other people in the booth were Jeff and Vic Lissome.

'We *know* it's been a bad day when Larry's driven to drink,' commented Brad, who was Vice President in charge of all trading and thus my only superior other than Mr Battle himself. Brad was a big, bluff man, good-looking in a rugged sort of way, who nevertheless wore clothes even more elegantly tailored than those of Mr Battle.

I slid in beside him.

'Not a bad day at all,' I said. 'Just couldn't resist seeing more of you guys.'

'I think he's forgetting about his two visitors today,' said Vic, who as usual was himself quite far along the path of forgetfulness. 'You guys must be in even worse shape than I thought.'

'We didn't do bad,' said Jeff. 'Especially compared to *last* week.' Jeff had an innocence that often meant that no secret and no loss was ever long kept from the curious public at Hubie's – or anywhere else Jeff went.

'What's this about visitors?' asked Brad. 'We getting some new clients?'

'Yeah, tell us, Larry,' said Vic. 'How many shares of the BB&P Fund did the FBI order?'

'FBI!?' echoed Brad. Both he and Jeff looked at me in astonishment.

'Yeah,' I said casually. 'They're investigating the largest case of insider trading in history and have reason to believe Jeff's involved.'

Jeff went so pale and looked so terrified that all three of us burst out into raucous laughter.

'So what was it all about?' Brad asked after we had all quieted down, although Jeff was as pale as before.

'They wanted to find someone I knew once,' I answered as casually as I could. 'I couldn't help them. It had nothing to do with finances.'

'Are you sure!?' asked Jeff, as if his life depended on it.

'I'm sure. And if we are involved in massive insider trading I sure as hell wish it would show up more on the bottom line.'

'Yeah,' said Brad, grinning broadly. 'Another few months like you've been having and we'll have to get Vic back in there, right, Vic?'

'He can have the fuckin' job,' said Vic, snorting into his now empty glass. 'It's all a fuckin' fake anyhow.'

'True,' said Brad, still grinning at me. 'But some of us are better at faking it than others.'

I spent the weekend, as I often had during the summer, at the Battle mansion on a hill overlooking the Hudson River in upstate New York. The place was originally built by the financier Jay Gould as an early-twentieth-century rural retreat. The fact that it had thirty rooms and resembled an eighteenth-century English manor house didn't seem to faze either Mr Gould or Mr Battle, both of whom looked upon the estate as roughing it. After all, trees could be seen, grass, wild animals (rabbits and an occasional deer) and even mountains – the distant Catskills looming across the river in the distance. The fact that they usually viewed these wonders past the heads of the household help waiting on them hand and foot didn't interfere at all with their sense of roughing it.

The mansion was ornate, the grounds gracious, the view of the Hudson River and distant mountains spectacular, and Mr Battle pointed all this out to every new guest and then never noticed any of it again. But someday, I hoped, if I could just stay on the straight and narrow path of upward mobility, it would all be mine!

But as I drove up the winding drive that Saturday morning in a cab from the train station I knew that chance was always trying to upset the applecart of my personal life with the same arbitrary interventions that ruined some of my most scientific trades. Accidental meetings, absurd attractions, arbitrary diseases, suddenly exposed secrets – life had a horrible tendency to undermine the orderly man with sudden chaos. The unexpected appearance of the FBI and my having to confess my father's existence to Mr Battle was a tiny tremor of warning that accident, like death and taxes, was always with us.

Now as the cab slowed to a halt opposite the ornate columns of the formal entrance, and the tall and lugubrious Hawkins came with slow dignity down the steps to greet me, I was both pleased by the opulence and a little depressed by it. I knew that the place would be so crawling with well-dressed people that life would seem as formal as a tea party. Mr Battle even insisted that Honoria and I sleep in separate bedrooms, whether from the illusion that we hadn't yet slept together, or to maintain the façade of Victorianism, I couldn't tell.

I got slowly out of the cab, paid off the cabbie and watched Hawkins pick up my suitcase and lead me up the steps. The 'family', Hawkins announced solemnly, was out back on the patio.

Although my whole march up the ladder of success led to precisely this elegant mansion owned by my boss and future father-in-law, something about it made me feel out of place. What was it? Why didn't I feel comfortable with the people who shared my vision of a life of reason, rapaciousness and riches? Why didn't I care more about the things I was supposed to care about? Why did Brad Burner's enthusiasm for various numbered or named Porsches or BMWs seem so trivial? I owned a Mercedes but only as part of my uniform of success. I honestly couldn't tell the difference between driving my Mercedes and driving a Honda Accord or Chevy Corsica, but knew if I began driving around in a Corsica I would soon be seen as on the way out.

I continued through the huge lower hallway to follow the formal and funereal man in black, then up the long winding stairs towards my guest bedroom. Along the staircase were hung paintings and drawings: a Matisse next to a Norman Rockwell; an oil portrait of a grinning Ronald Reagan next to what looked like a giant Rubens nude.

Why couldn't I appreciate my colleagues' obsession with their clothing, furniture, cars and connoisseurship of art? I myself owned three original oils by a famous avant-garde artist whose name I could never pronounce, but I thought of them like my car and suits – part of my necessary uniform. And I derived less pleasure from looking at my art – or anyone else's – than I did at looking at a sunset over the river. Since I hated spending a cent more than I had to, it pained me considerably to have to pay thousands of dollars for things I didn't really want. Looking at them as necessary business expenses, I deeply resented the IRS for not letting me deduct them from my income tax.

And the subtle differences between suits, sports cars, vacation spots, athletic clubs somehow escaped me. Mr Battle had almost ordered me to quit the Red Rider Athletic Club, pointing out with a subtle shudder that most of the people who belonged to it were athletes.

I had always assumed that I would have to spend time doing what I didn't really like doing in order to become rich and successful so I could then do what I *did* like doing. Instead, I was finding that success consisted of doing a lot of additional things I didn't like doing.

As I turned at the top of the stairs to head down the upper hall I suddenly said: 'What am I doing here, Hawkins?'

'Preparing for lunch, sir,' Hawkins replied without breaking stride.

'Ah, right.'

When Honoria arrived at my room to bring me down to meet the guests I embraced her with a pleased smile. Seeing her dressed with stunning casualness in a pool-blue jumpsuit that showed off her figure, I realized that I'd never caught her off guard: she was always groomed, coiffed, made-up and ready. As I held her my heart didn't leap, but my male vanity felt its usual surge of satisfaction: what a priceless acquisition! And mine! Or soon to be so. I gave her an extra squeeze.

'Is that Jap still on the make for you?' I asked after we'd exchanged a light kiss and were headed down the stairs.

'Oh, yes, last night he came on to me like an eager college sophomore,' she said gaily, linking her arm in mine. 'But today I think he's shifted his interest to Kim.'

'Kim?'

'Yes, you know, that kook cousin of mine whose escapades I've told you about.'

'Oh, her,' I said, looking to see if the Japanese were down in the hallway. 'I thought she moved to the west coast or something.'

'She did. She went there to see some famous guru.'

I vaguely remembered Honoria's telling me about some black sheep of the family who was shamefully interested in things like the I Ching, tarot, nature hikes and nuclear disarmament, and even more shamefully unable to hold a job or accumulate money.

'Oh, yeah,' I said as we headed through the hall towards the patio where some sort of meal was being served.

'But now she's back,' Honoria went on. 'Much to Daddy's disgust. And when she's not chatting with sexless spirits on some astral plane she's often enticing sexually charged bodies on this earthly plane. I think she's already got Akito salivating and – ah, speak of the devil.'

As we moved out on to the patio Mr Battle was standing near a large round table, and past him three figures were making their way up the lawn towards us. As I casually tried to brush down my hair in preparation for meeting them I was puzzled to see Mr Battle frowning at the approaching people as if in disapproval. As we came up beside him he turned to me and whispered fiercely: 'Be brilliant.' And added strangely, 'And ignore the girl.'

The girl. Walking with a jaunty bounce between the two neatly-dressed Japanese bankers and clutching them both firmly by the arms was a lovely young woman whose striking photograph I realized I had noticed once in one of the Battle albums. Dressed with heretical informality in sneakers, jeans and a sweatshirt, she was laughing easily at what the taller and more impressive of the two men had been saying. She had a glowing vitality that immediately made her seem out of place, impolite even, her vibrancy almost resembling that of a woman in heat.

Although the two Japanese were dressed identically in business suits, they were otherwise opposites, the one being tall and broad-shouldered with a thick head of wavy black hair, and the other short, plumpish, grey-haired and bespectacled. When the three grinning newcomers came to a halt near the table, Mr Battle bounded forward with a sudden warm smile.

'Ah, Mr Akito and Mr Namamuri,' he boomed. 'I hope you've had a pleasant outing.'

As he introduced the two men Kim looked at me with such mischievous boldness I worried my trousers were unbuttoned. I nevertheless put on a superficial smile and bowed to Akito's bow and pumped his hand with as much warmth as I could, which wasn't much since Akito had a grip whose vice-like crush implied long hours practising karate or some other fortifying regimen. We exchanged a few brief inanities about the markets and then turned back to the women.

'Don't I even get a "hi", Nori?' asked Kim, and, after the briefest of pauses, the two women embraced, Honoria smiling at Kim as might a mother at a lovable but incorrigible child. 'Nori' was the family nickname for Honoria and a vast improvement it was over the original, but Nori preferred Honoria, especially from her inferiors, which was almost everyone.

Laughing, Kim broke away from Honoria and, ignoring me, seated herself in a patio chair quickly held for her by the good-looking Japanese, Akito.

'Well, Kim,' said Honoria, her blue eyes intense with something, but whether pleasure, interest in her cousin's escapades, or combativeness, I couldn't tell. 'Where have you been?'

'Into New York last night,' Kim said. 'Then here this morning. Then Mr Akito kidnapped me as I arrived and insisted he show me the river.'

From behind her chair Akito smiled easily and, after his older colleague and Mr Battle had settled into chairs, seated himself next to Kim.

'The victim went willingly,' he said in barely accented English. 'It may even have been her idea.'

'Details,' said Kim. 'The point is we had a lovely morning, and – how are you, Uncle?' This last she addressed to Mr Battle, who looked as if he deeply disliked being called 'Uncle', which, I guessed, probably accounted for Kim's using the term.

'I'm fine, Kim,' he said with a scowl. 'I'm fine. I'm glad you've all enjoyed yourselves. Gentlemen, have you had lunch?'

'Miss Castelli introduced us to a most interesting pizza restaurant,' said Akito. 'Part of a chain, as I understand it.' I was impressed that his little half-smile indicated absolutely no suggestion of what he might be thinking about the merits of eating at the local Pizza Hut.

'How are you, Nori?' asked Kim, her wide brown eyes mischievously alert. 'Haven't you got a wedding coming up one of these days?'

'Oh, yes, I think you're right,' said Honoria. 'But in the winter, I believe. I'll have to check my calendar,' she added in a tone of heavy irony.

Kim finally turned her eyes on me, a glance that although little different from the one she'd bestowed on the others, nevertheless sent my heart unexpectedly racing ahead as if a fire alarm had been set off. Although Kim was smiling and her eyes were bright, I, though unaware of it at the time, was glaring at her: I knew chaos when I saw it.

'And you must be Larry,' she said. 'I bet you know the date. Nori says you've got a good head for figures.'

Since my head, if not my eyes, had been gaping at her breasts, which I was sure had been swaying bra-lessly beneath her loose sweatshirt, her statement that I had a good head for figures seemed to be some sort of *double entendre*. I flushed.

'February twenty-eighth,' I managed to answer.

'He wanted the twenty-ninth,' said Honoria, smiling. 'But I pointed out there was no such date.'

While everyone else smiled at this little hit, I felt another burst of annoyance. I knew that the invasion of Kim was a Saddam Hussein: a sudden, unexpected new element which was bound to upset the markets. Chaos had come.

— 8 —

The rest of the day only proved my first intuition was correct. When we ended up playing tennis for an hour and a half Kim continued to be provocative – in all senses of that word. While the rest of us dressed in trim white shorts, blouses, socks and tennis shoes, Kim came out as the feminine equivalent of Andre Agassi: scruffy sneakers, raggedy cut-off blue jeans, and a multicoloured T-shirt that looked like an explosion in a paint factory.

And her playing style was no better. Whereas Honoria and I had competitive spirits of Superbowl quality – she'd been taking lessons from the age of six – Kim played as if she didn't have a care in the world. Honoria and I, partners, fought for every point as if our victory alone would stave off a nuclear holocaust, and Akito played the same way, racing and diving and grunting and grimacing with quite unJapanese passion.

But Kim played as if she were a child at a Sunday picnic, each point a lark. If she missed an easy overhead she smiled and shrugged. If she accidentally hit a woodshot that turned out to be a winner she laughed, not noting that her accidental winner was sending both Honoria and me into the kind of deep depression that normally takes years of therapy to overcome. Kim played hard but didn't seem to distinguish between her winners and her losers. Even Akito, lusting after her with his healthy male appetite, was clearly annoyed at her lack of devotion to beating the crap out of us. He tried to join in her smiles when she smiled and her laughter when she laughed, but his smile came out a grimace and his laughter like a sumo wrestler's grunt.

And I hated the way Kim frolicked around the court in her raggedy shorts and tight T-shirt, her breasts bouncing and swaying and doing all in their power to take my eyes off the ball. She was a few inches shorter than Honoria and more compact, with taut tanned legs that looked as if they belonged on a gymnast. And it also irked me that Akito often seemed as distracted by Kim's swoops and sways of breasts as I was. Chaos.

When it was over, Akito shook hands with us, the winners, with all the grace of his ancestors on the battleship *Missouri* at the end of World War II. But Kim bounded to the net as if greeting long-lost friends, her dark hair wild, sweaty and straggling about her face as if she'd almost drowned. Honoria, who had played twice as hard, although gleaming with perspiration, was nevertheless still as neat and dignified as a monarch greeting commoners at a royal reception.

Then later, when we were all having drinks on the patio, Kim showed up with a sweatshirt emblazoned with the logo 'Losers enjoy more free time', a clear affront to her guardian and all the right-thinking, high-earning people present.

'This Château Borgnini is one of a kind,' Mr Battle announced to one and all, holding up his glass so that the sunlight shimmered through it, giving it a deep purple glow. 'It's so expensive most French people don't even know it exists.'

'It is delightful,' pronounced Akito, with a smile and a slight bow of his head to his host.

'I prefer a cold beer,' said Kim. 'But it does look lovely in these glasses, that I admit.'

'Daddy bought it last spring in Paris,' said Honoria.

'It cost three hundred dollars a bottle,' announced Mr Battle proudly. 'You might give it a decent try.'

'I've always wondered what an eighty-dollar glass of wine would taste like,' said Kim, taking a small sip from a fresh goblet poured for her by Hawkins. She paused. 'And now I know.'

'Wonderful, isn't it?' suggested Mr Battle.

'Yes it is,' said Kim. 'I'm glad I've discovered something else I can do without.'

'Aren't you being a little ostentatiously philistine?' I said, annoyed at her rudeness. 'Most women I know would fake an orgasm from a single sip.'

'I save my fake orgasms for men,' said Kim, and poked Akito with an elbow to show she'd just made a good shot. Akito joined her in loud laughter.

'Oh, Kimsy, stop trying to shock us,' said Honoria, smiling. 'It's adolescent.'

'I know,' said Kim calmly, looking at me. 'But being surrounded by parents does that to me.'

'What happened to that guru you were so enthusiastic about?' Honoria asked, changing the subject.

'He was brilliant,' responded Kim, now drinking again from her beer. 'I decided I wasn't quite ready to become totally enlightened.'

'No?'

'I'm too young. I've got too many mistakes I haven't made yet. Enlightenment is for people who've grown tired of their mistakes.'

'What about people who never make mistakes?' asked Honoria ironically.

'They don't need enlightenment,' countered Kim. Then she smiled. 'Only friends.'

Mr Battle and Mr Namamuri, who had shown little interest in the subject of enlightenment, were now both standing.

'Ah, gentlemen,' said Mr Battle. 'Enough of this frivolity. If you would be kind enough to bathe and, uh, get dressed, Mr Namamuri and I would like to have a chat in the library . . . There's a jacuzzi down by the pool, Mr Akito, but . . . in half an hour if you don't mind' – this last directed to me as if I were the only one who might be delinquent.

With that he marched off with his older guest, and Akito and I, mere vice presidents, scurried off to do as we were bid.

Mr Battle's ornate study had ceiling-high bookcases on two whole walls, an impressive map of the world filling the third wall, and floor-to-ceiling windows on the fourth. As far as I could tell, Mr Battle himself rarely entered this room except to impress certain visitors. His actual working study was a smaller room near his bedroom which contained only quotron machines, stock tables and tax guides. Whenever I'd seen him in the formal study the old man liked to stare with quiet dignity at the rows of books, as if he might absorb their contents without actually bothering with reading. When I once asked him what books he had in his library, he'd turned and gazed at me for a long moment with his usual dignity, and replied: 'Hardcover'.

After Hawkins brought some brandy Mr Battle offered everyone a cigar, only the older Japanese accepting. I was baffled about what this meeting with the Japanese was all about. Mr Battle was the principal owner of the privately-held firm of BB&P and as far as I knew was not interested in selling any of his interest.

'Gentlemen,' he began, standing with dignity in front of his giant wall map of the earth as if he were Patton about to outline his latest offensive. 'I believe we may be able to help each other.'

It was indicative of Mr Battle's isolation from the common men of Wall Street that he was clearly unaware of the ancient joke that had been going around for months that Ivan Boesky always used this classic line as a preface to his requests for illegal insider information. The two Japanese bankers, sunk as deeply into huge cushioned chairs as I was, stared back at the grinning Mr Battle with their usual classic inscrutability.

'We need capital and you need our expertise,' Mr Battle went on. 'In particular in the area of futures trading. Although our dollar volume may be below that of other firms, I can say with pride that Mr Rhinehart here is at the cutting edge of futures trading, a man with vision and discipline, an asset for which other firms have envied us for years.'

I doubted that more than a handful of people on Wall Street had ever heard of Larry Rhinehart, and BB&P's futures trading operation was so small Merrill Lynch would probably account for it under 'misc. operations' and 'petty cash'. Would the Japs fall for this line?

'Your bank,' Mr Battle continued, pacing with slow dignity back and forth in front of the huge map, as if plotting the final outcome of a world war, 'wants access to a futures trading operation. We have one of the best. It is time to talk.'

Indeed.

Akito, dressed with almost unrealistically neat elegance, cleared his throat. Mr Battle looked at him politely.

'We would like to speak with Mr Rhinehart alone for a few moments if you could be so kind,' he said, then smiled and bowed his head slightly.

A flicker of doubt crossed Mr Battle's face before it was replaced with a smile.

'Of course, of course,' he said. 'Although, although . . . Of course!'

As we all stared at him expressionlessly Mr Battle looked a trifle upset at being kicked out of his own study, but with one final 'of course' he turned and strode with dignity from the room. As baffled as he, I sipped at my brandy and hoped I looked inscrutable.

As soon as the door closed with the minutest of dignified 'thumps', Akito rose, strode to the window and stared out a brief moment at the glorious gardens. I couldn't get over how Western Akito seemed; only his smooth olive complexion and slightly slanted eyes and inevitable collection of small bows identified him as Japanese. Otherwise, he was too large a man, too athletic, too handsome, and too interested in Kim to be a stereotypical Oriental. As I stared, the man suddenly wheeled and addressed me with a small bow and slight smile.

'Why do you gamble with your firm's money?' he asked softly.

My inscrutability, if it ever existed, was now shattered.

'Gamble?' I managed to reply.

'You risk you firm's money but guarantee profits to the clients. You can lose, the client cannot. Since no one can predict the direction of markets, you are gambling.' Although Akito again bowed slightly and was still smiling, the content of his words was like an artillery barrage. I could feel myself flush.

'Gamblers always lose,' I now snapped back. 'You may have noticed that I do not.'

'True,' said Mr Akito, 'and we wish to know why you do not.'

'Why?' I echoed, again baffled. 'Because I know what I'm doing. I use systems which – '

'Excuse me,' interrupted Mr Akito, 'but systems are bullshit. Systems do not work. Systems are gambling.'

He marched towards me across the deep carpet, his shiny narrow shoes sinking deeply in, as if he were crossing a lush lawn, and stopped a few feet away. Didn't the man know that the Japanese hate confrontation, hate directness, believe in saving everyone's face?

'We have noticed how in your trading when one of your trades loses money it seems to be always relatively small amounts,' Akito continued. 'But then every now and then you put larger sums into a trade and inevitably it seems these trades turn out to be profitable. We are alone now. We wish to know how you manage to avoid losing.'

Damn him! What the hell is he driving at!?

'By hard work, damn it!' I wanted to shout. And then I suddenly felt a quiet burst of joy: the bastards must really think I'm something if they suspect I must have a secret formula. Or did they think I was cheating in some way? Were they actually asking how I cheated?

I relaxed and let a quiet smile appear on my never inscrutable face.

'A lot of people would pay a lot of money to know the answer to that question,' I announced.

Akito, towering with unJapanese bulk, looked down at me with intense scrutiny.

'Yes,' he finally said. 'I believe they would.' He continued to look down at me.

'My official answer,' I went on, 'is that I have a knack for using some of the many technical systems for entering and leaving markets and for determining the amount of capital I put at risk for each trade.'

'Yes,' said Akito, '. . . a knack . . .' He turned briefly to Mr Namamuri, who was sunk so low in his easy chair and was so engulfed in cigar smoke that when I first followed Akito's gaze I thought it was a pile of smouldering rags with two shiny shoes attached. A voice miraculously emerged from the smoke.

'We . . . interested in buying your . . . "knack",' the old man said, his round face and thick glasses emerging briefly from the haze, then fading.

'But not,' said Akito, turning to stare down at me again, 'without having a clearer idea about what it is.'

But it was only a knack! A lot of damned hard work, some sharp brains, and a knack! I managed to meet Akito's blank gaze with my own nearest equivalent.

'Perhaps you have some theories about my knack,' I suggested.

'Perhaps,' said Akito.

'Well?'

Akito again turned to look at the older man, who from behind his cigar apparently released some smoke signals that Akito was able to interpret, although nothing I could catch.

'Our theories are irrelevant,' he said. 'Our bank is interested in creating a futures fund, possibly through your firm, a fund that would begin with approximately a hundred million dollars and expand from there. It is possible we would be interested in having you as one of the traders, possibly the chief trader. All this is possible, but not before we know all there is to know about . . . your knack.'

A hundred million dollars!! My God, with that amount of money you could affect markets, work them up and down like yo-yos!! And the chief trader! I'd be watched by everyone on the Street to see my every yawn, my every burp!! 'Rhinehart's just bought soybean oil!'

someone would report and the price of November bean oil would go through the roof!

I leaned back deeper into my chair, sipped my brandy and tried to keep my hands from shaking the tumbler. I attempted an exaggerated yawn.

'That's interesting,' I said. 'A big futures fund managed by my . . . knack . . .' I sipped at my brandy. The only trouble was if I started to try to tell Akito what I thought my knack consisted of – namely disciplined following of the technical indicators I'd developed – Akito would think me a fool or a liar – a fool if I thought my system would continue to work, or a liar because I was actually beating the markets with some kind of inside information. I wished desperately that I'd accepted Mr Battle's cigar so I could hide behind some smoke the way Namamuri was.

'It might make a quite profitable marriage,' Akito said, a soft smile crossing his face for the first time. 'Our capital and your . . . knack.'

Swallowing the last of my drink I stood up and strode forward and brazenly patted the huge Akito on the shoulder.

'It might, it might,' I said, grinning. 'But of course, as Mr Battle said, others have also expressed an interest in my knack. I'm afraid you'll have to give me a bit of time to think it over.'

'Oh, certainly,' said Akito, smiling politely. 'We totally understand. But you do see that we must have confidence in your . . . technical indicators before we could entrust such a large sum to your excellent guidance?'

'Oh, yeah. No sense in tossing away a hundred million on gambling.' I grinned again. A hundred million! Just to begin with! If only I had a saleable knack!

'Exactly,' said Akito, and he gave me a return smack on the back that sent me staggering several steps across the room like a drunk.

Namamuri's slitted eyes followed my staggering surge like those of a snake following a wounded mouse.

9

Although I went searching for Honoria to gloat with her about what a big deal the Japs thought I was, it turned out I wasn't given much chance to brag about my triumph. In the gardens out east of the mansion she and Kim were sitting on a stone bench overlooking a small pond on which four or five ducks swam in picturesque bucolic charm, but, from what the gardener said, probably shitting and pissing the pond into an unusual state of pollution. It was a lovely Indian summer afternoon, with a few early-fall leaves floating in the pond like tiny toy golden ships.

But Honoria and Kim were clearly oblivious to the weather. They were bent in fierce concentration over some document. Kim, still wet from a dip she'd taken in the pool, was wrapped in a gaudy striped towel over her black one-piece suit. When I approached, the two of them looked up at me with disturbing seriousness.

'Have you see this?' Honoria asked and handed me three photocopies of something.

At first I thought they were copies of some financial article and was thus unprepared to see some pages of the tabloid *World Star*.

'What's this all about?' I asked.

'Someone showed it to me in LA,' said Kim, who now began towelling her shoulder-length hair, wild with untamed natural curls. 'I recognized the name and remembered that Nori'd told me your father had an interesting past. He sounds great!'

When I looked carefully at the first page the main headline sent a chill through me: 'Dice Cult Creates Robots'. A lesser headline proclaimed modestly: 'I was a Random Sex Slave'. The next page was equally straightforward: 'Dice Commune Worships Chance and Chaos', and a subhead proclaimed: 'Mysterious Leader Still Sought.'

Standing in front of the bench I looked down balefully at Honoria, who looked back with her usual cool aplomb. Then I slowly lowered myself on to the bench next to her and read on.

According to former sex slave Anita Ransom, the commune brainwashed people into giving up their free will to the commands of dice. Diceguides forced everyone to break down habits and inhibitions and become random multiple personalities. Ms Ransom painted a lurid picture – cult indoctrination into a 'schizophrenic existence where you had to be somebody you weren't', 'where you could lose your life savings in a second, or make money by stealing or prostitution'. 'Nothing was taboo,' said Ms Ransom. 'People were doing everything!' The cult worship of their Dice Daddy Luke Rhinehart led to random 'contributions', orgies, and perhaps even some sort of Russian roulette human sacrifice. Luke himself appeared constantly in new disguises and personalities, a master fox, thus evading the FBI now for twenty years.

There were only two small photographs connected with the articles – one of Anita Ransom of sex-slave fame, who looked about as sexy and abused as a slightly stoned McDonald's counter clerk; and a second of Luke, a photo I immediately recognized as having been taken fifteen years earlier at Luke's trial. My father was smiling benevolently through his thick glasses at the camera, looking for all the world as threatening as a slightly tipsy stamp collector.

With a grunt I shoved the pages away on to Honoria's lap.

'Utter total bullshit crap,' I said, angry at the articles for both their lies and their probable truths.

'But such entertaining crap,' said Kim.

'I'm afraid that the accepted cliché is that where there's smoke there's fire,' said Honoria.

I looked at her and slowly shook my head.

'Jesus. And yesterday two FBI agents wanted to know if *I* knew anything about my father.'

When both women expressed surprise I had to fill them in on the interview, talking about it adding to my overall annoyance. When I'd finished, Kim was sitting on the edge of the bench in bright-eyed excitement, her soggy towel folded on her lap and her tanned legs stretched out in front of her, while Honoria was looking again at the pages.

'I hate to think what my father would think of this,' Honoria said after a pause, then turned to me. 'You've got to find your father. If he has anything to do with this nonsense you've got to convince him to stop.'

'Shit on that,' I snorted, the idea of wasting any time at all on my father having all the appeal of a barium enema.

'And if he's alive,' Honoria went on, 'you can find out what this is all about and get your father clear of this mess, maybe offer him some money, if that's what he needs.'

I stood up and strode away from the bench, staring bitterly at the cluster of ducks which had paddled over hoping for a handout. First my father deserts me when I need him, and now he seems to be returning when I least want him.

'I don't care about this fucking mess,' I snapped. 'As far as I'm concerned this man is not my father.'

'Unfortunately, his name *is* Luke Rhinehart,' commented Honoria.

'So?'

'So my father will go through the roof if he sees an article like this. If we can't clear it up there's no telling what he'll do about our getting married.'

'It's company policy,' I said, looking sullenly back at her, 'that my father is dead.'

'I'm afraid *this* father,' said Honoria wryly, holding up the xeroxed pages, 'is not dead.'

'But what can I do!?'

'Find him and kill him,' said Kim gaily. 'Isn't that the Freudian solution?'

I turned back to the ducks and the pond. 'It looks to me like a hornets' nest,' I finally said. 'And my father's already stung me enough.'

'But it would be an adventure,' protested Kim. 'When do we begin?'

'Begin? Begin what?' asked Mr Battle, abruptly appearing along the path alone.

'Begin to clear up the, uh, unpleasantness that may be brewing about Larry's father because of the FBI,' explained Honoria, casually folding the xeroxed pages of the article and shoving them into a pocket of her jacket. 'By going and finding him.'

49

'No, no, no,' said Mr Battle. 'That man should be buried, not dug up.'

Honoria blinked uncertainly at her father but then continued.

'And by finding and confronting his father,' she persisted, 'he could complete his relationship with the man and stop being insane on the subject.'

'Nonsense,' said Mr Battle. 'He's perfectly fine the way he is. I never understood why he bothers with psychiatrists anyway. Any man who can sell short November soybeans on Monday and buy them back on Friday for a two hundred per cent profit has no psychological problems whatsoever, believe me.'

'Thank you,' I said gloomily, now facing the three of them with my back to the ducks, who were squawking in discontent.

'If he weren't obsessed with his father he might have made three hundred per cent,' said Kim.

Mr Battle frowned as he considered the suggestion.

'Well . . . no, no,' he finally concluded. 'It may well be that Larry's brilliance as a trader depends on his complicated attitude towards his father. Perhaps a cure would ruin him.'

'Heaven forbid,' said Kim, winking at me.

'But Daddy,' protested Honoria. 'Think of how upsetting it would be to have Larry's father dragged back here in chains spouting his idiocies about dice – just when Larry and I are going to be married.'

'Well, perhaps,' said Mr Battle, scowling, 'but the easiest solution is news management – perhaps even prepare some papers proving he was an adopted child.'

While staring absently out at the ducks I found my irritation and confusion slowly coalescing into something firm and un-deviating: anger.

'Larry is perfect the way he is,' Mr Battle finally added.

'Except when he raves on about his father,' said Honoria.

After an awkward silence had stretched into too many seconds I turned back to the others.

'By God,' I said. 'I'm going to *find* the bastard!'

'That's terrific,' said Kim, springing up and running to give me an unexpected kiss on the cheek. 'You're going on a quest!'

'I say the Dice Man is better off dead,' Mr Battle muttered grimly.

'I do too,' I said firmly. 'And one way or the other I'm going to bury him.'

I stood there feeling angry, determined and noble.

Behind me the ducks continued to paddle and poop.

From Luke's Journal

Exactly what are the problems we humans would like to solve?

The problem of unhappiness. Men don't like being unhappy. Frowns are bad for the complexion.

The problem of death. Death is felt to be a drag. Its silence is suspicious, a bit malevolent maybe. It is considered somewhat too permanent.

The problem of failure. It's not considered as much fun as success, but seems to arrive more frequently.

The problem of pain. Ingrown toenails, arthritis, headaches: the body always seems to stay one step ahead of Extra-Strength Tylenol.

The problem of love: it doesn't last, isn't returned, or is returned too zealously and jealously.

The problem of purpose: we don't seem able to find one or, having found one, we lose interest too rapidly.

The problem of reality: it's never quite clear what it is. John's and Jane's always seem to differ. Today's reality is tomorrow's illusion. And today's illusion . . .

The problem of evil: usually other people's. Too many bad people are doing it to too few good people. God's police force is understaffed.

The problem of self: we can never quite figure out who we are or, having figured it out, find it pretty depressing.

The problem of enlightenment: we often want it, but seldom have it. We know there is some better way of life, know we're currently not living it, and want to get there from here.

Life, as the Buddha said, is a thousand follies. And the sage is he who plays with the thousand follies.

'There is one way to be wise,' said the Buddha.

  'What is it, O Master?'

  'To play the fool.'

10

What a weekend! Here I was being offered by the Japs a chance at wealth beyond my wildest daydreams while at the same time my engagement and job were under threat from my father's suddenly crawling back into the daylight.

And the threat was real. Mr Battle had tolerated my lack of wealth because I was showing some potential for rectifying the oversight, but there would be no way to rectify the Luke of the *World Star* and Lukedom. I didn't want to return to the struggles and humiliations of my college years, to have to start again at the bottom somewhere, especially in the middle of a recession. Frankly I liked getting Rolexes from Honoria on my birthday, and huge Christmas bonuses, and becoming a vice president when only twenty-six. It was all a fine revenge on my father, and I was determined not to let him come back and steal it all away. What would Akito and Namamuri think of making market decisions by casting dice – they even thought trying to follow technical indicators was gambling!

I had to figure out what I could say that would convince them that I had a more reliable knack than simply following technical indicators. Like every trader I daydreamed of having an insider at some government agency who could tip me off about key economic data that would send markets reeling in one direction or another. Unfortunately, the only government official I knew worked for the City Welfare Department, and the only inside info he ever dropped on me was the number of unwed mothers getting foodstamps.

And as if the weekend weren't complicated enough, I also had to deal with Kim. On Sunday I'd tried to escape from everyone by taking a sail on the river on my thirty-five-foot cutter, but Kim and Akito had showed up in the Battle speedboat. When Akito motored off to look at the ancient Hudson lighthouse I had a tantalizing conversation with Kim that strongly hinted that chaos was closing in.

'Nice-looking boat,' said Kim, bouncing into the small aft cockpit and looking bright-eyed around. She was dressed again in jeans and a red T-shirt with the same beaten-up sneakers she'd worn at tennis. 'How often do you use it – five or six times a year?'

'A little more than that,' I said, checking the sails as we ghosted slowly downwind in the light breeze. 'Actually I own only half of it.'

'I hope it's the half above water,' said Kim, smiling. She moved to peer down the companionway into the salon.

I looked at her rounded rear and grimaced. How I hated a behind like that, a cute behind that pretended it didn't know it was cute – one of the prime sources of chaos loose in the universe.

Kim turned back to me, shaking her head.

'I like canoes,' she said, sitting down again, this time on the settee opposite me.

'Me too.'

'Then why'd you buy this monster?' she asked.

'I thought you said it was nice,' I said, meeting her gaze evenly. What a little bitch.

'Well?'

'Because I can afford it,' I said.

'You can afford to help the poor too, or the arts. Done much of that lately?'

'Not much,' I said, wondering why she had it in for me – unless she was attracted to me as I was to her, and it was annoying her the way it was me.

She turned away and let her eyes follow Akito, slowly receding towards the lighthouse in the runabout.

'Me neither,' she said unexpectedly.

'Are you always this critical of people you meet?'

'No. Only a few. I can never understand why rich people spend money the way they do. Jerks can never give me an interesting answer. I thought you might.'

Akito had reached the lighthouse and seemed to be slowly circling it.

'I think we spend most of it in order to make sure we'll be able to have more to spend,' I answered quietly. 'And to make sure that other people know we have it.'

She nodded and looked away.

'What a waste,' she said.

'Why do you spend your money?' I asked.

She laughed.

'To eat,' she said. 'To keep the rain out. Say,' she added, turning suddenly serious, 'I think you ought to know that Honoria's a lot nicer than she seems.'

'Well, I would hope so,' I said, laughing.

'No, I mean it,' said Kim with unaccustomed sincerity. 'She comes across as cool and controlled, but I want to assure you, underneath all that is a heart of steel.'

This time we both laughed.

'She's the only rich relative that I ever have any real fun with — except some of the men, of course, who figure that since I'm usually penniless I must be easy. Nori's a little spoiled, but too bright to be a snob like the rest of them.'

'Thanks for the data,' I said, still grinning, 'although I'm not sure I'll quote you to her. By the way, where do you plan to work now that you're back east again?'

Akito was now on his way back.

'Beats me,' she said. 'I'm good at a lot of things, but most of them aren't marketable. I can chart an astrological sign, maybe get in touch with some spirit from some other dimension, but the esoteric is unfortunately not very interested in money.'

'Do the spirits ever tell you anything about the future?' I asked, smiling at myself for even now looking for an insider angle.

'Not really,' said Kim, as she stood and shaded her eyes to stare at the approaching Akito. 'She — the spirit — tells me to get off my butt and get a job, to stop living hand to mouth, stop mooching off rich Uncle William.' She turned to me with a smile, her damn eyes glowing as if she were approaching orgasm. 'No matter how many times I ask, it still tells me to work and settle down. A million spirits on the astral plane and I get a Republican free-enterpriser.' She shook her head.

I couldn't help smiling back.

'I might be able to find something for you — not necessarily at BB&P.'

'That'd be more mooching,' she said. 'Besides,' she added over her shoulder as she stood to greet the returning Akito, 'you've got your quest to worry about.'

'Oh, yes, that,' I said, although my gaze and thoughts were again on a cute behind.

— *11* —

But that evening, back alone in my East Village apartment, I did begin to worry about my quest. My father's fresh intrusion into my life wasn't as distressing as his ancient departure, but it was bad enough. The decision to *find* my father was exhilarating, much more a challenge than a burden, even though part of the thrill was the danger involved. If I ignored the FBI and the tabloid article then I'd have no control over what might explode next on to the public scene, not to mention what Mr Battle might do about it. On the other hand, if I actually found Luke, could I really hope to get him to cool it until I was safely married and had stashed away my first few million? It seemed doubtful.

And what if my father were innocent of Lukedom and of whatever the FBI was after him for, perhaps even leading a dull, conventional life that would satisfy Mr Battle that he was as good as dead? Maybe Luke was a harmless eccentric, being used by others for nefarious purposes. That was it! My father was a dupe, a fallguy! But I was a little depressed at this image of my father; I preferred the darker, more compelling image of some hidden malevolent power manipulating strings behind the scenes. Still, innocent dupe or harmless corpse were both solutions to the threat hanging over me.

As I paced back and forth across my large loft living room, from the wall of bookcases with scruffy paperbacks to my trading corner with computers and fax and reference books, I realized that I felt more engaged by this decision to find my father than I had by anything in years. It almost seemed as if I'd been treading water most of my life but now at last was starting to swim out at full power. Confronting my father and all he had done to poison my life — and was now doing again! — seemed right, seemed to energize my being in a way my trading and getting and spending wasn't. At last I was to meet the enemy. The great personal quest of my life had begun.

Larry's highly personal quest naturally included using his secretary, and Miss Claybell proved to be as efficient a demon digging into Luke Rhinehart's past as she was at digging into the dirt behind corporate reports. From the New York Library she brought Larry back copies of an amazing array of old newspaper and magazine articles about Luke and his dice followers, most from the early seventies; after that Luke dropped from sight. Occasionally they stumbled upon some reference to him in more recent articles or books about the counterculture of the sixties and early seventies, most references referring to him in the past tense – as if he were already dead.

In fact, Miss Claybell discovered two or three pulp magazines that did in fact report his death. One story had Luke tragically dying while wrestling with an alligator – a one chance in thirty-six option supposedly chosen by the dice. Since the alligator had ended up with the upper third of Luke's body, identification was a bit tenuous, but *The Investigator* was certain of the facts.

Another story had Luke dying of a heart attack while enjoying an orgy at one of his still existing dice centre communes. In this case, reported *The Nation's Reporter*, Luke's body had been cremated in an elaborate religious ceremony attended by all eighty of the commune members. One former 'bride' allegedly tried to throw herself on the funeral pyre, but was restrained by less fanatic hands.

There were also references to Dr Jake Ecstein, Luke's old friend and colleague, and to the numerous articles and books Jake had written in the seventies about chance and personality. But references to Jake too tailed off to nothing. The library seemed to be a dead end.

And in other ways too that week was an unproductive one for Larry. He was trading exactly as he had for most of the last four years, but remained in his trading slump. And knowing that the Nagasaki Somu Bank had invested fifteen million dollars in the BB&P Futures Fund didn't help Larry's peace of mind. Fifteen million had seemed like small potatoes when Mr Battle had given him the news on Monday, and it was also discouraging that the Japanese insisted that

Larry provide a complete accounting of every trade to good old Akito, who was staying on in New York as manager of their New York branch. Knowing that Akito and a many-billion-dollar bank were watching over his shoulder made each tiny reversal that week twice as painful as usual. Now, just when it would be most helpful for a few of his indicators to work like clockwork, they were working like Mexican jumping beans, only with even less reliable predictability.

Jeff Cannister came into Larry's office on Thursday of that week looking as hunched-over and pale as Larry had ever seen him.

'The sky is falling,' said Jeff blankly and, without another word, left as quickly as he'd entered.

Larry stared after him for a long moment and then had the uneasy feeling that Jeff had finally flipped: that the losses, which were unnerving the usually cool-headed Larry, had crushed the last remnant of sanity of the excitable Jeff. With reluctance and dread he shuffled out of his office to find Jeff and see just how serious it was.

Jeff was standing in the middle of the large open office area and staring blankly at a monitor in an unoccupied cubicle. Larry eased up to him cautiously.

'How's it going?' Larry asked with as much casualness as his frayed nerves could manufacture.

'The sky is falling,' said Jeff, in the same dull voice he'd used in the office, a nerve jumping in his jawline.

'Uh, how badly is it falling?' asked Larry carefully. 'Has it broken through support areas?'

Jeff continued to stare at the monitor for a long moment and then turned blankly to Larry.

'The centre will not hold,' Jeff announced dully.

'Which centre?' asked Larry, hoping no one was watching, no one hearing.

'*The* centre,' announced Jeff.

'Ahhh,' said Larry, 'that one.'

'The market's in free fall,' went on Jeff.

Larry glanced quickly at the monitor to reassure himself that Jeff was not reporting a factual condition of the market and saw that the stock market was doing nothing unusual. In fact, none of the futures markets was doing anything unusual either, unless you counted losing money for BB&P.

'Free fall,' echoed Larry nervously.

'The nail is in the coffin,' said Jeff.

'Ahhh.'

'The last helicopter has left the roof.'

Larry took Jeff gently by the elbow and began to steer him towards the elevators. There was a doctor on duty on the third floor, a psychiatrist actually, for exactly this sort of development.

'*Après moi, le déluge*,' said Jeff.

Larry smiled heartily at a Vice-President for Business Affairs whom they passed.

'Mighty Casey has struck out,' announced Jeff.

At the elevators Larry pushed the down button and waited impatiently. He suddenly realized that Jeff was the calmest Larry had ever seen him, pale and dull-eyed, but totally calm.

'The missiles have left their silos and no one remembers the recall code,' said Jeff, looking suddenly at Larry with a slight frown of worry.

'It's just war games,' Larry suggested.

Jeff stared at him for a minute, and then, as the elevator arrived, sighed.

'And worst of all,' said Jeff, and at last his face broke into its more familiar lines of anxiety and pain and his voice became a cry of anguish, 'our gold positions are down another point and a half.'

Of course as soon as Jeff began wailing uncontrollably about a point and a half movement in the price of gold, Larry knew he was totally sane and needed no medical help.

— *12* —

When Miss Claybell had exhausted the resources of the NY Public Library I had her begin calling the New York City Police Department to see if they were still involved in the case. Unfortunately, or fortunately, depending on what mood I was in, no one seemed ever to have heard of Luke Rhinehart, repeatedly suggesting to Miss Claybell that she try lost and found. When Miss Claybell asked about the Lieutenant Nathaniel Putt who had been a prominent pursuer of Luke twenty years before, no one had heard of Putt either. Finally she located a Detective Cooper in the 20th Precinct who was reputedly an old friend of Putt's, and he agreed to talk to me.

He turned out to be a hollow-voiced man who listened stonily until I mentioned the Dice Man.

'Oh, Jesus, him,' he said affably. 'That guy just about drove Putt into the loony bin.'

'You remember the case?'

'Sure,' said Cooper. 'I mean how many guys accused of something tell us the dice told them to do it? Drove Putt bananas. One day this guy Rhinehart would confess to half the things we were after him for, and the next he'd say the dice had told him to lie in confessing, but that now the truth was that he was innocent. 'Course the dice told him to say that too. Poor Putt.'

'Where might I find him?'

'Putt thought Rhinehart was a murderer, embezzler, rapist, forger, traffic violator and general all-round menace,' Cooper went on, ignoring the question. 'But until that time he helped those Commie radicals raid the TV station he could never prove anything. Had to go after him for breaking FCC regulations. Putt was on the case for seven months officially and two years after that on his own — after Rhinehart jumped bail.'

'Did he find any leads?'

'Not so you'd notice,' said Cooper. 'He got pretty closed-mouth about it after a while, though. A little nuts, you know? He told me once just before he left the force that he prayed every night that God would give the man what he deserved. "What's that?" I asked. "Castration and dismemberment," says Putt.' Detective Cooper laughed.

'Do you have any idea how I might locate this Mr Putt?' I pressed again, irritably.

'Sure,' said Cooper. 'Try the FBI. Putt got his law degree and joined the bureau. He likes to wear suits.'

I couldn't decide whether to pursue the Putt lead into the FBI or not. It seemed a little silly to go and ask them where Luke was when just two weeks before they had come to me with the same question. Instead I decided to see what I could find out from the *World Star*.

Kurt Lyman was a ton of fun. He received me in his office at the *World Star* with a hearty handshake and a big grin. He was a small wiry man whose conviviality seemed inconsistent with his slight build. His office was a mess and throughout our talk a chunky secretary kept scurrying in and out, scavenging for papers or notes either on the desk or in a file cabinet, but ignoring Lyman and me as if we were custodial help.

'So you're the guy's son, huh?' asked Lyman after he had motioned me to a chair still slightly buried in papers and had himself sprawled back in the tipback chair behind his desk. 'He must be raking in millions, right?'

'I wouldn't know,' I answered irritably. 'I haven't seen him in years and need to locate him.'

'Hey, if I had a daddy who was worshipped by thousands of assholes with money I'd want to find him too.'

I did a wondrous job of not showing active displeasure.

'You indicated in your article that no one seemed to know for sure where this Luke Rhinehart was,' I went on. 'Do you have any ideas about where I might look for my father or how I might find him? I assume you have a lot of material that you didn't include in your article.'

'Hey, I never even went to the place,' Lyman countered easily. 'The whole article is based on this girl who came to us. Even the photo of the church comes from some Polaroid she took when she was there.'

'Did she say she'd ever met this Luke Rhinehart?'

'Meet your father?' echoed Lyman, grinning. 'No, she says she met some people who claimed they had seen him in the commune – one girl even claimed the Big Dice Daddy fucked her in the orgy room – but our source herself never saw him.'

'Why didn't your paper send someone to the commune to dig up some more juicy stuff?'

'Funny you should ask,' said Lyman, poking at his nose with the eraser end of a pencil. 'Griggs wanted to go for it but seems the girl couldn't tell east from west or Paris from Pittsburgh. She says a girlfriend drove her there through a lot of back-country roads someplace down in Virginia or North Carolina or Kentucky. We spent about half an hour over some road maps with her and we might as well have been throwing darts. We couldn't narrow it down any better than a big circle of more than a hundred and fifty miles' diameter. Turns out she was asleep or stoned most of the way.'

'She doesn't sound like too reliable a source.'

'Reliable source!' snorted Lyman with a grin. 'Christ, compared to some of our sources she was integrity incarnate. She was simple, sincere and spacey. Everything in that article of mine is the God's truth by the standards of the *World Star*.'

'So the commune exists and people say that my father is there,' I suggested, looking at Lyman sceptically.

'Yep.'

'Is there a chance I can talk to the girl?'

'Sure, there's a chance,' said Lyman, tipping forward in his chair and vaguely shuffling among some of the papers on his desk. 'But not much of a one. She gave us a phone number in Pennsylvania where she said she was going, but when I phoned there a week ago to ask her something, they said she'd never showed up and they wanted nothing to do with her.'

'Can I have that phone number?' I asked.

Lyman was still groping absently at his papers.

'The number?' he said and finally looked up at me. 'Of course not,' he added. 'We have to protect our sources.'

— *13* —

More than two months before Larry had been visited by the FBI Jeff had known he could take it no more. He saw clearly that there was some Malignant Force permeating the financial markets that was perversely working to thwart his every move. Whenever he or Larry would be making a profit on a trade Jeff would be furiously wondering how this Malignant Force was using this temporary profit to trick them into a much greater loss. Jeff had concluded then that every profitable trade was in fact a demonic trick to lure Jeff on, to give him a false sense of hope, to make him believe that he still might possibly make money as a futures trader.

He couldn't tell Larry about his new discovery. Larry was an agnostic. Larry had no sense of the Divine which moved through and controlled all things, especially the Malignant Divine. But Jeff knew. Jeff was a believer. The Gods did not take kindly to mere humans presuming to be able to predict the future. And what was futures trading if not the arrogant act of a man thinking he could predict the direction of the price of something? The Greeks called it *hubris*. The Hebrews called it pride. The results were the same: the arrogant presumer ended up a cripple, a crackpot or a *clutz*.

Jeff had finally decided to do something to end his madness. No longer would he challenge the Gods' domain over the future. He would never again presume to know something that only the Gods could know. He would become religious. He would honour the Gods. He would acknowledge that only factual knowledge should or could be used to take an investment position. He solemnly vowed that he would never voluntarily trade again except on the basis of privileged insider information. That, he knew, the Gods could accept.

Cheating was not presumptuous. Indeed, the Gods expected it of man. Cheating was a man's way of acknowledging that he knew no way of beating the laws of chance. Cheating was, in fact, the rational man's answer to the great Mystery of Life. Some men of course simply surrendered to the laws of chance and let themselves be buried by random events, content to be rich or poor on the basis of something no more purposeful than the toss of a coin. Not Jeff. Not a full American. The American way was to attack the unexpected, eliminate the unexpected, control the unexpected. In the futures markets there was only one reliable way: you cheated.

It was an incredible breakthrough for Jeff when he had this religious conversion. He felt like a gay must feel who, after many years of trying to go straight, suddenly and finally gives in to his deepest desires, and becomes what he fundamentally is. He'd known for almost a year of a certain person, X, who was able to give insider information to certain people, information which tended to make those certain people look very brilliant to others who had no such means of being certain. It had filled Jeff with gloomy and agonized anguish to know that Pete Riddles of Shearson was getting promoted and doubling his bonus because he accepted that certain person's info, while Jeff, corrupted by the influence of Larry, still desperately believed that intelligence and skill could permit him to triumph over the future and futures and the Gods.

But then, luckily, Larry's system had begun to produce losses with almost the same dull consistency that it used to produce gains. The Gods were beginning to make their move on Larry. Jeff would save Larry. Jeff would confess his *hubris* to the Gods, agree never to challenge their domain over the future again, and make money for BB&P by cheating – the way every great American had made his success.

He had phoned the certain person for the first time two months before Larry's papa problems had come crashing down on him. He made his first trade based on insider information two weeks later. It had involved going short the Japanese yen the day before the US balance of trade figures were to be released. Since BB&P already were short some yen contracts Jeff was able to use his discretion to triple the position. The next day the BB&P Fund had its best profit in more than a month, and Larry had gloated that maybe their little slump was over.

Three weeks later Jeff had scored a smaller coup when 'X' had given him advance information on an FDA approval of an anti-Aids drug that would make a certain biotech stock soar. Jeff had quietly bought shares of the stock for various of his managed accounts and some call options also, mostly in his Aunt Mildrid's account. He'd mildly recommended the shares to Brad Burner, but not in a pushy way and Brad had ignored it. When the biostock shot up after the FDA approval of its drug, Jeff himself didn't make any money – in fact he lost some since he had to give 20 per cent of his profits in cash to 'X' – but his personal stock with Brad and his clients rose considerably. For a few mad moments Jeff almost relaxed.

Now Jeff was considering a new trade based on his third surreptitious phone call to his certain person. The information he'd been given was simple: at 10 A.M. the following Wednesday, an hour and a half after bond futures trading started, the government would release the beige book report on the state of the American economy. That report, so the certain person indicated, would show that the nation's economy was much weaker than expected. The bond market would rally. Bond futures might even soar. Jeff planned, over the next three trading days, to quadruple the long position in bond futures in the BB&P Fund and accumulate at least a million dollars of long-term government bonds for his clients and the house bond fund. In five days, if things were announced as the certain person said they would be, bond prices would rise sharply. So would bond futures.

Thus, humbly asking the Gods not to send an earthquake, revolution or presidential assassination between Friday and the following Wednesday at ten and thus mess up the works, Jeff promised the Gods to take his profits that day at noon. Far be it from him to predict what the market would do on its own without any advanced news from an insider.

From Luke's Journal

Socrates once won first prize in an Athenian quiz game by answering that he knew nothing, but his answer has won few prizes since. Men continue to be ignorant of their ignorance, illuded by illusions. Playliving begins with the assumption that men are fools and the wisest man is he who plays the role to the hilt. Men's lives are based 90 per cent on lies; about the other 10 per cent we don't yet know enough to be sure.

Illusion and inconsistency are the two great enemies of Truth and Honesty, those twin deities of Western man which have caged him in the house of boredom. Both are basic to man's fulfilment and happiness.

In living life freely any insight held more than the moment appropriate to it becomes an illusion and a snare. For every name, idea, insight applied over any period of time deadens that part of the universe it touches. To name is to experience. To name a part of the flow always the same way is to experience it always the same way and thus to die to life. To live freshly entails continually re-creating exerience, continually unlearning, continually destroying the old names, the old truths, and creating a new world and fresh experience by giving to the flow new names.

— *14* —

It had taken Miss Claybell more than a half dozen calls to locate
Agent Nathaniel Putt. He worked in the Washington bureau. When
Larry got back from his less than successful trip to Mr Lyman he
phoned Putt and told him who he was and what he wanted. Putt
said it might be helpful if they could meet. Larry decided this was
too important to delegate to Miss Claybell, and Honoria was tied
up, so he flew alone to Washington.

Putt turned out to be quite different from the image conjured up
by Detective Cooper's stories. He was a large florid man in his
fifties with a face that looked as if it had seen every crime ever
committed and was therefore a bit sceptical about the human race.
But he seemed subdued and only marginally interested in Luke
Rhinehart.

'You're his son, are you?' Putt asked, after seeming to browse
through some of the file he had brought out on Rhinehart.

'Yes, I am,' said Larry. 'I'd like to locate him.'

'Well, I can't see how we can help you,' said Putt. 'The bureau
was on the case for a few years but didn't come up with anything.
Then Carter got into office and discouraged us from chasing kooks
and suggested we consider crooks instead. The file's been inactive
for fifteen years – not closed but inactive.'

'But I thought – ' Larry began.

'Actually, old Luke here is still wanted on about a half dozen
federal charges. But he's probably long dead and buried. We got two
or three reports of his death . . . No corpse unfortunately.'

'But I thought – two weeks ago two agents who questioned me
said he was wanted for what he was doing now!'

Putt peered at Larry over his thick horn-rimmed glasses.

'What agents?' he asked.

'FBI agents,' Larry countered. 'Two tall skinny guys. One of them left me his card. Here . . .' He took out his wallet. 'See. A man named Hayes.'

Putt leaned forward to accept the card from Larry, sniffed at it, turned it over, and then shook his head.

'Oh, them,' he said. 'Just routine. The bureau has to follow up on every open case at least once every three years. They were just going through the motions.'

'It didn't seem that way to me,' Larry said.

'Nevertheless,' said Putt, slipping the card into the file. 'I'm afraid we can't help you locate Rhinehart.'

'What about his followers?' asked Larry. 'Didn't they form communities around the country – little dicedoms or something like that?'

'Oh, yeah,' said Putt, looking down at his file and then slipping back into his chair. 'According to the file here we sent agents into two or three of them.' As Putt perused the file the furrows on his brow grew and his flushed face flushed further. 'Seems that two of the agents left the agency without ever filing a report. The one agent who did file one claimed that nothing anyone ever said at this place was reliable so he had no new idea where Rhinehart might be.' A nervous tic rubberbanded twice across Putt's cheek and then subsided.

'But do you have the addresses of some of these places?'

Putt looked a long time at Larry and then excused himself for a few minutes. He was away half an hour.

When he returned he again stared a long moment at Larry.

'You're determined to find your father, are you?'

'I am,' said Larry.

'OK then,' said Putt. 'Maybe we can be of help. We're pretty sure that there's one of these dice centres still in existence. It's, ah, it's a place called Lukedom – but it's not on any map. We're not actually sure where it is – someplace in West Virginia or Tennessee we think, but since the case is inactive we haven't pursued it. You interested?'

'Of course,' said Larry. 'But that's not much to go on.'

'There's a lady,' said Putt. 'An Arlene Ecstein. She might know. She was Rhinehart's mistress or something back when everyone was crazy. Her husband was a big deal in the movement. We even think the husband, Jake Ecstein, might be behind some of these dice

69

communes. Anyway, if I were trying to find Rhinehart I'd question her.'

'I remember Mrs Ecstein,' said Larry, frowning. 'My God, she became the flakiest of them all.'

'Yeah,' said Putt. 'I think you're right. She's probably not too reliable.'

'You know where she is?'

'Got an address,' Putt replied, looking down at his file. 'It's five or six years old. Might help.'

After Agent Putt had escorted Larry to his door, walking with a big slow lumbering waddle, he closed the door slowly behind him. Then he slammed one fist into another and his eyes blazed. He almost leapt to his desk and punched out a number.

'Get me Macavoy!!' he barked. 'Get him in here!'

While he waited, he phoned to reserve a car for Macavoy and then began pacing back and forth. For fifteen years – ever since he'd been denied a promotion because of his failures on the case – he'd been after this guy Rhinehart and come up blank every time. He'd watched as the man's influence had waxed and waned, but always spreading pornography, promiscuity, Aids, herpes, dope, violence, unwed mothers and welfare cheats. Now his kid, who must be as nutty as his father but seemed to hide it better, had finally decided to try to find his old man. It could well be the break Putt had been looking for all these years.

When Macavoy entered he stood at polite attention until Putt turned to him. Macavoy was a deadly serious young man, an agent for only two years and convinced that two-thirds of being a successful agent lay in being steadily sombre and serious.

'Rhinehart's son has decided to try to find his father,' Putt announced gruffly, his bloodshot eyes blazing.

'How is this going to help us?' Macavoy asked.

'These dicequeers won't talk to cops or reporters or us,' Putt answered. 'But they may be willing to talk to someone whose last name is Rhinehart and happens to be the bastard's son.' Putt stopped pacing and made a facial expression which may have been a smile.

'I want you to put a loose tail on this kid,' he went on. 'Stick with him for as long as he's going after Rhinehart senior. Stick with him until he leads us to the old madman himself.'

'You mean Rhinehart senior?'

'That's right. Rhinehart. The worst threat to American society since Karl Marx.'

Macavoy nodded soberly.

— *15* —

Arlene Ecstein's phone number was in the Queens phone book, and it turned out she lived in Hempstead, Long Island, not exactly a bastion of kookiness. Larry was surprised on phoning her to find himself talking to a gentle grandmotherly woman who tended to babble on a bit about 'dear old Luke' and 'your wonderful mother', and 'wasn't it a shame . . .' and so on.

He reported his meeting with Putt and his follow-up phone call to Arlene and his memories of her to Honoria and Kim at the Battles' Upper East Side luxury apartment. Luke's seduction of Arlene had been his first dice decision, his first step on his 'downward path to self-destruction' as Larry put it, or 'first test of the malleability of the human soul' as Luke's followers had since put it. In any case, as Larry explained, Arlene had soon become a fanatic practitioner of the dicelife, blossoming from a frustrated and unfulfilled childless housewife to an earthy mother, career woman and 'slut' – the last word being Larry's interpretation of her subsequent dicelife. Larry hadn't seen her since he was a boy. At first Honoria had seemed put off by Larry's recitation, but when Kim seemed eager to meet Arlene, Honoria wisely decided she would go with her fiancé.

It turned out that Arlene lived in one half of a somewhat run-down duplex in a mostly white neighbourhood that looked as if it was struggling to maintain its dignity. The doorbell didn't work, so Larry had to bang several times on the old wooden door.

When it opened, Larry and a tense, wary Honoria found themselves facing a large, white-haired lady wearing a long brown dress with a black shawl thrown over her upper half. She peered at them through thick glasses and then smiled warmly.

'My, how you've grown,' she said, as if imitating every ancient relative since the beginning of time. 'I'd never have recognized you if you hadn't phoned first. How's your father?'

Of course that's what Larry wanted to know, so her asking was a bit of a setback. But Arlene didn't seem to expect an answer and went babbling happily on about the good old days and wasn't it a shame and sugar? milk? or lemon? in the tea. As Arlene bustled away towards her tiny kitchen Larry and Honoria exchanged discouraged looks from the deep ancient armchairs they found themselves buried in.

When Arlene had returned she served them lukewarm tea with some stale Stella Dora biscuits. Then with a loud groan she settled herself down into the overstuffed couch.

'The arthritis does get to one over the years,' she said. 'I hope it hasn't hit poor Luke.'

'We were wondering where Dr Rhinehart might be,' said Honoria, wanting to get to the point. 'Have you heard from him recently?'

'Oh, no,' said Arlene. 'Luke hasn't written or phoned me in years and years. He has to lie low, you know. The police are after him.'

'We know,' said Honoria. 'Where was he the last time he wrote or phoned?'

'Oh, that was years ago,' said Arlene, looking off into space. 'I'm sure he's moved since then.'

'Where was it?' asked Larry.

'Oh, here in New York, I guess,' Arlene answered. 'It's all rather vague now. He wasn't much for precision.'

'Where's your husband?' Honoria asked.

'Oh, Jake's down south, I think,' said Arlene. 'He's become a guru or priest or something, I hear, but still writing books. He'll never stop writing books.'

'I see,' said Honoria.

'He always wanted to be a king or a president, but I guess he's had to settle for a smaller kingdom.'

'And where exactly in the south?' asked Larry.

'Well, now, let me see,' said Arlene, frowning. 'A little town in Virginia I think . . . Not even on the map. Lukedom. Jake named it after your father.'

Larry and Honoria both sat up straighter in their chairs.

'Do you know where it is?' asked Honoria.

'Oh, my, no,' said Arlene. 'Jake says it's not on any map. That's why he had to send me instructions about how to get there.'

'You have instructions about how to get there!?' said Larry.

Arlene looked surprised.

'My goodness, that's right,' she said. 'I guess I do. I never went, so I never even bothered to read them, but I know he sent them. I wonder what I did with that letter.'

While Larry and Honoria sat on the edge of their chairs – or as close as the deep, broken-springed chairs would permit – and exchanged glances, Arlene bumbled up off the couch to putter around her desk, mumbling happy apologies for her sloppiness and finally returning with a big smile and a letter.

'See,' she said. 'I told you Jake had written instructions and here they are.' She adjusted her glasses and peered down at the paper. 'Lukedom. Dirt-road route to Lukedom. Were you thinking of visiting Jake?'

'Yes,' said Honoria. 'Larry is interested in seeing his father and we thought this little . . . village might have some people in it – Dr Ecstein, for example – who might have some idea where he is.'

'How nice!' said Arlene. 'You're going to see your father! Do say hello to him for me and tell that naughty man to write.'

Larry nodded, and a few minutes later, sketchmap in hand, he and Honoria said goodbye to Arlene. She wanted to have them take some of the stale Stella Dora cookies and offered to throw in some sort of frozen pie she had made the previous year, but they politely declined. She told them to give Jake a big kiss for her and tell him she was getting along just fine. She said she'd like to find Lukie too and give him a piece of her mind. She was still babbling away when they finally managed to leave.

Larry and Honoria edged carefully down the old wooden stairs into the smelly night of Hempstead and were soon back in Larry's Mercedes speeding towards Manhattan.

After Arlene had closed the door behind her two visitors, she grinned, shook her head, and began to shuffle back into the living room. Then she stopped in front of an old full-length mirror and looked at herself. She stretched and smiled again.

Then she reached up and began pulling at her white hair until, with a sudden wrench, the entire white wig came sliding off, revealing a mass of jet-black hair pinned down. After putting the white wig in a cardboard box with others on a closet shelf, she reached back and unpinned her hair, sending a cascade of

74

touched-up black hair down on to her shoulders. She shook her head and smiled.

She checked her watch, frowned and took off her black shawl. Then, as she began to walk with a decidedly younger step towards the bathroom she flipped her shawl into a bedroom as she passed. On the way she took off her thick glasses and left them on a shelf in the hall. In front of the mirror in the bathroom she began to insert contact lenses into her eyes. When she'd finished she began to apply 'the works', as she called the creams, mascaras, eyeshadow, line erasers, blushers that were any woman's staple when she wanted to look younger. This done, she left for the bedroom to change her clothes and prepare for her evening out.

But twenty minutes after Larry and Honoria had left there was a knock on the door of Arlene's duplex. It was Agent Macavoy. He had dutifully followed Larry's Mercedes and knew, when they had arrived at Browning Street in Hempstead, that the two were questioning Arlene Ecstein. After they'd left, he decided it might be worthwhile if he had a few words with the lady. If she told him what she'd told them it would simplify his surveillance.

The door was finally opened. A big-busted woman wearing a low-cut flaming-red dress and high heels greeted him with a slow smile. If Arlene had looked well into her fifties for Larry and Honoria, she looked closer to a well-preserved and heavily endowed forty now.

'Hi,' she said. 'What can I do for you?'

Agent Macavoy pulled out his FBI identification and held it in front of her face.

'Mrs Ecstein?' he said coldly. 'Macavoy, FBI. A few questions.'

Arlene didn't even glance at his ID, but simply swung the door open wide and invited him in.

'Sure,' said Arlene. 'I was just going out, but I love answering questions.' She walked over to her desk and, with her back to Macavoy – for a moment he worried that she might be going for a weapon – she seemed to fiddle with something there before turning. As she came towards him he saw that it was just a couple of dice.

'So,' she said, coming back up to him with a smile. 'What can I do for you?'

Macavoy halted at her approach and looked at her severely, hoping to put her in a properly respectful if not fearful frame of mind.

Arlene ran her tongue around her lips and idly rotated her

shoulders so that her breasts momentarily swelled up towards the neckline of her low-cut dress then receded – two round white tides swelling and receding.

'Few questions,' said Macavoy. 'Like did you tell your recent visitors where they might find – '

'My God, you're a hunk,' said Arlene, reaching her two hands up briefly to knead each of Macavoy's shoulders and eyeing him up and down. 'You work out every day?'

'Uh, every other day,' said Macavoy, taken aback and actually retreating a step. 'Uh, Luke Rhinehart, Mrs Ecstein. Did you – '

'No, no, more than that,' said Arlene, moving her hands inside his suit jacket to his chest and squeezing through his shirt the muscles around his nipples. 'You must have played football or lifted weights, right?'

Macavoy was retreating sideways now, into the living room.

'Basketball actually,' said Macavoy. 'But, uh, what did you tell – '

'And a belly like a steel wall,' said Arlene, whose fingers were kneading his abdomen as the two of them danced slowly from the hallway across the living room, Macavoy retreating, Arlene effortlessly advancing.

'Look, Mrs Ecstein, I – '

'And thighs like – '

'Aghhhh!!' said Macavoy as Arlene's fingers probed his inner thighs so suddenly he actually jumped, almost breaking their physical contact.

'. . . Great hard haunches of bullmeat,' concluded Arlene.

After meeting Arlene Ecstein I confess I began to have some doubts about my quest. Arlene was so harmless that it rubbed off on to Luke: I seemed to be making a mountain out of a molehill. Besides, I didn't see how I could spare the time to go down into the southern wilderness to search for a man who probably wasn't there. And a part of me was equally afraid he *would* be there. I passed over the first weekend I might have gone by escorting Honoria to a gala charity ball given by several old-line Wall Streeters as a way of showing their commitment to the needy – whether the 'needy' referred to those to whom a bit of the money raised eventually trickled down or to the socialites themselves was unclear.

The following week was a hectic one, marked primarily by Jeff's 'hunch' on bonds and bond futures proving to be a good one; our BB&P Futures Fund soared almost 6 per cent in one day. Akito phoned and complained he couldn't tell from my indicators why I'd taken such a large bond futures position and then, after making good profits in just two days, gone flat. I hemmed and hawed and concocted a series of mostly fictitious variables to disguise the fact that I'd taken a large position because one of my most unstable traders had a hunch, and gone flat for the same reason.

In his new strange state Jeff seemed to want to go flat in almost everything. It was like pulling teeth to get the poor man to go long or short anything, Jeff inevitably muttering darkly about risks and 'challenging the Gods', and only going away to execute the orders because he knew I'd have to fire him if he didn't.

But even as I pretended to throw myself into my trading and my life with Honoria I felt the pull of Lukedom. I finally decided that if I went the weekend before election day then even if I had to stay longer than two days at least the Tuesday of the election the markets would be closed and I'd miss only one day of trading.

Honoria didn't want to go with me. For one thing she couldn't afford to take any days off from Salomon Brothers, not even the Monday before election day. For another, that part of Virginia was the pits as far as she could tell. Lukedom appeared to be located at the far southern end of the state, buried in barren stripmine hills, probably surrounded by people who had starred in the film *Deliverance*. Kim seemed interested in going, but I knew that Honoria might not take too kindly to my travelling alone with Kim, so I pretended I didn't notice her interest.

Still, I decided to make one last effort to get Honoria to come with me. I arranged to meet her at 'Wipples', a fashionable financial district bar best known for having one whole wall on which customers had over the years written various stock, bond and futures recommendations. They also dated and signed them. 'Wipples' then saw to it that the best always remained, despite the efforts of their authors to remove them. Hence customers were able to note that one well-known Wall Street guru had urged clients to 'sell everything' in August 1982 just before stock were to take off like a missile launch. Another wrote in September 1987 that the market would hit 3,000 by mid-October. Instead it hit 1,750. But except for the wall – to which I'd wisely never contributed – the place was a simple, unpretentious bar that humbly charged all the traffic would bear.

Which was considerable. The bar had a reputation for being the place one went after a particularly brilliant or lucky financial coup, so going there implied one was brilliant or lucky. At any rate it implied you could afford to pay ten dollars for a shot of whisky, which certainly showed something.

When I arrived Kim was with Honoria, and wearing a dress, one of those new short spandex things, black, that hugged the body and begged you to watch each vibration. Since it was mid-thigh-length Kim's black-stockinged legs stuck invitingly out beneath the table. I hadn't seen much of her since she'd gotten a part-time job promoting some Upper East Side health club.

Honoria, like most of the other female patrons, was dressed in a more sedate and stylish manner, a mauve and white business suit which, with her blonde hair, was dramatic. As I sat down at the booth with them I couldn't help feel my male ego swell – the two foxiest ladies in the joint.

78

Kim, as far as I knew, normally avoided Wall Street types – except maybe the rebels and losers – and couldn't usually spend much time with Honoria, their lifestyles overlapping only in that both ate, slept and peed. As Honoria waved at me, I wondered vaguely why Kim was here.

I ordered the cheapest drink on the menu: I hated overpaying for a drink as much as overpaying for a security. Then I again urged Honoria to accompany me on my drive south to find my father.

'As I understand it,' Honoria responded, shaking her head with a mock groan, 'I am being asked to visit a hippie commune caught in some time warp left over from the sixties. Is that right?'

'Maybe,' I said. 'But I really don't care one way or another.'

'That Arlene Ecstein certainly didn't turn out to be a hippie,' suggested Kim.

'That's true,' said Honoria. 'If your father has degenerated into the male equivalent of Mrs Ecstein, then I suppose our worst worry would be that we'll be bored to death.'

'But it would be nice if some of the sixties was still alive today,' Kim went on. 'That two or three people still existed who weren't chained to chasing money and ripping each other off.'

'In those days,' said Honoria, 'parents were so stupidly liberal, their rebellious children didn't have to worry about money – doting parents sent moneygrams. Today we know better. Rebellious youth are disinherited before their hair even reaches the back of their neck. Reserve your compassion for condors and spotted owls.'

'Actually it's that we know better now,' I said, thinking that the sixties and my father were part of the same sickness. 'We want to make something of our lives instead of drifting with some flow that eventually strands us in a bog.'

'Yes, but the flowing and the bogs often seem so much more interesting than the upward march on the treadmill,' said Kim, grinning a challenge at me.

'Nonsense,' snapped Honoria, wriggling her bottom on the chair in annoyance. 'What's wrong with minding the store? Perhaps for you and the sixties the treadmill symbolizes repetitious drudgery. For us it symbolizes staying in shape and getting ahead.'

'Maybe so, but getting ahead for what?' countered Kim, her eyes getting brighter and a flush appearing on her cheeks. 'Staying in shape for what? As far as I can see people stay in shape in order to do better on the treadmill, and get ahead in order to get further ahead. Where's the joy? Where's the payoff?'

'The payoff is a six-figure income,' said Honoria. 'Not to mention that you yourself are being paid to get people to pay good money to use the treadmills.'

'Touché,' said Kim with a grin. 'But I'd still like to know if a place exists where people don't care about the amount of their income.'

'Oh, I'm sure you can find them all over,' conceded Honoria. 'And they're undoubtedly living in wrecks and hovels. You know, Kim, you might be living in one yourself if it weren't for us treadmill types.'

'Touché again!' Kim said. 'But remember, I often have lived in tents, teepees, shacks and hovels. I just visit you and Uncle Willy every now and then to get back to my roots.'

'You'd probably be right at home in Lukedom, then,' commented Honoria, signalling to a passing waiter for another drink.

'This is all very nice,' I interrupted, shaking my head at the sparring, and then addressing Honoria. 'But I'd still like you to come with me.' I reached across and took her hand and went on with an exaggerated seriousness. 'Come and console me as I plunge into the lower depths in an effort to redeem my long-lost father and win your hand in marriage.'

'Silly boy,' said Honoria, mollified. 'I think the myth insists the prince go off by himself and slay the dragon. He doesn't drag the princess along with him.'

'That's right,' agreed Kim. 'Maybe you should take me instead. I'll be Sancho Panza to your Don Quixote. And then maybe I'll stay in Lukedom and become a cube or whatever you call your father's followers.'

'I call them jerks,' I said.

'Yes, take Kim,' said Honoria, stiffening. 'She won't mind a little mud and diarrhoea and, fitting in, she might find out things you couldn't.'

'I'm not taking Kim,' I said firmly, fighting the racing of my pulse at the prospect. 'I want you to go – just for a few days. It'll certainly be more interesting than another trek upstate.'

'Perhaps,' said Honoria. As she paused to reconsider, she finished the last of her drink. 'Just until Sunday night. You promise?'

'Hey, I either find my father or get a lead or I don't. How long can it take to get an address?'

'You don't love me,' moped Kim exaggeratedly. 'You prefer your fiancée to me.'

'It can take a long time to get an address — as the FBI has discovered,' commented Honoria, her mind on the business trip and ignoring Kim's taunt.

'Well?' I persisted, still holding Honoria's hand.

'I suppose I'll have to come along just to keep you out of trouble,' sighed Honoria.

I smiled and released her hand.

'Good,' I announced, having managed to keep chaos again at bay.

Although also smiling, Kim shook her head.

'Lukedom will be wasted on you two,' said Kim. 'It'll be like sending two nuns to a Playboy mansion.'

'Or two Kims to a meeting of securities analysts,' countered Honoria, standing up to leave. 'But duty calls.'

'Says who?' said Kim.

On our drive south, Honoria and I stayed that first night at a small motel in northern Virginia, arriving at about ten, Honoria a trifle irritated that we'd passed up a Holiday Inn a half-hour earlier and had to settle for something called 'The Molvadian Motel' on the outskirts of nowhere. Actually the room was indistinguishable from one in a Holiday Inn — except perhaps to the two architects involved — and the television offerings were absolutely identical.

Being young and engaged, and intelligent and well brought up, we got right to it after quick showers and made hot and horny love for forty minutes. Then we found our attentions wandering to a PBS special on the greenhouse effect. This led us naturally to a serious discussion of the investment possibilities inherent in Long Island and Miami being three feet under water and the Berkshires becoming the new sun belt — possibly the new east coast line as well. We were both annoyed that the greenhouse effect would apparently take effect only very slowly over the next half-century, thus minimizing the possibilities of dramatic short-term capital gains.

Nevertheless, we concluded that we should be bullish on the American midwest and sell short the south east, since the latter was likely to become either a desert or part of the Atlantic Ocean, either of which alternatives would decrease its value. We discussed ways of selling short the south east but could think of nothing better than shorting the stock of Disney whose Disney World in Orlando, unless converted to an underwater theme park, would suffer a pronounced decrease in both gross and net. Cotton prices would soar. Companies involved in building bridges would do well. Perhaps boat-building would make a comeback.

We were soon as deeply engrossed in our speculations about how to play the greenhouse effect as we had been earlier in our lovemaking, the only difference being we reached no climax in our discussion. Instead Honoria suddenly found our speculations the most boring and unproductive thing she'd done in weeks and announced she was going to sleep. I made a few tentative pokes with various parts of my anatomy at various parts of hers, but receiving nothing more encouraging than a rather unsexy mooing sound, I soon rolled over to go to sleep. However, I spent the next fifteen minutes daydreaming about cornering the market in sugar beets just before the millions of acres of sugar beet fields were flooded, thus becoming the richest man in the world since the Hunt family. Vaguely, just as I fell asleep, I remembered that the Hunt brothers had recently declared bankruptcy.

From Luke's Journal

In the beginning was Chance, and Chance was with God and Chance was God: of this much we and sophisticated twentieth-century scientists are certain. While the old physics saw purpose, the new sees chance. When the old saw reassuring and ubiquitous causal nexus, the new sees ubiquitous randomness. When the old probed deeper they always found cause; when the modern physicist probes deeper he always finds chance.

'Was God playing dice when he created the universe?' *The New York Times* asked a Nobel Prize-winning biologist.

'Yes,' was the reply.

— *17* —

The next day we ploughed on. Crossing the flat heartland of the central valley of Virginia I concluded that after you'd seen one cornfield you'd seen them all – unless of course I was long or short corn futures, in which case I'd have gotten out of the car every thirty miles to measure the height of the corn.

After two hours I took over the driving and Honoria settled back into the passenger seat. But I continued a silent brooding that had begun at breakfast and Honoria apparently noticed it.

'You know,' she said, 'the reason you're all hung up about your father is the old cliché that you're probably more like him than you admit.'

'I'm nothing like him,' I said.

'Not in any way?' she persisted.

'I suppose we both like the excitement of taking risks,' I finally said. 'That's the only thing we have in common.'

'Taking risks?' said Honoria with a frown. 'How so?'

'That's my job!' I said with some exasperation. 'You know that. There are two kinds of trading in futures. As you know, the whole purpose of hedging is to reduce risk – a kind of insurance policy against other positions one has in other markets. But I'm not a hedger. Jeff is our firm's hedger. My job is to make money for clients by pure speculation.'

'Gambling, you mean.'

'It's not gambling!' I shot back, taking a hand off the wheel to gesture emphatically. 'It's intelligent risk-taking. I suppose you could call it loaded-dice risk-taking. Gamblers at something like roulette or craps rely totally on chance, whereas I rely on knowledge, skill and analysis to overcome chance.'

'But if your knowledge always beats out chance then there's no risk,' said Honoria with annoying reasonableness.

'Damn it,' I said. 'It's still risk-taking! I sometimes lose millions in a week! It's just that in the long run my knowledge and skill beat out the pure diceplayer – beat out chance.'

'You don't have to get so excited,' Honoria said, reaching forward to retrieve a map that had fallen on to the floor.

'Look at it this way,' I said a little more calmly. 'I like sailing in strong winds. That's risk-taking. But I like to prepare my boat carefully, have a skilled crew member aboard with me, and carry all the latest safety equipment. But it's still risk-taking – intelligent risk-taking.' I frowningly thought of my father. 'My father, on the other hand, also liked to sail. But he thought nothing of taking some junkheap out on to the ocean without charts or safety equipment or weather projections and with a crew that had never been further out to sea than a bathtub. That's what I call stupid risk-taking – gambling, if you will. And of course his dice decisions were the stupidest gambling of all.'

'I see what you're driving at,' said Honoria. 'But it seems to me that the whole meaning of risk-taking is that you subject yourself to . . .' she hesitated to say the word, maybe fearing it would provoke a diatribe, '. . . letting chance into your life.'

I didn't explode.

'Well, maybe,' I said. 'I guess my futures speculation is a . . . declaration of war against chance. But as you said, if chance were actually beaten, then the game and the risk and the fun would be over. Yeah, I see that, but my father somehow wants to turn that fact into some sort of worship of chance as the great liberator or life-enhancer. What he failed to admit was that too much chance is like too much order – it ruins the fun. The only thing worse than fascist order is total anarchy, and that's what diceliving leads to.'

'Well, I agree completely,' said Honoria.

'So,' I concluded, hoping I'd won whatever argument we'd been having, 'both my father and I enjoy risk-taking, enjoy – I admit it – the existence of chance, but I see it as an adversary that must be continually overcome while he saw it as a . . . as a . . .'

'As a friend whom he liked playing with,' finished Honoria.

'Mmmmm,' I muttered, feeling that somehow I hadn't won the argument quite as convincingly as I would have liked.

When I finally turned my car off the last paved highway shown on Arlene's map we were deep in the Blue Ridge Mountains of southern Virginia. The dirt road the sketchmap put us on was deeply rutted and narrow. It curved and climbed and dipped through spectacular fall scenery which neither Honoria nor I noticed in the least, both being too busy feeling annoyed at being lost and pummelled around by the ruts and potholes. My Mercedes bottomed out half a dozen times, was coated with a quarter-inch of dust, and hated going in low gear almost as much as I did. If I loved my car as much as did most healthy American men I'd have been in tears.

Finally the tortuous road spilled out on to a wider dirt road, and fifty yards from the intersection was a gate and a guardhouse with a tiny sign that said simply 'Lukedom'. We had arrived.

When we came to a halt near the guardhouse a young man emerged dressed in a uniform of some kind – military cap, jacket, boots and trousers, but each apparently of some different military service. He approached the window on my side with a decidedly unmilitary amble. I was already feeling annoyed.

He leaned down and peered in at us.

'Password?' he asked.

'Fuck the password,' I shot back. 'Just let us in.'

'No problem,' said the guard, amiably enough. 'But you have to give me the password.'

Honoria leaned towards the guard.

'Chance,' she said.

The guard shook his head but continued to lean in.

'Look, we don't know the password,' I said. 'All we wan – '

'You have to guess,' said the guard.

'Garbage,' I said.

The guard shook his head.

'You each get one more try,' he added helpfully.

'Dice,' said Honoria.

'Bullshit,' I suggested.

The guard peered down at a small green notebook that appeared in one hand.

'Close,' he said, 'but no cigar.' He straightened. 'The password is "February",' he said.

'February,' I echoed, wondering whether there was a method to the madness or if it was all a practical joke. 'All right then, "February". I've said it. Let us in.'

The guard looked in at me neutrally.

'I'm afraid there's a new password now,' he said, looking sympathetic.

It was some sort of test. There must be some mad method behind it.

'May I ask how you can change the password on a moment's notice?' I said. 'How will people who know the old one now know the new one?'

The guard shook his head sympathetically.

'A password isn't something you know,' he said. 'It's something you guess.'

'Jesus Christ!' muttered Honoria.

'Nope,' said the guard.

Honoria leaned across towards the guard.

'We really have to get into Lukedom and speak to a few officials,' she said with what I thought was remarkable composure. 'It will only take an hour or two. Can't you call someone who will let us in without our guessing a password?'

The guard shook his head.

'The only way I can let you in is if you guess the password or pass the test,' he said.

'We'll try the test,' said Honoria impatiently. Then under her breath she whispered, 'This is insane.'

'Certainly,' said the guard. Straightening, he leafed through the green book and finally settled on a page.

'There are four questions,' he said, and turned a page of his book as if checking for something. 'First question,' he went on. 'What is the difference between order and chance?'

'Order works and chance doesn't,' I shot back.

The guard peered in at Honoria. She was thinking hard.

'Order is the work of divine law,' she finally said. 'And chance is the work of the devil.'

The guard checked his green book, scowling considerably and clucking to himself.

'Well,' he finally said. 'I guess the foxy lady got that one,' he announced, looking not too pleased, then frowned his official frown. 'Second question: what is a human being?'

'An asshole,' I suggested.

After a pause Honoria echoed me: 'An asshole,' she said.

'Hey, both right!!' said the guard. 'You're doing good!' He smiled down at his book. 'Number three then: how can you tell when a man is really and truly being himself?'

'When he has an erection,' I said.

The guard nodded and peered in at Honoria.

'When he or she is a child,' said Honoria, looking as if she was getting into the quizzing game and even enjoying it.

The guard shook his head disappointedly. 'I should have warned you that the last two questions are stinkers. "You can tell when a man is really and truly being himself when his self disappears." ' The guard looked down doubtfully at Larry and Honoria. 'A real bitch, huh?'

He went back to his book.

'Last question, another stinker: "How many sides are there to a six-sided die?" '

'Six,' said Honoria.

'Hold it!' I shouted, suddenly remembering a riddle from high school. 'Hold it! This baby is mine. I remember the answer from the ninth grade. A six-sided solid has *two* sides: an inside and an outside. Two! Two is the answer!'

'Eight,' said the guard. 'Inside, outside and the other six sides.'

There was a rather profound and deadly silence.

'OK, then,' the guard went on, straightening. 'The lady passes and the man fails. Welcome to Lukedom, Miss.'

'Now, hold it,' I said, managing against overwhelming odds to maintain my dignity. 'This nonsense has gone far enough. I have to talk to some people in there and none of this Socratic gobbledegook is going to stop me.'

'The lady can enter and you can't,' replied the guard indifferently.

'Look, I have to see my father!' I insisted. 'I've just driven eight hundred miles! My father created this damn place!'

The guard frowned, then leaned down again to the window.

'What are you talking about?'

Honoria answered him.

'His father is Luke Rhinehart,' she said. 'The Dice Man.'

The guard looked suddenly very nervous.

'You . . . You're the son of Luke Rhinehart?'

I was distinctly annoyed that having Luke Rhinehart as my father might possibly do me some good.

'Yes,' I muttered irritably. 'I'm the son of Luke Rhinehart.'

The guard straightened.

'Wait here,' he said.

88

He disappeared back into the small wooden guardhouse. While he was there, Honoria and I looked at each other and then Honoria sneered.

'We've just driven eight hundred miles to be interviewed by an idiot, from a book written by an idiot, in order to get permission to enter a place undoubtedly populated by idiots.' She paused. 'I wonder what that makes us.'

I contributed a grimace.

The guard returned, marching towards the car with a newfound military bearing. He stopped by my driver's side and, standing exaggeratedly erect, saluted smartly.

'The son of Luke Rhinehart is welcome to Lukedom,' he announced in a deep voice. 'Enter.'

He turned and marched to the gate, gave both sides a gentle push and they swung open. Scowling, I pulled the car forward. As it moved by, the guard saluted smartly. Honoria shook her head in disbelief. I think we were both in a slight state of shock.

The road we were now on — smooth, wide and well-maintained — declined gently towards a large cluster of wooden houses nestled in a lovely valley, bursting with the yellows and reds of fall leaves. It ran alongside a mountain stream that made everything seem as sanely idyllic as the guard had seemed insanely demonic. Then we saw the first house.

It was a house. It was a two-storey clapboard rustic house. A woman in the yard was tending a flowerbed. She looked normal. We drove slowly by. How come she didn't have two heads?

Further on there was a farmhouse and barns, with at least two dozen cows slopping around in some muck waiting to be fed. Further yet, a field with half a dozen big tents and teepees. Long-skirted women and long-haired men made it look like a hippie enclave from the seventies. A couple of children were flying a kite, a cluster of long-hairs seemed to be passing around a pipe, and rock music could be heard in the distance. There was everything but frisbees.

'Oh, no,' said Honoria. 'I think we're entering a time warp. I thought Reagan had outlawed teepees.'

'That first house looked normal enough,' I said.

'Probably owned by one of the zoo-keepers,' said Honoria, who looked as if she was assessing whom she might call on for help if needed.

The village itself at first glance seemed normal, but only at first. It had clearly been a mining town at some time in the past, and the buildings were of the most uninspired wooden construction, square and boxy and old, but most of them renovated and well kept. There was a drugstore and deli and bank and hardware store and bar and people in the streets. Honoria, who had herself never met a 'hippie', was suspicious of anyone who vaguely might have had something to do with drugs now or in the past. The streets of the Big Apple were enough evidence for her that those people were not to be trusted whatever they called themselves.

We pulled into an area designated 'Parking' and stopped. Except for a large unlabelled delivery truck outside a grocery store there had been no other cars on the street and were only two in the parking lot.

For a moment we just sat in the car.

'What do we do?' Honoria said. 'Ask for the mayor?'

'You don't suppose it's all a joke, do you?' I asked. 'Maybe that guard just ushered us through a gate that led through to some small town that everyone else approaches from a main road.'

'Welcome!' boomed a voice from beside us, causing Honoria to jump and let out a small scream. 'Welcome to Lukedom!'

'Oh, Jesus,' I moaned.

'Thank you,' said Honoria, getting out of the car. 'Isn't there an easier way to get here?'

'It's always hard to get here,' a large jovial man dressed in jeans and a pink T-shirt replied. 'But you made it. Let me take you to "Orientation".'

I got out too, slamming the car door shut.

'We need some information,' I said firmly. 'Who here would know all about this place and . . . and about Luke Rhinehart?'

'Got to go to "Orientation" first,' said the man, moving off. 'Maybe they'll tell you.' He ambled away, glancing back once with a smile of encouragement.

Honoria strode off after our greeter.

'Come on,' she said without looking back. 'Let's get it over with.'

As we followed our jovial greeter we began to notice that things were not as normal as they first appeared. Many of the stores had names playing on the words 'dice' or 'chance' or 'Luke'. A boutique was 'Difashions', a bar was the 'Snakeyes', the bank was the 'Lukedom Bank & Chance Co.'. A wooden, very New Englandy church across the street from us looked charmingly nineteenth-century except for the steeple: on the top was a neon green die rotating in the wind like a weather vane.

And I began to realize that the people weren't totally normal. They were dressed in too great a variety of styles for a simple country town. Some looked as if they'd just eaten at Luccis or Sardis while others looked as if they might be turned away from Burger King. Some women paraded down the sidewalk as if they were out on a fashion ramp in Paris while other women dressed like truck drivers or hippie retards.

When Honoria saw a fashionably-dressed woman walking sedately along the dirt path accompanied by a man in a business suit she paused to smile at me.

'Look,' she said. 'Either there are actually a few normal human beings living here or . . . tourists.' She groaned lightly when she realized the second alternative was more likely.

'Welcome Centre' was the sign over the large wooden building that our greeter had brought us to. It looked as if it might have been a warehouse in an earlier incarnation. We followed him in.

'Hi there!' beamed a vigorous young woman with mannish blonde-streaked hair and snapping brown eyes. She didn't quite smile but exuded a purposeful energy and control. 'I'm Wendy. Have you done any diceliving before?'

'I'm Larry Rhinehart,' I said, halting. 'We're not here for any of that crap; we're here to try to locate Luke Rhinehart.'

'That's wonderful!' Wendy replied with barely a blink. 'If you know it's shit you must have tried it?'

'We haven't tried it,' I snapped back. 'We don't want to try it. We just want to find someone who might help me locate my father.'

'Wonderful,' said Wendy, who seemed to find everything of a high quality. 'That would be Rabbi Ecstein. But you really ought to try die-ing: you'd benefit.'

I gave Wendy my best glare and then said softly: 'Where can I find Mr Ecstein?'

'The church, usually,' Wendy said brightly. 'Of course, like everyone else he may be someone else today.'

'Wonderful,' commented Honoria.

When we were out of Wendy's earshot, she whispered, 'That is one scary female . . .'

— *18* —

When Wendy released them they went looking for Luke Rhinehart's old friend and rival Dr Jake Ecstein. Jake had been a brilliant and eminent New York psychiatrist back in the late sixties and early seventies. Although his vibrant coarseness made him sometimes resemble a used-car salesman in a late-night TV ad, he was in fact a man who not only understood Freud considerably better than anyone, including Freud, but could brilliantly see how to convert this knowledge into fame and fortune. Jake was a successful yuppie long before a naïve world had even coined the word, much less realized that it was the wave of the (brief) future. Jake loved money and fame and saw his brilliance as a lucky talisman capable of converting knowledge into bucks.

He liked Luke Rhinehart but thought Luke was a jerk for having no interest in or aptitude for money. When Luke suddenly began behaving weirdly and doing strange things with his patients Jake worried about it, but didn't feel like doing anything about it until he heard Luke's theory about the human problem and its possible solution. That some people were stuck with one narrow personality and miserable as a result seemed reasonable to Jake. On the other hand, curing their misery by making decisions with dice, expanding each person's life so he could enjoy many different attitudes, beliefs and activities was clearly weird. But when patients began to respond to this therapy and Luke began to get a little famous, Jake decided Luke might be on to something. Far be it from him (Jake) to challenge the eternal idiocy of human beings. If they found happiness with dice then Jake would become the most brilliant dice therapist of them all. And he did.

By the time the disgrace and disapperance of Luke caused the whole movement to crash, Jake had become too fascinated by chance and multiplicity to go back to his old life. He found that fame and fortune were strangely irrelevant, especially since he had lost both. He, like Luke, lost his psychiatric practice, his wealth, his reputation, his wife and family, and all those friends who were so drawn to him because of his fame and fortune. And for the last fifteen years he, like Luke, had essentially disappeared, although he still poured out a prodigious series of articles, case histories and books on personality theory and modes of therapy, the only difference being he had them published under a half-dozen aliases.

Larry and Honoria found him, as predicted, in the church, which was as unconventional inside as was the die on the steeple outside. Although there were bench pews and a stage with an altar, the stained-glass windows had pictures not only of Christ and Buddha but of Moses and Mohammed and a few other dark-skinned men Larry didn't recognize. And one, Larry suddenly realized with suppressed rage, which was clearly of Luke Rhinehart.

In addition to crosses and six-sided stars on the walls there were also dice. And – Larry and Honoria both had to stare at it for several seconds to be sure – a huge tapestry depicting the Last Supper: thirteen bearded men arranged around a long table, but in the centre, in place of Jesus was a bearded Luke, and instead of eating, the thirteen all seemed to be playing dice.

Honoria poked Larry and gestured towards the tapestry.

'I'm glad you father isn't a megalomaniac,' she said.

'Larry, baby, long time no see!'

A grey-haired portly man with thick glasses came wobbling down the aisle towards them, arms outspread, a big smile on his face. Dressed completely in black, he stopped several feet from Larry and cocked his head to one side.

'Hard to believe you're the same little fella I used to totally ignore back when Luke was still acting like your papa,' he said, still smiling. 'You've gotten big, and from the looks of that car out there you're doing all right for yourself, huh?' He winked. 'And this gorgeous lady here's all right too. Luke would be proud.'

'You're . . . Dr Ecstein?' Larry asked.

'Call me Uncle Jake,' said Jake. 'That's what your father used to try to get you to call me back in the good old days.'

'Where's my father?'

'He's fine, I guess,' said Jake, suddenly bounding forward and grabbing Larry's lifeless hand and pumping it vigorously. 'Lost a little hair over the years, but – '

'Where is he?'

'Here and there, there and here; aren't you going to introduce me? Your gal here must be embarrassed.'

Larry pulled his hand free from Jake's and stared down at the smaller man.

'I'm not his gal,' announced Honoria. 'I'm Honoria Battle. We haven't much time to waste here, Dr Ecstein, so if you could just steer us to Larry's father we'd appreciate it.'

'Hey, terrific. I'm Jake Ecstein,' said Jake. 'Used to be a psychiatrist and am now a healer of souls. Also Larry's sometime Uncle. You can call me "Master" or, if you're feeling Jewish, Rabbi.' He laughed.

'Where's my father?' insisted Larry.

'Hey hey,' Jake said, bouncing away from Larry and Honoria towards the altar. 'I haven't seen you in almost fifteen, sixteen years and you're all business.'

'I want to know where he is!'

Jake stopped near the altar and turned. He was suddenly serious. He cleared his throat and folded his two hands over his belly in a somewhat reverential pose.

'It's not that easy, my son,' he said.

'I don't care whether it's hard or easy,' said Larry. 'Just tell me all you know.'

Jake shook his head and looked either sad or devout.

'No, no, my son,' he countered. 'Luke has left very explicit instructions about who is to be told about him or about where he might be, and it isn't simple, not simple at all.'

Larry moved closer to him, Honoria following reluctantly.

'Then you *know* where he is?'

'Didn't say that,' Jake replied, looking a little sly. 'I just said that Luke has set up definite . . . steps before I can tell anyone anything I might know about him.'

'I'm his son!'

'Oh, yes, oh, yes,' said Jake. 'Luke said you might be along one of these decades and he said to treat you just like the rest.'

'How nice of him!' Larry blurted.

'Well, maybe,' said Jake. 'Maybe not. Anyway, if you want to know more about him and where he might be you have to follow the rules.'

'Fuck the rules!' said Larry.

'I'm afraid it's the only way,' said Jake.

Larry turned to Honoria as if for help against the flood of insanity that kept rushing at him. Honoria shook her head and shrugged.

'I warned you,' she said, folding her arms.

'What are these rules you're talking about?' Larry asked.

Jake raised his hands off his belly and rubbed them together in front of him. Then he raised them further, palms pressed together as if about to begin a prayer, and held them just beneath his chin.

'Well, there are really only two, I guess,' he said. 'And not hard at all – assuming you really want to find out more about Luke.'

'The rules!' muttered Larry.

'Ground rules actually,' said Jake. 'The first one is that you must live here in Lukedom for at least a week.' He stopped and suddenly beamed at Larry and Honoria.

'A week!' said Honoria. 'My God, the markets could collapse in a week! I've got a job!'

'That's the first ground rule,' said Jake. 'Just live here in our community for at least a week.'

'Go on,' said Larry.

A slight frown appeared on Jake's round face. He sniffed.

'Well, number two . . . number two is a little trickier,' he said. 'You must . . . you must undergo training with one of our dice-guides.'

'Absolutely not,' said Larry.

'You don't have to agree to anything,' Jake interrupted hastily. 'I mean you can make fun of the guide and everything he says and does, that's fine, but you have to undergo the brief . . . training.'

'I won't do it,' Larry said. 'I'm not hanging out here for a week even if I were sure it would let me find my father the next day.'

'Nor I,' announced Honoria. 'We're too old for die-per training.' And she rolled her eyes at her bad pun.

'It's really not bad,' Jake urged. 'Just give it a try.'

'No. I'd like to find my father, but I'm not going to give in to his sick ways to do it.'

This time Jake was silent and Honoria began to move restlessly away.

'Hey, wait a minute,' said Larry, after he himself had begun to move towards the door. He came back towards Jake. 'Say, Dr Ecstein . . .' he began musingly.

'Master Ecstein, please,' Jake interrupted happily. 'Or Father Ecstein, or Rabbi.'

Larry shook his head.

'Master Ecstein . . . You know I'm Luke's son. You can see how important it is that I find my father. Can't you make an exception?'

'Nope.'

'But why don't you cast the dice to determine whether you make an exception or not?'

Jake's eyes narrowed suspiciously.

'Mmmmm,' he said.

'You really should,' Larry went on, smiling at his hoisting a diceperson with his own petard. 'It's an important decision and you ought to let the Lord Chance have an opportunity to speak.'

'Mmmmm.'

'Let's go, Larry, we'll find another way,' said Honoria. She was watching Jake, who was staring at the floor, his hands again folded over his ample belly. She came up and took Larry's hand and began to lead him out of the church.

'OK,' said Jake. 'You got it. I'll consult the dice.'

Jake marched smartly up three steps to the stage and then over to the altar. There he picked up a large, four-inch per side green die with some sort of battery-operated light inside that made it glow eerily. Jake began to mumble something that sounded suspiciously like Latin being pronounced by a retarded aborigine. Then he announced: 'Odd I'll make an exception, even I won't.'

As he raised the green die above his head, he concluded with 'Thy Will be done . . .' then dropped the die onto the altar in front of him.

He looked at it.

'Nope, a six,' he said. 'You have to follow the two ground rules.'

19

I must admit that the meeting with Jake left me shaken. Somehow I must have imagined that it would be relatively simple to locate my father once I'd found Lukedom or Jake. I'd forgotten that my father believed that easy solutions never lead to growth: that life had to be hard in order to get interesting.

Honoria was tired and irritable; all she wanted to do was leave as fast as possible, and I didn't blame her. But when we got to the parking lot the Mercedes was gone. We stared in confusion at the empty spot.

'The dice said he ought to borrow the car,' the chubby man who'd initially greeted us explained. 'Rick likes to give the dice that particular option.'

'But I've got the keys,' I said. 'And the car's got a sophisticated anti-theft device.'

'Rick never uses keys,' said the man. 'Lack of challenge, he says. He used to instal those device things.'

'You mean you just stood there while some hotwire artist broke into our car and took it off for a joy ride,' said Honoria.

'I don't meddle,' said the man.

'This is ridiculous,' she said. 'Where's the police station?'

'Two blocks down on your left,' said the man.

The police station was no more than a two-room shack stuck between two larger clapboard houses. A man in a blue uniform with a star announced he was the chief, but when we stated our problem he shook his head sadly.

'He's a troublemaker, that one,' he said. 'I'll arrest him soon's he gets back.'

'You've got to be kidding,' said Honoria. 'When will that be?'

'Before midnight,' said the chief. 'Those are the rules.'

'He's done this before?' asked Honoria, like me still grappling with the abnormality of it all.

'I'm afraid so,' the chief answered. 'He's got a record longer than Pretty Boy Floyd's. 'Course he doesn't mean any harm. Just a teenager trying to find himself.'

'Well, tell him to find himself with someone else's car,' I said. 'And if there's the slightest scratch on it I'm suing your town.'

'Yep,' said the police chief. 'Lots of luck.'

We retreated from the police station and wandered down the street, both trying to control our frustration and anger.

'I can't believe it!' said Honoria.

'Goddamn it, that cop acted as if stealing my car was some game.'

'He didn't act much like a cop.'

'You don't let people run off with a fifty-thousand-dollar car.'

'If they let people steal,' said Honoria, stopping and glaring at me as if I were personally responsible, 'what else are they allowed to do until midnight?'

'Ah, shit,' I said, 'I don't know and I don't care. We don't seem to be getting anyplace towards finding my father.'

'We should leave.'

I laughed.

'Absolutely. All we need is my car.'

Eventually we realized we were stuck and decided to spend the night at the local hotel. Assuming the car was returned as promised, we'd leave the next morning. It was possible we might still learn something before we left.

The Do Dice Inn appeared to be a normal small country hotel. The sample room we were shown was large and comfortable with old furnishings that reminded me vaguely of those at Arlene's. I was feeling irritable enough without this new reminder of my father.

We had dinner in the hotel restaurant, where both the service and food varied from good to godawful. Although my roast beef was tender and juicy the 'chef's sauce' was definitely Heinz ketchup. And the salad looked suspiciously as if it had been rescued from a garbage can.

'Do you think someone might let the dice tell him to poison us?' Honoria asked after we'd seen the salad and pushed it aside.

'No, no, they couldn't go that far,' I assured her, but we both poked and prodded the rest of our meal as if looking for hidden razor blades.

The bill was unique. Each item had a range of prices which were then chosen at random by the dieregister for each customer. My meal was: $0.15 for the soup, $13.50 for the garbage salad, $22.95 for the roast beef, and $4.00 for the coffee. Honoria's bill for essentially the same meal was $2.25 for the soup, $0.50 for the salad, $3.00 for the roast beef, and $0.05 for the coffee. Thus I had to pay $40.60, while her meal cost only $5.80.

'Do you take credit cards?' I asked the waiter, then realized I wasn't certain I wanted them to have my card in their hands for a single second.

'Oh, no, sir,' he said. 'I'm afraid not. Only cash or work vouchers.'

'Work vouchers?'

'Yes, sir. In case you might want to clean the floors or do the dishes or prepare the salads.'

'Jesus.'

'Yes, sir.'

He then made me cast a die to determine how much I tipped him.

Later, as we were passing through the bar area on the way out of the restaurant we had a new encounter that didn't help our dispositions.

'H-e-e-a-y, sweetheart, don't go,' said a grinning young man in a black leather jacket, jeans and cowboy boots. He was seated at the end of the bar and holding open his arms as if in greeting.

'I beg your pardon,' said Honoria, halting in front of him and tilting her head askance to give him a disdainful look. She was used to doubletakes and flattery, but not this type of approach from a rather crude-looking young man.

'I've been wanting to meet a fox like you all my life,' the young man went on, sliding off his seat to look her up and down with a nervous leer. 'Hi,' he said turning to me, his large brown eyes sparkling. 'You mind if I date her tonight?'

'That's very gallant, but Larry does not decide my fate just yet,' said Honoria coldly.

'Excellent,' he said, moving closer to Honoria. His smooth tanned skin, big brown eyes, mass of curly brown hair and babyish grin combined to make him look no more than seventeen or eighteen. 'What shall we do then? You want to go for a drive?'

'I'm on my way to bed,' announced Honoria firmly.

'All r-iiiight!! This is better than a wet dream. We'll skip the car ride. You're hot to trot, huh?'

'Larry, how long are you going to let this high-school dropout insult me?' Honoria asked me. 'Get me out of here!'

99

'I thought you were handling it,' I said, taking her elbow and trying to lead her away.

'Hey,' said Rick. 'I thought you were your own woman.'

'I am!' said Honoria, pulling away from me impatiently. 'I'm in no mood for any of this. I don't want to talk to you or see you, so just back off!'

'High-strung,' the young man said to me. 'A real handful, I bet.'

'Come on, let's go,' I said, again taking Honoria by the arm.

'Hit him!' she said, her voice rising.

'What!?'

'I said hit him! He's insulting us both.' She had her fists clenched and looked ready to hit him herself.

I turned back reluctantly to the teenager.

'Fuck off,' I said.

He was shaking his head sadly.

'I can't fight,' he said, adjusting his leather jacket as if to show that his neatness reduced his threat. 'I'm on probation. And all physical violence is against the rules here. You'll get in trouble if you hit me.'

'Hit him,' Honoria hissed at me.

'I've got to hit you,' I said stupidly.

'Go ahead,' he said, 'but don't blame me when they kick you out.'

'That's fine. I want to leave,' I said and, after a brief hesitation while I considered where and how hard to hit him, I swung a right fist in a short arc which ended striking the upper right part of the young man's chest. Although rocked by the blow he looked down at the area as if a small fly had just landed there.

'Let's go,' I said to Honoria.

'Are you free *tomorrow* night?!' he called after Honoria as we marched off.

By the time we made it to the room I was deeply depressed. First, I saw no way through the strange morass of Lukedom to find my father, and second, Honoria was livid. She was angry for coming to Lukedom, angry for my being so stupid as to want to come, and angry with the people of Lukedom for their concerted efforts to inconvenience or insult her.

I knew that when Honoria was angry the least bad strategy – there were no good strategies – was to remain silent. So we exchanged not a single word from the encounter with the leather jacket to our room

– our accommodations costing $48 for the night, roughly in the mid-range of the options the dice could have chosen.

While Honoria marched off to soak in a hot bath in a huge old clawfoot bathtub, I lay down on one of the sagging twin beds and brooded. I hated my father for setting things up in such a way that I had either to conform to his ways or give up the quest to find him. I supposed I could get a few days' leave out of Blair, Battle and Pike to stay on in Lukedom, but felt it would defeat the purpose of my quest if I compromised with Luke's ways before finding him.

If only there were some easier way to get Jake to tell us where he was. It still seemed logical that Luke might be hiding in Lukedom. The gate and guard might only be a camouflaged early-warning system to inform some central headquarters about who was trying to arrive. The more I thought about it the more I realized that I knew little about what might actually be going on here.

Honoria came out of the bathroom and climbed quickly into the other bed, ostentatiously pulling up the covers and turning her back to me.

'Please turn out the light,' she said. 'I just want to blot out everything.'

'I've been thinking,' I said, staring at the cracked ceiling.

'Don't,' said Honoria. 'I'd rather be buried in jello.'

'I think we should stay here tomorrow and look around,' I went on. 'It's Sunday, and a few more hours here can't hurt us.'

'Of course not,' said Honoria, her back still to me, 'we've already lost the Mercedes, been overcharged for bed and board, and I've got a chance to date the local teenage werewolf.'

From Luke's Journal

We sit in front of TV sets, we read the sacred tables of the baseball statistics, stock quotations, bank balances; we check the grades of children, loved ones, self; we measure salaries, complexions, grades, cars, penises, bosoms, square footage, frontage, savings, neighbour-hoods, nations – everything but vitality, which can't be measured and so is ignored. We measure and triumph or measure and fear; in either case we lose, for both are on a scale which is recognized as valid by only a few. Our triumphs and our tragedies are both mountains of the moment, to be turned at the toll of another hour to ant hills in the dust.

20

Agent Macavoy was doing his duty. He had followed Larry Rhinehart down Interstate 81, enjoying the lush motel Larry chose to stay in, the expense covered by the bureau, and then up and down that incredible dirt road, to the gate of Lukedom. There, however, he had encountered a setback. The guard. The password. The test questions.

Agent Macavoy did not know the password. He flunked the test. Of course the questions, like the password, had changed in the ten minutes since Larry and Honoria had passed through, and the test may have been harder. One question had been how many angels can dance on the head of a pin? Macavoy had hazarded a guess of six, shrewdly thinking it was dicepeople's favourite number (page sixteen of his briefing on dicepeople), but had been told by the guard that the answer was 'very few'.

Agent Macavoy had been turned away from Lukedom, but he was too dedicated an agent to let this deter him for long. He drove about a half mile and then, spotting a little track leading off into the woods, pulled his car in and parked. Here he disencumbered himself of all documents that might identify him as an FBI agent, hiding them under the driver's seat. Then, after locking the car and carrying only a small overnight bag with a single change of clothes, he marched back along the road towards Lukedom.

When the gate came distantly into view he set off through the woods. In another ten minutes he came to a low, run-down stretch of barbed wire fence with a dilapidated sign off to his right which, on closer inspection, read simply: 'Welcome. Abandon all ye who enter here.'

Macavoy, who felt that in leaving his FBI identification he had abandoned quite enough, entered. In half an hour he was walking down the main road into the village.

The bureau briefing file on Lukedom was not helpful. After all, only one of three agents sent to infiltrate it had ever returned. That agent's report was described as a little hysterical and was not included. The summary by his superiors indicated that Lukedom was occupied by up to two thousand people, many of them hippies who smoked dope and were unreliable. They played games which caused confusion. They worshipped dice. Questioning any of them was an unproductive endeavour because one of their principles seemed to be always to lie. There was a police force which kept a kind of order, and normal life seemed to go on. Some respectable citizens seemed to exist. How they coped with the kooks was not clear. If Luke Rhinehart had been there when Agent F— had infiltrated, he had kept well hidden. Rumours of his presence were rife but unsubstantiated.

As Macavoy strode down the centre of the main street – a dirt road still – his strongest impression was that this community was little different from the small North Carolina town in which he'd grown up.

He decided to go into the nearest bar to get the lay of the land. Macavoy was convinced that, despite his business suit, he could blend into a bar better than most agents because of his Irish heritage. He felt he knew the lingo.

The Lucky Seven Bar was not crowded on this summer afternoon and seemed as typical a small-town bar as any Macavoy had been in. He ordered a beer, a Bud to be exact. He then announced to the skinny old bartender: 'Hot today.'

'Yep,' the old guy replied.

'Nice little village you got here,' Macavoy added nonchalantly, looking around the bar as if it were itself the village.

'Yep,' said the old guy.

'I'm in real estate,' Macavoy said. 'Driving around looking for a way to make a buck.'

'Yep,' said the old guy.

'Got any suggestions?' Macavoy prompted.

'Nope.'

Macavoy wandered over to the corner where two guys were shooting pool with a young woman watching. Macavoy shot a pretty fair game himself and figured it would be a good way to break the ice. The bartender had not been a strong source of information.

He watched. The two men moved around the table with a certain awkward macho swagger and it thus took Macavoy about a minute to realize what he was seeing: the two worst pool players in the history of the world. One shooter would announce 'six ball in the side pocket' and not even come close to touching the six ball, much less propelling it towards the side pocket. The next shooter would study the table while letting smoke ooze up around his face from a dangling cigarette and announce 'four ball in corner pocket' and proceed to smash into the centre of a cluster and scatter just about everything except the four ball. At the rate they were going Macavoy would reach retirement before they ever got around to the eight ball.

'How they falling?' he ventured to the younger of the two players.

'Pretty shitty,' he answered. 'I'm not getting good caroms.'

Shit, he could get the best caroms God made and still not sink a golf ball in the ocean from two feet up the beach.

'What's a guy do for action in this town?' Macavoy asked next, purposely making his question vague.

'What you want?' the young guy countered.

'Hey, just something to do,' said Macavoy.

'You name it, Lukedom's got it,' said the young man. 'Fifteen ball in the side pocket.'

Macavoy tried the local diner next, and managed to engage a shrewd-looking man his own age in a conversation that went on for almost half an hour. Although Macavoy learned a great deal about raising chickens he still felt the essence of Lukedom was eluding him. These people seemed, well, retarded, but otherwise perfectly normal. The bill for his hamburger, french fries and a Coke seemed a little high: it was $58.99. He started to protest and then decided he didn't want to draw attention to himself. Besides, he'd bill it to the bureau.

The hotel room, on the other hand, was remarkably cheap: he got a real nice room – a little old-fashioned maybe – for only $13.50 a night, with TV and even a bed massage. He tossed his few belongings on to a chair and automatically switched on the television set as he strode into the bathroom. When he returned, he was surprised to see the President of the United States addressing the nation.

He was doubly surprised in that the President was Dwight David Eisenhower. He decided it must be some documentary, and though in theory Macavoy believed in the value of historical documentaries he began to search for a remote control so he could change the channel, when Chevy Chase began addressing the nation. Ike had been talking about some sort of military-industrial complex, but Chevy was talking about his ability to chew gum and walk at the same time. Maybe this was 'Saturday Night Live', but Ike had sure looked like Ike. Then Adolf Hitler was addressing his nation. He seemed to be getting a lot livelier response than Ike and seemed a lot more emotionally involved in what he was saying, but Macavoy didn't understand German and – then Oprah was addressing the nation – or at least her audience. She seemed to be concerned with transvestites who were prevented from being mothers. Macavoy was slightly interested in this subject but before Oprah could really clarify the issues involved, Sylvester Stallone was addressing . . . well, the camera, the audience.

Macavoy sat on the edge of the bed. What programme was this? Did this set have a built-in channel switcher? No, because everyone who appeared was just talking to the camera. Stallone was followed by Charlie Manson, who was followed by Pope John and then Phyllis Diller talking about mastectomies. Ronald Reagan told the beginning of an anecdote about a welfare mother who didn't get a job because the government paid her to get laid and have babies, and then Bill Moyers was talking about myths and Macavoy finally switched channels.

The cavalry was coming to the rescue. It wasn't yet clear whom they were rescuing, but the sound of the bugle, the yellow scarves trailing in the wind and the give-'em-hell look in John Wayne's eye made it clear some Indians were in trouble and some girl's heart would soon go pitty-pat. Canned laughter flooded over the shouts of the cavalrymen and the beating of the horses' hooves. A two-second image of a man spraying deodorant into an armpit interrupted the action and then the cavalry was upon the redskins and sending them fleeing in disarray. An immaculately coiffured frontier woman stared teary-eyed as the cavalry came riding in, the scene interrupted by another two-second image – this one from an X-rated film showing a woman being sandwiched by two grunting studs. As an Indian went plunging head first from his horse into the dust the canned laughter came flooding across the normal soundtrack and Macavoy wondered if his set had somehow crossed two channels – or three! Had that really been two men banging that blonde? Then a cartoon cat chased Jerry the mouse across the screen for a moment followed by a cavalry man after an Indian and then one miler chasing another miler in a track meet and then a pack of wolves pursuing an elk and Elmer Fudd after Bugs Bunny and a missile after a jet aeroplane and Macavoy simply sat on his bed and stared as one image followed another in haphazard order or ordered chaos, the sequences always seeming just on the edge of saying something but never quite being rational or articulate. It was almost as good as MTV.

An hour and a half later, when he finally turned off the TV set and went to sleep, Macavoy had determined that there were only three channels available on his TV set here in Lukedom, and none of them was like any other channel he had ever encountered. The News Channel – at least that's what it called itself – showed a President Kennedy news conference, a sports summary from 2 January 1968 reporting mostly on the bowl games, a financial report for 3 April 1976, the weather for 3 June 1955 in the midwest, a Time newsreel from the Korean War, and a variety of other items whose sole uniformity was that they all took place in the rather distant past.

The commercials on all three channels were a hodgepodge of segments of various commercials yoked together with the same random relativity of the programmes. They were utterly fascinating and utterly bewildering, especially since several were for products that Macavoy knew no longer existed.

As he fell asleep Macavoy was vaguely deciding to phone his cable company in Alexandria and see if they could sell him any of the three channels, especially the one that kept slipping X-rated scenes into 'All in the Family' and 'Cheers'.

21

After breakfast the next morning Honoria and I were both in better frames of mind. It helped that the Mercedes was back in the parking lot and had been washed and waxed since its little spin. On the front seat was a fifty-cent mint patty and a little note, which read simply: 'Thanks. She drives great! Rick.'

I carefully locked the car this time, but as I moved away the same chubby man commented simply: 'Won't do no good.'

'Well then, what say I hire you to keep an eye on it for me today?'

The man pulled something out of his pocket, squinted into the sky a moment, looked at his hand — it was a die he held — and shook his head.

'Nope,' he said.

Despite this irritating setback, Honoria and I agreed to spend the morning investigating. Although we hoped to find out something about Luke, we ended up finding out mostly about Lukedom.

We got most of our information from the local orientation centre. There we read that the town had been bought by the Dicelife Foundation back in 1975 and undergone various incarnations since. It had begun as an anarchic dice centre in which everyone was supposed to be letting chance influence most of their decisions. Chaos and anarchy followed, and the centre closed down in little more than two years. A total failure, I concluded smugly. After that the site had apparently remained abandoned for most of the next decade.

In 1987 it was reoccupied by some of Luke's followers, and in '88 Lukedom's present incarnation had begun as a highly structured community of people living mostly unstructured lives. Since the five thousand acres of Lukedom were owned by the company that created the community, Lukedom was theoretically private land and mostly self-governing. As far as I could tell, those who lived in Lukedom rarely interacted with anyone outside the community.

There were about two thousand people of all ages now staying in Lukedom. A tiny few had been here almost sixteen years, others only weeks or months. There were a few working farms, a school, a health centre – most of the ingredients of a small self-sufficient community. Some members had paid large fees to enter and/or paid large monthly fees to remain, while others paid little or nothing. I was surprised to learn that some people here hadn't used the dice to make decisions in years: it apparently wasn't required. Others were being trained in expanding role-playing possibilities through chance, and a few nuts were running wild with the dice. After an orientation period of from a week to a month, everyone was free to run their own lives, with or without the personal use of the dice.

The basic principle of the community seemed to be flexibility. Most members had to let the dice choose what job they took, for a given afternoon or day or week or month, from among the jobs listed as available by Orientation's daily computer printout. Living quarters, although more permanent than jobs, might be periodically changed by chance. The laws and rules of Lukedom were also changed sporadically by chance, as if the community itself were a personality in danger of becoming stodgy and stuck.

Although everyone had a great deal of freedom to experiment with their lives, there were societal limits on this experimentation. If you stole a car – there were actually only a few cars in Lukedom and few roads to drive on – you had to return it within twelve hours – thank God. If you robbed someone of anything else you had to return it within twenty-four hours. No physical violence of any kind was allowed – on penalty of being exiled. You could be sexually promiscuous, but the male had always to use a condom. There were frequent 'special' days or hours in which everyone was expected to bring in a harvest or build a house or be their normal selves or live the life of another person for the special time. Controlled chaos, I concluded – as if chaos could ever be controlled.

Still, although I grunted and grimaced as I absorbed all this, I was impressed. Individual diceliving was one thing, but Lukedom seemed to be trying to create a home where people could be more flexible and various than in normal societies. In theory it was interesting. I was almost proud of dear old Dad. In practice I was sure it was as ridiculous and destructive as everything else he'd done.

After our stint in the orientation centre and another at the local library, notable for having half the books placed on shelves at random, Honoria and I agreed to split up. I wanted to try to get into Jake's office to find something there that might hint at Luke's whereabouts. Honoria decided she would make a foray to the main administration offices next to the orientation building. We agreed to meet for lunch at two o'clock at the Hazard Inn, an impressive hotel we'd passed on the way to the library.

Since it was Sunday there were religious services taking place in the Church of the Die. Outside was a neat little bulletin board listing the weekend services: Saturday morning Temple Meeting; 8.00 A.M. Sunday, Catholic Mass; 9.00 A.M. Jehovah's Witnesses; 10.00 A.M. Sufi Dancing; 11.00 A.M. Worship of Chance; noon: Random Rites; 1.00 P.M. Native American Rites; 2.00 P.M. Dionysian Rites. I wondered why they left out poor Zoroaster and Odin.

When I arrived at a little before eleven, the church was filling with people apparently intent on 'worshipping chance' – whatever horror that meant. I snuck around to the back of the building and found an entrance there. I wandered along a hall behind the raised altar part of the church, opening doors off the hallway and finding nothing interesting until I came to 'Master Ecstein's Office'.

Inside were books, tapes, computers and file cabinets – exactly what I was looking for. I quickly examined the correspondence on Jake's desk but found nothing of help – several fan letters praising Jake or Lukedom, letters of inquiry about Lukedom, and a letter from some Psychiatrists' Association reminding Jake to pay his dues. One letter was from someone wanting to write to Luke Rhinehart, could Jake help? At first I was excited by this discovery but then realized there was no way Jake would tell a stranger where Luke was.

The first filing cabinet seemed to be filled with case histories of people's use of chance in their lives and some of Jake's articles on the cases. The second contained a collection of more articles about the dicelife, dice therapies, theories of chance and chaos and multiplicity, some by Jake, some by others. The bottom one, labelled business and finance, was locked.

I wondered whether a locked file cabinet in an office and building and town that seemed lax about locking anything might be significant. In addition, financial information might give me the names and addresses of dozens of other people or entities associated with Jake or Lukedom.

I spent another few minutes going through the desk drawers and even began scrounging through the waste-paper basket. There I noticed some strange stamps on one envelope and saw that it was postmarked 'Tokyo' – and without any return address. I thought no more about it until at the very bottom I came across a second such envelope, similarly postmarked, dated only two days earlier. Yet I hadn't seen any correspondence from anyone or anything from Tokyo.

Tokyo? The Japanese were the most sensible and orderly people on earth. Why would anyone there have anything to do with something as inefficient, unprofitable and totally American as Jake Ecstein and Lukedom? Or my father?

I poured the contents of the basket on to the floor and began searching for the letters that had been in the envelopes, but found nothing, nor on Jake's desk either. I then tried to force open the third drawer of the file cabinet, but couldn't. But in it might be the answer. I'd have to return better prepared. Reluctantly I left.

Out in the hall, I was surprised to hear through the wall the whole congregation belting out something that sounded like a Negro spiritual, having a jazzy tempo and high spirit foreign to more traditional Christian music. I decided to make my way around to the front of the church and sit in for a few moments.

As I slipped inside I was disappointed that the lively music came to an end. As they seated themselves the congregation, filling only about a third of the church – perhaps a hundred in all – seemed to be glowing from banging out the spiritual. They were of all ages and in all manner of dress, and scattered throughout the pews. I walked unobstrusively down a side aisle just as a tall good-looking man rose from beside Jake and went to the altar. He was dressed incongruously in a smart grey business suit and blue tie.

I guessed that it was just my luck to arrive for the passing of the plate, but it was worse. As people around me began the ritual preliminary coughing, I realized I'd arrived just in time for the weekly sermon.

'All ways of liberation start with slavery,' the big man began, speaking without notes and staring benevolently out over the congregation. He had a clipped, snobbish-sounding English accent.

'Convents and monasteries are the Catholic way of destroying the self so that the spirit may live. They exist with a rigid hierarchy and rigid rules and discipline. Their first principle is the total submission of the nun and monk – to God and to the religious order.'

'That's right,' a man in the front row commented.

'In the East, total obedience to the guru is also the first principle of discipleship. The seeker surrenders his will to his teacher, knowing that his own will is the very heart of his enslavement. Giving up one's freedom is, paradoxically, the *sine qua non* of proceeding on the path to liberation.'

'Bullshit,' a voice countered from the back of the room, and a few heads turned to look at the man – but without much surprise.

'The reason this overt enslavement is necessary,' the big Englishman went on, speaking as if he hadn't been interrupted, 'is that as men normally live, their enslavement is hidden. They are enslaved by their past, by their sense of self, by their need for certainty and consistency, by their illusions. The purpose of our enslavement is to free you from your hidden masters so that when we end our overt mastery over you, you will be, for the first time in your lives, free.'

'That's all very nice,' said the loud voice from the back, 'but I bet you never let us go free.'

I was surprised that there was so little concern about the heckling on the part of either the speaker or of the congregation; both seemed to take it as normal.

'Oh, we do, we do,' the Englishman said with a smile. 'We give you periods of freedom even here in your training, periods that permit both us and you to see how much you have become aware of, and free from, the enslavement to traditional thinking and traditional selfhood. We call such periods "recess" – the spiritual equivalent of what you call here a bar's "Happy Hour" – and they are much loved by us all.'

'Amen, amen,' said a chorus of voices.

'Enslavement is in reality just another word for discipline, for training, for education,' the speaker went on, now pacing back and forth at the edge of the raised stage and in front of the altar. 'Instead of teaching you certain skills that let you work at a high level within the established society, here we try to free you from the domination of society so that you can play with the established norms and values rather than be run by them. Normal education teaches conformity and accommodation; ours teaches detachment and flexibility. With the normal diploma one can become a successful business executive. With ours one can become a business executive – or not become one – and change the system – or not change it – succeed in the system – or not succeed – succeed in undoing the system, or in not undoing it. With the normal diploma you remain limited to the norms and values that society offers. With the second you are free to create new norms and values and thus create a new society.'

A second chorus of 'Amens' met this little bit.

'In traditional education you are limited to the dominant values of the society and to lives consistent with conforming to or rebelling against these values. With our education you become free to create new values and new lives unrestricted by the dominant norms. We aim not at making a "better" person or "better" society, at least in traditional terms. Our values are limited to three: playfulness, flexibility and multiplicity. We honour the playful over the serious, the many over the one, and the flexible over the rigid. But that is only to say that we value freedom.

'The dice and chance are simply a method for creating a variety of yeses and a variety of nos; for creating flexibility where rigidity is the norm, for creating play where seriousness is the norm.'

More 'Amens'.

'All happy and fulfilled people have one secret in common: they have all learned to surrender. The only happy and fulfilled Christians are those who have learned to surrender to the spirit of Christ or to the will of God. Their lives are a joyful yea-saying to whatever befalls them because they have faith in God – they surrender to whatever He does, no matter how it may seem evil on the level of their personal values. They may fight the evil or lament it, but they will accept it as the Will of God – and that is the source of their happiness.

'The unhappy man is he who refuses to surrender to something or someone, even to himself! A total egotist may be a happy man: he has surrendered totally to the will of himself – who is infallible.'

'I bet that means you,' commented the heckler in the rear, and someone in the front row snickered. The speaker only smiled.

'So too there are those who find happiness by surrender to institutions – to the army or the church or the family. Such surrenders are confusing because some might say such people crave *order*, but we say that what they crave is surrender. Our "institution" here does not offer order – quite the contrary – but it does demand surrender, and we find that this is the secret of our success because it is the secret of human happiness.

'Of course, we will take you beyond surrender to freedom, where your surrender is of a different nature. In the early stages you surrender to our will or to the will of the die – a specific force which you experience as outside of yourselves. Later, there will be no surrender because there will be no individual separate from the society in which you play. The child at play is not in a state of surrender but rather in a state of unity. Surrender can only exist in a state of duality. As long as the dualities exist just so long will surrender be the secret of human happiness. But once the dual world is broken down in an individual, then there is no one left to surrender and no one or nothing to surrender to.'

'Right on, Preacher,' shouted a woman's voice from the middle of the church.

I was annoyed, mostly, I realized, because I was impressed by the seriousness of the man's talk. It might be nonsense, but it was intelligent nonsense. And the people in the congregation listened with quiet intensity. I watched one woman so closely that the next thing I knew the Englishman had finished his sermon and the whole congregation was standing up. Jake now stood at the altar, and at his signal he and the whole congregation began reciting.

'In the Beginning was Chance,' Jake's voice boomed out over the voices of the others, but was drowned out as the recitation continued. 'And Chance was with God and Chance was God. Lo, though we walk through the Valley of the Shadow of Death, we shall fear no evil, for the Lord Chance watches over us . . . We shall never question the wisdom of Chance. His Ways are inscrutable. He leads us by the hand into an Abyss and, lo, it is a fertile plain. We stagger beneath the burden he places upon us, and behold, we suddenly soar. Let us enclose the Die in our hand and let the Lord Chance enclose us in His.'

As I stood in some shock at this sudden religisizing of what had been pretty intellectual stuff, I abruptly became aware that the sermon and service were over. People were leaving. A little shaken by the whole thing, I followed.

On the steps of the church, Jake and the Englishman who had preached the sermon were greeting the parishioners as they left. I joined the line.

'Hi there, Larry,' said Jake, when my turn came. 'Great sermon, huh? And, say, this is Michael Way, or Master Way on most Sundays.'

I shook hands with Way, a big man in his thirties with a rugged, weather-beaten face and thick rust-coloured hair already streaked with grey. He looked as if he played rugby and enjoyed it.

'You know this is a cult you're creating here,' I said to them.

'Oh, sure,' said Jake. 'But our cult differs from others because we train our guys to leave the cult. Our "graduates" don't need to hang out with cult members or with other graduates. They go back into society – hey, I might even say they disappear back into society – and they almost never try to snare people into our so-called cult.'

'Then how do you ever get anyone to come to this madhouse?' I countered.

'The world has never lacked for dissatisfied people,' said Way. 'Never lacked for seekers, for intelligent people who sense that something is very wrong with the way we live our lives.'

'Dissatisfied maybe,' I said. 'But not crazy.' And I moved on down the steps and away.

22

Honoria had no luck at the administration building. The Dicelife Foundation, she was told, no longer existed, and the present funding of Lukedom was through private donations – presumably, Honoria thought, the guest residents. So she decided to take a more direct approach.

She told the secretary that she was interested in being able to write to Luke Rhinehart. How could she get his address? Sorry, they couldn't help. Well, could they forward a letter to Luke if she left it with them? The secretary didn't think so. Well, where could she find out more about Luke Rhinehart's life and philosophy? Perhaps Jake Ecstein or Michael Way might help. They would both be at the church about this hour.

Honoria wasn't interested in talking to Jake again nor in duplicating Larry's trip to the church, so she moved on.

When she passed a little café with two immaculately-dressed ladies sipping tea in a window seat, she impulsively entered. She ordered tea from the counter and then, her supreme sense of worth carrying her forward, asked the two ladies if she might join them.

After they smilingly urged her to sit, Honoria immediately decided that she had found two kindred souls. Their hairstyles, make-up, dress, the very way they carried their cups of tea to their mouths, blared forth breeding. After a few brief pleasantries about the tea and the surprisingly fine china it was being served from, Honoria got to the point.

'I've only been here a few days,' she said, 'and I still haven't met Luke Rhinehart. Have you?'

'Oh, yes,' said the taller and slightly older of the two, a distinguished and dignified middle-aged lady. 'Many times. He can be a dear.'

'Or an asshole,' said the other, bringing her teacup to her lips with classic elegance.

Although surprised at this breach of tea etiquette, Honoria managed a smile. The second woman, now that Honoria looked at her more closely, definitely was not quite as refined as the first, her hair being a bit too obviously dyed.

'But how does one get to meet him?' she asked casually.

'Oh, it just happens,' said the dignified lady. 'Often when you least expect it.'

'And usually when you least want it,' said the other, grinning.

'But . . . if one wanted to initiate such a meeting?' Honoria asked.

'Oh, I don't think so,' said the first. 'It just isn't done. Luke is just too elusive.'

'How . . . elusive?' asked Honoria, feeling that she was on the brink of a breakthrough.

'Oh, he's just never the same,' the woman answered. 'He can change his clothes, his looks.'

'Usually for the worst,' commented the second.

'Is there any place in particular one might visit and expect he might show up there?' Honoria prodded.

The two women exchanged glances and then the older one shrugged.

'The Hazard Inn, I suppose,' she said. 'Everyone ends up there.'

A lead, a lead. The conversation continued for another half-hour and Honoria probed but picked up nothing else of interest. The two women had been at Lukedom for about six months and lived 'usually' in a house a few blocks away. They apparently held a variety of jobs.

After thanking them, Honoria went on her way, stopping briefly to window-shop in a small boutique with stunningly up-to-date fashions mixed in with utter garbage. Then it was on to the Hazard Inn.

The exterior of the building was quite impressive: eighty years ago it must have been the grandest thing in town. Indeed it still was: a grand old Victorian hotel that had been reasonably restored to something of its old splendour. Honoria marched briskly up the steps.

The lobby of the Hazard Inn was, however, something of a shock.

Many of the guests looked as if they were just coming off the back lot of a grade-B movie set or had been issued elaborate costumes for some sort of party. There was a man dressed as Superman, a clown, two nuns, two women who seemed to have every article of clothing and every mannerism of blatant hookers, a rabbi, one football player and several men who looked as if they might be Hell's Angels. Although the few normal-looking people seemed at ease, Honoria wasn't. She took one long look and then wheeled to leave.

She went out on to the porch feeling distinctly ill-at-ease. If Luke Rhinehart was in there she wasn't sure she wanted to meet him.

As she stood wondering what to do next she noticed a disconcertingly well-built hunk striding down the sidewalk trailed by several people, mostly women, staring up at him adoringly. Not only was he good-looking, but he was dressed impeccably in a suit that might have been stolen from William Fanshawe Battle III's own huge walk-in closet. As he waved off his hangers-on at least two of them said 'Thank you, Mr Way' and 'See you later, Michael.' So this was the other bigwig.

As the man bounded up the stairs of the inn, looking as if he owned it all, Honoria stepped casually up to meet him.

'Mr Way?' she asked with her best smile.

'Absolutely, my dear,' he answered, stopping and smiling. 'What can I do for you?'

'If you've got a moment,' she said. 'Perhaps you can help me with a few questions I have. My name is Honoria Battle.'

'It's a pleasure,' he said. 'Certainly, yes, I do have a moment. Tea?'

Tea was about the last thing in the world that Honoria wanted at this point, but she greeted the invitation with a smile worthy of an invitation to a coronation.

'Why, thank you, that would be wonderful.'

Michael Way smoothly took Honoria by the elbow and steered her back into the lobby. He was such a big man, and so sure of himself, that he immediately made Honoria feel ultra-feminine. As they entered and crossed the lobby, now filled with a slightly different but equally bizarre melange of people, including several men crawling around on the floor behaving like some sort of animal, this time with her best front of *sang froid* Honoria marched through the show towards what she hoped would be a normal coffee shop.

It *was* a normal coffee shop and, being on the arm of what she believed was the best-looking, best-dressed, and most intelligent man in all of Lukedom, Honoria felt particularly attractive and desirable as they entered.

They took a chair overlooking a playground in the back of the inn. For some reason, the playground – containing swings, slides, teeterboards, sandboxes and jungle gyms – was occupied mostly by adults. Honoria tried not to stare at the grandmotherly types swinging skywards, their skirts billowing, or the two middle-aged men arguing in the sandbox over rights of way for their trucks.

As they ordered and began talking, Way continued to impress Honoria: even more than his having been a star rugby player at Oxford was the fact that he'd gotten a law degree from Harvard. She immediately began to discuss the philosophy of Lukedom as if it actually interested her and might have some merit. Finally she casually asked how she might meet Luke Rhinehart.

'You know,' he said in response, 'it's possible that Luke doesn't exist.'

'What do you mean?' she asked.

'I mean both that he may be dead and, on the other hand, that he may never have existed.'

'Well, he certainly existed,' returned Honoria. 'His son is one proof, and I've already met several people who actually have met him, recently – *they* certainly feel he's alive.'

'Yes, but he may not exist the way people think he does,' Way went on. 'Certainly from what you were telling me, the Luke that Larry is carrying around in his mind doesn't exist, wouldn't you agree?'

'Oh, in that way,' said Honoria. 'I quite agree.'

'Isn't that wonderful,' said Way, gesturing at the middle-aged men and women playing on the jungle gym and in the sandbox outside their window.

Honoria managed a smile.

'Oh, yes,' she said. 'I love to see older people playing with children.'

'Shall we join them?' asked Mr Way.

The prospect of grubbing in the sand or contorting in a jungle gym in her new business suit did not appeal to Honoria.

'Oh, not now, I guess,' she replied with a bright smile.

'We'll have to get you some play clothes,' suggested Mr Way, looking at her suit as if it had been soiled.

'What about yours?' she returned.

'Definitely,' Way agreed. 'I just put it on as a long shot for my Sunday sermon.'

'Aren't you a businessman?'

'Sometimes,' he said, 'but thankfully not too often. How about you, are you often a child?'

Honoria's head tilted to one side questioningly.

'For eleven years I was,' she said, smiling.

'I mean these days,' he said. 'Don't you feel the need to be a child at times?'

'No,' she answered. 'As you can see, I'm all grown up now and don't see the need for it.'

'What do you feel the need of?' Way asked, looking at her directly.

'Of simply being who I am,' she answered, becoming annoyed with his questioning.

'And who are you?' he asked.

She was silent a moment and then said: 'Can't you tell?'

'No, I can't, actually,' he countered easily. 'Although my major interest is in opening people up to who they are.'

'You make us sound like cans of tomato soup,' said Honoria, clenching and unclenching her fingers. 'I don't need opening up.'

'Of course not,' said Way. 'That's why you're getting upset and balling your hands into fists.'

Michael Way was rapidly losing his appeal.

'I've got itchy palms. I always get them when talking to a boor.'

'That's fine, but what have I said or done to make you call me a boor?'

Honoria reached for the glass of water and got hold of herself. Somehow she was not coming off the way she wanted to. She had definitely lost her cool. After taking a leisurely swallow she looked up at him with her most brilliant smile.

'Nothing, of course,' she said. 'I'm afraid our long auto trip yesterday and our car's being stolen with all our luggage has made me unusually sensitive. You *do* come across a bit like a truck backing into my Porsche. But please forgive me.'

'Great comeback,' said Way, grinning. 'Would you like me to tell you why all these people in the lobby are in costumes?'

'Not really,' she replied.

'It might lead you closer to finding Dr Rhinehart,' said Way.

Honoria couldn't tell from his expression whether he was bullshitting her or not.

'All right, then, yes,' she said.

The Hazard Inn, it turned out, was patterned somewhat after the original dice centres that Luke Rhinehart had created back in the good old days of the sixties and early seventies, when kooks were given a chance to carry their kookiness to its logical extreme. Over the reception desk were three signs: 'Anybody can be anybody', 'Die-ing is the way of life', and 'This Truth above all: Fake it'. Apparently all who came were expected to experiment with different role-playing.

As Honoria followed Mr Way down the main hallway what she saw made her increasingly tense and suspicious, wondering whether this Oxford man and Harvard lawyer was about to force her into some terrifying act and claim it was for her own benefit. Each room off the hallway was a 'playroom', each with its own labels, some harmless-sounding, others bizarre, and yet others threatening. There was a Rec Room, a Creativity Room, a Meditation Room on the one hand, but then a Slaves' Quarters, a Children's Playroom, a Death Room, a Madhouse, an Emotional Roulette Room, something called the Pit, a Random Body Room, a Love–Hate Room – even a Room Room. According to Way each was specially designed for people to express themselves in the way the room's environment encouraged.

'Just a moment,' said Honoria, coming to a halt when she noticed the Death Room. 'Exactly where are we going?'

'With your permission,' said Way, smiling, 'I'd like to introduce you to one of our techniques – nothing physical or dangerous, I assure you. And no one will be watching except me, and I don't count.' He laughed. 'I'd just like to help you in seeing what this place is all about.'

'No force, no gimmicks, no whips or handcuffs?' Honoria asked, beginning to relax.

'The only enemy you'll find will be yourself,' he commented, returning her smile. He then took her arm and led her on and into the Love–Hate Room.

On two of the windowless walls were soft flowing murals, peaceful and gentle, presumably representing the mood of love. The other two walls were filled with violent colours and sharp angles, surreal images of weapons and faces contorted with hatred, headless animals linked by chains, screaming skulls – the usual nightmares of modern art. The only furniture in the room were six double chairs, each having two seats yoked together in such a way that the two people sitting in them had to face each other with their knees touching. Way led Honoria over to one pair and motioned for her to sit.

He explained to her that playing love–hate was simple. Each person chose from three to six people, then let a die choose one, and a second die choose whether the emotion to be felt and expressed towards that person was love or hate. One of the persons always available as an option was the person sitting opposite you. If the die chose your father to love or hate you were to see the individual opposite you as that father and express the emotion directly at him or her.

Michael Way went first. He listed as his three options to love or hate himself, Honoria and his mother. The die chose Honoria and then chose love.

So for the next two minutes Mr Way expressed his love for Honoria. His eyes softened, he reached forward and took her hand, and when he spoke, it was in a soft, husky voice.

'I love you, Honoria,' he began simply but with such apparent feeling that Honoria felt herself flush. 'You're the most beautiful being I've ever known. You move like some great princess, carrying yourself proudly, your lovely eyes looking at things as a queen surveys her kingdom . . . And yet . . .' (and here he reached up and caressed her face) '. . . beneath the sweet lushness of your sensual abundance I sense a little girl frightened of herself . . . frightened of all the respect and power the woman Honoria has, frightened that the little girl might not be able to handle it . . . And I love this little girl in you too, Honoria, love you that you so bravely keep her hidden . . . Love you that . . .'

By the time the automatic timer signalled the end of the two minutes, Honoria felt tears glistening in her eyes. She rarely cried.

Way stopped as abruptly as he had begun, becoming neutral as quickly as he had become passionate.

122

'Your turn,' he said, pushing back his mop of curly hair.

Honoria listed Mr Way and Larry and her father as the three options and the die chose Larry. The next die also chose love.

Honoria sat silently for several seconds, aware that the seconds were silently ticking away as she groped to try to express the feelings of love.

'I love you, Larry,' she finally said hesitantly, but in a voice that might just as well have been announcing her going to the drugstore to pick up some Extra Strength Tylenol. 'You're exactly the man I've always dreamed of marrying . . . handsome . . . successful . . . ambitious . . . I love . . . the way you . . . get excited . . . about your futures trading . . . You, your soul, I love . . . except of course your father . . . I mean I love . . . I love the way . . . I love your . . . abilities . . .'

Honoria, confused and a little shaken, lapsed into silence. The timer finally indicated the end of the two minutes.

'I take it you don't actually have much feeling for this Larry fellow,' commented Mr Way.

'No, I . . . I'm finding this not at all easy.'

'Don't worry about it,' said Way. 'You're doing fine. My turn.'

Way then was randomly told to hate his father.

In the next two minutes he directed such an incredible barrage of venom, hatred and rage against Honoria (his father) that she found herself pressing herself against her chair to escape, chilled to her core. His face became contorted, his fists clenched; he drooled, shouted, glared, his body rearing at her like a wild dog chained just out of the reach of its prey. When he was finished Honoria was so frightened she urinated slightly in her pants.

It took Way a little longer to recover from expressing hatred than it had love. Finally, he sighed and said again to Honoria: 'Your turn.'

Honoria was so upset she wasn't sure she could go on, but didn't want to confess that she had been so moved.

This time the die chose Honoria herself to be the object of her own emotion and again chose love as the emotion to be expressed.

She relaxed just a bit. Love for herself – that should be a snap. She sat up straighter in her chair, and took two deep breaths, trying to relax further but aware of a high level of anxiety lying like lead in her stomach. Let's see, Michael Way was supposed now to be her. She must express her love for herself at him. As she looked at him her jaw felt frozen, her whole self felt suddenly frozen.

'Honoria, you're wonderful,' she began after a ten- or fifteen-second pause. 'You're one of the most accomplished women I've ever known.' Again, even as she spoke, she realized that the voice was all wrong – it sounded like one society matron talking to another about one of their daughters. She stopped and cleared her throat, stirring uncomfortably in her chair.

'I love you, Honoria . . .' she began again, her effort at expressing love coming out stiltedly. 'You have created for yourself exactly the life . . . you dreamed of . . . You are bright, successful, beautiful, rich . . . You can do anything you want to, the sky's the limit!' Honoria was barking out the words like a marine sergeant stirring a young recruit to toughness. 'You . . . are a fantastic woman! A beautiful woman! Men pursue you, lust for you! Other women envy you! You are a queen! You are – '

Honoria broke off, aware that there hadn't been a drop of love in anything she'd felt or said. She felt only a tense numbness, then anger, at first undirected, and then suddenly and satisfyingly, directed at Mr Way. The timer at last signalled the time limit had passed.

'What incredible crap this all is!' said Honoria, prying herself out of the chair and standing. 'I can't act, and never said I could! And I make no claim to being able to conjure up emotions like a robot.'

'Oh, no, Honoria,' Mr Way said gently. 'You know – '

'I know that you're a psychological bully!!' she said, her voice quavering. 'That's what I know!'

When Way stood and reached out a comforting hand, she brushed it aside and rushed from the room.

23

After leaving the church, I spent an unproductive hour trying to talk to people and get a sense of Lukedom or a hint about my father, but got nowhere. The only interesting conversation I had was with the guy who had stolen my car, who turned out also to be the teenage werewolf who had accosted Honoria in the bar. He introduced himself as Rick and wanted to compliment me about the Mercedes.

'You know I'd never hurt your car,' Rick assured me as I decided to head over to the Hazard Inn to meet Honoria. 'Stealing cars is just part of my trying to expand my talents.'

'Well, expand your talents with someone else's car,' I said, hurrying my pace.

'I was a pretty shy teenager when I got here four months ago,' Rick went on earnestly. 'Chicks scared me shitless and I could barely drive. But I keep challenging myself to expand.'

'Good. Keep it up. But not with my car.'

'Now I can be either a cool dude or a nerd,' Rick continued with increasing enthusiasm. 'I can handle cars and cycles and even the big bulldozer over at the south construction site. If you just trust the dice, it's amazing what things you can do you never knew about!'

'Ever let the dice choose walking?' I asked irritably.

'Hey, sure!' Rick reassured him. 'The dice had me run a six-minute mile!' As I strode on even faster, Rick had to hurry to keep up. 'What have the dice told you to do?' he asked.

'To leave this place as soon as possible,' I announced and left Rick in the dust.

A minute later I met Honoria just outside the inn, striding down the stairs as if in the midst of a fire drill.

'Hi,' I said. 'What's happening? Aren't we going to eat?'

'We're leaving,' Honoria announced, her soprano voice higher than normal. She didn't even slow down as she strode past me to head for the Do Dice Inn. Baffled, I hurried after her.

'What's the matter?' I asked as I pulled up beside her. 'What happened?'

'Nothing happened!' she returned. 'I've just decided I don't like this place. We're leaving.'

'But I think I've got a lead,' I persisted. 'In Jake's office at the church – '

'Screw your leads!' she snapped back, careening around the corner and continuing at full throttle the last hundred feet towards the Do Dice Inn.

Stunned at her upset, I hurried after her.

Inside our hotel room, Honoria began flinging her clothing into her three expensive pieces of luggage while I numbly began to pack my one suitcase.

'Are you saying a prayer over that sweater?' Honoria snapped at me. I'd been holding a sweater over my case for half a minute.

I shook my head.

'I don't think we should go, Nori,' I said. 'I've got to stay at least until I can get into the file cab – '

'Well I'm going!' Honoria interrupted wildly. 'And going now! You can continue your sick search for your father back in New York – where I'm in no danger of being browbeaten by philosophical fullbacks or propositioned by teenage car thieves.'

'But here is where – '

'Hire a private detective! We're going.' Honoria snapped closed the last of her three bags, a bra strap dangling out of it like a tail, and began to get into her raincoat inside out.

I dropped the sweater into the suitcase but then just stared down at it.

'What are you standing there for?' Honoria said. 'Help me!'

Scowling, I went around the bed and helped her the rest of the way into her raincoat.

'Look, Nori,' I said. 'You can go. I know you want to get back to work tomorrow morning. I'll drive you to an airport or you can take the car, but I've got to stay at least another day.'

Honoria had gone to the vanity to scoop the last of her cosmetics into her shoulder bag, but paused to glare at me.

'You can't mean it,' she said. 'I've had one upsetting experience after another since arriving here. And I want to go home!'

'I know, I know,' I said, coming up to her to take her in my arms, but as I approached and saw how stiff and cold she stood I felt like a small sailboat gliding towards an iceberg. 'And I'll help you, but I myself – '

'If you don't come with me now,' said Honoria, pulling away from my embrace, 'our engagement is off! I won't marry a man who loves his neurosis more than me!'

I again tried to go to her and again she retreated, backing towards the door as if I were a potential rapist.

'If you love me, you'll give up this silly quest and come this minute!' she said, stamping impatiently.

I finally turned away, went to the near bed and slid her other two bags on to the floor. I left my own suitcase open on the other bed.

'I can see I mean nothing to you,' Honoria said quietly, her face flushed. She stared for a moment at her engagement ring and shakily pulled it off her finger. Then, with a scream, she threw it at me, sending it sailing past my shoulder against a bureau and on to the floor.

'You can have it back,' she hissed. 'It's as phoney as your love!' she said.

'Look, Honoria,' I began. 'Can't you see – '

'My jeweller said the diamond was flawed!' she interrupted and, head high, swung her blonde hair to leave.

'Just bring my bags,' she added as she disappeared out into the hall.

Outside, the Mercedes was, as usual, missing.

'I knew it!' Honoria moaned, as she stood amid her bags at the edge of the street. 'This whole place is just a vast conspiracy to drive people crazy!'

As Honoria continued to rail, for some reason I felt like giggling, but managed to control myself and go to phone a cab. However, the bartender informed me that cabs couldn't come into Lukedom since no cabbie had ever guessed the password. Even as I again suppressed giggles, I wondered vaguely how people managed to leave when I saw out the window that my Mercedes had magically appeared from nowhere and that Honoria was getting in. When I saw that the person helping Honoria with her luggage was Rick, I hurried out.

As I came trotting down the wooden steps of the inn, Rick had finished throwing Honoria's bags in the trunk of the car and was blithely getting into the driver's side. Honoria was pulling the passenger door closed behind her.

I rushed up to the car to lean in to peer past Rick to Honoria.

'What are you doing!?' I asked. 'Don't you remember who this is!?'

'Of course I do,' said Honoria, her eyes a haze of hysteria. 'He's an admirer. He adores me. And he has promised to serve my every need, which is more than I can say for my last admirer.'

'I told you she was feisty,' said Rick, smiling up at me.

'Where are you going?' I asked.

'Rick said he'll drive me to the nearest airport,' said Honoria. 'And I believe him.'

'I'll do it,' I said. 'It's my car, for Christ's sake.'

'Hey, man, your time is too valuable,' said Rick.

I stared at the grinning young man in disbelief. On the other hand, my time *was* valuable.

'Any chance you'll bring the car back?' I asked sardonically.

'Sure, man,' said Rick happily. 'These are the best wheels we've had in Lukedom since I've been here!'

'I'll phone you tonight,' I said reluctantly to Honoria, straightening and standing back from the car.

'Don't bother,' said Honoria, turning her face away.

'You can phone *me*,' Rick said to me with a grin, the engine running now and ready. 'Although I don't actually have a phone.' And, in a shower of stones, he roared away.

— 24 —

For Honoria, the drive to the Wickstown airport was a trifle unnerving. Rick approached every curve on the windy dirt road as if it were the finish line of the Daytona 500 and, on the main highway, he came up behind each car as if it were parked, and roared past in similar fashion.

At the airport she was dismayed to find that all flights to anywhere that might get her back to New York were ended for the day, Sunday flights being limited. She collapsed on to a bench while Rick rushed off to see what he could do.

He came back twenty minutes later with a big grin.

'Got you a plane,' he announced, gathering up her three bags.

'You're a doll!' Honoria said, leaping up with the first burst of happiness since meeting Way. 'But how — '

'It's a special charter,' announced Rick, bounding along ahead of Honoria despite the three bags. 'Not sure of the cost.'

'Oh, hang the cost!' said Honoria. 'That's why rich people get rich.'

Rick led her out of the main building and in among a cluster of small planes, coming up finally to a small two-engine Cessna, its door already open.

'Here we are,' he announced. 'Flight 006 for good old La Guardia.' He tossed the three bags up into the plane and then helped Honoria to board.

'Little cramped, I'm afraid,' Rick said as he pulled himself up behind her.

There were in fact only four seats in the passenger area and Honoria happily sat herself down on the front one on the right.

'This is fine,' she said. 'When does the plane leave?'

Rick looked at his watch.

'About five minutes, I think.'

Honoria looked out the window towards the main building, hoping to see the pilot or the flight attendants on their way. Rick poked his head into the pilot's area and then disappeared inside. She thought it nervy of him to do so, but based on her two encounters with him, nerve was not something he lacked.

She opened her handbag and took out a mirror and some lipstick. She'd been biting her lip steadily since her encounter with Way. She heard an engine sputter and roar off to the left and at first assumed that it was that of a nearby aeroplane. Then the right engine on her own plane — just outside her window — spun, coughed and then roared into motion.

My God, what was Rick doing!!?

Honoria started to undo her seat buckle, her mouth agape and lipstick rolling to the floor.

'Uh, this is your pilot speaking,' came a deep reassuring male voice, much deeper than Rick's although somehow similar. 'We're cleared for take-off at sixteen hundred hours . . .' Abruptly the plane lurched forward like a drunk who has suddenly decided in which direction to head. Honoria was thrown back, grabbing desperately at the arms of her seat.

'Estimated flight time to New York,' continued the deep voice from the speaker system, 'is three and a half hours. We'll be flying at about ten thousand feet . . . At two hundred knots.'

A 'fasten seatbelt' sign began flashing reassuringly on a panel in front of her and Honoria hopefully rebuckled herself in. Could someone who spoke so comfortingly and knowledgeably and deeply about altitude and knots and estimated flight time not be a pilot? Despite the clamouring of her common sense, which she was aware had deserted her totally much earlier in the afternoon, Honoria settled back a little deeper into her seat, her eyes noticing the parked planes they were taxiing past.

Then the Cessna made an abrupt right turn and headed down another concrete path that Honoria assumed was a runway, although on the other side of the plane she might have been worried to see a line of parked cars and several people staring at the taxiing Cessna in disbelief.

'We're cleared for take-off, folks,' came the pilot's voice, still seeming to Honoria to be much too deep for Rick and yet somehow so like his. 'So make sure your seatbelts are fastened . . .' The plane now quickly swung around one hundred and eighty degrees and its engines began to roar in earnest.

'. . . And your seats in an upright position . . . 'cause, Baby, *here we go!!!*'

There was no mistaking Rick's voice now, nor the squealing of the wheels as the plane surged forward.

Eyes wide as saucers, fingers digging into the armrests, Honoria began mumbling for the first time in twenty years her childhood prayers.

The Cessna roared down the access road directly towards a late-model BMW which quickly showed the manoevrability for which German engineering is famous by making a right-angle turn out of the way of the oncoming plane and into a parking place between a pick-up and a Ford van which, unfortunately, was not wide enough, and the BMW had to wedge itself in by ploughing the two other vehicle sideways and out. The driver thus avoided the plane but was trapped inside the BMW for the next six hours.

The Cessna became airborne just in time to avoid a Cadillac which was crossing the access road at that point.

The Cessna continued to gain altitude, just managing to miss the control tower itself. Since the two air traffic controllers on duty did not normally monitor access roads for aircraft taking off, they never saw the plane coming, and when it passed across in front of their tower only ten feet away, they were both left in a state of shock.

As the Cessna continued to climb, Honoria was quite impressed with the take-off, much smoother than those of most small planes she'd flown in. Below her on the ground she could see a cluster of people wildly moving their arms. Sitting back in her seat and beginning to relax, Honoria smiled and waved back.

That evening at the Battle apartment Mr Battle was enjoying a rare moment of leisure in front of the rerun of the film *Patton* when Honoria burst into the room and, with a loud groan, collapsed on the couch. Kim and the housekeeper, both looking concerned, hastened in after her.

'Nori!!' Mr Battle said. 'You're back!?'

Honoria sprawled arms akimbo on the couch, staring vacantly out into the room. She looked drugged or shell-shocked. Kim ran over and knelt in front of her, taking one of her hands.

'What's the matter?' Kim asked.

Honoria simply stared out into the room.

Mr Battle rose with great dignity and restraint and walked over to stand looking down at his daughter.

'That will be all, Elsie,' he said to the housekeeper. 'I'll call if we need you.'

'Yes, sir.'

After Elsie had left, Mr Battle turned back to his daughter.

'Where's Larry?' asked Mr Battle.

'In hell, as far as I'm concerned,' said Honoria.

'What happened!?' pressed Kim.

Honoria came out of her trance to lean towards Kim.

'You have no idea what it's like in Lukedom,' she said. 'Nothing's reliable.'

'But where's Larry?' persisted Mr Battle.

'I don't want to talk about it,' said Honoria, collapsing back into the couch.

'Is he still there?' asked Kim.

'He deserted me,' said Honoria. 'He's somehow been infected with dice measles!'

'And he's still there?' persisted Mr Battle.

'Be serious,' said Kim, standing with a frown. 'You left and he stayed?' she asked.

'I begged him to come. He refused. I want nothing more to do with him.'

'Nonsense, my dear,' said Mr Battle. 'Larry may be temporarily deranged, but that's no reason – '

'I've broken our engagement and given him back his imitation ring,' said Honoria.

'You didn't!?' said Kim.

'I did,' said Honoria. 'I should have done it years ago.'

'You've only been engaged for two months,' Kim reminded her.

'I made a mistake.'

'Nonsense, Daughter, you – '

'I was kidnapped. I almost died.'

'Kidnapped!?' Kim exclaimed.

'How did you almost die?' asked Mr Battle with a frown.

'I trusted a teenage rapist.'

'What happened?!'

'A kamikaze madman from that horrible place kidnapped me into an aeroplane and then tried to commit hari-kari by landing on the Long Island Expressway.'

'That's impossible!' said Mr Battle. 'What about traffic?'

Honoria settled for a scream.

From Luke's Journal

Ah, the human charade. What fun it would be if the players only knew they were playing! In the theatre if an actor begins to 'live' his role, to 'become' the character he is playing, we call him insane. But in life we actors take all our roles seriously, 'live' each one, 'become' each one and are, accordingly, insane.

To live we must play roles. The question is only whether we let the roles play us or let us play the roles. When a role plays us we become absorbed in it, identified with it. Its loss is our loss; its triumph, our triumph. We take it seriously. We suffer.

Why did nature build into humans this destructive, anti-joy original sin element of seriousness? Without it men might float like a butterfly, sting like a bee. With seriousness we float like elephants and sting like fleas.

25

It took me a couple of hours to recover from Honoria's departure. At first I maturely tried to drown my worries in a few drinks at the inn bar but was distracted by people coming up to me and starting conversations that seemed to interest them but not me. I regretted letting Honoria go, wishing that I'd gone with her or had insisted we stay until the next morning. I knew I'd never shake the deep anxiety I was feeling until I got back to Honoria, Wall Street and sanity. If I was to achieve anything from this disastrous trip then I had to try to learn all I could in the next few hours and to hell with the consequences. Since normal laws obviously didn't hold sway in Lukedom even if I were caught red-handed breaking into Jake's office, so what? The worst thing Lukedom would do to me was kick me out!

So I dropped into the town hardware store and purchased a small crowbar, a hacksaw, a flashlight and even a set of skeleton keys, though I doubted they'd fit any lock I might get interested in. It was too bad Rick wasn't back from the airport: he could probably steal anything without all this hardware.

After dinner, when it was fully dark, I marched over to the church which, thankfully, was lightless and seemed deserted. The side door was locked but the main door to the church itself was unlocked! I wandered down the central aisle and up past the altar and off to the right where I saw a passageway. Sure enough it led down a short hall to a door which was, *voilà!*, unlocked. I recognized the new hallway as the one leading to Jake's office.

The office door was locked and none of the skeleton keys fitted, but I grinned. I then took great pleasure in using the crowbar to split the door open, happy to see the lock dangling nicely askew when I was finished.

Inside, I went to the desk to see if anything interesting was there that hadn't been in the office on Sunday. There was some new correspondence, but again nothing but fan letters, inquiries, psychiatric pamphlets and a letter of insider gossip.

I then attacked the locked drawer of the file cabinet. Again the crowbar did the trick, leaving the lock a hapless clump of metal on the floor and the whole front plate of the cabinet swaying in the wind, fastened now only on one side.

But the files themselves were less fun. They were arranged chronologically, starting in 1975, thick files for the early years, then a decade of thin ones, then thick files again for the last three years. I began browsing through 1990 for references to my father but was disappointed to find none whatsoever. As I continued scanning various documents I gradually became aware of references to DI, capitalized but without periods. Whether DI was a person or an organization wasn't clear, but whoever or whatever it was, DI was an important contributor to Lukedom – especially money. Most references to DI were in connection with receiving or requesting funds.

This was clearly important, but nothing I read indicated where or in what manner this DI existed, human or institutional.

After a half-hour I tired of scanning documents in the dim light of my flashlight and went to the waste-paper basket. After spilling the contents on to the floor I was about to kneel down to make a search when I realized someone had turned on the hall light.

Footsteps began echoing down the hall towards me. A man was humming. I remained frozen, standing next to the open and battered file cabinet, my feet buried in the sea of trash from the waste-paper basket, staring at the open and damaged office door.

Jake arrived, switched on the office light and stopped to stare at me.

'Jesus,' said Jake. 'What a mess!'

I looked down at the jumble I was standing in, then back at Jake.

'Looks like a break-in,' said Jake, fingering the broken lock of his door. 'You notice anyone?'

I stared at Jake.

'Notice?'

'Yeah,' said Jake, finally entering and taking a seat in his desk chair. 'Anyone leaving when you came into the building?'

'Uh, no.'

'Jesus, the guy left his crowbar,' said Jake, taking hold of the instrument I'd left on Jake's desk. 'Can you get fingerprints from metal?'

'I don't think so,' I said, trying casually to hold my flashlight behind my back.

'Hell, who cares?' said Jake. 'There's nothing worth stealing in here anyhow. Probably just some random dice decision.'

'It was me,' I at last blurted.

'You made a random dice decision?' said Jake, looking up. 'That's great!'

'I broke in here,' I continued, beginning at last to feel something, namely annoyance. 'It's me who wrecked the file cabinet and spilled the trash.'

'That's terrific!' said Jake, swinging around in his chair and beaming at me. 'What else did the dice tell you to do?'

'It wasn't the dice!' I snapped. 'I broke in here to try to find out something about my father!'

Jake frowned.

'Oh,' he said. 'And you didn't ask the dice if it was a good idea?'

'No.'

'Oh.'

'Who or what is DI?' I asked aggressively.

'Ah.'

'And who's writing you from Tokyo?'

'Ah, ha.'

'Well?'

Jake continued frowning and finally emitted a big sigh.

'You'll never get anyplace without the dice,' he said sadly. 'As long as you make your own decisions you'll look in all the wrong places. You expect to find a letter from Luke in there?'

'I didn't know what I'd find,' I said, kneeling now and beginning to put the trash back in the basket. 'I just knew you weren't helping but that you must know where Luke is.'

'Hey, I'm helping!' insisted Jake, bending forward in his chair to help with the clean-up. 'You've already been here two days and only need another five for me to give you a real lead. You're just not patient.'

'What's DI?' I asked Larry, standing and irritably reclaiming my crowbar from the desk.

Jake looked up without expression for a long moment, then sighed.

'I can tell you in five days. Tomorrow morning you have to start work with your diceguide. He – or maybe it'll be a she – will really let you know what's what.'

'I already know what's what.'

'Sure,' said Jake, 'and he'll teach you what else can be what if you just give it a chance.'

I glared at Jake for a long moment and then marched out. I didn't even bother to reclaim my hacksaw.

26

Alone in an unaccustomed bed, listening to startling and unnerving sounds, I slept badly and was awakened by a cacophony of bird calls, caws, coos and warbles that made me wonder how anyone in the country ever managed to sleep past daybreak. I was used to getting up at seven each morning to catch the results of the overnight trading in Tokyo, but the birds must have been even more interested in the markets since they started at six. Wobbly, blurry-eyed, I dressed and went down the stairs to pretend to conform to Lukedom and see what I could find.

The dicetrainer turned out to be a she – the young woman in purple slacks and matching print top who had found everything 'wonderful' at the orientation centre. This morning she was dressed in a severe grey suit and her name was no longer Wendy. She introduced herself as Ms Kalb, Kathy Kalb. It was her task, she announced, to let you people – there were ten or eleven others besides me – discover how we could enrich our lives by letting chance come in.

The class – if that's what it was – took place in a small room in the back of the orientation building. There were thirteen or fourteen old school desk-chairs and a small lectern. Kathy paced in front of the students, a half-dozen sitting in each of the first two rows, and me alone in the third. I thought it was all very shabby. I almost felt embarrassed for my father. *This* was all that was left of the Dice Man's legacy? A flaky female in a run-down back room preaching about letting chance, like a poor man's holy ghost, into our lives? And to find Luke I was going to have to sit through it!

Kathy, it turned out, was no fool. She knew what she was talking about, cared what she was talking about, and didn't give a damn if we were stupid or resisting or fawning or what we were. She made it clear in her manner that everyone was a total fool and that the only salvation lay in flexible multiple foolishness rather than rigid single foolishness.

'Die-ing is simple,' she began. 'Instead of doing what your usual self wants to do, list some other options that a small part of you feels might be possible or interesting, and then cast a die to choose from among them. At the simplest level the dice choose among films, books, clothing, food, friends and activities open to you at a given time. At a more challenging level, the dice come to choose *how* you act, which kind of person you pretend to be – which kind of person you in effect *are*.'

She strode back and forth in front of us, stopping to peer intensely first at one person and then another.

'Our basic principles are also simple. First, all humans in complex and contradictory societies are filled with many inconsistent attitudes and desires. The normal self fights these contradictions and is miserable. The wise man embraces them and flows.

'Secondly, to go from the cage of a single self to the amusement park of multiple living you need to exercise, to play games which break down your self-imposed limitations, to permit the expression of a variety of emotions, talents and ways of living.

'Of course the killing of your self is almost as difficult as physical suicide – although generally more rewarding. Here in Lukedom we've made this process easier by creating an environment where inconsistency and multiple role-playing is the norm, where no one cares who you are or what you did in the past. Here you can use new names, masks and costumes to enhance your role-playing. This immersion in an environment in which many people are changing their lives as often as their clothes, and where they have no expectation that you will be the same person day after day, should help to release you from the pressure to be your "usual" self.

'Just die,' she continued, moving back to the centre of the room and seeming to address everyone rather than one person in particular. 'Let go. Cease being you. I don't care if you're here hoping to find salvation, success in the outside business world, orgies, or to locate Luke Rhinehart, you won't get what you want no matter what you do unless you die, let go, cease to exist. Give up the asshole you think you are and try being a new one. Notice the improvement – no, notice nothing, just be . . .

'The dice are nothing special,' she went on, resuming her pacing, glaring, stopping, spitting out some words, caressing others. 'Just a gimmick to dramatize the arbitrariness of decision-making. If you flip a coin to decide which movie to go to you are letting go of a small piece of the dominant jerk you think you are. If you flip a coin to decide how you're going to behave with your boss you're letting go of a bigger piece. Flipping dice is a gimmick to help you let go of larger and larger pieces of your self. So don't get addicted. The diceperson can be as big a jerk as the next, so you've got to give him up too . . .'

I was surprised at the way I began to be interested in her spiel. I'd sat down filled with anticipatory resentment, had at first internally criticized Ms Kalb's dress, speaking voice and verbal style, but then gradually found my mind being engaged by what she was saying, perhaps because she so clearly didn't give a damn whether I approved or not. I had never given any serious thought to what my father had been about, except to reject it out of hand, but she was getting through. She acted as if she were providing a service that people could take or leave as they saw fit, and she couldn't care less.

'It's easy to cheat at diceliving,' she went on. 'Everyone does it all the time. You simply say to yourself that the basic lovable jerk you are is still intact, but that because it's trendy or convenient or fun you're now going to pretend for an hour or a day to be a new, different jerk . . .

'Won't work,' she announced after a brief pause. 'Life is strange: it only really works when you lose awareness of who you are and immerse yourself in an act, a role, a life. Surrender to the roll of roles, surrender to each new act, surrender to newness and change . . .'

After about an hour of Kathy's talking and answering questions, she broke the group up into smaller units. We were given specific assignments, some to do with jobs during the rest of the day, some to do with more training with other guides. Kathy, aka Wendy, then took me on personally in a one-on-one session that didn't go quite as I liked.

'What are you afraid of losing?' she began abruptly, sitting opposite me only inches away in the ridiculous desk-chairs that passed for seating arrangements. We were now alone in the room and I was ill-at-ease, trying to pretend to go along with all this while on the one hand having to fight *really* going along with it, and absolutely refusing to go along with it on the other.

'Nothing, that I'm aware of,' I answered, trying a half-smile that implied I was looking forward to playing whatever silly games she might suggest.

'Good,' she countered. 'Get undressed.'

'Beg pardon?'

'Take off all your clothes,' she said. 'Stand nude in front of me.'

I looked at her, calculating. What had this to do with the dicelife? Was this some sort of personal test? Did I pass it by undressing or by not undressing?

'I'll have to consult the dice,' I said, with sudden inspiration. I took out the green die I'd been given at the beginning of the session and idly shook it in my right hand.

'If the die falls a "six",' I announced, adopting again my half-smile, 'I'll undress. If it doesn't, I won't.'

'Fine,' said Kathy.

I dropped the die on the desk part of my chair: a 'three'.

'Well, well,' I said. 'It looks like I remain the well-dressed man.'

'Fine. What are you afraid of losing?' She gazed at me without the least decipherable expression, waiting.

I was unable to suppress a tiny grimace.

'Nothing . . . that I'm aware of,' I repeated.

'Fine,' said Kathy. 'Give me a cheque for two thousand dollars.'

Two thousand dollars. I found myself wondering how she'd arrived at that particular figure. If she'd said a hundred dollars I might have made out the cheque with a yawn; if she's said a hundred thousand dollars, I'd have simply shaken my head. Two thousand, though. What kind of a test was this?

'I'll have to consult the die,' I said after a long hesitation.

'Fine.'

'If it's a "six" I'll give you a cheque for two thousand dollars,' I said. 'If not, I won't.' I dropped the die. I noticed that Kathy didn't even bother to look at the result. It was a 'one'. I was still solvent.

'So,' she said even before I announced the result. 'What are you afraid of losing?'

This time I paused to consider what was going on.

'Well,' I finally said, 'quite a few things, I guess.' Her expression didn't change: not a single flicker of triumph in response to my changed answer.

'For one thing I'm afraid of being made a fool of. By standing nude in front of a sexless woman just because she tells me to. Or giving away money in a silly way. I'm sure there are others.'

She stared at me a moment.

'And what would you lose if you lost what you're afraid of losing?' she asked.

I frowned. Was I stuck in a dialogue with Gertrude Stein? I would lose what I lost when I lost it. What did she mean?

'What would you lose if you were made a fool of?' she asked, as if hearing my unspoken question.

'Dignity . . . self-respect . . .' I suggested. 'Sense of being a reasonable man.'

'Fine,' said Kathy. 'What would you lose if you lost your dignity?'

'My dignity,' I countered quickly, feeling a little annoyed.

'How much is your dignity worth?'

Damn it! Where was this conversation going?

'What do you mean?'

'I mean how much, in dollars,' she explained, 'would someone have to pay you to lose your dignity?'

'Depends on how much of my dignity I had to lose,' I answered, smiling.

'Fine,' she said. 'How much to undress and stand nude in front of me?'

I let out a deep breath, becoming aware as I did that I must be tense.

'Oh, maybe . . . three hundred dollars,' I said. 'I'm an easy lay.'

'Fine,' she said and pulled out a small purse from her suit jacket pocket. Barely looking at it, she drew out three hundred-dollar bills. 'Here's three hundred dollars. Take off all your clothes.'

Jesus H. Christ. How had my father managed to bring me to this? Was Luke behind her, staying awake all night thinking up things to make me do the next day?

I felt my face flushing, not from embarrassment but from anger and indecision.

'But now . . .' I began tentatively, 'I'm afraid of losing my dignity by accepting three hundred dollars for undressing.' I hesitated a moment more and then grinned.

'That loss of dignity is worth, oh, another three hundred dollars,' I said in triumph.

'Fine,' she said. 'And so on. I assume another piece of your dignity would be at risk if you accepted three hundred dollars for accepting three hundred dollars, and so on. It appears you have something of an infinitely regressing dignity.'

'So it appears,' I said, feeling I'd squirmed off the hook.

'Fine,' she shot back. 'Take off all your clothes.'

Here we go again.

'Beg pardon?'

'Here is the three hundred dollars,' she said. 'Take off all your clothes.'

'But I told you, I have other dignities which also have their price.'

She looked at me neutrally.

'Tell me, what do you gain by having dignity?' she finally asked.

Oh, Jesus, Jesus. I felt like a guilty man in the witness stand being harassed by a clever prosecutor. I let out another big sigh.

'I don't have the faintest idea,' I said.

'Tell me, do you think I could undress and stand naked in front of you?'

I knew the answer.

'I think you could.'

'And, in your eyes, would I lose dignity?'

'Maybe, maybe not.'

She stood up then and began to undress. In less than a minute she had taken off all of her clothes, placed them neatly in her chair and was standing naked in front of me. She was an attractive woman, but like most human bodies, hers had its flaws: a mole here, a little too much flab there, breasts that didn't quite fit any of my images of perfection. Nevertheless she stood in front of me with precisely the same expression she'd had earlier. There was no doubt at all that she had as much dignity now as before, perhaps even more. Definitely more.

'You don't lose any dignity,' I commented in a low voice.

'Fine,' she said, and turned to begin to dress. 'Then you too might undress in such a way that it would involve not losing any dignity, right?'

'Right.' I felt the prosecutor, half-naked as she might now be, was closing in for the kill.

'Then doing something foolish – as I have just done,' she concluded, still buttoning her blouse, 'can be an act of strength and dignity.'

'Yes,' I said, trying to re-establish the half-smile of superior irony.

'Why?'

Why? I felt briefly that I must have lost the drift of the discussion.

'Why?' I echoed.

'What was it about my standing nude that distinguished it from . . . a foolish standing nude?'

I thought about it.

'You so obviously don't care what anyone thinks,' I finally answered. 'You expect neither approval nor disapproval and don't care which comes. Others – the fools – would look as if they cared very much what people were thinking, and as if they were standing there against their will.'

'Let's assume I cast a die first to determine whether I undress and the die ordered my nakedness. Would my dignity be less?'

Now that was an interesting question.

'No,' I answered. 'I don't think so.'

'So it can't be simply free will,' she suggested. 'Then what is it?'

'I suppose,' I said, 'that what counts is your having confidence in what you're doing – no! No, it's not that. It's almost as if there wasn't any you there either to have confidence or not have it. You simply do things one after another but don't seem to score points as you do so. There's no evaluation going on.'

She nodded. I was beginning to feel now less like the defendant in a hopeless trial than like a schoolboy slowly learning from a no-nonsense teacher.

'Uncertainty . . . wobbling . . . vacillation – usually because of fears of evaluation,' I found myself continuing. 'These are the hallmarks of the fool, or the seeming fool at least.'

'Just doing what you're doing while you're doing it,' she confirmed. 'No matter how foolish or arbitrary it may be.' She paused and smiled.

'Get undressed,' she said.

27

After his chastening session with Kathy that Monday morning, Larry wandered out of the orientation building a little dazed and a little proud: he had managed to lose his dignity. He had stood naked in front of Kathy and not flushed. He'd given her back the three hundred dollars and not felt a fool – or rather felt like a fool but also felt like a fool for feeling a fool. He found himself looking to see if Rick had yet returned his car, but saw no sign of it. Then, with a sudden rush of anxiety, he realized the markets were open and were racing off in every direction without him. He had to phone Jeff.

With the cellular phone in his car not an option, he'd have to use the pay phone in the orientation lobby, which annoyed him considerably since it had very little privacy. He hurried back in and soon huddled himself in a corner, with his back to the room, and called Jeff.

He was still a little distracted by the session with Kathy so it took a little while before some of the things Jeff was telling him finally sunk in.

'What the fuck are you talking about!?' Larry said after Jeff had presented his new recommendations and Larry had finally grasped them. 'We can't go short that much oil!!'

'The price is way overvalued,' Jeff insisted. He was also hunkered down – in his cubicle at BB&P peering out at the other brokers and traders as if each one was a foreign spy. Sweat was pouring from all the usual pores and several that hadn't been used since adolescence. He had just received a new inside tip from X, the biggest ever, but couldn't tell Larry. 'The market's way overbought. I figure the President is bound to do something after the election that he's been hiding before the election. That's the political process. Almost any news that doesn't make it look like war for certain is bound to lead to a sell-off.'

'Then how come none of the other traders has figured this out,' Larry barked into the phone, trying to shout into the corner so that his voice would be muffled for the half-dozen others milling in the room behind him. He was wondering what had gotten into Jeff this time. Until two months ago, Jeff had never had a risky idea in his life, or if he had, he'd kept it carefully to himself. 'All our indicators are still on buy signals,' Larry continued. 'How can we justify suddenly selling?'

'The market is overbought,' said Jeff desperately.

'So what!? It can stay overbought for weeks. Let it sell off and trigger some sell signals, then we can talk about going short.'

'But you used to like to sell overbought markets!' Jeff persisted.

'That was before I'd taken several baths because the overbought markets kept going up and up and up,' hissed Larry, shuffling back and forth in the corner as far as the phone's short cord would permit and feeling caged.

Jeff cradled his phone closer to his cheek and crouched down even lower in his chair. He'd already gotten Larry to agree to cover shorts in the stock market and to go short a few gold contracts, but the key to it all was oil, going short oil. After they'd exchanged code words X had told him that a few days after the election the President was going to announce a new peace initiative, one that would have a credibility that would at least for a moment make people think that war would be avoided. If this happened, the price of oil, inflated by war scares, might fall 20 or 30 per cent in a day! Fortunes would be made! It was a futures trader's wet dream! Larry simply didn't understand that the Gods didn't like people who thought that the future was going to remain like the past. The Gods liked gamblers who believed only in luck and the Gods and cheating.

'Look,' Jeff finally said, lowering his voice. 'I've got a friend in the State Department.'

Larry, who had been staring out unseeing into the room and nervously scratching his back against the phone box, now froze in that position.

'You've got a friend in the State Department,' he said evenly.

'A fraternity brother,' said Jeff, deciding that if cheating was all right, lying must be too. 'I was at a party with him over the weekend. After he'd had a lot to drink, he let out that . . . well,

147

something that next week – after the election – will make the price of oil fall.'

For Larry, who didn't yet share Jeff's insight into why insider trading was moral, had to think about this. Strictly speaking, acting on information about some change of government policy that had not yet been announced did not constitute insider trading. For one thing there was normally no clear or necessary market play based on some vague government policy change. State Department leaks were not part of the Securities and Exchange Commission's mandate, the SEC figuring that such leaks were so common, and spread so widely, that 'insiders' constituted half of the investment community. Also, thought Larry, a drunken rumour was good luck, not insider trading. Even he would trade on some unpremeditated, gratuitous, but reliable bit of drunken insider information. It was paying for information, or trading such inside information in an unauthorized way, that was clearly wrong.

'May I ask what that something is that's going to make the price of oil fall?' Larry finally asked.

'A peace initiative,' Jeff mumbled.

Well, yes, that would do it.

'I see.'

'If my friend's right,' said Jeff, 'the profits will be enormous.'

'I would say so,' said Larry. 'Did your hunch about the T-Bonds come from this same guy?' he suddenly asked.

Jeff's body began running in all directions at once, which meant his teeth gritted, eyes bulged, face twitched, hands quivered and sweat glands, all two million of them, put in overtime.

'No, no,' he answered. 'This guy is State Department. He doesn't know beans about economics or bonds. He put all his money in condominiums.'

This last statement was a masterstroke, the sort of seemingly trivial detail that makes the liar's story ring absolutely true. On Wall Street in the early 1990s anyone who had put all their money into condominiums was clearly a complete ass – as opposed to the partial asses that everyone else was – except me and thee.

'OK,' said Larry. 'We go short two hundred December oil contracts – gradually, today and Wednesday, assuming the President will wait a decent day or two before telling the public what he wouldn't tell them during the election campaign. Put the stop . . . about fifty cents above the market. Let's see if we can make more off drunks than we can from ten years of experience and education.'

Jeff dared to smile.

'That's exactly it,' he said. 'I think we can.'

28

After talking to Jeff I felt oddly dislocated. Wandering away from the orientation building I looked around and found myself surrounded by huge mountains of pine trees with open meadows spread below, instead of huge mountains of concrete with layers of macadam below. As I walked along I felt myself moving back into the world of Lukedom where people were different and unpredictable and unique compared to the button-down world of Wall Street and Blair, Battle and Pike, where they were all crazy in the same ways. And the trades and figures Jeff and I had bandied about, which seemed to have such body and meaning in New York, seemed flimsy and artificial here in the mountains. Everything about Lukedom made money seem sort of silly, while everything in Wall Street made it seem like the only serious reality in the world. I knew Wall Street was right, and worried that if I stayed too long in Lukedom I might lose that compulsive calculating nature that had made me the hotspot I was.

And things didn't get better when I went back to the orientation centre after the break. I found that I was expected to let a die choose which of three 'chores' I'd do during the lunch hour: cook, serve table or mop up. The die chose the mop and, after I'd eaten a mediocre lunch, I had to clean up both the kitchen and dining area of the small orientation centre restaurant. So for the first time in my life I discovered the joys of mopping a kitchen floor.

In the afternoon I had to continue to endure my 'training', some with Kathy but most with the big English trainer Michael Way, and I hated it. While Kathy had made me feel like an inhibited prude, Way soon had me feeling like a philosophical pygmy.

Even the other people in the classes or on the street or in the restaurants began to depress me. No one seemed to care who I was. No one seemed to care I was a brilliant graduate of Wharton Business School earning close to two hundred thousand dollars a year; that the expensive clothes I wore were really mine and not some duds I'd borrowed from Lukedom's huge collection of clothing and costumes. It was depressing to be telling someone at the bar at the Do Die Inn how I'd made an incredible coup on the Japanese yen that had made BB&P millions, and then realize that the two men listening to me assumed it was all simply a bullshit role the dice had told me to play. And when a woman told me a really moving story about losing her only child to leukaemia I'd wanted to comfort her until she took out a die, flipped it across the bar and, in an entirely different tone of voice, told me I had a cute butt.

I realized I was feeling a consistent low level of anxiety. I'd often enough had anxiety caused by worrying about other people disapproving of who I was or what I did, but this was the first time I'd experienced a low level dread of not being sure *who* I was. Of course I knew who I was, but somehow the fact that no one else acknowledged or cared about who I thought I was was profoundly unsettling.

I felt such waves of loneliness I phoned Jeff two more times than I really had to, pretending I was worried about all the oil contracts. I also tried to phone Honoria at her office, wanting to apologize and redeclare my undying devotion to our union, but was told she was in a meeting.

Was it a real meeting? Was she talking to me? Were we no longer engaged? Had she really discovered that the magnificent two-carat diamond I'd given her had a minor flaw?

I became so depressed I even longed to meet my father again, just to have someone who would recognize me as Larry Rhinehart. Never had I realized how important it was to have people who were always around reminding you of who you are. Maybe Honoria was right: the place was designed to drive people crazy.

In mid-afternoon, after I'd been at last released from more intense one-on-one training which was giving me an inferiority complex, I was given a chance to choose six 'occupations for the day' from a list of over twenty. The list varied from bank manager to farmhand to housewife to babysitter to hardware store clerk and so on. Only one leapt out at me: administrative clerk; maybe I'd have a chance to browse through some other file cabinets. So I listed it as one of the six and then added five more: bank manager (why not start at the top?); babysitter (I'd have free time to follow the markets on CNBC-

FNN); hardware store clerk (maybe True Value would have a special on effective skeleton keys); telephone operator (maybe I'd overhear a phone call that would give me a lead); psychotherapist (I knew I'd enjoy playing god to some poor wimp the way Dr Bickers did to me); and sheriff's deputy (maybe I could find out how I could stop Rick from always taking off with my car).

I then cast a die. A 'three': babysitter.

The babysitting was a disaster. I'd assumed I would sit around reading the *Wall Street Journal* and catching up on the Monday markets on CNBC-FNN on television while the three children played with blocks on the living-room floor. It didn't work out that way.

I was given a hint of the trouble to come when the babysitter for the morning shift, a middle-aged woman named Dolores, looked rather frazzled as she passed over responsibility for the three young children, varying in age from two to seven. She practically ran from the house as soon as I took over.

Things got off to a bad start immediately. First of all the house had neither cable television (and thus a financial network) nor a telephone (and thus access to Jeff back in New York). Secondly, the children claimed they hadn't been fed since mid-morning snack and were circling the icebox and cupboards like a wolfpack closing in on a kill. Thirdly, I made the mistake of asking them what they wanted for lunch.

'Pizza' had seemed a reasonable request until I discovered that there was no frozen pizza, no leftover pizza, no nearby pizza parlour, and that I was expected to *make* a pizza. I quickly corrected the children on that expectation but was immediately labelled a liar by the oldest: 'You promised us we could have whatever we wanted!'

I tried to get the three kids to become hypnotized by the television set, but discovered that only one of the three channels had cartoons, and the cartoons were so bizarre that minutes after the kids had snuck away to try raiding the refrigerator again, I stood in front of the set hypnotized. In the middle of a manic cat chasing an over-confident mouse would appear Snow White singing away with the seven dwarfs, followed by Dumbo diving into a pool of water and then a video *Playboy* centrefold smiling shyly out at the kids in the slimmest of bikinis, followed by Batman getting tough with

Penguin, and then a beautiful two-minute scene of water gurgling down a mountain stream in autumn, the sunlight splashing such spectacular light and shadow and colour it was hypnotizing. I was only snapped out of my trance by the appearance of the three-year-old soaking-wet with blood that soon, thank God, turned out to be tomato juice.

I traipsed into the kitchen and tried throwing together three peanut butter and jelly sandwiches, but found that none of the children would eat them because I'd used 'crunchy' peanut butter and not smooth. To show them who was boss, I announced that they could make their own lunches and marched from the kitchen back to catch some more of the cartoons.

A half-hour later, after I'd discovered that the other channels were equally bizarre and equally fascinating, I was feeling pretty good, especially since there had been a beautiful silence from the kitchen. Then I smelled the smoke.

By the time the kids' mother returned from acting principal for over one hundred and fifty children she found her house looked as if another one hundred and fifty had run wild in it. I assured her there were only three, and hers, and that I was sorry I hadn't cleaned up as much as I'd wanted to. As the poor woman stared around at the devastation, she wondered apathetically just exactly what I thought I *had* cleaned up – perhaps I'd rearranged some area of neatness that looked out of place.

It was five o'clock when the mother rescued me from a fate worse than death, but I discovered my trials were not done. I was ordered to report for duty to the lobby of the Hazard Inn.

I was met there by a thin wiry man named Ray, who in a soft gentle voice, announced that he was another diceguide. My first response to the Hazard Inn with its lobby crowded with people spaced out in their individual movie scenarios was one of both annoyance and a sense of righteousness: this was what I expected all of Lukedom to be like. This was the sort of kookiedom that was my father's madness at its worst.

I grimly followed gentle Ray down the central hall, off which were the strangely titled rooms, most of which had their doors open. In the Yoga Room was nothing more threatening than a group of seven people on a huge mat all arching their backs and sticking their tongues out in what I assumed was some traditional yoga *asana*. One of the seven appeared to be a leader. I didn't see what yoga had to do with Lukedom, but Ray answered that it was a way of gaining new knowledge about one's body and of making the body flexible.

I peeked into the Art Room, where nothing more subversive was happening than a dozen people, ranging in age from sixty to five or six, messing around with paints and clays and that sort of thing. It looked like every art class I'd ever seen, although Ray said something about the teacher getting the students to let chance enter their work. I sneered. That's all modern art needed: more chaos.

The Death Room was not what I expected. When we stopped outside the closed door Ray explained that the groaning we were hearing from inside was the sounds of mourning by those within. He asked me to go inside and spend as much time as I wanted, but at least ten minutes, mourning for someone I had lost from my life. I hesitated, hating to be drawn into any of these games, even those that didn't involve dice, but decided at least to enter the room.

Inside, it was dimly lit by stands of candles on either side of a raised closed casket against the far wall. There were six mourners, five seated in various positions on the deeply padded floor, the sixth standing. Two were crying softly, one moaning, and the other three were silent, with bowed heads.

Ray had come in too and went forward to the casket, crossed himself, and stood with bowed head in front of it. The casket was a simple pine one, but looked well made, with nicely designed handles on the sides and a clear varnish making it glow in the candlelight.

I eased myself over to one side of the room and, feeling exhausted from my babysitting, sat down on the thick floor covering.

One of the previously silent mourners, a young woman, now went public with a long wail, almost a scream, and then broke into noisy sobs. I was annoyed. After a minute, Ray turned from the casket and walked slowly back into the middle of the room and also sat down. When I noticed the candlelight reflecting off the tears in Ray's eyes I felt first another burst of annoyance and then an inexplicable rush of grief.

I hadn't even thought of anyone to mourn!! Yet I had to stifle a sob! I quickly lowered my head to get a hold of myself. But the sounds of people crying and groaning in grief around me were too powerful – I could feel their emotion vibrate through me and pull me down into a pool of deep sadness. Even as tears welled into my eyes, I was mumbling, 'What the fuck!? What the fuck!?', fighting against the rising flood of grief.

But for whom?! For what?

It didn't seem to matter. As the tears and grief and sadness flowed through me, I thought of my mother on the morning of her car accident, vibrant, happy, busy and unknowing, and I groaned. And then the memory of my sister Evie, still alive, but so different from me, now living her circumscribed life in Trenton, telling me that afternoon with the rain falling gently around us that she didn't need any money, even as the beat-up car she was sitting in stalled and wouldn't start. I grieved for her and for the distance between us. When I suddenly thought of Luke, my grief ebbed as suddenly as it had flowed, replaced by anger. I would not be tricked by that man's madness into mourning him. But then the sobs and sniffles and cries from those around me overwhelmed the image of my father, again forcing me to remember my mother and weep once more.

In the next hour Ray took me into several other rooms, but none had the impact of the Death Room. I observed but didn't participate in the Emotional Roulette Room, was curious about but didn't enter the Prostitute–Client Room, and watched for ten minutes the people in the Childhood Room, off which was a playground where the childhood could be continued outdoors. There was something appealing about the adults playing with the blocks and the Lego and Nintendo and dolls. But when Ray suggested I get in there with the other adults and the few real children – who looked as if they were having a ball – and regress, I felt too wasted from the Death Room and declined.

Ray did get me involved in the Money Room, which was perhaps the most bizarre of all the rooms I'd seen. It consisted of an otherwise bare room lit by two harsh fluorescent lights and containing only a tiny wood stove, with a small live fire, and money: real dollar bills, and fives scattered over the entire floor of the room like windblown trash. There was only one other man in the room when we entered and he, like me, just stood and looked around in some incomprehension.

Ray handed me a die.

'In here,' he explained, 'there are really only two options: you let the die decide whether you are going to keep or destroy each cluster of money you pick up.'

I bent over and picked up a five and examined it. Damned if it didn't seem genuine.

'What for?' I asked. For me the amounts of money were so small as to be trivial.

'For the hell of it,' Ray replied with gentle smile.

'Hrhuh!' I said, and with the five in hand went over to the wood stove. Then I turned back to Ray. The other man in the room was watching me.

'What prevents someone from coming in here and simply taking all the money he needs?' I asked.

'Nothing,' said Ray. 'Although in this room all decisions must be made with the dice.'

'So if I say "odd" I take all these bills home with me and "even" I don't, I can do it?' I asked.

'Exactly,' said Ray. 'But of course if the die falls "odd" then you have to clear the whole room of all its money.'

I absorbed this. Money *was* used here in Lukedom. I had paid for my food, my room, even the crowbar. People must be able to leave the place. Although there probably wasn't more than a thousand dollars or so here, it did seem as if it might prove an expensive game for the owners of Lukedom.

I turned back to the stove and let the die decide the fate of my fiver. It ordered death by fire. I lifted the lid of the stove and started to place the bill into the coals, but stopped.

'Why waste the money?' I asked, turning to Ray with a scowl.

'What else is there to do with it?' asked Ray and then, with that strange seraphic smile, left the room.

I turned back to the stove, hesitated, and finally dropped the bill into the stove. When I saw it burning I felt very depressed.

By the time Ray released me from the Hazard Inn and I'd eaten and washed dishes for half an hour in 'Joe's' café, I was exhausted. And lonely. After going up to my room to take a shower I shuffled down the stairs to the inn's bar to solace myself with a drink.

When I remembered yesterday's spat with Honoria it seemed as if it had taken place back in the Middle Ages. I realized again that

Lukedom had the effect of making one's normal life seem trivial, not an effect I enjoyed. When I was finally able to concentrate a bit on Honoria I was angry at her insistence on her own way and saw no need to apologize for my insistence on my way. I wanted her to phone and be sweet and apologetic and witty and our engagement be back on. Then I realized that if the phone system in Lukedom was run like the babysitting system, then my chances of receiving a phone call were small. That depressed me a bit too: I felt isolated. Yet when I thought of Honoria's phoning and announcing that the engagement was back on and all was forgiven, I was surprised to find that such a scenario didn't exhilarate me as much as it should. Was it possible that I wanted Honoria like I wanted to be making half a million dollars a year – as a symbol of having arrived? But I loved her! Didn't I? The sex was good, we actually talked not only before, but even afterwards! How many men could say that about their fiancées!?

No, no, no, it was clear that this little tiff must be kept a little tiff. You don't sell a good stock just because some small part of you thinks there's an even better stock just over the counter.

I ended up trying to make phone contact with Honoria, both at her office and at the Battle apartment, but failed. So as I nursed a vodka and tonic I was feeling close to my low for the day, morosely trying to avoid talking to any of the weirdos and pretending-not-to-be-weirdos who occasionally approached me. Then who should come bubbling into the room but Kim.

From Luke's Journal

Nature's accidents are the universe's way of throwing chance into a system which would die of too much orderliness. Hurricanes, droughts, floods, volcanic eruptions are all Mother Nature's way of stirring up the pot to prevent stagnation and putrefaction.

A world without them would be a world of death. Floods, fires, eruptions, earthquakes all destroy and renew, kill and create, demolish and replant.

So too riots, revolutions and wars are societies' ways of throwing chance into their systems, which are dying of too much orderliness. And like nature's eruptions, these too destroy and renew, kill and create, demolish and replant.

And so too with individuals. Human beings need in their lives earthquakes and floods and riots and revolutions, or we grow as rigid and unmoving as corpses.

29

My heart, the little bastard, did a somersault. She seemed to be floating across the room toward me, vibrating with that sexy glow that seemed aimed to drive men (and especially me) crazy. Then I noticed that she was gaily walking arm in arm with Michael Way and the somersault flattened into a belly flop. As she approached, I stepped away from the bar to meet her.

'What are you doing here?' I asked, nodding a silent acknowledgement to Way. The fop was wearing Bond Street slacks with an Italian leather jacket and looked as if he was ready for a night in Beverly Hills. Kim was wearing jeans and a soft aqua sweater. 'Did Nori send you?' I then added with sudden confusion.

Instead of answering, Kim laughed and gave me a brief hug, then guided the three of us to a small booth. After Way ordered a round of drinks, Kim explained that she'd come to Lukedom out of her own curiosity. However, she had seen that Honoria was upset and wondered if I'd talked to her since our separation.

The subject depressed me and I hemmed and hawed about bothering to try to call her again until finally, sensing that for her own reasons Kim wanted me to phone, I dragged myself away to make the call.

At first Mr Battle, who answered the phone, gave me a lecture on the necessity of avoiding too tight stop loss orders, a strategy which could lead one to be stopped out of long-term winning positions. It took me most of a two-minute lecture to realize that Mr Battle wasn't talking about market trading, but about Honoria and I having been apparently stopped out of our engagement position, a position that Mr Battle saw as a long-term winner. He suggested that I 're-establish my "long" (engaged) position as soon as possible – before the market (Honoria) got away from me'.

'Let me speak to Nori,' I asked when Mr Battle ended his extended metaphor.

'Fine, my boy,' said Mr Battle. 'I shall go and get her.'

It took about a minute before Honoria's voice came on.

'Larry?' was all she said.

It was a good opening gambit, forcing me to make the first offer.

'Hi,' I said. 'How are you? Your trip back go all right?'

I too was stalling for time, but my innocent filler question was like stepping on a land mine.

'My trip back was a ride with Mad Max through the Thunderdome,' Honoria answered testily. 'And I hope your stay in Lukedom is the same.'

'Well, it is,' I said. 'I'm hating every minute of it. But I'm finding more and more suspicious things here. Did you know this place must produce its own TV programmes? Where can they possibly get the money?'

There was a silence. When two negotiators are really skilled they can talk for hours without either one of them saying anything.

'Look, I'm sorry about yesterday,' I said after several seconds of silence. 'Have you forgiven me a little?'

'A little,' said Honoria.

But she added nothing to that ambiguous statement.

'How do you feel about . . . us?' I asked next. Like all men, I approached the subject of feelings as tentatively as possible and hoped that the woman would have all the answers.

'I'm not sure but that we might be doing the right thing by calling it off.'

Did that mean she was still involved with me? Did that mean the engagement was back on but ought to be off? What *did* it mean?

'I don't blame you,' I said.

A new ploy: plead *nolo contendere* and throw myself on the mercy of the court. When I sensed Nori pulling away from me I desperately wanted her; when I sensed her needing me I wanted to withdraw. My subconscious was working overtime to force Honoria to make the decision.

'I'm really sorry I was so selfish and cruel,' I continued. 'I just felt that for both our sakes I've got to get in touch with my father before his actions hurt us.'

'I understand,' said Honoria. 'But I'm beginning to think it's not worth it. Why don't you forget the whole thing and just come back?'

Aha, it looked as if the engagement was back on – if I gave up my quest.

'I want to forget my father,' I said. 'But Bickers and most of my life have made it clear that I can't just do it. I've got to find him.'

The other end of the line was silent.

'It'll only take another full day at most,' I continued. 'Tomorrow's election day anyway.'

More silence.

'My father was right: you're fine the way you are,' said Honoria finally. 'You're making a mountain out of your molehill father. If you really loved me you'd return immediately.'

Good point, I thought. But still, I could see Honoria any time. This might be my only chance to find my father.

'But what about the possibility of scandal resurfacing about Luke just before our wedding?' I asked. 'Doesn't that concern you?'

'Yes,' said Honoria. 'It does. On the other hand, there are scandals and there are scandals.'

'Beg pardon?'

'I suppose I should have told you sooner,' she said in a quiet voice. 'I think I'm pregnant.'

I felt that my system was now definitely on overload. Lukedom, Honoria's anger, Jeff's bizarreness, Kim's arrival, and now Honoria's pregnancy! The data were coming too fast and furious for the technical indicators to keep up.

After a long silence in which I could hear Honoria's quiet breathing on the other end of the line, I finally spoke.

'You're . . . pregnant?'

'I haven't menstruated in seven weeks,' she said.

I had always had total confidence in Honoria's grand ability to avoid all unpleasant situations. I knew she'd stopped using the pill because of side-effects and that we had depended mostly on her using a diaphragm. I'd assumed that she was as good at using that as she was at everything else.

'Right,' I said, not sure after I'd said it what I was agreeing to. 'I, uh . . . Wow.'

Silence.

'Wow,' echoed Honoria. 'I would guess so.'

'I . . . I want to have children,' I managed.

'Do you? How nice. Too bad you have no uterus.'

'I . . . uh, mean have a family . . . be the father of my wife's child.'

'You don't sound too convinced,' she said. 'I think we'd better be a lot more certain than that . . .'

I sensed I wasn't responding to Honoria in a winning way. But what could I say!? We'd both agreed we wanted to postpone having children until we became bored with our success.

'What . . . do you plan to do about it?' I asked.

She let another silence fall into the thousand-mile space between us.

'I haven't decided,' she said.

Another silence.

'Look, I'm staying here through until tomorrow,' I said tensely, knowing it was taking a position she was likely to bombard. 'I should be back by Wednesday afternoon at the latest. We'll talk then.'

'Perhaps,' said Honoria. And she hung up.

Well. So.

A 1990 yuppie with four-hundred-dollar shoes, a Mercedes, a big sailboat, and yet still liable to a shotgun wedding! What was the sense of health, wealth and supercomputers if women could still announce they were pregnant?

I returned with considerable sobriety to the corner table where I'd left Kim and Mr Way. They looked up at me with curiosity.

'Everything's fine,' I announced, trying a grin. 'We patched it up. I'll probably be heading back to New York tomorrow night.' For some reason I said this all to Mr Way, as if he were the one who'd expressed an interest.

Kim greeted my words with a big grin.

'If everything's fine,' she said, 'I'd hate to see what you look like when things are lousy.'

'We still don't see eye to eye on everything and I guess it hurts me to disagree with her.'

'I'll bet,' said Kim. 'And if it didn't, she'd probably make sure it did.' She smiled at Way. 'Larry has an engagement made in heaven. Unfortunately, a large part of him suspects he doesn't like choir music.'

'Honoria's a brilliant woman,' said Way in his deep Oxford-accented voice as he abruptly rose from the table. 'Brilliant and beautiful. She has everything going for her except herself. Excuse me,' he added, leaning down to Kim, 'Ray seems to want to speak to me about something.' And he moved away through the tables towards the bar.

I now looked at Kim.

'How did you meet him?' I asked.

'At the orientation centre early in the afternoon,' she said. 'Doesn't he talk to all newcomers?'

'Only attractive women.'

Kim smiled, turned to follow Way's progress for a moment and then swung back to me.

'So Honoria hung up on you,' she said in a serious voice. 'In some ways you two are the perfect couple . . . but in others . . . you bring out the worst in each other.'

I looked at her morosely.

'That's only from my distorted value system,' said Kim. 'I mean if being highly competitive, financially ambitious, having expensive tastes and wanting to impress people are good traits then you bring out the best in each other.'

As I continued to examine the ice cubes in my drink I felt I wasn't prepared to handle that one.

'Look,' said Kim. 'I shouldn't be talking. I haven't exactly been a winner at romance myself. The men I end up attracted to usually bring out some of the worst in me too. I'm afraid Uncle William is right: I have an instinct for failure.'

'Is that one of his philosophical gems?' I asked.

'No, I'm afraid that's mine. What he actually said was that I'm a spoiled good-for-nothing who will never be good at anything I do.'

'He actually said that?' I asked, surprised that Mr Battle would be that explicitly cruel.

'I'm afraid I cause him a lot of pain,' said Kim, with an expression that was so new on her face that it took a moment for me to realize it was sadness. 'He so wants to like every Battle, no matter how distantly related. It can't be easy to be so generous to me and have me turn out the way I am.'

I felt that a compliment might be appropriate here and wondered whether Kim was scheming for one. But as I was considering it, she gazed at me as if deep in thought and continued: 'Not that I'm bad,' she mused. 'It's just that I'm so different from what he . . . wants.'

She shook her head and smiled ruefully. 'I like music and flowers and animals and far-out spiritual things and sex and goofing off – all the things that Uncle B. finds irrelevant or counter to the important things in life.'

I smiled.

'You're lucky,' I said. 'You find your enjoyments without having to pay for them.'

'Oh, I pay for them.'

'I mean pay big money, have to earn a lot to pay for them.'

'Oh, of course. I think making money is absurd – unless you enjoy it for its own sake. But, my God, when you read about Boesky and Milken and Levine and all those poor guys who cheated in order to earn a few more million than they were earning without cheating, and see how miserable they were and how they never seem to have had one happy moment spending their money – well, it makes you wonder if all you guys aren't sick.'

Again she was touching upon something I wasn't ready to think about too closely.

'They were neurotic,' I said. 'Some Wall Streeters have been known to spend a dollar or two with a smile on their faces.'

'Have you?'

'I enjoy my sailboat,' I said.

'Maybe,' she said, 'but the only sail you've ever told me about was in a friend's small catamaran. You didn't have to pay for that one.'

Way was abrubtly back standing at our table.

'I'd like to show you around a bit,' he said to Kim. 'Are you interested?'

Kim looked up in response and then over at me, who was feeling more than a little irritation at the man. First he drives Honoria away and then steals Kim. What was wrong with the women in London?

'I guess so,' said Kim. 'Want to join us?' she asked me.

I didn't want to join them.

'Have a great time,' I said. 'But don't believe a word he says,' I added.

Kim rose.

'Don't worry,' she said. 'I've already informed Michael that I am seduced by everything except arguments.'

With that little bit of provocation she took Way's arm and marched off.

'Michael' . . . 'seduced' – Was she as loose as she pretended? I felt a wave of self-pity wash over me. I'd show them. I'd show them. Absolutely. I ordered another drink.

30

I spent a restless night, not helped any by wondering where Kim was spending her night. And where Honoria was spending hers, though Nori wasn't chaos like Kim. My sleep wasn't helped any by someone in a room nearby singing all four stanzas of 'The Star-Spangled Banner', possibly to get into the *Guinness Book of Records* as the first person ever to do so. The singing was punctuated with the sporadic motif of voices shouting 'shut up!' and 'pipe down' and 'please stop it', a motif I was tempted to join but resisted.

In the morning I was hung over and depressed. If the Mercedes had finally gotten back from the airport I would leave. As I wobbled down the steps from my room – again wondering where Kim had spent the night – I pictured that pompous bastard Way having his way with her. The place was utterly corrupt.

With the Mercedes still nowhere in sight I actually felt a little relieved: since it would be hard to get out of here without my car, I had a good excuse to keep trying to dig into some of my unanswered questions. Where were those TV programmes coming from? Who created them? Who paid for them? How could Lukedom be so nonchalant about money? Could this complex community really be administered from that little warehouse administration building with only two computers? Was Jake really dealing with me based on age-old instructions from Luke or was he in daily contact with him?

I wandered along the street looking for a reasonably normal-looking café and settled for 'Joe's', which I felt I was beginning to know inside and out after doing the dishes and mopping up there.

I had barely sat down at the counter and taken the first sip from a cup of coffee when an attractive woman took the seat next to me and leaned around to look into my face.

'You're Larry Rhinehart,' she said, staring at me with large brown eyes, reminding me vaguely of Susan Sarandon.

'Sometimes,' I answered coyly. The place was contagious.

'I know your father,' she said simply.

Aha!

I lifted the cup of coffee to my mouth and took another sip.

'Really?' I said.

'He's here, you know,' she said.

'I . . . uh . . . know,' I said, searching her face for signs of sanity. 'That's why I'm here.'

'Have you seen him?' she asked, suddenly swinging her head quickly to glance at the door to the café.

'No. Matter of fact he seems to be avoiding me.'

She leaned her face in closer.

'He's watching you,' she announced.

'Oh?'

'He's never the same one day to the next,' she went on in a fierce whisper. 'But he's always watching us.'

'Watching everyone? Not just me?'

'Everyone. But especially you . . . and me.'

I shook my head, then tried a smile.

'And how do you know all this?' I asked her.

She straightened away from me.

'I know,' she answered. 'I see him every day.'

'Have you seen him today?'

'Yes.'

'Where?'

She leaned back and gave me a sweet mad smile.

'He's in this room right now.'

I held her mad look a second and then peered around the room: ten people, not one of whom contained the six-foot-four bulk that had been my father.

'I don't see him,' I said.

'Of course not – that's his way.'

My omelette arrived and I turned to it.

'He keeps himself invisible,' the woman continued.

'Goody-goody gumdrop for him,' I said, and at last began my breakfast.

As I walked slowly back along the street towards the orientation centre I decided that the woman was mad, she must be, but somehow couldn't shake the feeling that some core element of truth lay in what she said. How did she even know who I was? Had someone sent her to talk to me? Three days ago, why had the guard let me in after he'd made that phone call – without even checking for ID to confirm I was who I said I was? Someone had the power to let Larry Rhinehart in when the guard had decided to keep him out. Was it Jake? Or was it someone even more powerful than Jake?

Goddamn it! I was going to stay here in Lukedom even if Rick brought my car back.

When I saw Kim among the dozen students already in the classroom when I arrived I felt some sort of anticipatory excitement – my life seemed to be opening up. She was paired off with Ray, doing some sort of emotion-expressing game which had Kim looking at Ray with wide watery eyes and licking her lips – whether it was supposed to be love or a stomach upset I couldn't tell, but was annoyed with her for seeming, like everyone else in Lukedom, not to know I existed. She was dressed casually in jeans and a flowery sweatshirt. Her sneakers looked as if they might actually have been bought in the last year.

I sat in the back until the class finished the exercise – Kim at last turned and waved at me and smiled – and then we all listened to Kathy give a brief introduction to our next exercise: confrontational roulette.

It turned out that in confrontational roulette you let chance choose whom you have to confront – wife, husband, father, mother, God, devil, President, priest and so on. Then a person is randomly selected from volunteers to play the person confronted, playing the role after being given a brief background by the one doing the confronting. Kathy began pairing people off from dice throws with her class list, and I was annoyed to see Kim paired off with Ray, while I got a tall, bald-headed guy who gave his name as Abe Lister and looked like a retired funeral director.

'The die says I have to confront an imaginary you!' Kim said to me gaily as she and Ray were leaving the classroom. That was just what I needed: knowing Kim would be attacking me for my various flaws and doing it with another good-looking diceguide. How did she do it?!

The die picked from three options I gave it that I confront my father. It seemed such an appropriate choice I wondered if dear old Dad had supernatural powers and could influence the fall of dice. I wasn't too enthusiastic about the prospect and Kathy had to stand over me prodding to get me to give the bald-headed Abe Lister a basic background on my relations – or rather lack thereof – with Luke. Then she suggested that we have our confrontation outside while going for a walk in the woods.

'Well, Son,' said Baldy (as I thought of this guy). 'What's on your mind? You wanted to talk to me?'

I didn't have the slightest interest in the world in talking to the man, whether he were Baldy or Dad. I was angrily resentful that the whole charade was a waste of time.

'Yeah,' I said sarcastically as we entered a trail leading into the woods. 'I've been wanting to talk to you for years.'

'That's fine, Son,' said Baldy. 'I've wanted to talk to you too.'

'Bullshit!' I said. 'If you'd wanted to talk to me all you had to do was pick up a phone and call.'

'Ah . . . yes.'

'You're so wrapped up in yourself you don't even know I exist.'

'Oh, I do, Larry, I do,' protested Baldy. 'It's – '

'You don't! All you care about is your stupid theory about developing multiple personalities. Everything gets sacrificed to that – especially your family.'

'I have a career, just like any man. I admit that – '

'Career! You call throwing dice to decide who you are a career!?'

Baldy stopped on the path and glared at me.

'I had a calling!' he said. 'I did something unique with my life, something no man had ever done before. You should be proud of me!'

'You deserted me!' I protested. 'You sacrificed me and my mother and Evie for your fucking Dice Man calling!'

'I did! I admit it! But what would you have me do, stay around and ruin your lives with my experiments in randomness? Which is worse, a faithless fanatic who tortures those who love him by remaining in their lives, or a dead man, one who kills himself and disappears?'

My anger was slowly being melted down into depression. My father was eluding me now even as he had all my life.

'I'd have had you stay,' I said as we moved further along into the woods. 'I used to love the dice games you played with me. You know I did. I could have been diceboy to your Dice Man – Robin to your Batman. But you let Mom put a stop to it. You decided to go your own way and leave me behind.'

'The dice told me to stop urging you to play with the dice. It was – '

'The dice! Where was your heart!? Where was the father I loved?'

My bald-headed dad moved on, hands clasped behind his back like a pondering professor or a grieving funeral director.

'You can't have it both ways,' he finally said in his gravelly voice. 'My calling was to subject my soul to all the disparate forces within it, including the heartless forces. My calling took precedence over my heart. Where it called, I followed.'

'Out of my life . . . ' I said, my hands too clasped behind my back.

'Out of your life,' echoed my bald father. 'But not you out of mine.'

We walked on a while in silence.

'What does that mean?' I finally asked.

'I never stopped thinking about you, never stopped wanting to see you.'

'Liar! You could have seen me whenever you wanted.'

'When your mother died I wanted to come and take you to live with me, but you . . . told me to go to hell.'

I stopped and, remembering that awful day ten years earlier after my mother had been killed, began trembling.

'You . . . bastard,' I said.

'But why!?' he protested. 'I wanted to come for you!'

'But how could I say yes!? Not a word from you for almost five years and then a disembodied voice on the phone. I hated you! You were all that was false and selfish in the world. My mother had just died – alone and deserted like me. How could I betray everything I had thought and felt for years by saying yes to a disembodied devil pretending love after years of indifference?'

We were facing each other now, tears in our eyes.

'You . . . couldn't, of course,' he said huskily.

I looked at him through tear-distorted vision and took a deep sigh.

'But I wanted to . . . ' I finally whispered.

Agent Macavoy had been on the job. He had followed Larry faithfully for two days, getting yelled at and grieved over and yogied into a pretzel and fucked over by all sorts of weirdos who seemed to find him a nice object to act on.

He had been appalled at what a dismal amateur Larry was at trying to find out something about his father. He had seen Larry's initial reconnaissance trip to the church and then the trip there with the hacksaw and crowbar. My God, the man knew nothing about breaking and entering!! Macavoy himself had easily jemmied the lock to enter Jake's office and used one of his two dozen keys to get into the locked file cabinet. There was nothing there of use. But Larry!! The guy might just as well have used a hand grenade to get into the office and dynamite to get into the file cabinet! And then to get caught in the act!! Why, breaking and entering was kindergarten level stuff for the FBI, and Macavoy could feel nothing but contempt for Larry's ineptitude.

This Tuesday he had followed Larry and the tall bald-headed man out of the orientation building, across the street, up a narrow dirt road and into the woods. He hadn't been able to hear much of the early parts of the conversation because he was forced to keep his distance, but when they stopped at one point to confront each other angrily he had managed to sneak within thirty feet, hiding behind the trunk of a large fir tree. What he had heard had stunned him.

' . . . Your fucking Dice Man calling . . . I could have been diceboy to your Dice Man, Robin to your Batman . . .'

Although Macavoy hadn't got all of the next parts of their conversation he'd heard enough to realize that the tall older man was none other than Luke Rhinehart himself, snuck into Lukedom to see his long-lost son.

If Larry and Baldy had been trembling with their emotions there in the woods, Agent Macavoy was trembling with his. After dozens of agents had failed, he, James Macpherson Macavoy, had located the illusive, dissembling Luke Rhinehart.

When the two of them ended their talk and split up, Macavoy chose to follow Luke back to the orientation building. He waited an hour until the bald bastard had come out again. He then tailed him through the village to a house up a sidestreet: number six Boxcars Street, a modest two-family clapboard house perched up on cement blocks. The guy knew enough to live low key. Then he rushed to the nearest pay phone to call Putt at the Bureau.

'No, don't try to arrest him yourself,' Putt said after being filled in. 'I can be there with backups tomorrow – maybe even this evening . . . By two tomorrow afternoon we'll be ready to make the arrest.'

'Should I keep close to the father?'

'If you can,' said Putt after a pause. 'No, wait. I don't want to risk his getting wise to someone following him and have him take off. Let him go for now. You know where he's staying and what he looks like. We'll be able to locate him again after I get there with backups.'

'Right.'

'Meanwhile, contact the local authorities. See if they can provide some bodies for us. Don't tell them who we're after or exactly when you'll need them. Act as if it's a minor matter.'

'Right. Got it, chief.'

31

By the middle of her second day in Lukedom Kim realized that though she was excited by some of Lukedom's experiments, she was also disappointed at what she finally thought of as its 'institutionalized spontaneity'. Spontaneity should be spontaneous, and she wasn't sure it really worked when it was contrived by the dice or some diceguide. On the other hand, how else could you get unspontaneous people to be spontaneous?

She was flattered that Michael Way seemed to single her out for special attention, though after listening to him for hours she concluded that for all his attacks on the folly of ego and self, he had at least the trace of one of the biggest egos she'd ever known. Of course it could just be his high-toned English accent. Although he could make fun of himself, his 'spontaneity' sometimes seemed as controlled as most people's rationality.

The previous evening he'd taken her to the church, where she'd met Dr Ecstein. She couldn't help comparing him with the man she'd read about in *The Dice Man*, a copy of which she'd been reading since she arrived. All the fierce ambition he'd had twenty years before seemed gone; he was now more like a benevolent rabbi.

Then Michael had taken her on a moonlit jaunt along a stream that skirted the centre of town. If he was making a pass his technique seemed to be to show how wise he was.

The philosophy of ego-destruction was familiar to her from her interest in Eastern mysticisms. She saw that diceliving was a way to humiliate and break down the socialized self – a goal of several Eastern traditions. But it seemed more akin to LSD and the other powerful psychedelics that seekers had used two decades earlier – useful for some, dangerous for most.

So she argued with him a bit, made sure he noticed how intelligent and well read she was on these matters.

'But what brought you to all this?' she asked. 'Making a fool of yourself – as diceliving necessitates – seems awfully unEnglish.'

'Well, exactly,' he said easily. 'We English are much more tightly hammered into our square boxes by society than you Americans. So we need all the explosives we can find to break free.'

'Are there any places like this in England?'

He smiled – almost to himself.

'Oh, yes,' he answered. 'Actually more than here.'

'How come we don't read about them?' asked Kim.

'Ah, well, that's a question now, isn't it?'

Their wandering had brought them back towards the remaining lights of the village.

'Well, is there an answer?' asked Kim, suddenly aware of how tired she'd become.

'Yes, but I'm afraid it's hardly appropriate to give to casual Lukedom visitors – no offence intended.'

'Classified stuff, huh?' said Kim, and then added: 'Say, I just realized I need a place to stay tonight. Is there a dorm or something for newcomers, or a cheap motel?'

'Actually there are both,' said Way. 'There are cots at the orientation centre and rooms at two hotels in town. But you're welcome to stay at my place. I've two spare bedrooms.'

'No, thanks,' she found herself replying easily. 'I want to sample this place the way most people do. I'll try the dorm.'

She was happy to see him appear disappointed at her decision, and so wheeled away into the dorm before he could respond.

The next morning she'd gone to orientation and been 'trained' by a guide named Ray and another named Kathy. It had seemed like a cross between boot camp and an encounter session from the seventies. Again, she thought she saw what they were up to, but thought it was pretty strong medicine for most people. After the lunch break she'd cut her afternoon session and taken a short hike out of town. She visited the teepee village and met people she might well have met at some of the ashrams she'd visited. Many were indifferent to the dice business and were in Lukedom mainly because it was cheap. She felt a little uneasy thinking that living simply and cheaply and purposelessly in a teepee was probably where her life was heading.

When she returned to orientation she was randomly selected to man the cash register at the orientation restaurant for an hour. As she went through the motions of receiving the money and returning the change – it came to her much more easily than she had assumed it would – she thought about her feelings. She was surprised that despite all her listening to Michael and the other diceguides, she still had a strong resistance to using the dice. She could use them in silly little trivial ways or to show off, but when it came to doing something that might be really different for her, she drew back.

She tried to convince herself that she was already free and flexible and multiple without the dice, and that her resistance was reasonable. Nevertheless she sensed that she was strongly attached to her free-wheeling spirit and resisted appearing otherwise – options which the dice sometimes chose.

The main thing that disappointed her about Lukedom was that it didn't seem as much fun as Luke himself. She had finished Luke's *The Dice Man* and thought that though Luke sounded a little sick at times, he was fun! He was playful, a man who really did seem to have gotten rid of his ego, who didn't care what people thought of him or where the dice took him. But Lukedom seemed a rather serious place, more like many of the ashrams she had visited or lived in briefly over the years. Where could there ever be any spontaneous warmth or communication if everyone was on stage all the time trying on new roles? It was exhausting.

After her stint at the cash register, she grabbed a bite to eat, sitting with a young woman her age who had been in Lukedom for eight months. The woman seemed to be utterly serious about the need to free herself from feminine stereotypical role-playing and argued that Lukedom was offering the solution to the oppression of women. Kim could see that the breaking down of society's normal attitudes might be liberating for any of those oppressed by those attitudes, but she wondered what would emerge in its place. In Lukedom jobs and roles were so randomized that women were as likely to be carpenters, plumbers or bank presidents as men, and men cooks, housekeepers or babysitters. From a woman's point of view it was a clear improvement over most societies, although the plumbing must sometimes suffer. Susan, it turned out, was working for the next two months as crew boss of a gang of men and women renovating houses on the south edge of town and claimed she was better than any of them at her job.

After that talk, Kim sat down alone on a bench in the sun and finished off her iced tea from lunch.

She realized she was glad that Larry still seemed so . . . uneasy in her presence. Despite all his earnest efforts, he was hooked on her. And she was glad. One of her not-completely-hidden motives for coming to Lukedom, especially after Honoria gave him back his ring, was to be with Larry, to 'see what developed'. Despite his seeming to be the sort of man she usually made fun of, she liked Larry – probably more than 'liked'.

She felt a little guilty that she enjoyed seeing him struggling with his need for control against her, struggling to convince himself marrying Honoria was what he wanted. But depressing too. He had a lot of things in him waiting to break free, but she doubted they would ever make it. The reason she hadn't let herself get involved with him was not only Honoria, but because she feared Larry would make of their affair something melodramatic. He would be passionate and brooding, loving her for their physical connecting and hating her for taking him away from the straight and narrow path to fame and fortune he had set out for himself. She knew that being loved by a neurotic was a sure formula for misery. Larry would have to be miserable without her.

Although she had to admit she was sorely tempted.

32

I didn't go with my 'father' back to the orientation building, but instead turned back to hike along the stream that ran along the west edge of the community. There in the twenty-foot-deep cut through which the stream meandered I could escape the questioning of the diceguides about my confrontation with my 'father.' After a twenty-minute hike, stumbling over the rocks and boulders that contained the streambed, occasionally fighting through overgrown shrubs and brambles, I came to a huge boulder against which the water gurgled noisily. I sat down on a cluster of smaller stones and leaned back against the big boulder to stare at the water as it splashed its way through the maze of boulders and fallen logs towards me. Then I cried.

As I did I remembered – for the first time in years – how, when I was twelve, I had sobbed and kicked and raged when my mother had told me that Luke was probably never coming back again. I had raged both against Luke for leaving and against Mom for not having stopped it and for not being angrier at the desertion. I'd cried then because I loved him and had only good memories of him. And I guess I cried again that afternoon for the same reasons.

After a short while I stopped crying and suddenly smiled and shook my head. I spend half a lifetime hating a man, and then, because some bald-headed guy pretends to be him, I find that I love the man I hate. I wiped away the tears with the sleeve of my sweatshirt. Of course, I still hated him too.

But while thinking about the confrontation, I abruptly re-membered that when Abe Lister had been walking away back towards the town after we'd finished, a man had slipped out from behind a tree and begun walking casually after him. And by God, the man was one of the FBI men – the lanky one – that had come to see me five weeks earlier!

I had dimly known it was he when I first saw him, but in the midst of the emotional turmoil of the moment the presence of an FBI agent in Lukedom hadn't registered; now it did. What was going on? Was Abe Lister somehow an important lead to Luke himself?

I felt a shiver of excitement. Old Baldy had certainly known a lot more about Luke and our past relationship than I'd told him in the brief background I'd given before we were sent off to confront. He'd even known about Luke's phone call after Mom's accident: only Luke's closest associates could possibly know that! The FBI must have known that Lister was somehow important and sent an agent to follow him in their search for Luke. My father must be here!

Chance chose waiting on table in the orientation restaurant for my luncheon assignment; I supposed it was a step up from washing dishes. Little did I know. The people in the Lukedom community were probably no better or worse to wait on than those in the outside world, which means that I found them pretty unbearable. First I had to deal with the fact that the people I waited on didn't know I existed; I was R2-D2 with hair as far as they were concerned. They gave their orders with no more personal interest than they would had they been speaking into a McDonald's drive-in recessed microphone. And when I brought their orders they sometimes looked at the plate as if suspicious I was shortchanging them on the peas.

And tips. Although I thought I was superior to the pittances I might receive as tips, when a large table of six, whose chance-determined tab had come to a hundred and twenty dollars, didn't consult the dice and left me only a five-dollar bill, I was outraged. What nerve! What deadbeats! And I'd even brought them a second plate of rolls without being asked!

Back in orientation for an afternoon session I was annoyed to see Kim laughing with Ray as if they were old friends, even grabbing his hand briefly when making a point. When she saw me, however, she left Ray and came happily over to ask how my morning session had gone. I mumbled something vague, causing her to gaze up at me mischievously.

'Well, I had better luck confronting you,' she announced. 'Although I don't think Ray made a very convincing Larry – too soft.'

'Oh?' I said, reluctantly sitting in one of the stupid desk-chairs for the afternoon session.

Kim squeezed into a chair beside me, edging it closer to mine with a loud scratching sound.

'Essentially I accused you of desiring me and not doing anything about it,' she explained saucily. 'And accused myself of stringing you along without having decided how I feel about you.'

'I see,' I said, both pleased and annoyed at her pert frankness. 'And how did I respond?'

'You said you weren't about to mess up your life by giving in to a temporary lust,' she answered, smiling at me.

'Sounds reasonable,' I said, trying to maintain the traditional male coolness.

'That's what I said too,' said Kim. 'Although at the same time your reasonableness pisses me off.'

Our dialogue was broken by Kathy and Ray beginning the afternoon training with a lecture from Ray on the ways confronting archetypal figures in your life tended to free up aspects of your life that were stuck, and then a second shorter one from Kathy urging us to give as a regular option our living for a time without any role or personality. Ultimately, she suggested, once we were able to go from role to role or attitude to attitude by the whims of the dice, we'd in effect be able to be 'roleless' most of the time. Exactly what this 'roleless' state would be like wasn't clear.

I was paired up with the red-headed woman sitting in front of me for an exercise in trying to experience this rolelessness, but flunked it badly. When Ray then paired me up with Kim for her childhood 'confront', the same exercise I'd done in the morning, I felt anxiety – why, I didn't know. I was to play her father. Ray sat with us for about fifteen minutes, softly asking Kim to fill me in about her parents, particularly her father.

Kim cheerfully explained that her father was an artist, an oil painter, who had never quite made it in the art world, instead becoming a competent, if low-paid, layout artist for a series of ad agencies. Because he was nearly twenty years older than Kim's mother and more interested in oils than oil, he'd been considered by the Battles a disastrous choice for the young Susan Battle. As a result, despite all his efforts, he was usually snubbed. When he died of cancer at fifty-five it was considered by some to be the most socially acceptable thing he'd ever done.

Unfortunately Kim's mother almost immediately remarried – this time an even worse choice than her first: an elegant drifter whose major skill was making minor money in shady ways – penny stocks, disguised pyramid schemes, mail-order fraud, the usual small-time scams that men of wealth, who operate only on a grand scale, sneer at. Kim's mother's rehabilitation as a Battle thus lasted only the length of her brief widowhood; her new ostracism was total and final. Kim, the only child, was dragged with the couple from here to there for almost three years until Kim's mother died of a cancerous brain tumour. Her stepfather, with brisk efficiency, promptly mailed Kim back off east to her aged grandmother. Kim lived with her for three years and was then, when the grandmother died, passed on to Mr and Mrs William Fanshawe Battle III.

From that background I could understand Kim's love–hate relationship with the Battles, but still didn't see how I could effectively pretend to be her dad.

We were sent outside the building for our confront and immediately headed across the stream and a sloping meadow towards the long rolling mountain that was the eastern wall that enclosed Lukedom in its valley.

'You sold out,' Kim suddenly said to me as we clomped slowly through the knee-high grass.

For a moment I was taken aback, feeling she was talking about me instead of the long-ago father.

'Not at all,' I said. 'I was good at what I did and I made money – that's not selling out.'

'You let those Battles push you around all your life,' she went on with surprising ferocity, 'bowing and scraping for any scrap they'd let fall your way.'

'I had your mother to think about,' I said, after a pause. 'She needed them, and I went along.'

Kim halted at the edge of the field that lay at the base of the steeper slope at the beginning of the mountain and turned to me.

'Yes, but what did *you* want?' she said. 'Why couldn't you take her *your* way?'

I turned away, trying to get into the soul of someone who had a talent but let it moulder and die in order to . . . to what? To survive? To please his wife? To enjoy a higher society? Nothing quite rang true.

'I'm not sure why I – '

'You denied yourself!' Kim interrupted. 'You lived a lie! There would have been nothing wrong with trying to be a Battle if it was only something you really wanted!'

'What about you?' I shot back. 'You fit in even better than I ever did. Is it something *you* really want?'

'Yes! It is! I had enough of genteel poverty with my mother and that creep she remarried after Da – after you! The Battles may be silly and snobbish, but life's a lot easier with them than without them.'

'I don't get it,' I said, no longer sure whether I was talking to the dice student Kim or the normal Kim. 'How can you condemn your father – I mean condemn me – for doing what you say you're doing?'

She was standing with her hands on her hips glaring at me when she suddenly broke out into gay laughter.

'Damned if I know,' she said. 'I actually think I'm madder at him for dying than anything else.'

'You've forgotten our assignment.'

'Oh, piss on our assignment,' she said. 'I'm tired of this stuff. Let's climb the mountain.' Without further ado that's precisely what she started doing, heading off at an angle to pick up what looked to be the beginning of a trail off to our left. I happily followed.

We began following the slightest of indentations in the earth that marked a path through the low shrubs and large fir trees that grew on the mountainside. The climb was relatively easy, angling up for a way and then cutting back, sometimes with long runs, sometimes with rapid switchbacks. Kim led at first and I was content to follow, happy to be rid of the pressures of Lukedom, although wondering what exactly this climb had to do with finding my father. Kim's athletic body was having no trouble with the climb and I was surprised to note that her behind swinging back and forth in front of me lost its usual sexual aura, as we both threw ourselves into the simple pleasure of the climb.

When the path came to a fork, one faint trail angling upwards and the main trail turning on the level to the left, we stopped to catch our breaths and look upward to see where we were headed and then off to the left, wondering why the main trail went that way. When I looked along the main trail I saw someone disappear into a cave in the hillside. It was a glimpse so brief I wasn't certain I'd seen what I'd seen, the glimpse being questionable because the man was dressed in a suit. A suit entering a cave?

'Did you see that?' I asked Kim.

'The man going in the cave?' Kim responded, turning to me and wiping her brow on her sleeve with childlike unself-consciousness.

'Let's take a look.' I led the way along the level main trail towards where we thought we'd seen someone disappear. We soon came up to an old mine entrance with a huge, battered wooden door, padlocked firmly to an ancient beam. A larger weather-beaten sign warned: 'Danger. Keep Out'. The cave entrance was blocked off by the door and the thick-looking wooden walls on either side of it. Although the man had seemed to disappear precisely here, it looked as if the padlocked door hadn't been disturbed in years. But weren't there signs of foot scufflings near the wall to the left of the door?

'Is this where you saw the guy disappear?' I asked Kim, who was running her hands over the vertical slabs of wood.

'Yes, it was, damn it,' she said, continuing her examination.

Had it been an optical illusion? Did the man simply continue on the trail around a bend that made it appear that he'd entered a cave? No. No, Kim saw it the same way I did!

'Anything phoney about the wall?' I asked her when she finally turned away from her examination, her usually bright face furrowed with concentration. The wall consisted of thick vertical planks with irregular spaces between them, and cross-beam backings could sometimes be seen between the cracks.

'It's possible there's a hinged section someplace along here,' Kim said, glancing back at the wall. 'One that could be swung open from the inside so somebody could get in. But if there is I can't find it.'

I banged some of the vertical planks in a few places and the thuds indicated a solidity that would have prevented anyone walking through them. Then I turned to look down at the little village of Lukedom in the valley below.

'Think we're hallucinating?'

'Maybe,' said Kim, joining me looking down at Lukedom. 'But nothing here would really surprise me.'

Since we were already two-thirds of the way up the mountain, we decided to follow the infrequently-used branch of the trail and hike to the top.

As we climbed, the trail became thinner and less worn. Had the peak not been so close and Kim with me I might have turned back, but my natural competitive juices were flowing, especially when every time I turned back to check Kim's progress she was there just behind me, sweating, occasionally cursing when a foot slipped on the loose stones, but not stopping to rest except when I did.

The last hundred yards were up a narrow scree in an almost vertical rock wall that I knew we shouldn't be climbing but couldn't resist. The knees of my trousers and Kim's jeans were getting torn, as were the palms and fingers of our hands, but looking up we could see that the rock wall appeared to begin to level out towards the peak.

In one tight chimney formation it was only my six-foot height and long reach that permitted me to get a high handhold and pull myself, and then Kim, up. It was our first physical contact in the long climb, and I was surprised at how hot her small hand was and how fierce her grip. When I pulled her scrambling up on to the small shelf, she collapsed with a groan beside me, our thighs pressed together as we sat momentarily with our legs dangling over the ledge.

'Thanks', she said, smiling at me with sparkling eyes.

'We shouldn't be doing this, you know,' I said.

'I know,' she said, glowing.

Returning her grin, I struggled up to begin climbing the last of the narrow scree. The worst was over. Though we were both gasping for breath as we walked the final fifty feet up the bare rounded top of this part of the mountain, I was feeling better than I had in months – since a wonderful spring sail in a friend's catamaran when we'd almost capsized and given up on ever getting the boat back before dark. Mindless physical exertion with a touch of danger was a tonic. I felt like shouting, but settled for impulsively grabbing Kim's hand and squeezing it.

'Goddamn it, beats washing dishes at Joe's, doesn't it?' I said.

'Or listening to another lecture about self,' Kim agreed, as we continued hand in hand to the top shelf of rock.

From there we could look back down at Lukedom, some of which was now hidden by tall trees halfway down the mountain. The village looked tiny and insignificant. When we turned and looked down the opposite hillside, there didn't seem to be a town or house in sight, only a ranger's tower on the mountain across the valley, and in the valley a meandering stream and trees.

When I turned to Kim she was in the act of turning to me. We looked at each other and then were in each other's arms and kissing.

We were kissing. I had the tiniest memory of the hunger and desire in her eyes just before we embraced, but that memory was buried in the avalanche of passion and fulfilment I felt in crushing her against me and in our kissing. My whole being seemed to be saying 'It's about time!'

The roar was incredible; the whole universe seemed to be vibrating and screaming in unison, the air rushing around us as if we were hurtling through space. I had an image of being plunged into a Hemingway novel, but then began to be almost frightened at the power of what was happening – when Kim broke our kiss.

The roaring and rushing continued for a moment and then receded. As I looked at her in surprised adoration I became dimly aware that she was looking off to the left, and that the roaring was an aeroplane I now saw soaring just over the last of the south end of the mountain, the aeroplane that must have roared over us in the middle of our kiss.

Still holding each other, we briefly watched the plane recede into the sky. It was a strange moment: I felt like a man who in the midst of receiving the Nobel Prize finds the ceremony visited by a UFO; I was interested in getting on with the ceremony, but felt a UFO probably had to be commented on.

'What the hell was that?' I asked.

'An awfully nice kiss,' answered Kim, turning to smile up at me.

'I know, but where did that plane come from?'

We broke our embrace to move across the flat peak to the edge of the cliff on the west side of the mountain from which the plane had come. When we got as close to the edge as we dared, we looked directly down.

At first what I was seeing didn't register. There were no buildings, no cars, no people – just a long flat terrace cut into the side of the mountain, cut by man into this side of the mountain. Fifty yards in width, not a tree or boulder broke the neat flat terrace that ran for at least a half mile. I stared at it and stared at it and finally saw it. A small airstrip.

'Things get interestinger by the minute,' said Kim from beside me.

'But where's the airport?' I asked, still trying to absorb what I was seeing.

'In the mountain,' said Kim.

A small airfield. On a mountainside miles from any town or, as far as we could see, from any road. An airfield on which small planes could land and take off, leaving off passengers to do nothing in nowheresville.

Looking down on this strange strip of modern technology in the middle of wilderness, I knew that the people landing there weren't doing nothing in nowheresville.

'I bet if we hiked down there,' I said as we gazed down at the airstrip, 'we'd find another abandoned mine entrance with a rusty padlock and a sign saying "Danger. Keep Out".'

Kim nodded.

'And I doubt that people enter one mineshaft just to hike through the mountain to exit on the other side,' she said.

She was right. Under where we were standing, between the mine entrance on the Lukedom side and the airstrip on the other, were people. People doing something that they didn't want other people to know about.

Kim took my hand and we turned away back towards Lukedom.

'It figures,' she said. 'Lukedom is far too sophisticated a place to be run by those few people in administration and orientation.'

'But why hide things in a mountain?'

'Beats me,' said Kim.

It was almost six in the afternoon and getting dark. Though we agreed it was possible we could hike down to the airstrip and look around and then climb back over the mountain to Lukedom before dark, we decided not to. Our climbing the mountain was explainable, but not our nosing around the airstrip. Although I don't think either of us was afraid, we figured that the people who were keeping secrets might not take kindly to strangers wandering about on their airstrip.

So, in a subdued mood, we headed back down the mountain towards the village. I felt I was closer to finding my father than I'd ever been before. One of Lukedom's mottos was 'This truth above all: fake it'. In Lukedom a door that wasn't a door and a wall that wasn't a wall and a wilderness that wasn't a wilderness seemed just about par for the course.

33

An hour and a half later I sat in a corner of the Do Die Inn bar and waited for Kim. We had separated soon after getting back to the village to go to our respective rooms to bathe and change clothes. Being alone with a drink had reminded me that reality was getting a little complex and contradictory – just the way the prophets here in Lukedom said it was. I was in an outrageous community that apparently had something even more outrageous to hide. I was engaged to a woman I wanted to marry, and mightily tempted by a woman to whom I wasn't engaged and didn't want to marry. I thought my father was here in Lukedom, but hadn't yet a shred of clear evidence that this was so.

I knew that I would continue my investigations tomorrow and not return to New York until I had some answers to the questions that had arisen. Although I dreaded it, I realized I had to phone Honoria. In all this chaos a part of me knew where the solid land of my life lay and it wasn't in any of the people here in Lukedom.

As I sat in the safety of my little booth, I thought of the prospect of talking to Honoria with the wariness of an amateur exploring the subtleties of an electric switch-breaker box – live wires everywhere. It took me twenty minutes and two more drinks before I was befuddled enough to dare try it.

Unfortunately – I'd somehow imagined it would be otherwise – Honoria was at home; she even answered the phone. After the usual preliminary verbal sparring, I blurted out the awful truth.

'I'm on to something here, sweetheart,' I said. 'Something big. Got to stay. Least another day. Maybe Thursday.'

'Fine,' said Honoria. 'I'll see you when I see you.'

'You know how much I'd like to be back – '

But with her usual brisk efficiency Honoria had hung up. Indecisiveness was not one of her flaws.

I remained in the stuffy phone booth for another half minute listening to the dial tone.

Well. So. I was still in the doghouse.

As I walked back through the restaurant towards the bar I suddenly became aware that I was grinning!

How sick! A hundred thousand dollars a year had just hung up on me! A woman who stood to inherit most or all of twenty or thirty million dollars! The woman my boss was willing to let me marry if I could only manage to keep my father squelched! The boss responsible for determining my annual Christmas bonus, a bonus due in little more than six weeks!

I felt a wave of fear: I was stepping into no man's land. My future, that grand reliable railroad line across the country to riches, had suddenly gotten sidetracked, and where this new line went was anybody's guess, but it certainly wasn't aimed at the same glittering city on a hill.

Seeing Kim had arrived and was sitting enticingly in my booth awaiting me, I became the healthy male on the make and wondered how I should play it. Cool? Angry? Hurt? Hurt, I remembered vaguely, always played best with women. But Kim was wearing a lovely tight-fitting dress and had her hair looking almost under control. She was dazzling. But I must look hurt, hurt.

I walked slowly back to the booth and slid into the bench opposite her. For a moment I stared at the melting ice cubes in the dregs of my drink and tried to look melancholy.

'What are you looking so happy about?' asked Kim.

'Uh, what?'

'You came back looking like you just won the lottery. What happened?'

Somehow this conversation wasn't going quite the way I'd figured. I looked up at her trying to maintain what I had thought was my tragic expression.

Kim returned my gaze for a moment and then burst out laughing.

I thought I ought to try to look offended but then realized that I'd probably be no more successful with offended than I'd been with melancholy.

'I guess I'm not as upset as I thought that Honoria just hung up on me,' I said.

'Not upset! I knew you and Honoria had your little troubles, but I never guessed you were *suffering*.'

'We *aren't* suffering,' I protested. 'I don't know why I don't feel worse.'

Kim shook her head, still smiling.

'Worse,' she echoed sceptically. 'When you came back here I thought you were having an orgasm.'

I tried for a moment to look offended but finally gave up and laughed.

'I think you're being a little hard on me,' I said.

'I'm not being hard. I'm just trying to figure you out. And besides,' she went on, 'maybe I'm laughing because I'm feeling pretty good about things too, ever think of that?'

Hey, that's right!

'You don't want Honoria to marry me?' I asked.

'Of course not. You two'd just make life miserable for each other.'

'I see,' I said, stalling, as usual, for time.

'Your heart knows it, your body knows it, but your mind doesn't know itself from a hole in the ground.'

'Thanks.'

'If you were truly in love with Nori,' Kim went gaily on, 'you wouldn't be so attracted to me. But since messing around with your fiancée's cousin is against the rules, you've been sitting on it.' She paused. 'Not literally, I hope,' she added with a smile.

'I don't believe I'm having this conversation,' I said.

'You're not,' said Kim. 'I'm having it and you're trying to figure out what you're supposed to do about it.'

'I see,' I said, but was fairly sure I was, as usual, seeing very little.

Later, we ate dinner together and discussed what we'd found out about Lukedom. Like most men, I was more comfortable with subjects I was the expert on, so steered clear of talking about the possibilities of something happening between me and Kim. As I kept up what I hope was a witty (if superficial) conversation I had the feeling my life was reeling just a trifle out of control. My engagement was in danger, and primarily from a girl who represented precisely the chaos and spontaneity I'd structured my life to avoid.

'I've been thinking,' Kim announced much later, when we were the last two customers in the restaurant. She was toying with the last of some rather awful cake she'd ordered for dessert and looking at me with less mischievousness than usual.

'I think we're in Rome,' she went on.

I was wise enough not to challenge this statement, despite its seeming to have a certain inaccuracy to it.

'And thus should do as the Romans do,' she concluded.

I pulled my eyes away from her breasts, where they had inadvertently wandered, and tried to return her gaze with equal intellectual seriousness.

'This community,' she continued, 'is populated by people who play roles and games and use dice. Dr Ecstein insists you get into diceliving before he'll give you the information you came for. I think you should do it.'

'No,' I said.

'To begin with,' Kim went on, 'I must admit I find the idea of using dice to make decisions rather irrelevant.'

'Exactly.'

'But fun,' she added. ' . . . Serious fun.'

'No, I'm not going to let the dice decide anything of any importance.'

'Because it seems to me,' Kim said easily, as if my interjection had been of no more significance than a sneeze, 'that if you're going to overcome your father you must prove – to him and to yourself – that you can play his games but choose not to.'

'If I want to do something, I do it,' I said. 'If I don't want to do something I don't do it. Although I may pretend to diddle with the dice to play along with Jake Ecstein, I'll never really let them affect my life.'

'Chicken,' she said.

This was a new tack.

'You're afraid,' she went on quietly. 'The man I'm falling in love with, the great risk-taker, the man who likes to sail out into gales for the fun of it, who risks millions of dollars every day, is afraid to let a single six-sided cube move him even a single inch.'

This was going too far. To be called chicken by the woman who had just admitted she was falling in love with me and whose pants I wanted passionately to get into was too much to let pass. I tried to feel anger, but Kim was sitting across from me in the dim light, looking lovely, loving and lovable, and smiling at me with her infuriatingly mischievous smile. She was a mean teasing slut.

'I'm not afraid of the dice,' I said. 'I'm at war with them.'

'Then beat them!' she shot back. 'As it is, you're running away!'

'I'm not running away!'

'You are! If you're at war with your father and the dice, then let's see you fight! Beat Luke at his own game! Show him you reject his ways not because they're beyond you, but because you've tried them and know your way is better!'

Well. Kim's outburst, made with dramatic inflections from her fork, stopped me cold.

' . . . Use the dice . . . ' I mused aloud, 'just to show I can use the dice . . . '

'Exactly,' said Kim.

'It's as if my father is reaching back through time and space to taunt me with his ways.'

'Beat him!' Kim urged again. 'You think you're the best at whatever you undertake. Well then, be the best at dicing!'

'I could, you know,' I said softly. 'I'm no uptight stuck-in-the-mud. If I stick to the straight and narrow it's out of strength, not weakness.'

'That's right!' said Kim, suddenly leaning across the open space between us and taking hold of my right hand with hers. 'You can stay here, beat the dicepeople at dicing, find your father, and still be the best trader east of Kansas.'

'East of Guam,' I corrected.

We smiled at each other.

'So,' said Kim. Still smiling, she leaned back and wiped her mouth and flopped her napkin on to the table. Then she reached into the small bag she had brought with her, scrounged around in it and brought out two dice.

'Let's see what's on the agenda for tonight,' she said.

From Luke's Journal

Accident provides the growing power of all life. Men have always liked to think that life evolved because Someone Up There had control and purpose and directed change. The sage sees that life evolves from a much more admirable force: Chance. Control and purpose inherently limited the direction of change to the limits of the mind doing the controlling. Imagine, if you dare, that the creator of the universe was actually rational! Were God rational, 99 per cent of the universe would not have been created — certainly not human beings. No, no, no, it is quite clear that the only Creator who can lay claim to the absurdity and richness of life is Accident, is Chance.

34

Agent Nathaniel Putt arrived in Lukedom at 21.07 hours Tuesday evening, accompanied by Agent Robert Hayes. Two additional bureau men, Agents Rogers and Massiori, were due to arrive at 10.15 A.M. the following day. Putt had picked up his bureau car at the Wickstown airport at 18.36 hours and driven straight through to the guard gate with no more trouble than a broken right rear spring and dented right fender.

The gate guard, a middle-aged woman that evening, told him and Hayes that they had not known the password and, ten minutes later, that they both had badly failed the test. However, after making a phone call, she announced that since Putt was 'cute' she was waving them on in, nonchalantly recommending the Hazard Inn. She let Putt use her phone, and he called Macavoy and ordered him to meet them at the Hazard. Macavoy tried to protest, but Putt, exhausted from his flight and drive, curtly ordered him to be there.

Putt followed her directions and arrived at the Hazard at precisely the same moment that Macavoy came trotting up, gasping for breath. Putt had carefully prepared his identity: he was a Hollywood producer looking for shooting locations and agent Hayes was his go-fer, a role he had been practising for years. Putt parked their car on the empty street and handed his bag to Macavoy.

'Nathan Tupper,' he said to Macavoy. 'Bob here is Rob Siffel. Who are you?'

'Mac Voy,' said Macavoy. 'I'm looking for real-estate deals.'

'Find any?' asked Putt as they began to climb the stairs of the hotel. He looked doubtfully at the array of signs and then continued ahead of Macavoy up the stairs to the door.

The lobby wasn't crowded, but the guests looked a little strange. Several seemed to be wearing costumes and the rest looked as if they were wearing someone else's clothes.

Putt led his two men across the lobby and up to the desk. A distinguished man dressed in a tuxedo greeted him.

'Uh, yes,' said Putt. 'We'd like two separate rooms, one preferably a suite.'

'I'm sorry, sir,' said the man. 'We can't give you a room until we know who you are.'

'I'm Nathan Tupper,' said Putt smoothly. 'I'm a producer at Paramount out here looking for locations and – '

'Oh, no, sir, I mean who the dice tell you to be today.'

'Ahh,' said Putt, pulling his arm away from Macavoy who was trying to pull him aside. 'We're only here as observers. Producers looking for locations.'

'Certainly, Mr Tupper,' said the distinguished man. 'You'll find your clothes over there in the outfitting room.'

'No, no, no,' said Putt. 'Just some rooms.'

'I'm afraid you have to report first to the outfitting room,' said the man. 'Regulations, you know.'

'I warned you, sir,' said Macavoy, tugging again at Putt's sleeve as they moved off towards the outfitting room. 'Everyone who comes to this hotel has to pretend to play the game.'

'But for God's sake – '

'It has its advantages,' said Macavoy insistently. 'Even if you tried to tell people you're an agent, no one will believe you – unless the dice tell them to pretend to.'

'I'm not sure coming here for the night was such a good idea,' mumbled Putt.

Twenty minutes later, after Putt and Hayes had changed into costumes and been assigned rooms, and the dice had ordered Hayes to pay $6.32 for his and Putt $128.88 for his, Macavoy led them away, carrying their bags. As they moved down the long wide hallway Putt stared uneasily at the signs over each of the innumerable doors: Love Room, Money Room, even a Master–Slave Room. Macavoy, speaking over his shoulder, soberly explained.

'Along here are the playrooms – Therapy Room, Hate Room and so on. This Death Room, for example, is where people can go if they get killed or feel like having a funeral.'

Hayes hesitated next to the door marked 'Love Room' but then hurried on.

'Or,' continued Macavoy, 'you can go into there and give a eulogy or be a mourner.'

'For someone you don't know?' protested Putt.

'That seems to be beside the point,' Macavoy answered.

'I'm not sure we should be staying here,' said Putt again.

'This is a good place for us, Nat,' said Agent Hayes. 'No matter how weird we are we'll blend right in.'

Putt paused to glare back at him. Putt himself was now wearing tight-fitting jeans, an open-necked silk shirt, and several gold chains and medallions down his bare chest. He looked like an elderly down-and-out pimp and wasn't sure he liked Hayes's comment.

A woman dressed skimpily in a tight low blouse, hot pants and high heels, and wearing an extravagant blonde wig and garish make-up, now came up to Putt.

'Hi, big boy,' she said. 'Looking for some action?'

'Certainly not,' said Putt, growing a little red in the face. 'I'm an observer.'

'Like to watch, huh?' said the woman. 'Well, it'll cost a little extra, but – '

'Macavoy!!' shouted Putt.

Macavoy hurried back to his boss.

'Uh, it's Mr Voy, sir,' said Macavoy. 'Or Mac to my friends.'

'Tell this woman I'm not here.'

'Uh, look, baby, cool it,' said Macavoy. 'This is the famous Hollywood producer Nathan Tupper. You want a part in a picture then don't hassle him.'

The woman widened her eyes and then licked her lips.

'You do any X-rated?' she asked.

'No,' said Putt, pushing on by her.

'Let me take your phone number, Miss,' said Hayes quickly. 'Might have a part for you.'

As the woman smiled and Hayes took her number, Putt and Macavoy continued down the hall. Putt glared at the walls, which now contained various proverbs inscribed in religious-looking script: 'The Die is my shepherd, I shall not want', 'The Die giveth, the Die taketh away', 'Blessed be the name of the Lord Chance'.

Putt scowled.

After they had passed the Creativity Room, the Life Choices

Room, the Mother–Son Room, and the Room Room, they passed a big tough-looking cop outside the Jail Room.

'Good to see they have a jail and policemen around, anyway,' said Putt.

Macavoy frowned.

'Of course, in here those acting as cops aren't really cops,' he said.

'They're not!?' said Putt.

'Any real cops around here are probably dressed as jocks or pimps.'

When Macavoy became aware that he was staring at Putt's outrageous get-up he flushed and moved on.

— 35 —

Although I didn't remember agreeing to use the dice, after we'd finished eating I'd followed Kim up the inn stairs, and now she was sitting in the stuffed chair of my bedroom rubbing two dice together in her palms and beaming away like a ringmaster about to start the circus. Should I object? My basic self told me I mustn't permit my father's poison any further into my life, but the rest of me was shouting, 'Who gives a fuck?' There she was, bathed, beaming and beautiful, and only a fool would stick to technicalities. The trouble with arguing with a woman you loved – or rather, lusted after – was that you couldn't win. You either won the argument and lost the prize, or had to lose the argument to have any hope at the prize. It was the one important area of life where a man of reason learned to abandon his principles and forgo reason, justice and logical debate to opt for agreement and a sure fuck. I could inform her afterwards that I hadn't conceded any of her points.

'OK,' said Kim, 'I feel like being an animal. 'I'll let the die determine what animal I'll be.'

This wasn't exactly what I had expected or hoped for, and as I sat on the edge of the bed I wanted to protest.

'Will you join me?' asked Kim.

'As an animal?'

'Whatever,' she said, grinning impishly. 'Will you play dice games with me?'

I wanted to make love to her and felt I should order her out of my room. I hated using the dice even for whether I should brush my teeth or not, yet here was this sexy minx asking me to play dice games with her. I wanted to explain to her why it was sick, and yet thought it might be delightful. But mainly I wanted to make love to her.

'Sure,' I finally answered. 'As long as we don't get too serious.'

'That's the spirit,' she said. 'Supposedly the whole purpose of the dice is to kill seriousness.'

'Supposedly,' I said.

Kim abruptly looked away for a few concentrated moments and then flipped a die on to the badly worn rug at her feet. It was a 'three', whatever that meant.

'I'm a puppy,' she announced gaily and tossed the die to me. Then she plopped down on all fours and, after sniffing the air, crawled rapidly over to one corner of the room and poked her head in the straw waste-paper basket.

In her tight-fitting dress, which came to just above her knees, Kim's puppy looked more silly and sexy than puppyish. I looked from Kim's always fascinating behind to the die in my hand. If it fell an odd number I'd be a puppy too, an even I wouldn't.

The die fell five.

I slid off the bed on to the floor almost as rapidly as Kim had, crouching on all fours and wiggling my shoulders, then my butt, trying to become aware of my dog body. I stuck my tongue out and brought it back two or three times, my main memory of puppies being their tongues always being in evidence. Suddenly Kim's face was in mine, her nose poking at my nose and cheek. Before I could respond she moved along my side, rubbing me and wiggling her behind like an excited puppy.

When I began crawling after her, we began circling each other rapidly on all fours, each of us sniffing and trying to get our noses to the other's rear end. I was grinning but pursuing Kim's bouncing buttocks with a lot more than puppyish fervour until she finally stopped so abruptly my head banged into her right buttock, bringing me too to a happy halt.

After shaking my head as if I had long ears I wanted to clear away from my head, as she remained stationary I poked my nose into her dress at the cleft in her behind. When she pulled away, I swung away from her and at full speed race-crawled across the room, turned, and then raced back directly at her.

Kim crouched down with her hands flat in front of her and her behind in the air facing my approaching dash and, as I neared, scooted to the left to avoid me, knocking over the ancient floor lamp, which plopped down on its lampshade with enough force to kill the lightbulb.

'Yipe-yipe-yipe,' went Kim, and I swung around to chase after her.

Kim dashed-scrambled into one corner of the now dimly-lit room and crouched down behind the straw waste-paper basket with a mad gleam in her eye that looked for all the world like that of a mischievous puppy. I race-crawled straight at her, but just as I arrived she leapt up and came down on my back, sending the waste-paper basket tumbling.

I shook myself to unseat my puppy-friend straddling my back in reverse, and when that failed, collapsed and rolled over, sending Kim rolling off on to her back. I leapt up on to all fours and, seeing her lying on her back with her knees and arms raised – a puppy's surrender position – I leapt to her exposed neck, opening my mouth wide and letting her feel my teeth on her soft warm skin.

There was a moment of unreality as my puppy role and man role became confused, the white smoothness of her neck stirring me even as I shook my head as if trying to break the neck of some prey.

Kim began to whine in a doggy way and then abruptly rolled away on to all fours and dashed away, with me scrambling after her. She leapt up on to the stuffed chair and over the arm back on to the rug and I followed, the chair toppling over. Kim was zipping around the bed, her shoes long lost, her dress hiked high up on her thighs and her pantyhose much abused, me following, my tongue hanging out like a mutt or man in heat.

When Kim tried to scramble up on to the bed, I pounced on her stationary stockinged foot, grabbing a mouthful of toes that brought a long series of feminine 'Yipes' as she thrust with her other foot and made it up on to the bed. With a mighty male spring I followed, landing on the bed and with a second leap landing on Kim's back.

With another puppy 'Yipe' and then a series of whines she tried to roll her way out from under me, but with my face buried in the thick hair at her neck, I used my weight to hold her down, my hips thrusting rhythmically against her buttocks in an instinctive if not totally puppyish frenzy. I pawed the hair away from her neck and sunk my mouth to her skin, opening it wide to hold her helpless neck at my mercy.

With my teeth hard and my mouth wet against her neck she ceased her struggles, her puppyish whines slowly metamorphosing into womanly moans even as my threatened bite turned slowly into a deep kiss and sensual licking of her neck.

After a few delicious moments of this I stopped moving and lay panting on top of her, holding my head just away from her exposed neck. I could feel the rise and fall of her breathing beneath me.

'Puppies, even males, don't hump other puppies,' Kim announced in a voice muffled by her face being pressed down into the blankets of the bed.

I let out a low threatening growl, as if resentful of her unpuppyish behaviour.

'And puppies don't kiss the necks of their victims,' she added, voice still muffled.

I growled louder and again enclosed her helpless neck in my open jaw, my teeth pressing harder into her flesh.

'That's . . . (moan) more . . . (moan) like it . . . ' from Kim.

After another long moment, I finally raised my mouth away from her neck.

'Puppies don't speak English,' I announced.

Kim stirred beneath me.

'Not to each other maybe,' she said clearly, 'but to puppies who begin acting like humans they might.'

Smiling, I rolled off her and sat up on the bed.

'Puppies may not actually hump other puppies,' I explained, 'but they sometimes like to pretend to hump'.

Kim rolled over and smiled over at me, her hair a mess and her face glistening with perspiration.

'Your puppy wasn't exactly pretending,' she commented with an attempt at a leer.

I laughed.

'That was great,' I said.

'You were terrific,' Kim said, bringing herself up into a sitting position and pulling down her skirt. The knees of her pantyhose were torn, revealing abrasions and a bandage – the results of our struggle up the mountain scree. Then she leaned back to her elbows.

'Now,' she added, 'we'll have to let the dice decide whether and how we make love tonight.'

Smiling and relaxed, on first hearing her words I felt a warm surge of desire. Then I reacted to the word 'dice'.

'No!' I said, straightening. 'That's one thing the dice won't decide!'

'But you should be able to show your father you can play his games if you wanted to.'

199

'If I want to make love tonight,' Larry said, 'we'll make love. If not, not.'

Kim raised an eyebrow.

'No matter what I want, is that it?' she said.

'I'm not going to cast a die about anything serious.'

'The first option,' Kim said, ignoring me, 'could be that tonight I'll be your total sexual slave.'

Somehow that caught my attention. However, using the willpower that had made me a number-one trader, I continued to look stern.

'Of course, we also have to give the devil his due,' she went on easily. 'So if the dice comes up a "two" or "three" we sleep in our own separate rooms and are as celibate as nuns and priests.'

I couldn't stop an instinctive scowl.

'How come celibacy gets twice the chances of sexual slave?' I found myself asking.

'Risk-taking,' she answered. 'No pain, no gain.'

My mind, egged on by my loins, searched desperately for a good argument against giving any chance to the prospect of our not making love, but flailed and failed.

'If the dice rolls a "four",' continued Kim, 'we'll make natural instinctive love the way we would without any dice business.'

'Hear, hear,' I said.

'Why don't you create the last two options?' Kim suggested. 'It's only fair.'

'I create the last two options?'

'Right. What else shall we offer up to the dice?'

'It's "die",' I said with unaccountable irritation. 'If you're only going to toss one then it's called a "die".'

'Well?' Kim persisted.

'If it's a "five",' I finally said, 'I'm going to leave here and give up my search for my father.'

'That's a good one,' she said seriously. 'One more.'

I threw my feet off the bed and stared down at the rug. Now that I'd surrendered, the game was oppressing me. I felt like a man taking his first step down the slippery slide to hell. At that moment I didn't even feel much like making love. Was my father now in the process of making me impotent?

'You make up the last one,' I said dully.

'Let's see,' said Kim from behind me. 'I suppose we could let you be my sexual slave for the night.'

Was that good? Would a real stud permit such an option? Should I protest? While my mind bounced around these questions my prick stiffened, giving its assent and effectively overruling my mind.

'No . . . ' she said and looked around the room as if there were hints there that might help her. 'No, not that one. If it's a "six" we can make love, but no matter how much we want it you can never enter me – any part of me. We'll be virgin lovers.'

Shaking my head, I swung around to face her again on the bed. She was sitting up against the headboard gazing at me.

'No matter what the dice say,' she said with sudden seriousness, 'I think I love you.'

That little piece of lightning exploded through me but was energetically repelled, a healthy male fear of commitment being my instinctive response to the word 'love'.

'You plan to follow the die no matter what it falls?' I asked.

'Of course,' she answered. 'No risk, no reward. But let's say that if a lovemaking option is chosen it lasts for only two hours.'

Only two hours. Jesus. What sort of a woman was this?

'And we must obey,' she continued. 'To show your father your strength.'

'Shit,' I said.

'Good.' She began shaking the dice in the palms of her hand as if she'd been doing it for years.

I watched.

She shook the dice hard in the cup of her hands and dropped one on to the bedding between us. It was a 'one'.

The significance of the 'one' didn't register – the various options not being tightly linked in my mind with any number on the die – until Kim uncoiled from her sitting position and slowly crawled across the bedding towards me, finally falling forward on to her chest in front of me, burying her head near my feet and lap and clasping my ankles. Her golden-globed buttocks arched into the air in front of me.

'How may I serve you, Master?' asked Kim.

I decided to give the dicelife a try.

From Luke's Journal

Chance contains an element of order. Like a game of tennis, chance depends on the net and lines of order to play. Chance is the playful side of order. With two perfect tennis players — two totally consistent, rational, perfect players, there would be no game — no variety, no winners and losers. It is imperfection, randomness, chance that makes the game possible, makes life possible, makes happiness possible.

Humans perversely pursue order when in fact our health and happiness depend on both order and chance. Could we learn to introduce chance into our lives as intelligently as we try to introduce order, ah . . . then . . .

36

Love, at its best, is, of course, a form of madness. It is a euphoria in which not only the beloved is perfection incarnate but the whole world seems to be shining. It is a state in which we feel we are incapable of taking a false step since the Gods are clearly on our side. And besides, the beloved can and will approve even of our pimples. We can't lose.

The theory that one can't lose has, to say the least, a chequered history. In general, those who have lived by the theory have usually been disappointed. The universe, even in its most benevolent moods, tends to let the rains fall pretty much at random on the just and the unjust, on those who know they can't lose, and on those who know they can.

When Larry and Kim were awakened after three or four hours' sleep by an aspiring opera singer in the shower next door, they giggled and mooned dewy-eyed at each other and, after Kim had insisted on casting a die, made love again. When they were finished, they became aware that it was 8.30 in the morning and, in theory, they were already late for their breakfast clean-up assignment.

Kim leapt up and ran to the shower to begin the day. Larry, though as sated as a male can be when first involved with a passionate woman, was still inclined to remain in bed and waylay her when she came back again. So he lay back with his hands folded beneath his head and considered what life had wrought. What the die had wrought.

The die had been generous. Kim had been his sexual slave for two hours and then had commanded them – as if they needed commanding – to make natural and instinctive love. As far as Larry was concerned it was like being released from the anteroom of Heaven into the real thing. For though Kim as sexual slave was incredible, as instinctive woman she was incredibler. The sexual slave bit had let him express an uninhibited masculine power that pleased him considerably, although it sometimes had sadistic elements that disturbed him. And it let Kim express a total surrender of her mind and will that was both intoxicating for him, but again, somehow disturbing. Although in purely sexual terms they didn't do anything special, it was totally different.

Although at first he enjoyed ordering Kim about, after a while he found himself wanting to order her to be spontaneous, natural, innovative. He realized that he had wanted to make love to her since he'd first met her, but to *Kim*, to a very specific and special Kim, that he wanted to know who she was, to be intimate with her in every way, and the sexual slave game prevented that type of intimacy. He missed sexual initiatives and naturalnesss. Kim never did anything unless he commanded her to. She even suppressed most of her moans and groans until he ordered her to moan and groan. Then, of course, he worried that she was faking it.

And when the die released them from the slave game into naturalness he knew immediately that he was right. Kim threw herself at him with an unrestrained passion that awed him. Within minutes he knew how much he had missed by being her master. Now she would suddenly abandon a perfectly delightful position and manoeuvre him and herself into an even more delightful position. Now she laughed and joked and romped as if she were playing puppy again. Now she loved him with her body, her eyes and her words, and, naturally, Larry found it disturbing.

But marvellous. What a woman. When she finally appeared out of the bathroom dressed in jeans but with no bra or blouse on, he shook his head again in awe.

'Come here, my loving slave,' he growled.

'Not now,' she answered, continuing on to the chair where she had put her overnight bag. 'I want to get dressed.'

'Give me a chance,' he protested.

Kim turned to him with a smile, pulled a die out of her jeans, frowned momentarily in concentration, and then glanced into the palm of her hand.

'No more this morning, says the die,' she replied, and turned to bury her face in the blouse she pulled over her head.

And from that moment on, the day was all downhill. The first hint of trouble was that Kim seemed to associate the die with their newly discovered passion for each other.

'Chance has thrown us together,' she said gaily as he less than enthusiastically began dressing. 'And Chance will keep us together. Nothing will ever separate us.'

Larry might have conceded he was in love, but not *that* much.

'The dice had nothing to do with our – or rather they just let us do what we wanted to do anyway,' he said, pulling on his trousers. He felt groggy with sexual satiation and lack of sleep.

'They let us discover and express the deepest part of ourselves,' she insisted. 'We can freely experiment with other options because they'll never uncover a more basic us.'

'Fine,' said Larry, wondering how Kim managed to look so fresh and trim. 'In that case we can give up the dice since they're no longer necessary.'

'But you miss the point,' insisted Kim. 'If our relationship is sound then nothing chance chooses for us can weaken it. We can test ourselves!'

As they left the room and began clumping down the stairs of the old inn, Larry had not the slightest interest in testing himself or Kim or anyone. All he wanted was breakfast and a chance to go back to bed.

'Sweetheart,' he said, 'I have no – '

'Larry, Larry,' she interrupted, taking his arm as they reached the lobby. 'Remember the challenge! To be the best! Let yourself go!'

Larry let himself be led out the door into the warm sunshine, which immediately had him squinting and grimacing and wondering if he had also drunk too much.

'OK', she said as she released his arm. As they headed towards the café kitchen where they were already a half-hour late, she took out a die. 'If it's odd I'll spend every second of the morning with you; even, I won't.' Before Larry could muster more of a protest than a groan Kim shook a die and revealed the result in her palm: a 'six', even; she wouldn't.

In the hundred paces it took to reach the café she consulted her die two more times, and matters only got worse. First it picked a one-in-six shot and said in the morning she should do something outrageous. Then it picked another one-in-six shot from among several vaguely outrageous things and said she should try to proposition Michael Way.

205

That little gem came just outside the café. They both stood looking down at the stupid die in the palm of her hand absorbing what it implied, Larry so dull-witted from the night's exertions that it took him several seconds longer than Kim.

'Satisfied?' he said dully. 'The die is destructive. It can't be trusted any more than human beings.'

Kim stood in the sunlight looking down at her palm with a puzzled expression. Then she shrugged.

'It's stupid,' she said, 'but it must mean something. I suppose it's a test,' she added, shrugging again, and smiling at him.

'I want to eat,' announced Larry, assuming they were through with the dice business for a while and that Kim was aware, or soon would be, of her folly.

Although the café manager that morning insisted Larry do some dishes before having a cup of coffee or breakfast, Larry managed to sip some dregs from someone else's cup and filch three slabs of bacon and generally sample the café wares before officially being seated and granted his own plate and cup.

Kim did her assigned chores and ate her breakfast separately, but they left the café together and headed for the orientation centre. Larry didn't know whom he would question about what he and Kim had seen on the mountain, but it would be someone, and soon. Although slightly revived by coffee and food, he still felt dull. He took Kim's hand as they walked and, just outside orientation, whispered into her ear, 'You were magnificent.'

'You too,' whispered Kim and stretched up to rub her nose against his.

Inside her training room Larry was glad to collapse into the nearest chair, but Kim strode up to the front of the room to talk to Kathy. She returned a few moments later.

'He's working at home today,' she said.

Larry stared at her blankly.

'Who?' he asked.

'Michael. He's working at home.' She leaned over and kissed his forehead. 'Have faith. See you at lunch.' And with her usual energy she strode from the room.

Neither before, during or after lovemaking is the human mind a thing of great speed and precision. It tends to take a holiday during such periods, or certainly should, figuring correctly that other

206

elements of the being are on duty and the mind would just get in the way. So Larry sat a full ten seconds before his mind managed to make it clear that Kim was apparently on her way to proposition Michael Way. How could she!

His head aswirl, he remembered their night together, the fall of the die that had ignited it, and now of Kim letting another die send her off to Way. Was it all just a game to her!? Kim last night had been everything he had always dreamed of – and more, since his dream life was rather limited – yet she was going to try to see Way. She had told him with starry eyes and a juicy pussy that she loved him, yet she was going to see Way. She was the most fascinating, creative, uninhibited, warm, loving woman he'd ever known. And was going to see Way. Chaos had come.

That morning Macavoy had bad news for Agent Putt. He had been unable to relocate Luke Rhinehart. Someone else was now staying at number six Boxcars Street, and Rhinehart had failed to show up at the orientation building.

Putt took it calmly. He ordered each of the two new agents and Hayes out into the field to seek out Rhinehart in what Putt considered the four key areas: the orientation building, the parking lot (Rhinehart senior might make a run for it), the Hazard Hotel (the heartland of his demonic creation), and the guard gate (Rhinehart senior might make a run for it). Macavoy was to move around the town in general since only he might be able to recognize their prey. Each of the others was to pretend to be a seeker after the ultimate dicelife and express a longing to meet the real Luke Rhinehart. If anyone found him they were to stick to him until 14.00 hours and then either entice Rhinehart on some pretext to come to Putt's temporary headquarters in the Hazard Hotel lobby, or, if enticement didn't work, to bring him there by force. At 14.00 hours all agents were to report back to the lobby.

Agent Hayes was to go to local police headquarters and request that they send two men to the lobby at 14.00 hours to help control any disturbance from his followers when they made the arrest.

At 11.18 the agents dispersed on their assignments. Putt remained behind, seating himself in a comfortable lobby chair and puffing on his morning cigar. He didn't even let himself get upset at the sight of an elderly man dressed as Superman.

37

A few minutes after Kim had left I wandered out of the classroom into the bright sunshine of Lukedom, Kathy making no effort to stop me. I was headed down the street towards where I knew Way lived when Rick, dressed all in black leather, including a black leather riding cap and dark sunglasses, came up to me.

'I didn't know your father was in town,' he said. 'I'd really like to meet him.'

'What do you mean?' I asked, stopping.

'Some guy in a business suit said he'd heard the great man himself is here today,' said Rick. 'He wanted to meet him. Asked me where he was.'

'It's all just more bullshit,' I said, starting to walk further along the sidewalk towards Way's.

'Yeah, maybe, so my dice told me to tell him I'd last seen Luke in the Do Dice Inn hanging out with you. But then another well-dressed guy over at the pool hall asked me the same thing, said he *knows* Luke is here. Both the guys looked to me like narcs. Is your big dicedaddy really here?'

Looking at him, I wondered if Rick were playing another random role. There was no sense in asking him, of course, since whatever Rick said would be unreliable. The FBI stepping up their looking for my father?

'Yeah,' I said to Rick. 'My dad's here. But he's trying to lie low.'

'Hey, man, sure! That's great! Where's he at?'

'Can't tell you, pal,' I said, punching him playfully on the chest. 'It's a kind of test. My father wants to see who recognizes him first.'

'Excellent!'

As Rick turned and rushed off in the opposite direction, I continued on until I'd come to the small recently-built house of Michael Way. It was at the end of a street of the usual old renovated miners' houses – two-storey clapboard affairs with all the charm of shoeboxes. Way's house was a modern one-storey ranch house with a lot of glass.

There was no sign of life. No one there? I suddenly realized I didn't really want to find out. After a few seconds I turned around to walk back towards the centre of town. It was time to talk to Jake about the airfield and doors in the mountain.

When I located him in a large meeting room of the church, Master Ecstein was busy teaching three youngsters dice proverbs. The kids looked barely eligible for kindergarten.

'You've been playing games with me,' I said, ignoring the fact that I was interrupting.

'You bet!' said Jake. 'What does Luke have to say about playing games, boys?' he asked his three charges, who looked at him with adoring eagerness.

'We're all playing games,' answered the oldest boy brightly. 'But the wise man . . . learns to make his own rules.'

'You know where my father is,' I insisted.

'I do?'

'He's here. In Lukedom. Now.'

'He is?'

I couldn't be sure from Jake's responses whether he was lying or not.

'Say,' said Jake, shooing the boys off to another corner of the room. 'That lovely woman you brought with you phoned once last night and three times today.'

'Honoria?' I asked, momentarily knocked off track.

'That's her name,' said Jake. 'Great gal. Little highstrung maybe.'

'Did she say what she wanted?'

'Said to tell you – and this is the exact quote: "All forgiven. I want to have our baby."' Jake beamed at me. 'Congratulations.'

Jesus. What next? Jake's round grinning face stared up at me like some troll.

'The FBI is here in Lukedom,' I said to wipe the smile off the troll's face. 'They're about to arrest my father.'

'Hey, how about that!?' said Jake. 'Exciting times.'

'You don't believe me?'

''Course I do,' said Jake, taking me by the elbow and steering me out of the meeting room and into the hallway, glancing back at the boys as he did so.

'Aren't you going to try to protect him?'

'I'll certainly think about it.'

'And you might mention to him that I'm trying to see him.'

'If I see him,' said Jake, as we strolled down the hall.

'And do you think you'll see him?' I asked sarcastically.

'I doubt it,' said Jake.

'Damn it! I've been here almost a week!' I said, pulling myself out of Jake's grasp and halting. 'I've worked with diceguides and played some of your damn games. Now the FBI is here and you still haven't told me anything!'

'Four of them, right? And one has been here as long as you have.'

'You knew?'

'Oh, well,' said Jake, looking modest, and moving again down the hall. 'Not everything that happens here escapes our attention.'

'Does all this have something to do with the secret airfield and secret underground building up on the mountain?'

Jake came to a halt again, his cheerful, unperturbed manner at last broken. He had arrived at his office, which was open.

'Airfield?' he said with a frown. 'Underground building?'

'That's right,' I said, triumphant. 'A secret door in the wall of that old mine entrance on this side of the mountain, and undoubtedly another secret door on the other side where the airstrip is. And my father is there!'

'Wow. That's terrific! When did you find this out?'

'Yesterday afternoon,' I said.

'Actually,' said Jake, now moving briskly into his office, 'it was the early evening, wasn't it?'

Losing my smile I followed him slowly into the office.

'You acknowledge, then, that there's a secret building up there?' I pressed.

Jake sat down at his desk and pulled out a large wooden drawer on the right-hand side. He then swung around in his swivel chair and looked up at me with more seriousness than I'd ever seen in him.

'Sit down, Son,' said Jake. 'It's time we had a talk.'

'You're damn right.' I pulled a chair briskly over and sat opposite Jake.

Jake nodded, then turned back and pressed a button under the overhang of the desktop. He then reached into the large open drawer and seemed to slide something forward from the rear. He groped around for a while and then pulled out a small mahogany box. Swinging back to face me, he held the wooden box on his lap.

'You've done a fine job,' said Jake.

'Where's my father?'

'You're absolutely right about there being a building in that mountain,' said Jake, 'though we'd appreciate it if you'd keep it to yourself.'

'That depends. Are you going to tell me where my father is?'

Jake looked at me for a long moment and then sighed. He looked down at the mahogany box, jiggled it slightly there in his lap and sighed again.

'Yes,' he said. 'I am.'

'Well?'

Jake cleared his throat, looked again down at the box and then back at me.

'He's here,' said Jake.

'I know that. But where?'

'I mean here,' said Jake and he nodded at the box in his lap.

I looked at the box, then back at Jake.

'What are you talking about?'

Jake cleared his throat again, then slowly undid the tiny gold latch on the lid and opened the box. He then pulled his chair towards me and placed the open box in my lap.

Inside were two small worn green plastic dice and a larger bronze die of about two inches in each dimension. There was also an envelope.

'What's this, some sort of corny symbolism?' I said. 'My father exists in dice?'

'Actually,' said Jake. 'Your father is sealed up in that bronze die. His ashes, that is. Your father is dead.'

On the surface I felt only the tiniest of tremors reverberating at some level so deep I was only vaguely aware of it.

'Really,' I said coldly. 'How convenient.'

'Yes. It is convenient in some ways.'

'Why hasn't the waiting world been told?' I asked sarcastically.

'Oh, rumours of Luke's death abound. He's died at least a dozen times since he disappeared. Apparently one of the deaths must have taken.'

'You don't seem very disturbed by it.'

'No, no, not at all. Anyone who uses the dice is, as you know, quite a pain in the ass.'

'So why didn't you tell me this when I first arrived?'

'Ah, well,' said Jake, leaning back in his swivel chair and grinning. 'Luke always liked complications. He didn't want to keep things simple. This box and its contents are for you.'

Still not knowing what to believe, I looked down at the box: two plastic dice, the bronze die supposedly with Luke's ashes, and the envelope. I looked back at Jake.

'My father left these for me?'

'That's right.'

'The bastard!'

'He certainly didn't treat you right,' said Jake amiably, 'that's for sure. But still, you ought to open the envelope.'

I took the envelope out of the box. It was unsealed. I slid my finger into it and pulled out the contents: a single handwritten page with Luke's signature at the end. I looked up at Jake.

'Read it,' said Jake.

'You know its contents?'

'He consulted me about it,' said Jake. 'Yes, I've read it.'

I looked down and read the note:

Dear Larry,

I don't expect you to forgive me for leaving you and Lil and Evie so totally. Nevertheless, I've never stopped thinking of you and over the years have followed your life closely.

Now that I'm going, I want to leave you a final message, one I hope Jake will get to you when you're ready to receive it. Since messages should never be sent except when the receiver is ready, I may be gone a day, year, or decade when Jake finally decides the time is ripe.

The message is simple: carry on my work.

When Jakes gives you this, you probably won't be willing to do that. I understand. By abandoning you I closed you up to the possibilities of living that I offer, and it will take either age or misery to reopen you. But at least you're ready for the seed.

Someday carry on my work – for your own sake if not the world's. Jake – or his successor – will tell you more when you're ready.

Luke

I think I remained with my head down and eyes on the page long after I'd finished reading. A part of me felt that this was all a hoax, that this was just another test that my father and Jake had prepared for me as part of some initiation into God knew what. But I was also feeling a weight in the tummy that I supposed might have something to do with grief. I became aware I was violently jiggling my right foot. I finally looked up at Jake.

'Such a heartfelt apology,' I said. 'Such an outpouring of parental love.'

Jake shrugged.

'You have to read betweeen the lines,' he said.

'That's for sure. There's certainly nothing *in* the lines.'

'Your father never was big on saying the obvious,' said Jake.

'Is that supposed to mean it's obvious that he loved me?' I said bitterly.

'Maybe,' said Jake. 'Not many daddies think enough of their kids to want to leave their kingdom to them.'

'What's he mean he's been following my life?' I asked, stuffing the letter back into the envelope.

'Can't say,' said Jake. 'I guess it means what it says.'

'And if he knew I'd reject his offer even after you think I'm ready, then why make the offer?'

'Well, if I'd sent this to you three months ago, you'd have sneered and been happy your daddy was safely out of the way of your social life,' said Jake. 'Now, because of the things you've done and had happen to you lately, you may sneer, but your curiosity has been whetted. You now know your daddy hasn't just been playing games for twenty years – or rather the games he's been playing may be a little bigger than you thought.'

Still holding the box, its lid now closed, I stood up.

'No,' I said. 'I'm sorry . . . if my father is dead . . . but all the rest is . . . meaningless.'

'Yeah, I suppose so.'

'They've caught Luke!' said Rick, bursting into the room, out of breath. 'They've got him!'

I looked from Rick back down to Jake, who looked both surprised and worried.

'When? Where?' barked Jake.

'Just now,' said Rick, still gasping for breath. 'Two of those narcs were taking him to the Hazard Inn.'

I looked once more at a frowning Jake and then, tucking the wooden box under my arm, stepped around Rick and began running down the hall.

38

Nathanial Putt had grown tired of the crowd of eager believers who came to question him about whether he'd found Luke Rhinehart yet. It didn't bode well for his enterprise that by one o'clock the whole town knew they were looking for Luke, although it was encouraging that many who came into the lobby hoping to find Luke said that they themselves had seen or even talked to him within the last week. But Putt wondered why, if they had recently seen him they were so anxious to see him again.

By a quarter to two more than thirty people had gathered in the lobby, all chattering away. Since Putt had never been in this hotel in the early afternoon he had no idea whether this crowd was normal or abnormal. Come to think of it, everything at Lukedom was abnormal. Which meant the crowd was normal.

Putt felt dizzy for a moment from the way his mind was working and glanced nervously at his watch. The big clock that hung on one wall was of no use since – it had taken Putt about an hour to realize it – the clock ran backwards. It thus registered the correct time only twice a day – by accident. Like the newspapers Putt had seen. All the newspapers and magazines strewn around the tables and chairs of the lobby, and for sale in the local newsstand, were from one week to one decade old. Apparently the date of the day's daily newspaper was chosen at random by Lukedom's master computer. Putt himself had browsed for more than fifteen minutes in a copy of *Time* magazine before he realized that the fucking issue was two years old! Belfast, the Palestinians, congressional corruption, huge budget deficits – it seemed like today's news but was apparently two years old! Only when he read a paragraph that referred to San Francisco winning the Superbowl did he realize something was fishy.

There was a disturbance at the front entrance and suddenly a big man half staggered into the lobby, coming to a halt not far from Putt.

'I told you to keep your hands off me!' the man shouted back at a cluster of people entering behind him.

Putt then saw Agent Rogers and a Lukedom policeman among them, Rogers looking red-faced, dishevelled and sweating.

'Got him, Nat,' Rogers said harshly.

Putt stared at the figure before him for a long moment. He was a big man, a little over six feet tall, but slender and slump-shouldered. He had thinning grey hair and a hangdog expression. The poor guy had aged and shrunk so much in twenty years Putt could hardly recognize him. Had Rhinehart purposely transformed himself to avoid recognition?

'What's your name?' Putt asked him sharply.

'Who are you?' he demanded of Putt.

'I'm Agent Putt of the Federal Bureau of Investigation. Who are you?'

'Wouldn't you like to know,' he said.

'Several other people already identified him,' said Rogers. 'He even admitted it to me once – but before I told him who I was and read him his rights.'

Putt nodded.

'Sit down, Rhinehart,' Putt said. 'Has Agent Rogers read you your rights?'

'Yes,' said the man, 'but I'm not sure I remember them all.'

'So now you deny being Luke Rhinehart?' Putt asked him.

'Oh, no, I'm your man all right,' he said. 'But only sometimes.'

Sometimes. Naturally. Oh, Jesus, here we go.

Then there was another commotion and Hayes and Agent Massiori arrived. They had a prisoner too. When Putt saw this man he stood up.

The man they'd brought was older, naturally, and he'd lost a little weight, and his face was more lined and his hair thinner, but as he squinted through thick glasses at Putt, Putt felt a chill of recognition. This guy could be the real Rhinehart! Must be the real Rhinehart! He even had the same mad gleam in his eye. After twenty years! Justice triumphs!

Putt tried to remain calm.

'And I suppose you think you're Rhinehart too?' he asked the newer prisoner.

The man simply looked at Putt with a sly smile.

'He tried to escape,' said Agent Hayes.

'I'll bet he did,' said Putt, examining the man carefully, trying to feel again that chill of recognition which he had briefly felt on first seeing him. The face was definitely a little different, damn it.

'Had a little plastic surgery, I see,' Putt suggested.

The man smiled again and stroked his nose.

'You like it?' he said.

Putt frowned.

The voice seemed different too – although it was so long ago. . . . And Rhinehart was an actor, he could change his voice with no trouble at all. Putt turned to the tall mournful-looking local police chief who was standing attentively nearby.

'Well, Chief,' Putt asked. 'Do you recognize this man as the real Luke Rhinehart?'

The chief moved two steps forward to take a closer look at the man. He studied the other man carefully.

'Can't be sure, Mr Putt,' said the chief. 'I wouldn't want to call it one way or the other.'

Putt sighed.

Macavoy. Macavoy could identify him; he'd seen Rhinehart arguing with his son yesterday. Where the hell was Macavoy?

As if on cue, Macavoy burst through the surrounding spectators and gazed dazedly at the strange cluster of agents and suspects that stood in a semi-circle in front of Putt. Looking confused, he finally turned to stare at Putt.

'Well?' said Putt, narrowing his eyes at the stupid expression on Macavoy's face. 'Which one is the real Rhinehart?'

'The, uh, real Rhinehart?' Macavoy echoed dumbly.

'Yes. The man you saw yesterday arguing with his son.'

Macavoy looked dismally from one suspect to the next. A facial tic spurted across his cheek.

'Uh, that one, sir,' said Macavoy.

At first Putt thought he was pointing to the second man, the one that Putt had briefly felt must be the real Rhinehart. But something about the gloomy and reluctant way Macavoy pointed made Putt realize something was amiss.

'Which one?' he asked again.

Macavoy cleared his throat.

'That one,' he said. 'The police chief.'

Putt turned from Macavoy to look at the police chief, who turned and smiled at Putt. Putt tried to retain his dignity. The police chief looked as much like old Luke Rhinehart as Putt himself did.

'You're Luke Rhinehart too?' asked Putt dully.

'That was yesterday,' Abe Lister said with a frown. 'Today I'm the police chief.'

Putt nodded.

'And today I'm an FBI agent,' he said gloomily.

39

I arrived in the lobby of the Hazard Inn in time to see the comic fiasco of the three Luke Rhineharts and realize that the FBI had fallen victim to having too many informers and not enough information. I left.

As I emerged into the hot sunshine again, a twinge of fear made me realize that it might be better if I were not in Lukedom during a major FBI bust – the whole world of Lukedom was not something a Vice President and Chief Trader at BB&P should be associated with.

As I hurried back to collect my belongings at the inn, I suddenly saw Kim on the other side of the street walking in the same direction – with Way. I felt a burst of anger, then a dull depression: my father was dead and now so was Kim. I kept on walking, looking straight ahead. Inside the Do Die Inn I ran up the stairs to my room and began throwing my stuff into a suitcase, beginning with the mahogany box. I was just finishing up when Kim entered.

'What's happening?' she asked. She looked flushed and was breathing hard, as if she too had run up the stairs.

'I'm leaving,' I said. 'I found out what I came for, and I'm leaving.'

'You found your father!?'

'He's dead.' I snapped the suitcase shut and yanked it off the bed.

'Oh, no,' said Kim, looking shocked. 'I'm sorry.'

'It's the best thing that could have happened,' I said angrily. 'Hope you enjoy your stay.' I took a swift look around the room and headed for the door.

'Hey, wait for me!' said Kim, hurrying towards the closet, but I swung open the door and headed down the stairs.

In the heat of the Indian summer day I became aware that with my car gone and taxis unavailable fleeing Lukedom might not be easy. On the other hand, if I wanted to avoid being involved with the FBI and any scandal their arrests made, I'd better get out of the centre of the town.

As I tried to decide whether to hike out of town, Kim, lugging two light bags, came up beside me.

'Do you have a car?' she asked.

I ignored her, squinting off in the direction of the gate, vaguely hoping it would approach me rather than I have to approach it.

An Oldsmobile 88 pulled up beside us and came to a halt. It was Rick, wearing an incongruous grey fedora with his black leather outfit and dark glasses.

'You folks need a lift?' he asked, in a deeper voice than normal.

'Where's my car, you bastard!?' I said, wondering what past Karma had linked me with this archetypal source of chaos.

'Oh, sorry, Larry, it's still at the Wickstown airport.'

'It figures. And whose car have you stolen this time?' I asked, noticing that Kim had opened the rear door of the car and was wrestling her two large suitcases on to the back seat.

'Not sure,' said Rick. 'I found it hidden off the dirt road outside town when I was hitch-hiking back to Lukedom yesterday. Some cop's, I think.'

I moved around the front of the car to get in the passenger seat.

'Dare I ask where you're going?' I said, getting into the front seat.

'Well, I think I better be getting out of town to begin with,' he said as Kim and I slammed our respective doors. 'The FBI may be looking for your daddy, but there's also a federal warrant out for some hotshot who landed a plane on the Long Island Expressway. Where do you want to go?'

'To the airport,' I said. 'Or wherever you left my car.'

With a shower of stones Rick accelerated away.

Back at the Hazard Inn, Nathanial Putt was trying to maintain his dignity. He didn't relish having to explain to his superiors what he had hoped to achieve and have it compared with this comic fiasco. As he marched out with the other agents towards their cars he decided that the best solution was to change what he'd hoped to achieve. If he hadn't come to capture Rhinehart then it was no failure not to have captured Rhinehart. What if he had come to gather evidence against other miscreants for other violations of federal law, thus laying the groundwork for a future massive raid?

For example, what about all those Lukedomites impersonating law enforcement officers? What about those who had resisted arrest? What about their universal failure to collect state sales taxes? Desecration of a church? Operating premises for obscene purposes? Promoting probable orgies? Permitting teepees without proper sanitation? Why, in the Hazard Inn alone there must be enough crimes to fill a court docket for a decade. And what about lying to FBI agents and thus obstructing justice? Or operating eating establishments with improperly trained personnel? Charging $56.00 for a hamburger? My God, the whole of Lukedom was one vast network of crimes against the state! He had come to catch a bothersome flea but instead could gather the evidence for a future raid that would ensnare a whole pack of mad dogs that the flea had set to marauding! If he later was able to get indictments on a set of mad dogs, who would notice that he'd missed the flea?

'Macavoy!' Putt barked. 'Hayes! Rogers! It's time to take some depositions and photographs.'

'Sir?' said Rogers.

'Sir,' said Macavoy, 'someone's stolen my car.'

'What?'

'My car's missing, sir,' explained Macavoy. 'Uh, and I'm afraid my bureau papers were, uh, inside. Someone said it just left a few minutes ago.'

Putt glared at him.

'Good,' he finally said. 'We'll add car theft to their crimes. Take Rogers's car and go after the bastards.'

While Macavoy scurried off to begin pursuit, Putt turned to the other agents.

'We came here today for two purposes,' he said with great dignity. 'One was to see if Rhinehart was here and, if he was, to apprehend him. The second, more important purpose,' he went on after a brief pause, 'was to gather evidence against this community of criminals so that we soon will be able to put a final end to this travesty of the American way, by coming back later and arresting everyone here who has been breaking the law . . . '

The other agents were staring at him with some awe, but Putt, stern-faced, went on.

'Now before we leave, here's what I want you to do . . . '

*

After Agent Macavoy had picked up speed to ninety-five and set his red light flashing, he switched on his radio and in a sober staccato voice snapped out an All Points Bulletin.

'Attention, all Virginia State Police officers and local sheriff patrols in the vicinity of and south of Wickstown. A grey FBI Oldsmobile 88 has been stolen and is believed now to be heading north on Highway 295. This car may be being driven by a bogus person who may claim to be a bureau agent named Macavoy. He is probably unarmed but may be dangerous. Please apprehend. I repeat . . . '

Sitting again in his favourite pull-off spot on 295, Sheriff Hiram Pennaker listened to the APB and, a few minutes later, grinned as a grey Oldsmobile suddenly roared past him at ninety, its red light flashing. Sheriff Pennaker took off in pursuit.

Five minutes later he pulled the car over and cautiously approached.

Behind the wheel of the grey Oldsmobile was a dishevelled, nervous-looking guy, a little wild-eyed.

Sheriff Pennaker carefully unholstered his revolver.

'For God's sake, Officer,' the man shouted as he approached. 'I'm an FBI agent in hot pursuit!'

'I see,' said the sheriff. 'And your name?'

'I'm Agent James Macavoy, Washington Bureau,' Macavoy replied rapidly, squirming in his seat in impatience. 'I'm after – '

'And your identification?' Sheriff Pennaker asked, tightening his grip on his revolver.

The man suddenly stopped squirming and looked out at the sheriff with sudden fear.

' . . . Identification?' he asked in a suddenly weak voice.

'Yeah,' said Sheriff Pennaker, backing away from the car and holding his aim tightly on the bogus FBI agent. 'Identification.'

'Oh.'

Larry's downhill day reached its nadir after they arrived at the Wickstown airport. He and Kim had not exchanged a word on the drive, Larry dozing off and on most of the way. It was after four when they arrived and found Larry's car was actually where Rick had left it, undoubtedly benefiting from Rick's being elsewhere during its brief stay. In his fatigued state Larry now felt the Mercedes to be a burden; he wanted to board a plane and be whisked painlessly back to Manhattan. And in fact as he stood gasping for breath from a brief sprint to the airport's single ticket window he discovered he was just in time for the last flight to Washington, DC and a connecting flight to New York.

'Can I hire you to drive my car back to New York?' he asked Rick, who had ambled up to the window in less haste.

'Sure,' said Rick. 'The Olds is a little hot anyway.'

Kim had arrived also and when Larry turned to her she met his gaze without expression.

'What are your plans?' he asked her coldly.

She simply continued to gaze at him, the only change in her expressionless demeanour being the watering of her eyes. Then she turned to Rick.

'Can I hitch a ride with you?' she asked.

'Hey, sure,' said Rick, grinning. And then, to Larry he added: 'Hey, man, I'm glad you got such good taste in women. Hope you don't mind I keep stealing them.'

'My pleasure,' said Larry, turning angrily back to the ticket lady to book a flight for one to New York.

As he stood with his back to them Larry became aware of Rick and Kim moving away, their voices fading towards the main set of doors. When he could stand it no longer he turned to sneak a peek.

He saw Rick holding open the door for Kim who, as she was about to exit, looked back. Larry had a fierce impulse to shout, run to her, beat her brains in, make wonderful love to her and totally ignore her until she apologized. He nodded vaguely in her direction and turned back to the ticket lady.

From Luke's Journal

Somehow somewhere human beings seem to have built into them an unhappiness-creating mechanism. A few people seem to have escaped the mechanism, either because they never had it or they do something to eliminate it or override it or ignore it. But finding the mechanism isn't easy. Since the sickness permeates everything we do it must be inherent in everything we do — in the very way we think about ourselves and our lives, in the way we make or don't make decisions, in the way we see or experience life, in the very way we try to cure ourselves. There is something fundamentally wrong with the way we normally live our lives and we'd sort of like to find out what it is.

40

As the intelligent reader knows, New York City and Lukedom, although similar in some ways, have their differences. For one thing I was expected to show up for the same job every day at the same time and in the same place. And with the same personality. For another, in New York people tend to turn up in the same clothes and saying and doing the same things each time you meet them. In New York when you meet the vice president of a bank you can be pretty sure he's a vice president of a bank and will remain so for at least a few more months, a security lacking in Lukedom.

In New York when you pick up the daily newspaper and read that a Palestinian has killed a Jew or a Jew a Palestinian, you can be sure that the death has occurred within the last few days and not two years ago, or ten, or fifty, as in the papers at Lukedom. And when you turn on your television set you can be pretty sure that Cliff Clayburn will not suddenly be involved in a six-second orgy with several licentious mailman groupies. And if a woman declares her love for you you can be certain that it was because at least for the moment she felt that way, and not because some damn die told her to say so and will tell her to go after someone else the next day.

On one level I felt a sense of relief at escaping Lukedom and being back with the regularity and reliability – such as it is – of the madness of Manhattan. When Jeff greeted me that first Thursday morning biting his nails and bemoaning the fact that the President still hadn't declared his peace initiative and that we were thus losing money on our positions, I felt like embracing him – it was like refinding a favourite teddy bear. When Miss Claybell briskly handed me a typed summary of every transaction in our various managed accounts since I'd been gone, I wanted to hug her too: the world was rounding into order again.

I was even glad to see Mr Battle, though Mr Battle was not his usual pompous, friendly self. He was now merely pompous. After making me wait in the outer office for twenty minutes he greeted me with distinct chilliness. He was not pleased that I'd been away from the trading desk for almost a week and thus lost the firm money. He was also not pleased that I hadn't monitored more carefully my most important single position – Honoria.

I have to confess, dear reader, that Mr Battle's frowning lecture frightened me. The simple fact of being back at my old job in the hyperkinetic rat-race of Manhattan was making me desperate to get things right with my job and my fiancée. I felt as I did when I sensed a magnificent investment opportunity slipping away: I had to grab it now before I 'missed the boat'.

When I invited Honoria to my apartment that night and she came, I was tremendously relieved to see her. Dressed with her usual simple elegance, she listened quietly as I poured out an apology for having deserted her when she left Lukedom. I climaxed this by pulling out my (flawed) engagement ring and offering it to her, begging her to accept me back in her good graces.

Honoria sat silently for what felt like a long time, her left hand resting lifelessly in mine, the ring still held in my right.

Finally, she gave my hand a small squeeze and assured me how happy she was that we were back together, even how much she'd missed me. But when she finally took the ring she said perhaps we should wait a week or two before she actually began wearing it: I was expected to suffer a bit more before being pronounced fully rehabilitated.

We sat side by side and hand in hand on the couch and she listened with uncharacteristic interest to my story about Lukedom – my initial clues about Luke, the gift of my father's ashes, and the FBI's arrival. Although I left Kim out of the story, Honoria didn't at first ask about her. When I'd finished, she squeezed my hand.

'I'm so happy your father turned out dead,' she said. 'Aren't you?'

Actually it was a question I'd been studiously avoiding since receiving the urn from Jake. Since rushing away from Lukedom I'd thrown myself compulsively back into my old life.

'Well, yes,' I said after a pause. 'It ends my quest.'

'And it ends any concern we may have about his making an embarrassing re-entry into your life.'

'. . . Yes,' I said, although I knew I still had doubts about the truth of the matter.

'And psychologically,' continued Honoria, giving my hand its fifth squeeze, 'your encounter in Lukedom with your father's follies has probably liberated you from his influence just as completely as meeting him in the flesh would have.'

'. . . Yes.'

'What do you plan to do with his ashes?'

'I haven't decided,' I said, feeling uncomfortable. 'Everything's happened so fast I'm still at sea on a lot of things.'

Honoria hesitated, but then went in for another squeeze.

'I hope you're not at sea about us,' she said softly, looking demurely down at our linked hands.

'Uh . . . no.'

'And I hope Kim didn't pester you down there,' she added.

At the first mention of Kim I evaded Honoria's eyes, especially since at first I thought her reference to 'down there' referred to my loins and not to Lukedom.

'No', I replied. 'She came and went her own way.'

'She began pursuing you from the first time you met,' said Honoria. 'But I never thought she'd stoop to running after you to Lukedom.'

'I guess she thought you and I had broken up.'

'That's no excuse for diving at your cock the first time it appears unprotected.'

I blinked in astonishment, having, in the subdued mood created by her feminine softness, forgotten her penchant for the salty, if slightly stilted, comment.

'. . . Yes,' I managed.

That night our remarkably nice lovemaking made me feel flattered, depressed and guilty, but whether my guilt was towards Honoria because of Kim in Lukedom, or towards Kim for what I was doing that night, I wasn't then capable of knowing.

That next morning, Friday, Kim phoned me at my office. When Miss Claybell told me she was on the line I felt a strange surge of sadness and didn't know whether I should take the call or not, but did.

'I wanted to see what you were up to,' said Kim. 'I take it you're returning to your old life.'

227

'I . . . I wasn't aware I'd left it,' I said, at the sound of her voice again feeling that strange surge of sadness.

'You weren't? Funny. I remember someone who let his finacée go packing and seemed rather giddy when he thought he was rid of her.'

I let a silence hang on the line. I knew I hadn't really confronted my strange elation at Honoria's hanging up on me in Lukedom. On the other hand, Kim was chaos. No matter how much I might feel for her she could only mean the end of what my whole life had been aiming at.

'Lukedom has a tendency to make people act in unusual ways,' I finally said. 'I . . . wanted you, and Lukedom let us . . . enjoy each other.'

'Reallly?' said Kim. 'I thought it was a lot more than that . . . a lot more, and I'm sorry that my going to Michael's that morning has soured you on what we were creating. It was stupid of me, and I owe you an apology, but you should have known that even if the dice had chosen a one-in-thirty-six shot and I'd decided to follow it and slept with him it wouldn't have changed what we'd discovered the night before. Nothing can change that.'

That fucking sadness began flowing through me like some fast-acting depressant and I sensed my stupid eyes tearing.

'I'm engaged to Honoria,' I managed. 'I shouldn't have . . . done what I did.'

This time there was a silence from Kim.

'Well,' she finally said in a soft voice that I sensed was close to cracking, 'if you and Honoria are back together . . . then I guess I'm gone. I . . . I never intended to . . . interfere . . . even if your relationship with her seems phoney . . . and built on quicksand.'

Again there was a long silence on the line.

'I'm sorry,' I finally said.

Another silence.

'Me too,' her almost inaudible voice said, and she hung up.

The moment the line went dead I wanted her back, wanted to shout not just my apology but acknowledge that it was *her* I loved, that it was *her* —

Suddenly Jeff was in the office, looking not just frightened — he always looked frightened — but in a state of catatonia: eyes glazed and bulging, mouth agape, shoulders hunched, spittle in the corner of his mouth.

228

'What's the matter!?' I shouted.

Jeff stood there just inside the office door, the frenzied trading floor a frenetic blur behind him, and slowly shook his head, eyes still glazed, the saliva now definitely advancing to the drool stage.

'The sky has fallen . . . ' he managed.

Oh, well, was that all, I thought – just another minor freakout. I went around my desk towards Jeff to comfort him.

'The President has betrayed us,' Jeff added in a mumble, bringing me to a halt.

'What do you mean?'

'His peace initiative . . . ' mumbled Jeff, still staring nowhere at no one, 'is sending four hundred thousand troops to Arabia.'

— *41* —

Before the elections of November 1990, the President of the US had sent, after Iraq's invasion of Kuwait, approximately one hundred thousand men to the Middle East, for purely defensive purposes of course, to defend Saudi Arabia from an unprovoked attack from Iraq and thus causing long gas lines in the US. Then that Friday, three days after the election, he announced that the Pentagon was planning to send an additional three hundred thousand American troops to defend Saudi Arabia.

Quadrupling the military forces in the region was not exactly what one would normally call a peace initiative. Of course, the President, like so many leaders before him, assured one and all that this huge increase in military force was solely for defensive purposes, although why one hundred thousand men had constituted sufficient defence on 4 November and on 8 November the number became four hundred thousand wasn't explained.

In any case, Wall Street, which knows the difference between a peace initiative and the beginning of a war, acted accordingly. The stock market sagged, gold rose, and oil, good old oil, which was highly overbought, went zooming higher. The BB&P futures fund suffered a devastating loss, fully 15 per cent of the fund's asset value.

That morning Larry first had to suffer through a long session with Mr Battle, who paced and brooded and questioned and lamented and could hardly believe what had happened.

'No, no, no,' Mr Battle said for about the thirteenth time, 'this can't go on. For three years nothing like this has ever happened. I can't believe it. Are you sure you made those trades? I thought you'd developed systems that eliminated any such catastrophic losses!? Why, why, why? No, no, no . . . ' And so on.

Then he and Jeff huddled in the custodians' rest room, a place both more secure and somehow more fitting for their present status. Or at least Jeff huddled. Larry raged.

'Phone the bastard!' Larry shouted. 'Find out what the hell he thought he was talking about!'

'I can't!'

'What do you mean, you can't! He has a phone, doesn't he? He's still alive, isn't he? Or did someone else who took his tip already wipe him out?!'

'I . . . I . . . I . . . '

'Jesus, first it's no, no, no, and now I, I, I. Has everyone begun speaking in triplets? Why can't you reach him?'

Jeff just stared up at him open-mouthed and afraid.

'Well!?'

'I . . . I just can't.'

Then it hit Larry, completely and clearly.

'It wasn't a State Department friend, was it?' he asked softly.

' . . . No . . . '

'It was someone feeding you inside stuff on a regular basis.'

'Yes.'

'He can get in touch with you, but you can't get in touch with him.'

'Yes.'

'You were double-crossed.'

' . . . I'm not sure . . . '

'You're a complete asshole.'

' . . . Yes.'

— *42* —

Misery loves company, so Jeff and I, who rarely saw each other outside the office in happier days, now began to hang out together. This tendency was aided quite a bit in that no one else wanted to hang out with either of us. Although incurring notable losses is not as contagious or fatal as the black plague, on Wall Street it is treated much the same. Lesser people might enjoy being with those who are bigger losers than they, but successful people know that the aura of losing is communicable, and that if A hangs out with B and B is a loser, then, by definition, A must also be a loser. I knew that Jeff and I were in trouble when the custodians ordered us to stop using the custodians' rest room. It was hard to see how much lower we could sink.

But the Battle family began to work on it. Their doors too began to swing closed or prove unusually sticky to open. At first Honoria seemed as aghast at the huge losses in oil futures as I was. But even as she tried to comfort me, I could see she was looking at me as if I'd suddenly gone totally bald and toothless: I suddenly wasn't the man she thought she knew. And when I incurred further losses the next week in my everyday trading, I could tell people were beginning to sniff the odour of a loser, an odour, I knew, that no amount of expensive cologne, powerful deodorant or past triumphs could hide.

Suddenly Honoria had a lot of work over weekends. Salomon Brothers seemed to have an outbreak of evening meetings that prevented her coming over to my apartment, where in the past we'd enjoyed my becoming a bull and going long and using maximum leverage, and Honoria making an opening offer, splitting her stock, getting her fill, and short squeezing, all leading to powerful upward thrusts in all the important markets and a final go-for-broke consummation of the merger. Honoria began implying that it might be desirable if I spent more time diddling with my technical indicators and less diddling with hers.

All this was rather depressing. Jeff had finally broken down and admitted that for his two earlier coups he'd been relying on someone with inside information, and though this man claimed Jeff had misunderstood his instructions, he had clearly double-crossed Jeff on the 'peace initiative', probably to permit X to double his own profits. I was almost relieved that my most horrific losses had been caused not by the sporadic unreliability of my technical work but by someone actually defrauding me. I gloomily told Jeff to pretend not to suspect X and to keep the lines of communication open. I think he assumed that it was because I wanted to join the ranks of cheaters, and was a little disappointed in me. I was actually driven by a more human motive: I wanted revenge.

No matter how chaotic and abnormal my five days in Lukedom had been, such chaos there was normal. That first week back in Manhattan was worse: the beginning of chaos in what for many years had been gleaming order. Even as I felt my world collapsing around me I tried desperately to be my old self again, that is, the man I'd been most of my adult life, the exception being those few stupid days when I'd gone a little crazy in Lukedom.

I left my father's plastic dice and bronze die with ashes in the mahogany box and placed it neatly at the back of a top shelf of my study bookcase, so recessed that no one would ever notice it and ask embarrassing questions. Although Honoria was quite happy Luke Rhinehart was dead, my feelings remained confused.

First of all, I didn't entirely believe that he *was* dead. Second, when I did somewhat believe that he might be dead, my feelings varied from a vague sadness to a bitter smile. In either case I felt no sense of completion. I still resented him for abandoning me years before and now resented him additionally for daring to make a claim on me, a claim he'd in no way earned. The idea that I had to prove myself worthy of my father seemed grossly unfair. I fantasized shouting at him that it was *he*, the father, who should go through a period of trial before deserving reconciliation with me rather than vice versa. I should set up a series of tests that would force him to prove that he was stable, reliable, consistent, unchanging, predictable – as regular as a healthy set of bowels. That would teach the bastard.

All through November things slid further and further downhill. On those rare occasions that Honoria agreed to see me she insisted on going over my technical work to see what I might be doing wrong. When I tried to talk about the coming child she grew silent, implying that having a baby was not something she intended to get excited about until it came. When I approached her with straight male lust my kisses were returned with such tightness and lack of juice it was like kissing two thin strips of boiled leather.

I began to acknowledge how much I missed Kim, but a few phone calls failed to locate her.

Thank God she was a slut. Otherwise I'd feel I had really lost someone important. Of course I continued to long for my slut and soon was madder at her for not letting me locate her than for her sluttishness. I alternated between longing achingly for Kim and longing greedily for a full return to Honoria's good graces; between lusting for a great trading coup and wanting to dynamite Wall Street and take to sea in my sailboat. In brief, I behaved like a frustrated child. In the end, I began, quite decisively, to mope.

I began standing late at night staring into my medicine cabinet and wondering exactly how many of my various sedatives I'd have to take to earn the big sleep. Once, during a cab strike when I'd been forced to use the subway, I found myself late in the evening on the edge of the platform staring down at the tracks, thinking how easy it would be to time my leap a few seconds before the speeding express train raced in. And there was almost no one around to notice or care, the platform being almost empty. Tears of self-pity welling in my eyes, I edged closer yet.

In the distance came the muffled roar of the approaching train. Hearing it, I became convinced that not only could I jump but that I would. That'll show 'em!! I felt the strange thrill-chill of exhilaration-terror of the martyrish adolescent as I moved to the very edge of the platform and watched the train come barrelling out of the black maw to my left and tear towards me.

Suddenly there was an arm around my neck and something poking in my back and I was pulled roughly away from the track. So fast did this happen that it was only half a minute later that I realized that two young thugs had pulled out my wallet, ripped off my watch and were sprinting away down the platform and up some stairs. The express train had rushed on past without me. In Manhattan it's never possible to do anything in peace.

As the gloomy days continued I didn't know which was worse: the times my colleagues totally avoided me or the times I actually spent with them. Once, too depressed to face sharing another downer lunch with Jeff, I shuffled down Broad Street and unthinkingly entered the first restaurant I came to, only to be greeted by a surprised Mr Battle and Brad Burner, who were apparently having lunch with some banker friend of theirs. They looked deeply embarrassed, but when I admitted that I was alone Mr Battle insisted I join them.

After we'd been served our cocktails and hors d'oeuvres and ordered our dinners, the conversation was barrelling forward about, naturally, money. Although we were seated at a small round table, I felt separated from the rest. In the middle of the ongoing conversation I finally found myself participating. Sort of.

'I'm burned out,' I announced glumly to no one in particular.

'That's very good,' Mr Battle said to Brad, continuing their discussion. 'Who could ask for anything more.'

'Exactly,' said Brad. 'I think we may as much as double our position. It's a kind of hidden monopoly without government regulation.'

'All our work seems so ineffectual,' I continued, staring out into nowhere.

'That's the key,' said Mr Battle. 'And the fact that no one realizes it.'

'I'm sick of pretending we know what we're doing, when half the time we're only the blind leading the blind.'

'It's the whole secret of successful investing,' announced Brad to Mr Battle with a note of satisfaction.

'Let's see,' said a befuddled waiter, arriving with our lunches. 'You, sir, are the veal . . . and you the stuffed shrimp?'

'No, no, no,' said Mr Battle. 'I'm the stuffed shrimp.'

'And I'm the crabmeat salad,' announced the banker.

'I'm a helpless pawn in a game being played by dunces,' I announced dully to the waiter.

'Prawn, sir? I . . . I'll have to recheck my order.'

'Larry gets the chicken,' said Mr Battle irritably.

'How you doin' today, Lair?' said Brad, as if noticing me for the first time but digging vigorously into his veal.

'I'm at zero.'

'Great,' said Brad, watching the waiter pour some fresh wine in his glass. 'Our model portfolio is up another 3 per cent this week.'

'I'm frozen in a sea of muck,' I continued in the same dull monotone.

'Eat your chicken,' said Mr Battle irritably.

'I don't want chicken,' I said, now noticing the plump breast stewing in its sauces on my plate.

'Really?' said the banker. 'What do you want?'

'A new life,' I said.

'Not on the menu,' snapped Mr Battle.

43

As if the Gods hadn't been able to figure enough ways to make me a loser, they came up with a new one. On the workday before the Thanksgiving holiday in late November Honoria, perhaps making up for not inviting me to her father's Hudson River estate for the long weekend, agreed to have lunch with me in a little restaurant in the Village. I had vague hopes of perhaps receiving a little feminine sympathy, when Honoria, as the dessert was served, made a quiet little announcement.

'Oh, by the way,' she said with the matter-of-factness of a woman reporting on the condition of her laundry, 'I'm not pregnant.'

I'd been trying to be lively and positive so as to show I wasn't the loser everyone thought I was, and was caught with a bright fake smile and, slow on the uptake, held it as I stared at her.

'You're not . . . pregnant . . . ?' I finally managed, still with my frozen grin.

'No,' Honoria said smiling politely as the waiter brought her mousse and two coffees. 'Apparently I was mistaken earlier.'

'You were mistaken . . . '

'Yes. In fact, I'm having my period right now.'

'You're having your period.'

'Yes . . . Ummm, this mousse is delicious.'

'After three months you're having another period.'

'Yes. Quite amazing. Probably stress-related.'

'You have a three-month-long stress-related false pregnancy but now you're having a period . . . '

'Yes . . . '

'What did your gynaecologist say?'

'I never saw him . . . You want a taste of this mousse?'

'You, who normally have a regular physical check-up every other week, didn't bother to see your gynaecologist even though you thought you were pregnant.'

'Things have been quite busy lately.'

During this exchange my smile had quite definitely been erased. My coffee cup had been lowered. My hands were in my lap mashing my napkin into a tiny ball and, unconsciously, I was leaning increasingly forward towards Honoria, who, equally unconsciously, was easing her chair backwards and now protecting her face by holding her coffee cup to her lips.

'You had an abortion,' I finally whispered.

'I was never pregnant,' she countered coldly.

We stared at each other. There would be no feminine comfort for me on this day, and no pretending I wasn't a loser.

I wandered back to my office that afternoon feeling lower than I could ever remember. I felt as if I, with my failures, rather than Honoria, had killed our child. In my office I could barely function. Even if my eyes were on the monitor all I saw were a bunch of noodles swimming rapidly across the ocean of blue screen. I wondered if there was ever a finish line.

My gloom was interrupted late in the day by a nervous Miss Claybell announcing that some woman, who refused to give her name, actually wanted to open an account with me – my first new client for weeks.

'She says she wants to invest some money with Blair, Battle and Pike,' said Miss Claybell with her usual nervous efficiency. 'And she won't do it unless she can do it with you.'

'Well, she obviously must be in love with my recent track record,' I said sarcastically. 'Show her in.'

I was halfway out of my chair to meet my new client when Miss Claybell ushered in a woman who looked utterly unlike any woman I'd ever seen and yet was vaguely familiar. She had on an extravagant blonde wig and was dressed as if for some artsy cocktail party, her black leather skirt so short that fully half her body seemed to fall below the hemline. But her face, despite all the garish make-up, was that of a woman at least in her forties.

'You like it?' the woman asked, placing a hand on one hip and posing in a cliché position of sexual enticement. 'It was a six-to-one shot that I usually only wear when I want to frighten or entice sixty-year-old bankers.'

'Mrs Ecstein!' I said, suddenly recognizing her despite the fact that her hair colour and style, clothing and personal manner were all fifteen years younger than when I'd last met her. I moved around the chair to greet her. 'I didn't recognize you at first.'

'I left Grandma Ecstein at home today,' she said with a smile. 'Say, you've got quite a place here,' she went on, looking around at my impressive high-tech office. 'You must be making a lot of money.'

'Not lately,' I said. 'Or rather, all for my clients, all for my clients.'

'I'll bet.' Without being asked, Arlene pulled up a chair and threw herself back into it with an exaggerated sigh of comfort. When she crossed her legs, her black-stockinged knees stared up at me like a pair of black Siamese twins.

'Jake tells me you took a little holiday down in the mountains of Virginia,' she went on, as I went back to my seat behind the desk. 'Have a good time?'

'That wasn't exactly why I went.'

'I know, but did you enjoy yourself?' she persisted.

'It was a business trip,' I countered coldly. 'I accomplished my business and now I'm back.'

'Find Luke?'

'My father is apparently dead.'

'Says who?'

'Says your husband.'

'Oh, come on, you must have been in Lukedom long enough to know you can't trust anything anyone says there, least of all Jake.'

Arlene was looking at me with friendly interest, like a bawdy aunt discussing my dating life.

'He seemed intensely serious when he conveyed the information,' I said. 'Unless I get evidence to the contrary I must assume my father is dead.'

'What did Jake say?'

Reluctantly I told her what Jake had said and given to me, including the contents of Luke's letter. Arlene listened intently and then, when I was done, burst into a deep gravelly guffaw, shaking her head as if in disbelief.

'Oh, not that old "sacred die" gimmick,' she said, still shaking her head. 'I thought they'd given up on that ten years ago.'

'What are you talking about?'

'People have been given the sacred die of a dearly departed Luke for decades,' she explained smiling. 'Sometimes it's supposed to contain the holy remains of the great man himself and at others it's supposed to be his personal die, used only for his most momentous dice decisions. There must be dozens of men and women rolling through life convinced they're the designated heir of Lord Luke. Or rather were. I'm sure most of them long ago gave up on the effort. You have to be awfully big to fill Luke's shoes.'

'I see.'

'Of course, far as I know none of them were given personal letters signed by Luke himself, passing on the mantle. That must be a new wrinkle Jake added just for you.'

'And is my father still alive?' I asked.

'Far as I know, he is,' said Arlene indifferently. 'I talked to him on the phone just four months ago.'

That, I quickly calculated, wasn't long before I'd gone and met Arlene in Hempstead.

'That isn't what you told me at the time,' I said coldly.

'Of course it wasn't,' she replied happily. 'If I'd told you the truth then you'd never have found your father.'

'I haven't found him!'

'Maybe not quite,' she responded. 'But you've got a chance now. Then you were totally out of it.'

I sat behind my desk and stared at this ridiculous woman who was quite merrily admitting that she and her ex-husband were playing lying games with me and showing not remorse but pleasure.

'I understand you wish to invest some money with Blair, Battle and Pike,' I said with quiet distaste. 'How –

'With you, Larry,' Arlene insisted. 'I want to invest money with you. Or rather, not invest so much, speculate – that's the term I think – I want you to speculate with my money. Gamble. Play with it. Have fun with it.'

'I'm afraid I can't do that,' I replied. 'We at Blair, Battle and Pike have a fiduciary responsibility – '

'To bullshit your clients and pretend you're investing – I understand that,' interrupted Arlene gaily. 'But you also have a fiduciary responsibility to do with my money what I ask you to do with it, and I'm asking you to gamble with it. I expect you to try to win with your gambling, look for the best odds, but then put it on the line and let the wheel spin or the dice roll. I wouldn't be giving this money to you if I couldn't afford to lose it.'

I couldn't help smiling. How many times had I had to sit through long hypocritical interviews with clients in which they tried to reassure themselves that I, Larry, could somehow guarantee a 20 per cent return per annum with no risk, and I, without promising anything, equally tried to create the very impression they so desperately wanted to receive.

'How much money do you have to invest – gamble with, I mean?'

Arlene pulled a large purse up from behind her chair and set it on her lap. She opened it and peered in.

'Two hundred dollars,' she said with sudden seriousness.

'Two hundred dollars,' I echoed, not knowing whether to laugh or cry. That might just cover the cost of opening an account.

'To start with,' added Arlene, now pawing around inside the huge purse and then suddenly thrusting two one-hundred-dollar bills towards me and dropping them on the desk. Then she again dove into her purse.

'Then, when this cheque clears,' she went on, finally pulling out a cheque, 'you can gamble with this two hundred thousand.'

Two hundred thousand. When Arlene also reached forward and dropped the cheque on my desk I couldn't resist sliding my chair forward and reaching across and picking it up. It was a Hempstead National Bank cheque signed by Arlene Ecstein and made out to Larry Rhinehart. It was correctly dated. The cheque had Arlene's name and address engraved across the top. For two hundred thousand dollars.

'Uh, you should have made it out to Blair, Battle and Pike,' I said quietly.

'I want it to be quite clear that it's with you that I'm gambling my money,' Arlene said. 'You'll have to work it out with your company if you want to put it into one of their accounts that you manage.'

'Why?'

'Why what?' asked Arlene innocently.

'Why me? Why this much money? Why now? Why all this emphasis on gambling and not investing? Why tell me my father is still alive? Why even bother to come and see me?'

'Oh, dear, you are an old busybody, aren't you?' she said with another of her deep guffaws.

241

When I silently waited for an answer, Arlene stood up.

'Your father once said something very wise,' she announced, 'something in general he did very rarely. He said that there's only one honest answer to the question "why"?'

'And what's that?'

'Accidents will happen,' Arlene answered serenely. 'Everything beyond that is all bullshit.'

She turned to leave but swung her head back for one last comment.

'That last bit about bullshit is my contribution,' she explained. 'Luke only uses profanity when he's in a bad mood.'

And she walked to the door and was gone.

44

Alone in my apartment that evening was perhaps the low point of the life I'd been leading for twenty-eight years and been expecting to lead for another fifty if my indicators hadn't begun to fail and Jeff hadn't discovered the joys of cheating and Kim hadn't blazed into my life and the FBI hadn't begun making appearances and my father hadn't resurfaced and died and then been resurrected and my engagement didn't blink on and off like a light with a loose connection, and my baby get conceived and unconceived with such sudden unreliability. I knew I couldn't go on with this old life.

But where was the alternative? And who cared? Not Blair, Battle and Pike, that was for sure. I'd be lucky if they let me stay on as a second-string account executive.

Not Honoria. One bad day at the office and our baby disappeared so fast she must have had it pulled out even before Mr Potter had had time to phone me and complain about the fund's losses.

And not my friends. What friends? The only one voluntarily talking to me in the last month was Jeff, and he talked to me just so we could exercise our tongues.

And not Kim. Just because I got a trifle irritated when she let the dice send her to Way, she had disappeared, not even giving me a chance to apologize, not that I would, she being the slut she was.

And not family. What family? My sister was a stranger and my father, he – he – he – he, hmmmm, he . . . didn't care . . . one . . . fig . . . Or did he? Was that letter genuine? And if it was, did it mean he cared? Was he really alive, or was Arlene just playing a new variation on some game?

The ashes. Were there really ashes in the bronze die? If there were, did that prove anything? If there weren't, did that prove anything?

I slogged out of my kitchen where I'd been morosely brooding over some straight bourbon and went to my study. I pulled a chair over and climbed up to retrieve the mahogany box from the top of the bookcase. It was the first time I'd touched it since putting it there a month earlier.

I carried the box over to the desk and, leaning over, opened it. There they were: the large bronze die, the two little green plastic dice, supposedly my father's first pair, and the folded note.

How does one open a six-sided cube made of bronze? It seemed seamless. I could crush it with a sledgehammer, but that seemed a little sacrilegious if my father's ashes were inside. Not that the man didn't deserve a bashing. Could I melt bronze? My metallurgical knowledge was limited, but lacking a blowtorch, my ignorance was probably academic. How about a hacksaw? Could it cut through bronze? Again my knowledge failed me, but in this case I actually owned a hacksaw, one left behind a year earlier by an absent-minded plumber, or rather by a plumber so rich after collecting the bill he sent me that bothering to travel to my apartment to retrieve a hacksaw would have represented a major waste of time and money.

It took me five minutes to locate this valuable tool, stored neatly with a pair of rubber boots and two rusty screwdrivers. Then I immediately jammed the cube against the side of the desk and began to saw.

Bronze is cuttable. I decided to concentrate on a corner, to cut off a corner. I could then see if there was anything inside. Ten minutes later, with still no sign of my father dribbling out through the long crack the saw was making, I successfully cut off one small corner of the cube.

I turned the cube in my hand and tried to pour Daddy out on to the desk. But if Luke's remains were in there, they must be clinging to the sides like frightened fleas.

I then held the cube up to the desk lamp and peaked inside.

Aha.

There was a slip of paper in there.

Now I had to locate a pair of tweezers and try to pull the paper out through the small hole. I was so totally engaged in the physical challenge of solving my little puzzle that it wasn't until I'd located some small tweezers and managed to pull a small scrap of paper from the die that I realized that maybe I was about to learn something momentous. I read the note.

'Good boy. You're getting closer. Time to begin chancing it. As ever, Dad.'

Talkative son-of-a-bitch. Demonstrative too. 'As ever' – boy, did that take nerve! And 'Dad'! After fifteen years it's suddenly 'Dad' again!

'Time to begin chancing it'! Over my dead body!!

Then, even as my mind was running out scatalogical insults, and my hands were balling up the note and flinging it across the room, my stupid chest began heaving out huge sobs, and my eyes pouring out a tide of salt water. I collapsed back into my desk-chair.

My father was alive. Not only was he alive but in some obscure and undoubtedly sick way actually seemed interested in me. How many daddies cared enough to write? I sat in the desk-chair and let my eyes water, feeling like a little boy who at long last has been recognized and praised by his father after years of neglect. There were tears of happiness intermingled with the general deluge of less clearly motivated tears. My father might be crazy, might have been heartless, might still be showing a certain restraint in his apparent interest and affection, but the fact was that in my world of late 1990, Luke was just about the only one who seemed to give a damn.

Not that much of this emotional interpretation made it past the heaving chest and flowing tears to enter my consciousness. I was still muttering 'The dirty bastard' and 'Shit, shit, shit' and other totally uncreative obscenities even while my heart was feeling that it had had a hit of parental warmth missing for at least a decade. I never had been too good at knowing what was going on with myself.

Of course, crying, enjoyable as it is, especially for men, who don't get to do it as often as women, finally, like all good things, has to come to an end. Sniffles. Snorts. Big sighs. Drying of eyes followed by minor tearing. There's a whole rigmarole that we humans go through when we come down off the high of a good cry, and I went through it. The process finally ended with my marching off back to the kitchen to check the level of my bottle of bourbon.

So. Dice Daddy lives. He may even want to see me. He is findable, maybe. He wants me to use his green dice. Fuck it. Fuck it. He's alive. He may even want to see me. He may even have sent Arlene! He may even have been at Lukedom! The bastard! The dirty betraying bastard!! . . . Daddy . . . Daddy!!!

My thought processes over the next hour or so would win no Nobel Prize for rationality or coherence but they did the job. I felt that my seemingly eternal effort to deny my father had reached a dead end; I couldn't go on. I could shoot myself, but that would be too permanent a solution. I'd have to kill myself the other way, the way Luke had, and see what grew to replace the hollow shell that was all that was left of controlled, rational me.

At midnight I left the kitchen, walked back to my study and picked up the two green plastic dice. What did I have to lose by using the dice?

I soon found out.

From Luke's Journal

The tendency of every living creature is homeostatic — it attempts to stabilize its relation to its environment at the simplest level possible. It wants security, stability and simplicity.

The tendency of chance, on the other hand, is to create insecurity, instability and complexity. Yet, living forms evolve through chance, not homeostasis. Life evolves through mutations — scientific terminology for the play of chance. Mutations are sudden, 'unexplained' altered forms of any given species. They are accidents. All living creatures evolve through accident.

Cultural changes occur in the same way as do biological changes: sudden accidental developments which either survive and alter the culture, fail and die out, or succeed, alter the culture, but perhaps so burden it for survival that the culture dies out (extinction of the species). The invention of electricity is a mutation which succeeded and altered the cultures which adapted to it. The invention of rockets capable of going to the moon or transporting warheads to distant societies may — fifty years from now — be seen as a mutation which was tried for a while and then abandoned, proving to be ultimately useless for the culture. (It could also prove to be as profoundly significant as the invention of electricity.)

And personal evolution also occurs through chance. Human beings change significantly not so much through normal 'growth', but rather through sudden dramatic 'abnormal', 'unhealthy', 'irregular' accidents. In biology, without accident we have a universe of amoebae. In culture, without accident we have a universe of primitive societies. In man, without accident we have a universe of normal clods.

— 45 —

The next morning Larry woke up a new man. The simple act of no longer trying to be who he'd been trying so unsuccessfully to be for the last many months gave him an exhilaration he hadn't felt in years. It helped that he realized that he'd come close to killing himself. As a result, experiencing a new dawn, even through the soot of Manhattan, was bliss.

The dice opted for his taking the subway to work, and though it wasn't exactly his first choice (not going to work at all had that honour), he found himself chatting inanely with several sleepy New Yorkers pressed flesh to flesh who listened to him in dull-eyed befuddlement, figuring Larry was clearly from out of town and would probably be ripped off four times before he ever got to where he was going.

When he came to his outer office and saw Miss Claybell meticulously applying a thin line of lipstick to her equally thin lips, he felt a surge of love for her, especially when she looked up in embarrassment and sung out her traditional greeting: 'Oh, good morning, Mr Rhinehart!'

She alone in these last two months had not deserted him, greeting him always the same, whether he lost a million or broke even.

'My God,' he said to her, stopping at her desk. 'I never realized what a beautiful woman you are.'

Miss Claybell's habitual smile of greeting was frozen on her face by surprise. She blinked but could not speak.

'I don't know whether it's the suit you're wearing or the incredible glow on your face,' he went on, peering at her intently. 'But . . . beautiful, beautiful . . . '

Larry strode on past her into his inner office, leaving Miss Claybell, for the rest of the morning, in a state of inefficiency she had never known.

Inside he consulted his monitors, checked some items in *Investor's Daily*, and ran some data through one of his chart programs tracking gold. Then he stopped, frowned, and leaned back in his chair. So. So what?

For his own account, he decided, he would buy or sell twenty December S&P futures at the market, and let the die tell him whether he should buy the futures or sell them, and where he should place his stop loss order. Theoretically the technical indicators he'd just looked at were bearish on the market, and Larry hoped the die would say 'sell'. With odd meaning buy and even sell, the die fell a three: buy. He gave the die a few more options regarding stops and then picked up the phone and got Jeff on the line to give him the order.

'I don't get it,' said Jeff. 'I thought our indicators were bearish. Didn't you say the market was going to drop to twenty-five hundred?'

'Yeah ... yeah, but uh,' Larry began, fingering his dice. 'I've developed some new software,' he went on, rubbing one die against his belly. 'Complicated indicator. Tell you all about it at lunch.'

'But in the BB&P Fund you're short those same futures!'

'Details, details,' said Larry, feeling a little giddy. 'I follow our base technical indicators for the fund but feel free to experiment with other indicators in my own account. Just do it.'

'Got any other brainstorms?' asked Jeff.

'I don't know, let me see,' Larry answered. He then asked the die whether he had any other brainstorms and it answered with a five: yes. Gold. He'd go long or short gold. Same ballgame. The die said buy gold. That should please Jeff. Maybe he should do this in the BB&P Fund. What did the die think of that idea? The die said with a four that it liked it. Larry told Jeff his new indicator was suggesting they go long twenty December gold contracts with appropriate stops in the fund.

'When did we finally get a stronger buy signal?' asked Jeff, sounding a little nervous. Of course Jeff always sounded nervous.

'About ten seconds ago,' answered Larry, grinning.

'Really?' asked Jeff. 'That's great! I told you we should be buying gold.'

'Well, my new indicator just agreed with you.'

'I'm glad you finally upgraded your software,' said Jeff.

'So am I,' said Larry, and they were through.

He spent the next hour going over all the positions in the Futures Fund and letting the dice decide what to do – buy more, sell, sell more, hold – and also let the dice pick the stops. This wasn't random trading as had been the two positions he'd taken earlier with Jeff. Now Larry was letting the dice choose between options that his indicators themselves took no strong position on. Indicators never said any more than 'probably' and it was Larry who decided whether to translate each 'probably' into a definite buy or sell, and who decided the extent of the position. Now he let chance decide. On the basis of his trading over the last half-year he guessed that he himself had some inherent flaw that was leading to his consistent slow losses. The dice would eliminate that flaw. Of course, the dice might have a few dozen of their own.

When he was working on his computer he called in Miss Claybell and told her to print it out and send copies to Jeff and the other traders.

'And one other thing,' he added to her as she was leaving. 'There's a woman named Kim Castelli who used to live with the Battles. Call their house and find out how I can get in touch with her. Don't take no for an answer. Tell them her bonds have matured – that ought to do it.'

'Yes, sir,' said Miss Claybell.

'Gonna be a big day,' Larry concluded.

'Oh, yes it is!' Miss Claybell said, perhaps still in a state of euphoria from Larry's earlier references to her beauty. 'It is!'

It was a big day. Not more than ten minutes after Miss Claybell had sent around his sheet of new orders in all the markets his office began to receive unaccustomed traffic and his phone began to ring, Jeff first, of course, Jeff being able to smell disaster faster than any known creature, even where there was none.

'Is this your new software?' he asked without preliminaries after marching into Larry's office, waving the list of new orders.

'It is,' said Larry. 'What do you think?'

Jeff stopped, lowered the list and began looking at it again.

'Interesting,' he finally said. 'I don't really see any pattern in this, but I sure as hell saw it wasn't our old pattern.'

'Exactly,' said Larry.

Two other traders phoned to ask if there were any misprints in the orders, and, being reassured, went about their obedient way. 'Twas not theirs to reason why.

Neither Brad nor Mr Battle phoned or visited. Larry's orders didn't interest them, only the results at the end of the day. *Then* they would look at the orders.

But Mr Akito phoned from his East Village bank, and only when Larry recognized his voice did he remember that Miss Claybell had been ordered by Mr Battle to fax him each morning's orders and each day's results. Akito, true to the Japanese stereotype, was on the job.

'You have changed your trading tactics,' Akito said with no more introduction than Jeff had given.

'That's right,' said Larry. 'We've finally become operational on a system that I've been working on for four years.'

'So . . . you are changing your . . . knack.'

'Exactly. And the drawdowns of the past few months will soon be a thing of the past.'

'That would be nice,' said Akito. 'Mr Namamuri has not been impressed with what has happened to our fifteen million dollars in your fund.'

'Absolutely embarrassing,' agreed Larry. 'But you have to look at the long-term picture. Every year I've ended up with a profit.'

'Except this year.'

'This year is not yet over.'

'You plan to increase asset value almost 16 per cent in a month?'

'Hey,' said Larry. 'I lost that much in a single day.'

'Ah, yes.'

'How's the old tennis?'

'Six-two, six-three, six-one yesterday,' answered Akito. 'I am now ranked number one hundred and fifty-six in my country.'

'That's great! Didn't know Japan had that many players. I think I'm ranked somewhere near the two hundred million level here.'

'You are strange today,' said Akito.

'The new software,' said Larry. 'I'm using it in my personal life, too.'

'Ahhh.'

The BB&P Futures Fund made money that day. Larry's personal account made even more, since the stock market, for reasons of its own, went up, as the dice had said, and not down, as Larry's scientific indicators had said. Of course there had been many profitable trading days over Larry's extended losing period, but not one quite as decisively on the upside as this – 2½ per cent overall. At the end of the day even Mr Battle phoned.

Of course his primary purpose in calling, he explained, was to question Larry as to why he was long stock market futures in his individual discretionary accounts and short such futures in the BB&P Fund.

'Collecting commissions,' Larry answered promptly.

Mr Battle thought about that a long time and finally managed: 'But not churning the accounts, I trust,' he said firmly.

'Absolutely not,' said Larry, although it certainly seemed to him that being long and short the same futures in different accounts and thus making money only on commissions couldn't be anything else.

— 46 —

Miss Claybell, with her usual persistent efficiency, managed to pry out of Hawkins a phone number of Kim's employer and then even learned from calling there that Kim would probably be at the Big Apple midtown Manhattan salon that afternoon until eight in the evening.

When the day's trading was over I considered my options. I thought I should probably phone Kim first and find out how the ground lay, but the die, given fifty-fifty odds, said 'no', don't phone. Should I go there right away, or after dinner, or wait for the weekend? The die, more rash than I, chose from those three that I go right away.

I took a cab up to the Big Apple Health Spa on Seventh Avenue. I'd only vaguely heard of this particular chain of health clubs but was fairly certain it was not on Mr Battle's approved list. The very name 'Big Apple' had the sort of bluff common man lingo that could only mean down-scale clientele – which probably meant they had muscles.

Although the neighbourhood outside of the building on Seventh near 47th Street was not reassuring, inside there was a pleasant lobby. An attractive receptionist confirmed that Kim was on the premises, probably in the main exercise room. The place had a pool and handball courts and even a computer-simulated golf game. Not bad.

The exercise room was full. Using the machines were a variety of men and women of a surprising range of ages, though most in their thirties, and a few so scantily clad as to take one's mind off building more than one muscle. As I moved through the maze of machines I felt self-conscious in suit and tie, and rather resented everyone working so hard on their bodies when I didn't.

Then I finally spotted Kim: she was dressed in a skin-tight black thongsuit over flesh-coloured leotards that came high up on each hip and revealed enough of the golden globes so that at least three men, theoretically grunting away on their Nautilus machines, were watching her as if her buttocks contained a winning lottery number. I felt a one-two punch to my heart and loins that stopped me dead in my tracks.

She was talking to a man wearing only shorts and a tanktop who looked as if he not only competed in the Mr Universe Contest but probably won. The two of them together looked like a God and Goddess casually discussing which humans they were going to fuck over that day. As the hunk chatted with Kim he was absent-mindedly juggling in one hand a twenty-five-pound weight as if it was a child's stuffed doll.

After I managed to get fresh control over my legs and came up to her, Kim turned with a polite smile that froze on her face in surprise – she clearly hadn't been expecting me. Then, the smile disappearing, she flushed and turned back to Mr Universe.

'Well, thanks for the advice, Ed,' Kim said to him. 'I know we have to do something.' Then she turned back to me.

'How can I help you, sir?' she asked with an exaggeratedly false smile.

Deflated, I looked at her for signs of her usual vitality and warmth. Her hair was tied back on top of her head and she was wearing little make-up. With that leotard on her I guessed no one would ever get to her face anyway.

'Well, for a starter, by being a bit more friendly,' I said, wondering what had happened to the Kim of my dreams.

She moved off at an angle away from Mr Universe and I followed.

'The last time I saw you,' said Kim, not looking at me, 'you weren't even talking to me.'

'I was being a fool,' I acknowledged.

Kim came to a halt against an unused Nautilus machine and finally turned to me.

'And now you're not?' she asked.

'Well – in a new way now,' I said, smiling.

Kim nodded and smiled at a man who greeted her as he passed by and then turned her attention back to me.

'And why are you here?' she asked, looking at me quizzically.

Kim Kim Kim, it's me! Larry! The man of Lukedom! Your sexual master and untiring lover!

'To see you,' I said, wondering if she'd totally forgotten me. 'To get back together with you. To play dice games with you.'

'Dice games!?' she said, and suddenly looked to her right as if afraid someone might overhear.

'My father's alive,' I said, glad to have gotten some response from her other than indifference. 'The report of his death was apparently exaggerated.'

'I . . . that's wonderful!' she said, her expression, if not friendly, at least now natural. 'How'd you find out?'

'I opened up the bronze die that supposedly held his remains and it contained a note from him that said I was getting closer.'

'He's playing games with you,' she said, appearing concerned.

'Of course. But for some reason I no longer mind. I think he expects me to do what you suggested – beat him at his own game. So I'm dicing.'

Kim studied me a moment and then laughed, that marvellous glow returning to her face for the first time.

'You aren't!'

'You doubt it?' I asked, a bit nonplussed at her response.

'But what about your job? What about Honoria?'

'Details, details.'

'Oh, no, you're in *big* trouble.'

'Want to join me?'

'In big trouble?'

'Whatever.'

She gazed at me for a long moment, the liveliness back in her face and eyes.

'Hey, Kim, when you get a moment I could use some help,' interrupted another muscular man as he sauntered by wearing a weight-lifting leotard that exposed almost as much buttock as Kim's. What was this place, a soft-porn show?

'You know if you really play your father's dice game,' she finally said with great seriousness, 'your old life is over.'

'I hope so,' I said, suddenly laughing.

'And you won't be exactly able to control what happens to us,' she added.

Considering this, I frowned.

'I think it was you who said if we're really meant for each other, then we'll survive whatever temptations the dice throw us into.'

She shook her head.

'I never used a cliché like "meant for each other",' she said. 'And it was *me* who was being a fool then. Both about the dice and maybe about you.'

'Maybe?' I said, moving closer to her. 'I'm at least still a maybe?'

Still shaking her head, Kim moved slightly away.

'I'm probably a one-in-six shot, right? You promise to love honour and obey until the dice falls a "four". I'm not sure what you think you're offering.'

'I'm diceplaying until I find my father or he finds me. After that, who knows? The world! Or maybe even dinner and a night out.'

'And your job? Honoria?' Kim asked again.

'I'm a free man now. Let the chips fall where they may.'

'That you can count on,' said Kim, again studying me. Then, for no reason I could see, she suddenly softened and moved closer to me.

'But it's good to see you,' she added in a whisper.

'I've really missed you,' I said. We stood as close together as possible without touching, I not daring to let my hands go around her since I knew I couldn't stop them diving for her buttocks. Then Kim stepped back and smiled at me with her usual mischievousness.

'So what's on the dice agenda today?' she asked.

'I don't know,' I said, 'but I'd like to give thirty-five chances out of thirty-six that it involves you, me and a bed.'

'And I thought you were a risk-taker,' she said with a smile. 'But I've got a room-mate,' she added, suddenly frowning, 'and I'm dating another guy. And . . . I'm not quite as . . . sure of us as I was that night in Lukedom.'

I confess, dear reader, that my heart sank at those words. Having lost Honoria, had I now lost Kim too?

But I managed to nod.

'I suppose that's . . . fair enough,' I said. 'But I'd still like to see you.'

'Sure,' she said, and unexpectedly came up and kissed me on the cheek before walking away towards the exit from the exercise area. As she left she gave her behind one exaggerated swing and as she did, added over her shoulder: 'Take a good look.'

I followed, noting as I walked another muscular behemoth

straining under a machine but managing to follow Kim's passage.

'Eat your heart out, fella,' I said and sauntered on.

Kim couldn't get off work until 7.30, a two-hour wait that I managed to survive only by leaving the health club and following a lot of trivial dice choices that had me making random purchases from random shops – I ended up with a hand calculator, a five-dollar packet of underwear and a small .22 automatic – and seeing ten minutes of random movies – one of them X-rated, which didn't help my ability to wait calmly for Kim.

At 7.30 she emerged into the lobby of the Big Apple dressed casually in a deep-brown pants suit and a raggedy-looking winter coat. I was awfully glad to see her.

We had a romantic candlelit dinner in a small Italian restaurant Kim knew, three blocks from the spa. She explained that the die back in Lukedom had chosen an option that she *proposition* Michael Way, not that she actually sleep with him. If he'd accepted her proposition, which he didn't, then she would still have been free to leave, or to consult a die about whether she should leave.

Frankly I was feeling too much joy in her presence to hear much of what she was saying. The glow in her eyes – from joy in being with me, I felt – made her words irrelevant. And for some reason the only thing that mattered from Lukedom was the marvellous day and night we'd spent together there.

But at ten o'clock, as we were standing outside the restaurant, Kim came up and planted a soft kiss on my cheek. I didn't let her escape, grabbing her in my arms and squeezing her to me.

'Ahhhh,' I groaned and, when I felt her hugging me in return, whispered: 'God, it's so good to hold you again.'

We remained embracing against a dingy wall next to the restaurant, the few passers-by eyeing us with Manhattan's customary indifference. Then Kim sighed and gently moved to separate herself, looking up at me as starry-eyed as I assumed I was, but then, after giving me another soft kiss on the cheek, she broke away.

'I've really enjoyed seeing you again,' she said simply, 'but I'd like to go home now, and alone.'

I was in that male state of anticipatory euphoria when a man thinks an evening is going to end just the way he wants with the woman he wants, and so was stunned into momentary silence. I felt vaguely outraged: how dare she act like a normal woman instead of like the girl of my dreams?

'You'll survive,' said Kim with a sudden smile at my surprise. 'And I hope you'll call again. It's just I don't want to move quite as fast as we moved in Lukedom.'

'Maybe we should check your decision with the dice,' I suggested with sudden animation.

She responded by cocking her head to one side and examining me carefully with a sceptical half-smile.

'Well, you can let chance have a say,' she finally said. 'My dice are in temporary retirement.'

'Fine,' I said, pulling out a green die. 'If it's odd I insist on sleeping in your apartment tonight – with you or without you.'

I rubbed the die between my palms, took it in my right fist and then opened my fingers palm up to see how the die lay. A one.

'Shall we take a cab?' I asked, smiling.

Kim's apartment in Brooklyn was a mess. There were not only clothes and books and cassettes scattered all over but several cats playing with happy abandon with these clothes, books and cassettes. Kim assured me that most of the stuff belonged to her room-mate, but Kim's bedroom wasn't much of an improvement. Here it was mostly books and magazines that seemed to have no home, the single wooden bookcase overflowing. Clothes were stacked neatly on top of the one bureau and the small closet was so full it looked as if the door couldn't close.

'All my worldly possessions,' she announced, gesturing extravagantly at the mess. 'I keep trying to simplify my life but keep spotting blouses or books I can't resist.'

'You need to hire a new maid,' I said.

'Oh, I will, I will,' said Kim, coming towards me. 'The poor girl's impossible.'

And then we kissed, the kind of long deep kiss that leaves strong men weak-kneed and weak women on their backs. Somehow we both remained standing. Kim broke away.

'We've got a futon in the living-room closet,' she said, staggering away from me.

'Mmmm,' I said and took out the green die. 'Odd I sleep on the

258

futon, even I sleep in your bed.'

'What about me?'

The die, bless it, fell a four: Kim's bed.

'I decide for me, you have to decide for you,' I said and cheerfully began to undress.

Shaking her head with a small smile, Kim left the bedroom, returning five minutes later with a tray with a pot of tea and a pint of brandy. With me naked under the covers, she peeled down to panties and a long oversized t-shirt and sat on her side of the bed. While my loin system stirred restlessly we talked about what had happened to us since Lukedom.

She told me that after getting back she'd moved out of the Battle household without telling anyone where she was going, and tried drowning her sorrow in work. Her job involved whisking herself around three boroughs visiting the eight clubs and encouraging clients to sign up for everything the clubs had to offer: yoga, aerobics, meditation, guided weightlifting, Nautilus, swimming, handball, golf lessons, whirlpool treatments, volleyball.

She said she'd first been intrigued by me when she saw me sitting out there alone in my sailboat on the Hudson that first afternoon; anyone who would use lack of wind as an excuse to avoid the Battles could not be all bad, she said. I said I'd first been intrigued by her when she leaned over to look down the companionway hatch into the boat's salon. I didn't elaborate, but she grinned knowingly.

She admitted she resented me for being such a fool about Way and the love we'd found that first night in Lukedom, a love which I seemed to suppress when confronted with the possible loss of several million dollars. What was a few million dollars to a man who really loved her? Nothing, she said playfully.

After leaving the Battles without saying where she was going or what she was doing, she had felt martyrish, hoping that I was missing her, yearning for her, desperate for her, perhaps even launching a major quest for her. After two weeks, however, she began to feel like the lover who kills herself to make the beloved suffer. Lying in the grave of Brooklyn she began to have second thoughts. She decided that a trip back to the Battle penthouse where she might accidentally leave a phone number or address might perhaps be in order. Although lovers were expected to overcome numerous obstacles before winning the beloved, they needed occasional clues along the way. Women have been dropping hand-kerchiefs for millennia, who was she to break the tradition? Together we laughed.

After she cleared away the tea and brandy and our talk seemed to be flagging, she turned off all but one dim bedside lamp and climbed in under the sheets.

Feeling like a saint, but one who plans to give up sainthood at the earliest possible moment, I lay on my back beside her. It was a wonderful moment, because I knew one way or another bliss seemed inevitable. But then, unfortunately, I remembered the dice. In the same rash blind overconfidence that had afflicted Kim in Lukedom after our first night of lovemaking, I decided to consult the dice – in this case about how we should make love.

The die, never one always to make wise choices, picked the option that to honour Kim's feeling that we should go slower this time, we would make love but without penetration or climax. As soon as the die had spoken I was over on top of Kim and we were intertwined in a blissful kiss.

I thought this command of infinite foreplay was marvellous – for about fifteen minutes. Then I began to have my doubts. Kissing and fondling are fine in their place, and no relationship should be without them. However, the Lord God had intended them as appetizers preparatory to the main course, and I was certain if I could get Miss Claybell to research the Old Testament with her usual thoroughness that it would be revealed that God had quite specifically listed what we were doing – or rather what we were not doing no matter how much we both wanted it – as a sin, if not a major Sodom or Gomorrah sin, then at least a minor plague sin.

Kim, writhing and gasping and groaning and generally doing everything that a woman could to make a desperate situation desperater, insisted, when I could get her to speak coherently, that we must follow the die choice, no matter how painful. That might be what her mouth was saying, I thought, feeling her hot rounded writhing female abomination of temptation, but the rest of her obviously agreed with me.

After about forty minutes my mind, ever obedient to the prodding of my prick, suddenly had a brilliant thought: Kim was testing me. If I really loved her I would take her here and now and show my love was more powerful than any plastic cube. With a great groan of satisfaction at the power of rationalization I spread Kim's legs and plunged into her, an act that was greeted with unbridled enthusiasm by Kim's body, even as her mouth mumbled something that came out vaguely like 'Wah are u doon?' It didn't take long for us both to break the die's command against climaxes, and I collapsed on top of her with feelings of relief and triumph: man is master of his fate and captain of his soul.

And victim of his animal appetites, as Kim pointed out to me when she had recovered sufficiently from her ecstasy to feel like uttering a rational thought. If I couldn't follow a simple little dice option that was scheduled to last only a few hours what kind of a man was I?

'A normal man,' I answered, lying on my back with a contented smile.

'Exactly,' said Kim, sitting up with sudden animation. 'You're just like you always are, you're just like everybody else, and there's no challenge to grow, to change, to discover new aspects of yourself.'

'I had discovered all the impossible levels of frustration I'm capable of,' I said, 'and wanted to pass on to new aspects of myself.'

'I'm serious,' said Kim. 'You're only going to be doing this dicing for a few weeks. The least you can do is do it right.'

Unfortunately, I found myself agreeing. I would show my father I could win, then drop the dice as a game I had mastered and moved on from.

Still, I was sure that if there were a God in heaven and He had seen what I had done, He was looking down on me with approval.

Despite their having had an up couple of trading days Larry and Jeff were still not welcome in the custodians' rest room. So after Jeff told Larry that he'd been re-contacted by his insider X, they huddled in a booth at a local tavern frequented primarily by secretaries, maintenance men, couriers, and an occasional trader or two plotting some illicit scheme. Larry and Jeff ordered a couple of double bourbons and began their plotting.

'This is what the dirty bastard told me,' said Jeff, holding a single piece of paper in trembling hands. He was still violently bitter whenever he thought of how he'd been screwed by the post-election troop build-up. 'On noon next Wednesday the Treasury is going to issue a report unexpectedly indicating that the economy is growing much faster than previous indicators had implied, that the recession is definitely bottoming and that the negative effects on the economy of the rise in oil prices are much less than previously estimated.'

Jeff looked up. 'He says this will make the stock market bounce up at least twenty points and maybe more and make bonds probably sell off.'

Larry nodded, feeling a little disappointed. It was nowhere near the bombshell that the supposed peace initiative was, but still it was the sort of advanced information that for a futures trader or stock speculator could mean millions.

'To double-cross the double-crosser,' Larry began as Jeff waited for his response, 'we have to figure a way to make the market do the opposite of what this tip is going to make it do. We can't stop the release of the Treasury report – at least I assume we can't – but we might be able to pre-empt it. After all, this news is only a minor hand grenade maybe good for twenty up points on the Dow. What we need is a small bomb that will be good for forty or fifty points on the downside.'

At first Jeff was smiling at the prospect of revenge, but then, when he realized that Larry was suggesting they manipulate the market, he was appalled. This was not straightforward insider trading – a religious recognition of man's normal ignorance and thus an acknowledgement of the Gods. No, this was usurping the Gods' power of controlling the markets. This was blasphemy! And illegal!

'We can't do that,' he protested. 'That's market manipulation.'

'It's illegal,' agreed Larry. 'And it's unethical, but it's the only way we can get back at the bastard who screwed us.'

'But if we get caught, we'll be kicked off the Street for months!'

'That may be true,' said Larry, 'but revenge will be ours. And there's a lot can be done even off the Street with the profits we may make.'

'But they'd be illicit profits,' Jeff persisted in horror, 'profits generated by altering the normal course of history.'

Larry studied Jeff, wondering where this sudden burst of morality was coming from. Here was a guy who had used illegal paid-for insider information to cheat three times and try to cheat a fourth, lecturing him on morality.

'Men make history,' he said. 'In this case, us.'

Jeff took another long swallow of his bourbon, but didn't reply.

'Look,' said Larry. 'Here's how we have to think. Let's suppose the tip was that Upjohn was coming out with unexpectedly lower earnings, a report that the insider thinks will lead to a 2 or 3 per cent sell-off. But just before the release of the earnings report we get a report on the wire that an Upjohn researcher has come up with a cure for the common cold. Bingo! The stock soars and no one even notices the earnings report until after it's discovered that the common cold still lives.'

Jeff brooded.

'We have to come up with something like that that'll knock the whole market off its feet next Wednesday,' Larry added.

'We shoot the President,' suggested Jeff suddenly.

Larry considered.

'Possibly, possibly,' he said. 'Of course rumours about the President's being shot are so common it's like crying wolf too often.'

'I mean really shoot him,' persisted Jeff, his eyes showing a sudden enthusiasm for the project. Ever since the President's failure to start a real peace initiative after the election had crossed him up, Jeff had had it in not only for X but also for the President.

Larry scowled.

'Steady, Jeff,' he said. 'we're only going to create a momentary illusion of reality that will have a profound momentary effect on the market, not try to really change the world. Besides, I thought you voted for Bush.'

'I did,' said Jeff. 'That's why I want to shoot him.'

'Aim lower,' said Larry. 'Something less radical but almost as devastating.'

'We give him Aids,' suggested Jeff.

Larry considered it.

'Aids might do it,' he mused. 'It's so totally far-out and such a basic cultural fear that people will tend to believe it despite their common sense.'

'I've got a friend that's infected,' said Jeff. 'We could get him to give us some of his blood and take it to Wash – '

'Jeff, Jeff,' Larry interrupted, putting a soothing hand on the arm of his friend. 'We're not going to do *anything* to the President, do you understand?'

'We're not?' said Jeff, looking let down.

'No. We're going to get something into the minds of Wall Street – stronger than rumour – that will make them sell stocks Tuesday morning. Something that will take long enough before being cleared up to wipe out X and let us make a little money on the opposite side.'

'Oh.'

'Now this week the President has a cold, so his health is somewhat on the public's mind. Aids might be just the ticket.'

Jeff returned to his bourbon, apparently losing some of his interest in the discussion now that it was dealing only with illusion and not reality.

'First, in the usual Street manner, we might on Monday float a few rumours that the President is more seriously ill than the White House is letting on. The Street will ignore them because such rumours are a dime a dozen – if a week passes without at least one rumour about a dying, dead, or almost assassinated President, then the Street starts to worry that he may *really* be ill.'

Larry, now talking more to himself than to Jeff, took a long slow swig of his bourbon.

'But that plants the seed that we'll make sprout on Wednesday morning,' he continued. He stopped to lower his glass and stare directly at Jeff, who was poking his nose down into his glass as if dipping for a cherry or seeking the Holy Grail.

'Somehow on that day,' Larry went on, 'we have to get it on the Reuters wire that the President's press spokesman denies that the President has the Aids disease and insists that he only has the HIV virus – "in its earliest stages". A White House investigation into the source of this leak is being made. The President's doctors will hold a news conference at Bethesda Naval Hospital at 1 P.M.' Larry paused.

'Jesus,' he concluded, 'that should be good for at least sixty Dow points on the downside.'

Jeff held an ice cube up between his thumb and forefinger and examined it as if it might contain the Aids virus.

'What do you think?' asked Larry.

'Who cares about money?' said Jeff, still involved with his ice cube. 'The world's only real hope is to shoot the President.'

Larry began to realize that BB&P would soon be in the market for a new Assistant Trader.

'Besides,' added Jeff, lowering the cube to his glass, 'you'll never get anything on to a Reuters wire. If it could be done, it would have been done long ago.'

Jeff had a point. Larry didn't know where Reuters originated but he was sure that putting a bogus story on their wire was next to impossible; otherwise it would have been done a hundred times by now. He knew that since the first caveman opened a stock exchange in 3,600 B.C. traders had been telling lies to manipulate the price of a stock or stocks they were interested in. Nowadays, with communications between cities and nations almost instantaneous, lying was more difficult than in the good old days. Then you might publish a lying story and before the slow pace of communication permitted its refutation have the market do what you wanted it to do. But today the ticker, the Reuters wire, and CNN and CNBC-FNN all had up-to-the-second live coverage of every lie. If a man just trying to make a decent buck threw out a rumour that the President had been shot, the next thing you knew there was the President live on CNN slashing away at a golf ball or jogging along a path looking like death warmed over. Why, it was so bad that a man might still be in the first paragraph of his lie when a spokes-man was appearing on CNN refuting it. What this meant was that

Larry had to create a lie that would make the refutation seem to be a confirmation – at least for a while. But how?

'Any ideas?' Larry asked Jeff, aware that Jeff probably wasn't privy to his line of thinking.

'It's simple,' announced Jeff, apparently following his own line. 'You let the doctor do the talking.'

'The doctor?' echoed Larry.

'The doctor,' said Jeff. 'No one can refute a doctor.'

After Larry let the die decide whether he should pursue this plan to thwart X and, thankfully, the die gave its permission, he called up Kim and told her he'd appreciate it if she would give him a hand in a little scheme he was working on. She met him in a coffee shop in midtown, and over hot chocolate and tea the two of them discussed possible scenarios. It turned out *she* had insider information that they could use. A doctor at a well-known midtown clinic used the computerized golf course at one of her spas every Wednesday and Friday mornings between ten and eleven. If they could find an actor who . . . And Kim knew an actor, a gay activist down on his luck who would leap at a chance to play a role that would screw the establishment. He'd even done guerrilla theatre work in the seventies. If they needed others this gay guy would be able to get them.

So drowning themselves in hot chocolate and tea they plotted and planned, plotted and planned. It was almost as good as sex.

But not quite.

From Luke's Journal

Since we're usually under the illusion that we know and have the truth, lying is a good habit to get into. By lying we're freed from the illusion of being right. Whenever I think I'm a sage I cause nothing but misery, for myself and others.

Lying is held in ill-repute primarily because people usually lie to protect their old egos, rather than to create new ones. Lying to try to seem consistent, either with oneself or with others, is an act of fear. Lying to create something new – and therefore inconsistent with our usual selves – is an act of creativity and aliveness. The first builds more bars on the cage; the second bends them apart so one can walk free.

'I don't have any personal history,' once said the Yaqui clown (and sage) Don Juan. 'One day I found out that personal history was no longer necessary for me and, like drinking, I dropped it.'

— 48 —

On Tuesday morning at 10 A.M. in a small anteroom of the Manhattan Diagnostic Clinic a small press conference was held. About a half-dozen radio and television stations had sent crews when they had received anonymous tips that a major story was about to break on President Bush's health. Present also were reporters from several of the major daily newspapers and wire services. About thirty people were packed into the small room, which, as far as the clinic knew, was being reserved by their Dr Donaldson to give a small talk to interns on 'The Pancreas: Then and Now'. The receptionist was a bit surprised at the sudden appearance of a crowd of excited reporters and camera crews but pointed them to the appropriate room. Far be it from her to know the precise value of the pancreas.

At 10 A.M. a dignified middle-aged man with a bushy grey beard and wearing a suit and a white coat entered the room, accompanied by a uniformed man whose stitched insignia identified him as an MDC security guard. The man went to the front of the room and stood behind the microphone that was already in place there. Cameras began flashing. Other mikes were shoved into the doctor's face. He blinked out at the lights for a moment, looking a little overwhelmed by the spectacle.

'My name is Dr Martin Luther Donaldson,' he announced in a firm, dignified voice. 'And I am chief pathologist here at the Manhattan Diagnostic Clinic. I am speaking out today because the White House effort to hide the truth about the President's health is counter-productive to our country's learning the truth about Aids and the normal lives people infected with the Aids virus may lead.'

The reporters leaned in closer, not quite believing what they were hearing.

'From the President's blood and tissue samples sent to us from Bethesda Naval Hospital I can say with total certainty that there is no truth to the rumour that President Bush presently has symptoms of the Aids disease.'

Dr Donaldson, or in any case the speaker, paused to let that little gem sink in to the thick skulls of his listeners.

'The President's doctors are convinced – and I share their belief – that his present cold is no more than the usual seasonal infliction and is no more severe than it would normally be. The blood tests completed here at MDC show no deficiency in his antibody count, the count still being within the range of the normal. We, or his doctors in Washington, will, of course, monitor it closely and keep you informed. We can expect that the President may live on free from the disease for many years . . . '

There was the beginning of an uproar among the assembled members of the press as the implications of all this began to sink in, two reporters breaking ranks and dashing for the door.

'The President's mind has not and will not be affected,' the doctor went on with stern dignity ' – at least not perhaps until the terminal stages, when he may become depressed.'

Although the cameramen continued to look at the doctor with that indifference that comes from living life totally detached from everything except getting the action centred, in focus and shooting only within prescribed union hours, the reporters were now staring at him with mostly open mouths.

'To summarize, while infected with the HIV virus, the President is not yet ill. He can continue to function in his office for the foreseeable future. And the White House effort to suppress this information is a disservice to the American people.

'Any questions?'

There were a few. Since twenty reporters were shouting at once, the good doctor could decide for himself which question, if any, he heard.

'Neither the President nor his physicians have been able to determine how he obtained the virus,' the doctor said next, although no one had been able to catch a single articulate question from the chaos of shouting. 'Blood transfusions are the obvious first suspect.'

Scramble, scramble, shout, shout – more reporters already racing out the door, others straining to get their questions heard.

'No, Mrs Bush has not been infected,' the doctor announced sternly. 'The President does believe in practising safe sex.'

Scramble, scramble, shout, shout.

'Yes, the doctors at Bethesda will confirm all this now that I have broken the story,' said Dr Donaldson. 'No, I don't know whether the White House will continue to stonewall it or not.'

Scramble, scramble, shout, shout, but the good doctor, microphones in his face, flashbulbs popping, retained his composure.

'No,' he announced with his stern seriousness. 'We have no knowledge of the President's sexual habits, and none about whether he engages in anal intercourse.'

Back at BB&P Larry watched the ticker that morning as if the Lord himself were about to speak for the first time in two thousand years. He had given his morning marching orders, accompanied by a pile of statistical manure to justify them, but his positions all presupposed a short sharp break in the stock market, a 'flight-to-quality' boost to T-Bills and maybe T-Bond futures, and a possible bump up in gold. The Treasury report that X knew about was scheduled to break at twelve, so if something on the President's health didn't come out before then, BB&P would get clobbered. As the stock market continued to rise mildly that morning – presumably on the continued buying of X's insiders, Larry's team at BB&P continued to sell into it.

Then, at 10.40 (ten minutes after the news conference at Manhattan Diagnostic Clinic had concluded) Larry noticed a sudden small swoon taking place in S&P stock market futures: someone was selling the futures rather heavily; but still nothing on the news wire to explain it.

Stocks themselves began to sell off over the next twenty minutes although nothing on any wire could account for it and the sell-off was steady rather than abrupt. It looked as if someone besides BB&P had gotten the news about the President's little problem before the item hit the ticker. Certainly the selling of BB&P alone wasn't enough to cause it – they were too small, Larry knew. Then at 10.57 Reuters spoke across the wire into thousands of brokerage houses across the country:

'Manhattan doctor reports President Bush infected by but not yet ill with HIV virus. Condemns White House stonewalling. Fitzwater to reply.'

It was all downhill from there, both for the ease of Larry's day and for the stock market. An airpocket opened up under the stock market futures and they were down 1 per cent while people tried to figure what the hell the Reuters item actually meant. Then the eleven o'clock news on several local radio stations gave brief reports of the news conference: a Manhattan doctor who heads the diagnostic lab of a well-known Manhattan clinic claims that President Bush has the Aids virus and that the White House has been trying to hide it.

As it turned out, Larry covered his shorts far too early, not having sufficient faith in the gullibility and irrationality of the investment community. Long after BB&P had bought back all their positions at nice profits the market continued to fall. It got so bad that for one horrible moment Larry became convinced that the President *did* have Aids and that Larry had just happened to uncover the stonewalling by accident.

Then he got control of himself and ordered his troops to buy, buy like crazy, and profit when the panic was over.

Spokesman Fitzwater's initial denial – 'The President does not have Aids and we don't know who this Dr Donaldson is,' rang false because reporters had already determined that Dr Donaldson was really the chief diagnostician at the Manhattan clinic and a well-respected member of his field.

The spokesman's next effort was 'We'll get back to you on this', and it wasn't too successful: especially since he was pale and shaking when he made it, his words sent the market down another twenty points.

It wasn't until about fifteen minutes after noon, when reporters began to hear that the Dr Donaldson who appeared on noontime local TV channel news was not the Dr Donaldson known and loved (and hated) by his colleagues at the Manhattan Clinic, that some cracks in the story began to appear. Still it took until 1.10 for the clinic to deny that the man who had given the news conference was *their* Dr Donaldson, who, it appeared, had at the time of the press conference been playing golf on a simulated course in lower Manhattan and knew nothing about any tests of the President's blood. When at 1.25 Reuters shot across its wire, 'President's Aids possible hoax', the stock market began to rally, and by the end of the day was only slightly lower than where it had begun. Larry's troops made even more money on the rally than they had on the fall.

And, of course, a minor news item at noon about the US economy being stronger than initially indicated had been totally ignored by the market.

The BB&P Futures Fund gained 14 per cent in asset value that day, its best single day on record – almost matching its worst day on record of a month before. The fund made almost as much as Jeff's Aunt Mildred. Arlene Ecstein's account, which had begun at $200,000, was now at $284,000. It apparently pays to tell your broker to gamble with your money.

The only other noteworthy event occurred late in the afternoon just after the markets had closed: Jeff had another one of his little breakdowns. He suddenly began wandering through the exhausted and triumphant traders and brokers of BB&P, a huge mad grin on his face and shouting over and over, 'Larry gave the President Aids! Larry gave the President Aids!'

After Larry's brilliant financial triumphs of that day his friends and colleagues were ready to credit him with almost demonic powers, but not in their wildest dreams did they think he could ever do *that*.

After the highly profitable countercoup against X Brad Burner now dropped in every now and then to say hello, as if I were a human being again. Brokers, whose noses had seemed always to be stuck in their monitors when I passed, now looked up at me and shouted a hello. After our triumph Jeff and I were no longer Mutt and Jeff or Huff and Puff, but now 'Morgan and Gould'. What higher praise could there be?

So high had my prestige risen after my great countercoup against X that Mr Battle invited me to the weekly high-stakes poker game he played in with several of his wealthy colleagues, an honour never before bestowed on a mere employee. I'd often played poker with Mr Battle and Honoria and assorted guests at weekends on the Hudson, but this was another level entirely.

The afternoon before the big event I wondered how I might get the dice to improve my poker game. By nature I was a conservative player, betting each hand according to what I thought the odds of its being a winner were. I never bluffed. I could see that letting a die influence my play might introduce an unpredictability into my game that I knew I lacked. So I decided that before each hand I would surreptitiously check a die in my lap and if it showed a 'six' I would bluff, no matter how good or bad the cards.

We played in the game room of Mr Battle's Manhattan apartment. The other players were Mr Battle, Brad Burner, Mr Potter, two Wall Street tycoons in their fifties, and Jeff, who I had insisted be invited too.

Dice or no dice, bluff or no bluff, near the end of the evening I was over eighteen hundred dollars behind. As chance would have it, I'd had mostly strong hands when the die had ordered me to bluff so that the fact that I thought I was bluffing was not apparent to the other players. However, in this seven card stud game, the die had opted that I bluff, and unfortunately the hand I was being dealt was abysmal. Nevertheless, from the first I bet as if my two hole cards were four aces. Mr Battle and I were involved in a betting war, one that I could see was going to be quite costly.

Jeff, who'd folded, was standing behind me, watching intently. A huge pile of chips and money was in the pot in the centre of the table, and what was left seemed mostly to be in front of Mr Battle and Brad Burner. Jeff, the two older tycoons and Mr Potter eyed the huge pot with awe.

Scowling and fingering his chips, Brad finally folded over his four face-up cards.

'Too rich for my blood,' he said.

On the table in front of Mr Battle were seven cards, three face-down, and face-up two kings and two queens. Larry's hand showed only a ten and nine of hearts, the two of clubs and the two of diamonds – a junky-looking hand to say the least.

Mr Battle was sweating profusely as he squinted down at my lousy hand, then took a careful peek at his own hole cards. It didn't take the wisdom of Solomon to know he had a full house.

The dice had me dressed that evening in an unusually flashy silk shirt open down my chest, and I was smoking a cigar, the smoke rising in classic fashion past my face. I felt like Clint Eastwood, but checking the junk I had face-down I knew I was Clint without any guns. Nevertheless I stared coolly at Mr Battle.

'He's bluffing, Bill,' said Mr Potter. 'Clobber him.'

'Really, Mr Potter?' I said. 'How about you and I make a little side bet – say twenty thousand dollars?'

Mr Potter looked startled and distinctly uneasy.

'I, uh, didn't know you had that much money,' he said.

'I will after this hand,' I said.

Mr Battle was watching me intently through half-closed eyes and still sweating.

'In the times I've played poker with you,' he finally said, 'not once have you been fool enough to bluff against what I'm showing.'

'It's your bet, big boy,' I said. 'How about it, Mr Potter, twenty thousand?'

'I believe house rules are no side bets.'

'I'll be gentle,' said Mr Battle, his face twitching. 'I bet five hundred dollars.'

'Good. I raise five thousand.'

As I began to count out most of the bills and chips in front of me and push them into the pot, the three onlookers burst out into mumbled oaths and gasps. Mr Battle's hand went to his heart.

Everyone but me leaned forward to stare down again at my four cards showing only junk.

'Jesus, Larry,' said Jeff. 'You *can't* have four twos or a straight flush. The odds against it – '

'Are considerable,' I said. 'Come on. Let's see your money, sir. You can't lose.'

Mr Battle peered at me shrewdly.

'You want me to think that your betting is part of your strange behaviour lately, so I'll think you're bluffing and call you – and lose five thousand.'

'Just put your money in, bossman, then we'll all see.'

Mr Battle's face twitched one more time and then he smiled with sudden relief.

'I believe in the unchanging solidity of your soul,' he announced calmly. 'I fold.'

As all stared at me, Mr Battle turned over his cards and I began to rake in the huge pot. Then Mr Potter reached forward and frantically began turning over my three hole cards.

He stared at them in disbelief. Jeff stared at them in disbelief. Brad and the two tycoons stared at them in disbelief. Mr Battle stared at them in horror.

'He's . . . got nothing,' murmured Mr Potter.

'That . . . is . . . absolutely the worst poker hand,' said Brad in awe, 'that I have ever seen.'

Mr Battle straightened himself in his chair and looked at me with cold dignity.

'You're a sick man, Larry,' he said. 'I just hope you don't invest our money with as little sense.'

'Only sometimes,' I said, grinning and raking in the pot. 'And if I'm sick, I now can afford better therapy.'

As they left the Battle apartment that night about ten, Larry explained to Jeff how he used the dice to improve not only his trading but also his poker playing. Jeff was speechless. Carried away with his success at the poker, Larry wanted to show Jeff in action how the dice worked and, since he happened to have one of his random purchases from three weeks before in his coat pocket, gave the dice three outrageous options and the die chose one: they were to go to the South Bronx and do the deed there. Jeff, who had been somewhat excited when he first learned of the use of dice, was now appalled.

Nevertheless, Larry dragged Jeff off with him to Harlem, the dice apparently feeling that Jeff should learn to confront his fears head on in order to bury them. Jeff definitely preferred burying them. He didn't know exactly what Larry was up to – Larry having mumbled his options and the results – but saw very little profit potential in 137th Street in the Bronx. Little did he know.

The cabbie that drove them there that late evening, a middle-aged man named Spinio with a thick Brooklyn accent (a native American cab driver!), was equally sceptical.

'You sure this where you want to be, buddy?' he asked when Larry tentatively said that this looked as if it might be a nice place to stop. Even in the darkness only sporadically broken by an occasional surviving streetlight, it looked a little like Berlin in about 1945 except that the survivors, unlike those back then, didn't seem to have much to do.

'We're looking for new experience,' Larry replied as he handed the driver the fare and pushed open his door.

The driver looked nervously at a cluster of young Hispanics loitering under a streetlight.

'Yeah,' he said. 'Probably your last.'

When Jeff had also reluctantly slid over and out of the cab, the cabbie burned rubber in pulling away and zooming off, his 'Off Duty' sign suddenly blazing forth like a Hatteras lighthouse.

Larry and Jeff were both wearing very expensive and nicely tailored overcoats. As they began walking slowly along the sidewalk, Jeff squirming up close to Larry's shoulder like a bear cub sticking close to mom, they passed two shabbily-dressed black men barely visible in the dim light leaning up against an abandoned building. A third man was lying against the building, seemingly dead or sleeping. The two standing men blinked at Larry and Jeff unbelievingly.

'Why couldn't the dice have sent us someplace safe?' asked Jeff. 'Life Belfast or Baghdad.'

'These guys have never been given a chance,' said Larry, strolling down the dark street as if it were Regent Street in London. 'They're victims of our unjust society.'

'I know,' said Jeff, 'but as an active member of the oppressing class I'd rather be someplace else.'

Three tough-looking black men in their twenties came swaggering along the sidewalk towards Larry and Jeff, eyeing them speculatively. Larry strolled leisurely onwards, even smiling at them as they neared, with Jeff huddled at his elbow, glancing nervously back over his shoulder. He was hoping to see several squad cars of police or perhaps a marine helicopter with two dozen green berets, but saw only indifferent loiterers.

The three big men stopped directly in front of Larry and Jeff, who were forced to halt, and grinned at them.

'Hey, man, what's happening'?' asked the smallest of the three. One of them seemed highly agitated, bouncing from one foot to the other and rolling his head as if trying to get it to fit right on his shoulders. The other two looked more menacing, their hands stuffed in their somewhat threadbare coat pockets.

'Looking for some action?' asked the biggest of the men, still grinning.

'We're fine,' Jeff squeaked. 'Just getting some fresh air.'

'Yeah . . . ' said the second man.

'I watch "The Bill Cosby Show",' Jeff said reassuringly.

Larry looked at the three men and slowly shook his head.

'I'm afraid this is your unlucky night,' he announced.

'Yeah?' drawled the big man, his grin fading and his face taking on an alert menace. 'How's that?'

Larry drew from his elegant coat pocket his small .32 automatic.

'I'm afraid this is a stick-up.'

'Shit, man,' said the hyper black man, bouncing on his toes and clearly needing a fix. 'We don't wanna buy no gun.'

But the eyes of the two men who were in fairly good touch with reality widened in disbelief as they looked from the two elegantly-dressed businessmen to Larry's gun and back again.

'Fuck, man, you got to be kidding,' said the big man.

'Jesus, Larry, what are you doing!?' Jeff squeaked, pulling at his elbow like a child who has desperately to go to the bathroom.

Larry took a threatening step closer to the men, moving his gun slowly back and forth from the one to the other.

'I gave a hundred dollars to the NAACP in eighty-seven,' Jeff said to them, hoping to dissociate himself from Larry's madness.

'My boss ordered it,' Larry said quietly. 'Your wallets, please.'

As the hyper black man continued to bounce on his toes and roll his head, happily indifferent to the trials and tribulations of his friends, the other two, in shock, slowly began groping for their wallets, managing reluctantly to pull them out.

'You a cop?' asked the smaller of the two as Larry took his wallet. 'You must be a cop. Hey, man, we didn't steal this money.'

'Yeah, man,' said the second. 'Our ladies gave it to us – pocket money, man, you got no right.'

Larry removed the numerous bills from the two wallets and handed them back.

'What about your friend?' he asked politely, gesturing with his automatic at the dancing junkie.

'Shit, man, you lucky to find a nickle on Willy,' the big man said. 'Money go through him into shit so fast you don't see it, man.'

'Well, thanks, I'm really sorry about this, but take this as a warning,' said Larry, slowly backing away, Jeff now hidden behind him and backing in tandem. 'The streets of New York are not safe.'

Larry gestured with his gun for the black men to be off in the other direction and then turned and led Jeff away.

Although it took two additional appearances of Larry's little .32 to ensure their safe escape with their illicit earnings back to the slightly safer streets of the West Side of Manhattan, they made it back.

Jeff found that confronting his fears head on was, as he had suspected all along, even less fun than living with them slightly buried. Larry could only think of the two black men he had robbed: what was the world coming to when rich white honkies began coming to Harlem and robbing decent black men at gunpoint? The extent of God's injustice must seem infinite.

— 50 —

Since the discovery that his father was probably alive and through the chaos of his diceplay Larry had continued to try to locate his father. He had set Miss Claybell to trying to discover a reality behind the initials 'DI' that he'd discovered in Jake's files. She'd come up with a Venezuelan company named Distributo Innovato whose monogram was DI, but its business was distributing wholesale food to supermarkets. An Italian company 'DI' provided clerical garb to the Vatican. A London DI was Davis and Inges, a small brokerage house specializing in government bonds. A Tokyo DI aroused Larry's interest but it turned out to be unlikely too: a giant company in design and consulting that did billions of dollars' worth of business with many leading companies not only in Japan but in the US and Europe as well. It seemed to have nothing to do with Luke Rhinehart, Lukedom or dice.

So with it looking as if his efforts at finding his father were blocked and as if the gay actor and friend who had pulled off the coup impersonations were not going to be caught, Larry found himself taking stock.

Except for the limitation that the dicer had an obligation not to disrupt the healthy aspects of his life, he was quite happy to let himself go. He enjoyed seeing the shock on people's faces when he did something unexpected. He loved the reputation he was getting for being eccentric; it gave him a freedom to expand his usual way of doing things. If everyone saw everyone else as an inconsistent eccentric what a wonderful zany world it would be! People could be lively and playful and absurd and stupid and brilliant and yet not have to be that way every day!

Of course he knew that in some sense he was living on borrowed time. He was making money for his firm and himself and thus was a winner. Winners, in America, could be eccentrics, kooks, jerks, bastards – almost anything they wanted – as long as they remained winners. But if they ever began losing and became losers, then, ah, then they became simply jerks to be avoided, or bastards to be chastised, or eccentrics to be pitied. In any case, the loser, no matter what his characteristics, was soon an outsider, exiled from the winners with a swiftness that was testimony to the efficiency of the free-enterprise system.

Kim had begun urging Larry to use the dice to develop new aspects of himself and soon had him taking karate lessons at the Big Apple, practising meditation, going to an opera, buying used clothes and actually wearing them, giving money to people, and reading novels, spiritual books and other writing that didn't have numbers in it and offer a profit potential.

The dice chose a few other interesting options as well. It opted for his selling his Mercedes, and buying – from the six options offered it – a used Chevy Corsica. It ordered him to sell two of the three paintings he owned of the soon-to-be-world-famous avant-garde artist, and buy a dozen new paintings that he actually liked – for one-third the price. He lost five thousand dollars in selling his two soon-to-be-world-famous masterpieces and concluded that the art market was as unreliable as the stock market. The die rejected an option that he try to sell his apartment, and another that he buy a summer place in the Hamptons.

Larry gradually became aware that his approach to using the dice was different from his father's. He felt that he was a scientist, while his father, for all the pretensions about 'exploring the malleability of the human soul', was at best an amateur, an artist rather than a true experimenter. Larry kept computerized records of his dice decisions and their results, records as careful and complete as those he had once kept of his financial ups and downs. He theorized that by introducing chance into his trading he was enabling himself to eliminate the usual human emotions that sway a trader's decisions and lead to losing streaks. He felt that a trader on a hot streak should not let chance tamper with his patterns, but a loser could only gain by letting the dice loose on what the technical indicators were suggesting.

So, too, if a man was winning in his personal relationships then the dice should only be used occasionally, as a kind of *agent provocateur* to keep the pot boiling and make sure stagnation didn't set in. But where a man was losing – in a job or in lifeless relationships – then it made sense to bring chance in to shake things up.

But Larry was uncertain about what he really wanted for himself and his life. On the one hand, he sometimes longed to re-establish the life that he'd had before Lukedom and his trading losses had destroyed his engagement and jeopardized his job, but on the other, he wanted to blow it all to smithereens. He loved his times with Kim, loved sailing with her, hiking New York streets, playing all sorts of dice games, even working out with her among the behemoths. He enjoyed her passionately and very probably loved her. But what did that mean?

And on the other hand, there were her grungy Brooklyn living arrangements and her tacky job, one which showed both her total estrangement from the science of making money and her disturbing tendency towards flirtatiousness. When he complained about the nature of her work it got him nowhere.

'Your job's only one step above a call girl for some escort service!' he had once spouted to her.

'No, it's several steps below, as you'd know if you saw my pay cheques.'

'My God, have you *been* a call girl!?'

'Nice girls don't kiss and tell,' said Kim.

And little counterhits like that made her seem frighteningly experienced, even if she had a freshness that belied it.

And Larry even wondered sometimes if her mind was rational. When he tried to discuss his futures trading Kim's eyes began to glaze over before he'd gotten much beyond the opening quotes. Anything to do with numbers seemed to push the off button in her mind. Larry's heart and body might prefer Kim, but the rational man said that if he knew what was good for him, he would forsake chaos, no matter how alluring, and find someone like Honoria, who came with bundles of boodle and a mind that loved thinking in decimal points.

And so he was living a waffling life, one definitely against his principles of reason and order. He was seeing Kim three or four nights a week, making fierce love to her, but uncertain if he wanted anything more than that. But he was also giving the dice the option of his asking other women out. And after his infamous market countercoup, Honoria telephoned and congratulated him. Was she open to seeing him again? My God, come to think of it she still had his ring! So when the die chose an option that he take Honoria out to lunch and 'see what happens' he did, but at the lunch Honoria was aloof, clearly waiting for him to make the first move, and his dice didn't give him the go-ahead.

When he told Kim about these dates, he was relieved that she simply shook her head and said, 'Go ahead.'

'I am not going to let you romanticize the competition,' she told him, 'which is what you'd do if I tried to prevent you from seeing Honoria or any other woman. I know it can't be easy to give up what she can offer you, but . . . ' and she grinned, 'you may end up finding it's a lot easier to give up that than what I can offer you.'

'And what can you offer?' asked Larry.

'Me,' said a challenging Kim.

Nothing like a little overconfidence.

Of course Kim was a woman, so one time when he showed up unexpectedly at one of the clubs after a woman he'd had a date with had stood him up he found Kim in a supply room in tears. She claimed she was crying because she felt like crying, but Larry, in one of his rare moments of insight, guessed that she couldn't understand how he could still be ambivalent towards her.

Neither could Larry.

But the dice began to clarify matters. They chose a one-in-thirty-six shot that he write Kim a love sonnet and, though she spent ten minutes suggesting various subtle ways the poem might be improved, Larry could tell she was pleased. She became kittenishly feminine and incredibly sexy and he would have raped her on the spot if the spot hadn't been the dirty-towel room at her midtown health spa.

And then the die chose a one-in-six shot and ordered him to buy Kim a five-thousand-dollar gold necklace and take her to one of the most expensive restaurants in the city, a place famous equally for its snobbish clientele and outrageous prices. This was the first time he had given Kim *any* gift or even taken her to a high-priced restaurant.

Larry was somewhat depressed that the dice seemed to have a tendency to choose expensive options. If they hadn't also been making the very money he was being forced to spend he might have lodged a formal complaint. Seated opposite Kim at a small, exquisite table, where everything around them glittered expensively, he tried not to think how much it was going to cost. A bottle of champagne – one that even Mr Battle might have bragged about – rested glowingly in a bucket of ice. A vase of roses stood on one side of their table.

Kim, dressed in what for her was expensive luxury, but was in fact only a simple but elegant cocktail dress she'd bought at T.J. Maxx, was fingering the necklace that lay in modest splendour on her lovely bosom. Her face was flushed with pleasure.

'I can hardly believe it,' she said. 'I didn't think I could be a sucker for something like this. But it's so beautiful. It even looks real.'

'It better be real,' said Larry a little irritably.

'I've never known you to show such extravagance,' she added.

'Neither have I.'

'Maybe this is a side of you the dice ought to develop more strongly,' she went on, looking at him playfully. 'Maybe I'll find I like the hundred-dollar wines better than draught beer and gold necklaces better than my usual costume jewellery.'

'Shame on you,' said Larry. 'Where are your values!?'

'And this restaurant,' she said. 'The one time I mentioned it you shuddered.'

'Not as much as I'm shuddering now,' said Larry, who had picked up the menu and was looking at the prices. It was poster size, its extensive area apparently needed to contain all the zeros.

'What shall we order?' asked Kim, picking up her menu.

'God knows,' Larry said. 'Let's hope they have bread and water.'

Afterwards Kim invited him back to her apartment in Brooklyn and they made marvellous love. While Larry lay back in post-coital bliss, Kim gaily went and brought in a tray with a pot of tea and a pint of some sweet liqueur, and they got into a discussion of Larry's diceplay. He felt his dicing would lead either to his finding his father or to his father's coming to him, but he was determined to avoid the error his father had made in creating wild options that let the dice ruin his marriage and his family.

'And who or what is this family that you're so determined to protect?' asked Kim, puzzled. She was sitting up against the headboard of the bed, wearing only a white T-shirt that managed to highlight what it covered and not cover much else. She was holding a saucer and cup of tea.

Larry thought about it and then moved so that he could look at her more directly.

'It's you,' he said. 'You're now my family.'

Those nice words were good for some spilled tea and a long kiss. When they had wiped up the dampness, Kim, teary-eyed, said that those were the nicest words anyone had ever said to her.

'It means I love you,' said Larry.

'Don't undercut your good line,' said Kim, wiping her eyes and smiling with her more normal mischievousness. 'Dozens of men tell me they love me, but none has ever before said I'm family. That's almost a proposal.'

That gave even dewy-eyed Larry a slight start.

'Almost a proposal,' he said quickly. 'But notice that I avoided the real thing.'

'Naturally,' said Kim. 'I haven't manoeuvred you into it yet.'

— *51* —

Reality, with its infallible nose for a human being who begins to get too cocky, took a good sniff at me and went to work. One evening, when Kim had to work until eleven, the dice picked at random that I read a book by Ram Dass extolling the spiritual value of service, of giving, of sainthood. Before I knew what I was doing, I found that from various do-good options I'd given the die, it had chosen that for one whole day I try to be a complete saint.

I felt a burst of excitement, but then began to fear that although sainthood was fine and dandy in books, in life it might not work out too well, especially on Wall Street. When Kim came home I quickly made love to her before the start of my saintly day at midnight necessitated celibacy. I wasn't sure what a saint's attitude towards lovemaking would be, but doubted it would be as favourable as mine.

Kim, of course, was enthusiastic about my becoming a saint and urged me to take it all the way, to let myself go, to pray, give and serve every second of the following day.

I spent a restless night, but began the next morning with a sincere prayer to the Lord God Almighty, a Being with whom I'd been in only remote and sporadic communication most of my life. I prayed that I be able to discover and express the saint in myself, and obey God's will in all that I did.

The prayer had an unexpected elevating effect. I felt love not only for Kim but even for the cats, whose habit of tearing my socks to ribbons had begun to annoy me. And even for Judy, Kim's roommate, whose fierce feminism I didn't normally find endearing, a feminism so strong it made Kim seem a conservative homebody in comparison. I gave Judy a hug that morning that the poor woman had no way of interpreting; I think she concluded that Kim and I had had a fight and I was coming on to her. She righteously pushed me away.

The mood still hadn't worn off when I reached the office. I found I was smiling benevolently at one and all. When I saw that some of the men looked so uptight that if the Dow opened a point lower that morning they might disintegrate I had all I could do to resist hugging them.

When I saw Jeff leaning over a monitor at a trader's desk and staring with the intensity of a man watching a surgeon operate on his wife's heart, saw him watching and yet knew that most of the markets hadn't even opened yet, I felt a rush of love and pity that could not be held in check.

When Jeff looked up and saw me, his face grimaced into what I'm sure Jeff thought was a welcoming smile but was more like the nervous tic of a man having a noose placed over his head. I went up to embrace him, throwing open my arms with a glowing smile.

Jeff, whose day-to-day expression normally varied only from worry to terror, revealed something I'd never seen before: confusion. Was I undergoing a seizure? An attack of indigestion? The effects of too many tranquillizers? Jeff was too astounded to move in time to avoid the bear hug that I now captured him in, but he was together enough to stand rigidly within it, so that I had the feeling I was embracing a thick concrete slab.

'Relax, Jeff, relax,' I said, as I released my prisoner and took a step back to look warmly into his eyes. 'Why don't you take the day off and . . . go to the ocean.'

I was firing him: I'm sure that was the only explanation Jeff could find for this mad embrace and even madder suggestion. A day off!? A trader take a day off!? Traders did not take days off. Traders knew that they were like the legendary Wally Pipp who took a day off from the Yankees once in the 1920s, was replaced on the field by Lou Gherig, and never played again. Traders had been known to survive gunshot wounds by muggers but still stagger in to make sure nothing happened in the markets while they weren't there.

'Bean oil is up again,' replied Jeff, looking as if he hoped I'd simply taken too many tranquillizers. Jeff had done that once and thought that having the March bonds go a full point against him was funny! After that he'd never taken another tranquillizer, and was proud to tell everyone he'd never found anything funny since.

'Of course bean oil is up,' I said benevolently, wondering why Jeff cared. 'And if it weren't, it would be down.'

Definitely too many tranquillizers, Jeff concluded and began to ease away.

'The important thing,' I went on, 'is to do our simple best in order to make more money to give to the poor.'

'Right,' said Jeff, glancing at the man whose monitor he'd been staring at. The man was too sleepy to notice what was going on. He was a stockbroker, not a futures trader, and thus could afford to be sleepy and afford not to know what was going on.

'And please, Jeff,' I continued, 'remember that the things of this world are but trifles, that whether we make money or lose money is but a speck of dust in the eye of the universe.'

Of course whether we made or lost money *was* the fucking universe, and every trader knew it, or if he didn't he was soon losing money and was even sooner no longer a trader. Jeff scurried away to his own private cubicle and I continued on to my office.

In preparing the morning trades I knew I had to let moral principles be uppermost in my mind, and I'm afraid I probably overdid it. I ordered my men to buy wheat because it was the source of the staff of life, to sell cattle and pork bellies because they were being cruelly butchered for mere money, to sell the D-mark to punish the Germans for the Second World War, but buy the Swiss franc to encourage neutrality. I had them sell oil futures to cut down pollution, but buy bond futures to support the Government's effort to clean up the pollution. As for the stock market I saw that most of the companies owned in the various BB&P-managed accounts were definitely sources of evil and would have to be sold – the tobacco stocks, oils, paper companies, advertising firms, chemical companies, banks, all defence stocks, the auto stocks – by the time I was finished I'd come up with sell orders on most of the thirty Dow Industrials, pausing only over dear old Procter and Gamble, until I remembered they produced aerosol products that were causing the ozone holes that were frying penguins all over the world.

By the time I was done, it was quite clear that my indicators must have come up with a major sell signal: my morning trading orders seemed to contain nothing but 'sells'. At first some brokers either phoned or tried to ease into my office to check on the validity of or reasoning behind my sell orders, but after one or two reported that I seemed stoned out of my mind and couldn't be shaken from my sell orders, they ceased their efforts. The word spread, first through

BB&P, then out into other brokerage houses: Larry Rhinehart was selling. I, one of the most creative traders to come along in years, was selling. The stock market opened lower and headed south.

A half-hour later Mr Battle was standing behind his huge glass pingpong-table desk and looking with fear in his eyes at Larry.

'I don't know what you're talking about,' he said nervously.

Larry, eyes glowing, yearned to communicate.

'It's simple,' he said. 'To begin to cleanse your soul you simply begin to give your fortune away to the poor.'

'Nonsense,' said Mr Battle. 'That's unconstitutional.'

'In time you will be able to surrender all of your worldly goods – '

'Stop saying that!'

'So that your spirit will be free to – '

'No, no, no!' snapped Mr Battle, putting his hands up to cover his ears. 'I've worked hard for thirty years to earn my money and I don't believe in giving any of it away except when the Federal government reimburses me with tax write-offs.'

'But the holy book itself says that it is harder for a rich man to enter heaven than for a camel – '

'I don't care about any holy book!' exploded Mr Battle with near panic. 'Or camels either! What's wrong with you!? Money is the whole purpose in life!'

Larry felt a surge of sadness as he saw the fear-filled Mr Battle, and he slowly began to move around the desk towards him.

'But dear sweet sir,' he said earnestly, 'I feel such overwhelming love for you.'

Mr Battle blinked at the approaching Larry and went into a frightened crouch.

'If you knew how giving up everything would cleanse your spirit . . . ' continued Larry.

Mr Battle, now in terror, began backing away around the other side of his desk as Larry, arms outstretched, continued to move towards him, his face lit with the characteristic glow of the totally mad.

As he went around the far corner of his desk Mr Battle began desperately to punch at his desk phone.

'Miss Riggers, get security! Get security!'

But with Larry almost upon him, Mr Battle finally had no choice: he began jogging towards the door.

Security and Mr Battle ended up concluding that Larry was no immediate threat to the community, a conclusion considerably aided by the fact that the stock market was down over thirty points and Larry had saved the firm's clients hundreds of thousands of dollars by selling on the opening. Rumours were rife on Wall Street that Larry Rhinehart had some inside information that would break later in the day and send stocks down fifty points. To protect themselves, a lot of people sold, thus sending the Dow down fifty points.

When Larry announced at noon that he was taking the afternoon off, panic swept through the upper and lower echelons of BB&P. What should they do? Sell more? Begin buying back at these lower prices? This was a volatile day; it was Larry's duty to stay at his post and monitor things. Larry tried to ease their concerns.

'Take no thought for the morrow,' he suggested. 'Do the lilies of the field worry? Does a sparrow fall without God watching? Surely the good Lord can keep an eye on cotton futures.' As for the stocks that they'd sold at the opening, they were all 'bad', and thus should not be bought back. Larry left, and behind him the word went out: don't buy, the rout will continue.

Larry went to his bank four doors down and withdrew five thousand dollars in cash, all in tens and twenties. It was time to put his charitable feelings into practice. He had no clear plan, just the knowledge that he had to give.

Out on Broad Street, crowded now at midday, he felt suddenly self-conscious, suddenly aware of his normal being of Larry Rhinehart, aware of being dressed like a normal Wall Streeter in suit, tie and brightly shined shoes. Passing a small import-export shop with exotic-looking clothes in the window he impulsively marched in. Ten minutes later he less impulsively walked out, now wearing over his suit a brown robe that was something of a cross between a Mexican serape, a choir robe and a Franciscan monk's robe. In any case, it definitely muddied the image of a Wall Street tycoon.

Back on the street, he was again overwhelmed with doubt, meaning that all his old habitual feelings and attitudes came surfing in, judging what he was about to do as idiotic. Larry had been, like every man who was healthy, wealthy and wise, blind to the millions of his fellow creatures who were not healthy, wealthy and wise. Like most Wall Streeters he was normally perfectly capable of stepping over the body of a homeless man in mid-sidewalk not only without missing a stride but without missing a decimal point in the financial figures he was tossing around in his mind or with a colleague. The homeless scattered in such rich abundance about the city had become objects of such grim familiarity as garbage cans and windblown debris and were considered no more significant.

Had there been only a hundred homeless citizens, New Yorkers would have wailed and rallied together to develop programmes to care for them. But with hundreds of thousands of the homeless, and wailing and programmes having been tried for many years with no measurable effect, New Yorkers did what all healthy, wealthy and wise humans do when confronted with suffering that they haven't directly caused and can't see how they can significantly help: they stopped seeing it. Or, when they did see it, they felt mightily annoyed both with the sufferers and those public officials who couldn't devise a programme to get the sufferers out of sight.

On most occasions Larry gave more generously than most — handing out dollar bills with a guilty commiserating nod and scurrying on. But today he stopped in the middle of the crowded sidewalk and, head down, tried to pray himself back into the role of saint.

'Lord, I have pledged today to be a saint,' he said to himself. 'I need your help. Inspire me to think always and only of others . . . no matter how stupid it makes me feel . . . ' Yes, that was exactly it. He repeated the words to himself until he could feel again the old rush of love for poor mankind. He reached under his brown robe and drew out the first fistful of tens.

He began to move slowly along the sidewalk, heading north, and every now and then reached out to offer a ten-dollar bill to one of the approaching New Yorkers who looked particularly unloved, whether rich-looking or poor. But New Yorkers have had long experience of what people do or want on their sidewalks and most immediately swerved to avoid him, pulling away as if from a leper offering his disease.

'Bless you, my son,' he said to one young man who looked as if he were close to tears. 'Please take this.'

The young man veered away.

'Bug off, buddy,' he said.

Finally one man absent-mindedly took the ten that Larry was offering and, as Larry continued on, stared at it, fingered it, held it up to the light and finally, shrugging, dropped it in a litter basket he was passing.

Two or three others took the ten and after examining it, also shrugged, stared back at Larry, then pocketed the ten and moved on. In Manhattan the unexpected is the norm.

'Bless you, my dear,' Larry said to an attractive and innocent-looking young woman approaching him. 'Please take this.'

The girl stopped in fear, stared briefly at the dewy-eyed Larry, then made a sharp right turn to cross the street, causing a car to brake to a screeching halt and the cab behind it to crash into its rear. Larry walked obliviously on.

When Larry tried to give to a distinguished but sad-looking older man, the man moved cautiously around Larry.

'I already gave at the office,' he said.

In the first hour of his walk through the Wall Street area heading north Larry was able to give away more than fifty of his tens and twenties, most of which were kept. Then his trek began to take him out away from the financial district and towards the Bowery. When on the less crowded First Avenue Larry offered a ten to a wiry young black man the man stopped and eyed Larry suspiciously.

'What's this for?' he asked.

'For you, my son,' said Larry. 'For your needs.'

'Dis is entrapment, you know. I ain't offered you nothing.'

'I want nothing, my son,' said Larry. 'Only to give you my love.'

'I knew it.'

'I mean Platonic love, my son,' explained Larry glowingly.

'I don't do none of that kinky shit,' said the young black man and wheeled away.

By the time he reached the Bowery Larry had attracted a following. As he moved along the litter-ridden, derelict-ridden street, a large group of winos, down-and-outs, and homeless followed him, each clutching a few ten-dollar bills. As Larry leaned down to give a sleeping or drunken derelict crumpled against a wall one of his bills, one of his escort would swoop down and snap it away so fast the poor victim, befuddled in some cases perhaps by alcohol, concluded the ten-dollar bill had only been a brief mirage.

But all good things must come to an end and, finally, Larry reached into his pockets and, after coming up with a few scattered bills, realized he was broke. As he dug fruitlessly into his pockets the trailing derelicts clustered closer.

'You run out of blessings, kid?' asked one old man.

'All I have are the clothes on my back,' announced Larry solemnly.

'I'll take the robe!' shouted a woman.

'The shoes!' shouted the wiry man.

'Me the shirt!' cried another.

Soon Larry disappeared in the excited throng surrounding him.

When Larry returned to the offices of BB&P at 4.30 that afternoon it was a momentous occasion. Unbeknownst to him the stock market had decided that day – with only the slightest of nudges from Larry's minor selling – to collapse, to take one of its infamous brief freefalls that make strong men weep and weak men weepier. Not only that, but staff-of-life wheat had rallied, and cruel cattle, hog and pork belly futures gone down. The people of BB&P knew that their clients had mostly avoided the worst consequences of the stock market fall, thanks to Larry's brilliant morning marching orders. And his trading in the agricultural futures was nothing short of miraculous. So that when he suddenly appeared after his four-hour disappearance, the roomful of brokers and traders and clients were prepared to burst into cheers.

Unfortunately, Larry had emerged from the elevators dressed only in his underpants, socks and a torn and dirty T-shirt, and accompanied by two New York City policemen.

It was a momentous occasion. All work in BB&P came to a halt as one and all turned to stare at their returning ?hero?, who stood, in his shorts, gazing at them benevolently from between the two cops.

What happened next is a tribute to the fearless and undeviating value system of lower Manhattan. Lesser men would have seen a man who was a little crazy, dressed as if he was ready for Bellevue, in the custody of police. The workforce at BB&P saw through all this. They saw a man who had just saved (and thus made) a ton of money.

After perhaps a ten-second hesitation to remember their value system, the men and women of BB&P burst into applause, then cheers. They hailed the conquering hero.

The conquering hero blessed them.

From Luke's Journal

With Chance there are no limits on change since there is no reason or purpose or morality to limit them. When Chance rolls out her developmental Dice – whether biologically, culturally or individually – she rolls out failure after failure after failure, and then, once a day, decade or millennium, rolls out a combination that the most intelligent and purposeful of creators could never have imagined or produced.

As long as the individual takes himself or his society seriously, then there must be control and purpose, and the possibilities of change are limited. When the flow of individuals and societies are seen as elaborate games, then the changing of the rules in order to make the games more fun, more challenging, more interesting, becomes a more acceptable possibility. Of course men today usually take their games themselves with such seriousness that rule changes are almost as difficult to come by as modifying Moses's ten commandments.

52

By the end of that afternoon I was intoxicated with doing good. I was mad, of course, insane by most standard definitions, because I was letting some saintly force within me that normally never got expressed run wild over my usual selves.

After I'd sent Miss Claybell out to buy me some new clothes – simple garb for a simple person: black sweat-pants and sweatshirt and sneakers made in Bulgaria – I spent the last part of the afternoon in my office, not to go over my supposedly miraculous indicators as my colleagues assumed, but to write out cheques for various charities, some on my own account, others on BB&P's behalf. By the time I was done I'd given away close to a hundred and fifty thousand dollars, half from me, half from BB&P. Although it had just been the Christmas season, a part of me wasn't absolutely sure Mr Battle would approve.

As I busily worked giving away the firm's funds various people came in to congratulate me on the day's trading – Brad and Jeff and even Vic Lissome. Vic even admired my black sweat-pants and shirt.

'I'd give anything to be able to dress like that,' said Vic lugubriously and then weaved his way out of the office for some refreshment.

By the time I'd finished my acts of charity the offices were mostly empty and it was seven in the evening. As I serenely stood up to leave I became aware of someone standing in the doorway: it was Honoria.

We hadn't had much contact since my descent into the dicelife, just the one formal and unsatisfactory evening out and two or three phone calls. As she stood silently in my doorway, dressed in a simpler and less elegant dress than was her usual style – a stodgy grey and a bit baggy even – all my conflicts about whether to re-establish my old life or to blow it to smithereens came rushing in.

We were both silent for almost twenty seconds, the only sound the hum of dormant computers and monitors being used by dedicated type-A personalities.

'I have to see you,' she announced. 'Have you eaten?'

'How . . . did you know I was here this late?' I asked.

'I've been waiting down in the lobby since 5.30.'

Somehow the picture of Honoria waiting in a lobby for anyone reawoke the saint; I hurried over and put my arm around her.

'I'm sorry,' I said. 'What's the trouble?'

She stood stiffly in my arms, her eyes not meeting mine but looking past me as if studying a stock monitor.

'You haven't phoned me in almost two weeks,' she said in a low voice.

'I'm sorry. I've been leading a selfish life.'

Honoria now turned slightly in my loose embrace and for the first time looked up into my eyes.

'I've been selfish too,' she said, still in that low, unauthoritative voice that seemed so different. 'I let your . . . financial troubles . . . alienate me when I should have been there for you, supporting you in your hour of need.'

'No, it was my fault. I took my losses too seriously. I forgot that getting and spending is all chaff on the wind. I should have called you.'

Honoria began to search my eyes, apparently thrown a little off balance by my responses.

'I . . . I have something . . . rather . . . strange to tell you,' she said, and again, after her long searching of my eyes, she lowered her face. 'It may upset you.'

'Go ahead and tell me,' I said, squeezing her shoulder. 'Nothing will upset me. I'm really happy to see you again.' In the mood I was in that day I was overjoyed to see just about everyone.

'Oh, Larry, I've been such a selfish shit,' she said, her head averted. 'You're the only decent person in my life and I've thrown you away. You can never love me again.'

'Nori, I'll always love you.'

Again Honoria raised her head to search my eyes, then sighed.

'I'm pregnant,' she said.

Even a saint gets knocked off kilter every now and then: I stared down at her in frozen benevolence.

'I was never . . . unpregnant,' Honoria continued. 'I lied to you that time last month. After I saw how upset you were I couldn't go through with the abortion I'd planned.'

'It's . . . our child?'

'Of course,' she said, a brief hint of the usual Honoria steel getting into her voice.

I stepped back to look down at her belly, hidden by the loose grey dress she was wearing.

'That's . . . wonderful,' I said.

'I'm going to have the child,' she said, reverting to her modest soft voice. 'I hope that will please you.'

'Of course it does. It would be monstrous to do otherwise.'

After an awkward silence she dared to look up and slowly raise her left hand and hold it out for my inspection. On the fourth finger she was again wearing my engagement ring. I felt a wave of dizziness: Kim Kim Kim! What's happening!? Save me!!

'You're engaged!' I said stupidly.

'I hope so,' she said, lowering her hand to gaze at the ring.

'That's great,' I said and, with a sick smile on my face, wheeled away to grope for support at my desk.

'Daddy thinks we can still arrange the wedding for 28 February,' Honoria said, looking relieved that I was acting with an understanding that passed all understanding.

I was reeling: I seemed trapped in a nightmare with some stranger self controlling the storyline in ways that portended disaster. Still, some deep basic dice man integrity was keeping me faithful to my temporary saintly role.

'Wonderful!' I managed and then turned back to face her. 'But first I have to tell you a few things . . . confess a few sins.' The 94 per cent of me that wasn't a saint began screaming at me to shut up. Honoria simply smiled at me, probably happy to be able to forgive me my little peccadilloes as I'd forgiven her hers.

'I'm afraid I may not be a worthy husband for you,' I continued in a low voice.

Honoria, standing only a few feet away, showed no response other than a brief narrowing of her eyes.

'I've been doing some . . . diceliving . . . like my dad . . . ' I began. 'And . . . having an affair with Kim.' Shut up, shut up, shut up! shouted several of my normal selves, but the saint rambled on.

297

'We've been fornicating many times a day and . . . enjoying it – horribly.'

This time Honoria's eyes flashed, her body becoming straight and rigid.

'However,' I went on, 'since I'm the father of your child I'll of course do whatever you want – marry you or not, even though, well, I'm obviously unworthy.'

Honoria was now the old Honoria, standing erect and proud, her head raised.

'You're a bastard!' she said.

'You're right.'

Her eyes narrowed and I sensed her wondering whether I was trying to wiggle out of my responsibilities by declaring myself a sinner. She got hold of herself.

'Perhaps you are,' she said quietly. 'But I will not deny our child having a father.'

'You're right, of course,' I said. The 94 per cent of me that knew its ass from a hole in the ground buried its head in a pillow and groaned.

'You are that father,' she continued coldly, 'and I expect you to assume all your responsibilities. Clearly you must totally break with Kim. If you ever sleep with her after today you'll never see me, the child or, I'm sure, your job again.'

'Ahhh . . . '

'But that's just common sense,' she said with a sudden unexpected relaxation of her fierce posture and tone. 'I'm being too negative. I must remember that I told you I wasn't pregnant and haven't been as warm to you as I might have been, so your little fling is both understandable and forgivable.' She reached forward and took one of my hands and looked up at me with a small smile. 'Just never again.'

The saint was in shock. So were all my other mes. I stood there and with superhuman effort managed to avoid reeling.

'Of course,' I said.

53

Reader, reader, reader, what had I wrought? I had anticipated that Kim was chaos and that my father's ways were chaos, but never in my worst imaginings did I anticipate what chaos was like. The advantage of building walls around your normal mainstream self is that all the other yous are locked out and can't usually do much more than pound on the walls and wail. But now that I'd begun knocking down those walls and letting a few of my other selves run free into existence I was finding that it's inconvenient to be more than one person. Lukedom might be organized to let my mes exist, but not Manhattan, and certainly not Honoria.

I retreated that night alone to my East Village apartment in such a state of confusion that not only couldn't the saint function but neither could any of my other selves. I handled a phone call from Kim by saying I wasn't feeling well, a statement of unequivocal truth. At midnight I was still awake and still uncertain what I wanted to do with my life. Did I lust for Kim or love her? Was it moral to marry Honoria or immoral to marry her if I didn't love her? Was it wise to marry Honoria and thus keep my job and fulfil the long-held masterplan of the rational, ordered man, or did wisdom rather lie in giving up her, my job, and my masterplan and follow my heart (or was it my loins?) to whatever life would bring with Kim?

I wondered if my father had ever faced a moment like this in his disintegration. Were my mother and our family and his job his straight and narrow path to unhappiness that he found he had to give up? If that was so, then my deserting Honoria and the unborn child would be my abandoning a child just as he had done – only when the poor child was only five inches long instead of five feet. It infuriated me to see this link. Was my not marrying Honoria really the same as his abandoning Lil after a marriage of almost thirteen years? Was my abandoning an unborn child the same as his –

Seeing these horrible parallels tended to make me want to repudiate my father, the dice, and – by some sort of association I wasn't sure of – Kim, and reaffirm my old life. But other forces, equally strong, pulled me towards my father and Kim.

In any case, that night I put my father's green dice back in the box Jake had given me and stuck it back up on a high shelf of the bookcase. Whatever was to come was going to be my decision (but which me?). I would continue to lead my usual business life, but would tell both Honoria and Kim that I was on a personal spiritual retreat that would last all week and which would prevent me from seeing either of them. This would seem to be irrational nonsense but would be completely consistent with the irrationality of most of the rest of my recent life.

Honoria took my 'retreat' in her stride, apparently thinking it was the same saintly me that she'd confronted that evening in my office, but Kim was angry. She resented my not telling her exactly what was going on and, when I wouldn't go into any detail, hung up on me.

So I tried to throw myself into my trading. It happened to be in the middle of January of 1991 and the United States government had given Iraq until 15 January to make a graceful exit from Kuwait, the oil well that it was hurriedly pumping dry. While politicians debated what the President might do on the 15 January deadline, Wall Street knew: he would blast the bastards back into the Stone Age. You don't ship fifty billion dollars' worth of men and materiel five thousand miles and then let them rust. You use them as soon as you can.

I found myself unmoved by the excitement felt by traders both in BB&P and elsewhere. For weeks I'd been experiencing what others would call 'burnout', but which in my case was something worse: I was beginning not to care about making money, whether my trades made money or lost it.

I continued to go through the motions, monitoring and adjusting my indicators, once or twice even flipping a coin to decide, but for the first time in my life I wasn't bothering to keep my own records on a daily or even a weekly basis. The fact was, although neither I nor my colleagues were aware of it at the time, my trading had barely been breaking even except for the day my saintliness had scored its great coup. However, my reputation had grown so big since the President's Aids day that everyone assumed I was doing well even when I wasn't: they noted and talked about my winning trades and ignored the losers.

Jeff, I learned, had entered a new stage too, a stage of tranquillity. The words 'Jeff' and 'tranquillity' had been, of course, absolute opposites for as long as Jeff had been a human being, but after he'd discovered dicetrading, he confided in me, all his worries and fears and nightmares disappeared. He had gotten in touch with the voice of God. Being in touch with the voice of God permitted him to know precisely what the Gods wanted, and whatever the Gods wanted must be, as far as he could see, exactly what he should want.

This religious insight had come early in his dicetrading. He'd huddled in his cubicle hiding his list of options and his dice from the other traders and let chance choose what trades he was to make. He had first prayed that he do nothing to challenge the Gods' exclusive right to know the future. His initial trading had been mixed: some trades had made money and some had lost. But it was a sharp, normally painful loss in gold futures that had given Jeff his insight, salvation and peace of mind. After a die told him to go long and the market had then begun to sell off he had naturally begun biting his lips, his nails and his tongue, bouncing on both feet and wringing his hands. Then he saw it.

The Gods controlled the fall of the die; They wanted him to go long even though They knew the market was going to sell off; it was Their Will that he lose on this particular trade! There was nothing he could do about it; it was Their Will!

Jeff said he felt a sudden release from two decades of tension: the Gods controlled everything and therefore Jeff could relax; nothing he could do could change Their Plans; he was putty in Their Hands. But by bowing to Their Will he was one of Their Favourites. He might lose on gold today, might lose again for a week, a month, a year! but in the long run the Gods would honour his subservience and take care of him. At that moment he became one with the flow of the universe and a happy man. The dice were the Instruments of the Gods, the ultimate surrender of man's presumption, and thus the vehicle of Jeff's salvation.

From that moment on he became as absurdly serene as he had been absurdly nervous. He moved around the offices of BB&P like a man who had not only taken several tranquillizers, smoked some powerful pot and was slightly brain-damaged, but also like one who has inside information denied to all other men, inside information that will permit him always to win while others falter. That was exactly how Jeff felt.

The other traders, not knowing what I knew, watched him with awe. This was my right-hand man, and they could see now why the two of us were so successful. Somehow Jeff had an infallible inside source. When one trader challenged Jeff, Jeff just nodded serenely and said: 'And *my* Inside Source is never wrong.'

The other traders could only look on in envy and awe.

Just as most traders anticipated, the war started promptly on the sixteenth, and the markets gyrated wildly. While others raced around the trading room in a state of near hysteria I indifferently made some adjustments and placed my orders. With Jeff gliding through the office like a serene angel (or as a lobotomized freak, as one trader claimed) and I showing not much more concern, our reputations as infallible insiders grew. But I found it all rather boring.

Not so for Mr Battle. Mr Battle loved war, especially when his side had all the best weapons, men and materiel, and, as an added bonus, even had right on its side. And even more especially when it looked as if the enemy, Iraq, was pulling a rope-a-dope strategy of letting themselves get clobbered until the US ran out of ammunition, an event that Mr Battle calculated wouldn't occur until the twenty-third century. Never had a war been so lopsided. Never had Mr Battle dared to hope that the trillions spent on the military over several decades would actually get to be used. Guns were being fired! Bombs were being dropped! Missiles! And without more than a handful of Caucasians dying! It was a warrior's wet dream.

It also helped that after the first day the stock market was soaring and all his clients and brokers were making money. Wars are always more enjoyable when you're making money.

And the Japanese bankers were finally coming round. They had been quite impressed by my remarkable December comeback. Although for some reason they still couldn't figure out my knack, they were coming to New York to complete the negotiations that would lead to their making a major capital investment in BB&P and hire BB&P to manage a major futures fund they would develop.

Mr Battle decided to throw a party. He would throw the biggest party of his life to celebrate the war and the invasion of the Japanese and his having in his future son-in-law the most acute trader since Jerry 'Fix It' Smoot. He would invite the Japanese bankers and everyone who was anyone on Wall Street.

— *54* —

The decisive day of my life occurred at the Battle country estate overlooking the Hudson on the day that William Fanshawe Battle III held his First Annual War Party. Actually he called it, on the advice from his PR department, a 'Celebration of the Triumph of the Human Spirit'.

He'd invited Mr Sato, the President of the Nagasaki Sumo Bank, his wife, and two senior vice presidents, good old Akito and Mr Namamuri, to spend the whole weekend at the estate, the better to impress them with the quality of his friends and business associates. Mr Battle seemed to feel that one of his chief selling points to them was my increasingly inexplicable knack, and he hoped my scientific approach to trading would be the seal to the deal he wanted to make.

At a private *tête-à-tête* a little before noon he impressed upon me how important this party was to the success of BB&P and urged me to be at my most charming and technical. I nodded.

The party was scheduled to begin officially at two o'clock and last until God knew when. It was an eclectic party, to say the least. Guests could play poker, baccarat, or watch the war on CNN on any of the four conveniently located television sets. They could eat at any of five buffet tables or drink from any of three bars, all colourfully prepared by Celeste's Heavenly Hosts. They could dance to a band that had promised no heavy metal, or swim in the heated indoor pool. They could even talk.

Kim had not been invited to the party, for reasons that seemed obvious to all concerned. The night before, she and I had had a phone tiff about my going to the party without her. I told her I was still on my 'spiritual retreat' and going solely as part of my job and not to be with Honoria. After a long silence on the line Kim had then spoken with quiet anger: 'When are you going to start creating your own life again?' she said softly. 'I'm getting a little tired of your shilly-shallying!'

'I know and I'm sorry,' I said. 'But whatever move I make next will irrevocably affect the rest of my life. I'd sort of like to know what I'm doing when I'm doing it.'

'Human beings never know what they're doing when they're doing it,' she countered. 'The smart ones just go ahead and do it anyway.'

And she hung up. Since Honoria had hung up on me three times that week for roughly the same reason – my sitting on the fence – I was used to it and no longer wondered if the phone company had cut us off.

Having been ordered by Mr Battle to arrive early, I wandered through the rooms feeling very detached from the proceedings. I was feeling more out of place than ever, a stranger accidentally plopped down in a life I'd never intended.

When I met Honoria in a hallway we greeted each other cautiously, both wondering the same thing: whether I was going to marry her and live happily ever after with the Battle millions or be a fool and do something else.

When I wandered into the kitchen I was surprised to see Kim busily laying out food on one of the half-dozen serving carts. She was dressed in the blue and white uniform of Celeste's Heavenly Hosts. I approached her almost as warily as I had Honoria.

'What are you doing here?' I asked.

'What's it look like?' she answered. 'I am earning my living.'

'I mean – '

'Me and the die figured out that if you can't get in the front door, there's always the back one,' she said. 'So I convinced Celeste she could use someone like me who knew the inside of this place.'

'But why?'

'I didn't think you should be unsupervised at a party like this,' she said with one of her mischievous smiles.

'Ah,' I said.

'Don't worry,' she said. 'You won't even notice me.' And with that she went back to spreading out what looked to be egg rolls.

'Mr Rhinehart, sir?' said the suddenly appearing Hawkins. 'A Mrs Ecstein has arrived and would like to see you.'

I turned reluctantly away from Kim and trailed after Hawkins, wondering what the unpredictable Arlene was up to this time. I knew she'd been invited to the party – after all, she was one of BB&P's better new clients – but wondered why she was asking for me.

Arlene greeted me just outside the main kitchen in one of her younger versions, with dark hair and wearing a conservative business suit. She was also carrying a ridiculously large and apparently full plastic shopping bag.

When I came up to her she handed me a copy of the *New York Post*.

'Have you seen this?' she asked pleasantly, as if sharing some amusing society item.

I never read the *Post* and, this being Saturday, hadn't actually seen any newspaper. The *Post* page-one headline was its usual succinct self: 'FEDS FLUSH FLAKES'. And then a smaller headline: 'FBI and DEA officials raid dice communes'.

I began reading. Page three indicated that officers from several federal and state agencies varying from drug enforcement to the IRS had raided three illegal communes – Lukedom in Virginia, Chanceton in Colorado, and Dice in California. They'd arrested over one hundred people, including Jake Ecstein. One article painted a sewery picture of life at the communes: slavery, brainwashing, cult religion, random sex, religious sacrilege, gross overcharging at restaurants, tax evasion, and rampant car theft. There was supposedly fanatical cult worship of the masterfiend Luke, who allegedly just escaped from the raid on Lukedom only minutes before it began.

The two *Post* articles were more restrained than the *World Star* article of four months earlier, but not by much. The only new contribution I noted in my quick browsing was to suggest that my father had a secret cadre of thousands of underground followers who had infiltrated important sections of American life. FBI official Putt claimed that the bureau was gathering evidence that indicated secret dice men in various banks were seeding bank computers with random elements that had led to many cases of masses of money being erroneously shifted from one account to another, with thousands of people spending or vanishing with the unexpected windfall before the errors were caught. He also claimed that dicepeople in the US and various state governments had intervened in the decision process to bring about all sorts of bizarre decisions that 'normal, rational' government would never have made –

although how the bizarre decisions of normal rational governments could be distinguished from dice decisions Putt didn't make clear.

An IRS official claimed that the two hundred thousand erroneous tax refunds the IRS had sent out the previous year had been the result of another nefarious dicing infiltrator. And the Virginia State Police were looking into the probability that dicepeople in Lukedom were running one of the largest car-theft rings in the east. On the other hand, as far as I could see, there was no mention of finding any underground hideout under Lukedom's mountain.

The *Post* had three photographs, one of three hippie women smiling vacantly in front of a teepee; a second of two sober-looking FBI agents manhandling a cheerful-looking Jake; and a third, naturally, of Luke Rhinehart, the same old photo taken many years earlier of Luke smiling benevolently at the camera.

I shook my head.

'It blames it all on Luke,' I said. 'But my father wasn't even there.'

'Oh, well, a little fiction never hurt anyone,' said Arlene sedately. 'Besides, I saw several sentences that verged on accuracy.'

'You've been there?' I asked.

'Oh, yes. I take my vacations at one or the other — it's like going home.'

'I'm sorry about your husband,' I said.

'Oh, don't worry about Jake. He's just happy to be back on page one again. If all of life is an act, then it's nice to have a larger audience to play to.'

'*Have you seen this*!?' shouted Mr Battle, storming down the hall toward us brandishing a copy of the *Post* like a subpoena. 'This is horrible!'

'I don't think my father has been to these places in years,' I said.

'It makes no difference! His name is associated with this lunacy! What will the Japanese think!? You've got to change your last name!'

'The Japanese don't care about anything in the *Post*,' I said. 'They never read anything that doesn't have at least half the text in numbers.'

'Well, the least you can do,' persisted Mr Battle, 'is issue a statement totally dissociating yourself from your father and this lunatic dice business.'

'Well, I'm certainly willing to dissociate myself from my father but — '

'Larry,' interrupted Arlene, handing me the paper and pointing. 'I think maybe you should read this.' She was pointing to the last paragraph of the long article, a paragraph which, in my first browsing, I hadn't read. With Mr Battle peering over my shoulder, I now did.

'Agents said that Wall Street speculator Larry Rhinehart, the son of Luke Rhinehart, had recently spent a week in Lukedom, apparently preparing new financing for the community.'

'Deny it!' boomed Mr Battle. 'You were in my house every day that week!'

Arlene pulled me away from my distraught boss and, again speaking as if she were just sharing light gossip, let fall another bombshell.

'And did you know that Lukedom does all its banking through the Nagasaki Sumo Bank?' she asked.

'You mean . . . Akito . . . !?'

'Just thought you'd be interested.'

'We'll sue the *Post*!' interrupted Mr Battle, pulling me away from Arlene. 'They have no right to mention our firm! We never finance anybody!'

I pulled myself from Mr Battle and wandered away. Chaos was making another comeback.

55

The guests began to arrive, and nothing quiets the passions of civilized people faster than the arrival of their guests. Mr Battle, who had been raving at noon, was smiling warmly and radiating welcome and goodwill by two. Larry, who was frightened and upset at noon, changed into his most conservative business suit and by two was ready to impress the Japanese with his brilliance and reliability.

It had been agreed that the subject of Luke and the dice communes should not be mentioned, and that if others brought it up, it was to be dismissed as idle gossip or old news or totally trivial. Mr Battle was prepared to say that Luke Rhinehart was actually Larry's stepfather and that Larry had refused to have anything to do with him for fifteen years. Larry may have briefly visited Lukedom, but only in an effort to rescue his distant cousin Kim who had been lured there by false advertising. The idea that Larry had gone there on a quest to find his father to tell him off was not one that stood up to close scrutiny; Mr Battle dismissed it out of hand.

Honoria, now dressed in a lovely, flowing, figure-masking off-the-shoulder red dress, saw Larry briefly before the guests began arriving. She gave him her sympathy about the *Post* story and assured him that she wasn't going to let that prevent her from marrying her baby's father.

'Since they still haven't caught him,' she added matter-of-factly, 'my father thinks you may be able to weather this *Post* thing. However, we do think it's best you deny ever being in Lukedom. Who will believe the word of one of those dicepeople against yours?'

Right. Who indeed?

'Dicepeople are very unreliable,' he said with bitter mischief, suddenly aware that he and the enemy were one. And then the guests began to flood in.

When Larry saw Akito he went straight to him and asked whether his bank was handling Lukedom's affairs. Akito responded by smiling blandly and bowing his head.

'Oh, yes,' he said. 'Good client.'

'And do they get their financing from you?'

'Oh, no. We're just middleman.'

'The funds come from a company called DI, right?'

Akito simply smiled and bowed again.

'I can say nothing about DI,' he said.

'I thought I was your hotshot trader friend!'

'Of course, but this company is very particular about its privacy.'

'I'll bet it is,' said Larry, wheeling away.

The guests continued to arrive. All the leading lights of Blair, Battle and Pike were there, including Brad and Jeff and even Vic Lissome; there were all the firm's wealthiest clients, including Mr Potter and Arlene, who had inexplicably reincarnated herself in her blonde wig and an odd sequined dress that made her look like a retired madam. There were all of Honoria's business associates at Salomon Brothers, many of the males flocking around her like bees to honey. Dr Bickers wandered in, looking serious and morose like a good therapist. Agent Macavoy came disguised as a conservative banker and thus looked not unlike an FBI agent. Putt turned out to be working with Celeste's Heavenly Hosts, disguised as a waiter, but being so alert and narrow-eyed he resembled an ageing pervert with his eye out for boys.

Mr and Mrs Sato and Namamuri were there, Mr Sato with a personal translator always at his side. Mr Sato was the head of the Nagasaki Sumo Bank, a slight intense man with fiery eyes who always looked as if he was about to spring at something. The Japanese mingled humbly and shrewdly with the bankers and investors and brokers, bowing and smiling and knowing that this party, like the war it celebrated, was all only the brave front of the pitiful American giant in decline.

At first this vast panorama of society mingled together with precisely that mixture of wit and wisdom that Mr Battle always hoped for. Larry spoke with deep seriousness (he was trying to keep his mind off the *Post* article) to Mr Sato and his translator about the necessity of always monitoring one's technical indicators and updating the software. He assured them that the collapsing Tokyo stock market was only in a temporary bull market correction, telling them this not because it was what he thought but because it wasn't considered good salesmanship to tell people whose money you were after that their booming nation's economy was built on quicksand.

Jeff spoke passionately to Akito about the necessity of throwing out charts and software, ignoring technical indicators, and developing faith in the Gods. He assured Akito that the collapsing Tokyo stock market was not just a bull market correction but probably the long overdue Divine Retribution.

Honoria circulated, telling anyone who asked that she and Larry were a happy twosome again and that rumours that their engagement had been broken off or the wedding postponed were sheer fabrications.

Jeff began playing poker, letting a die determine how much he bet on each round; the other players soon feared he was a ringer. Some of the younger crowd decided to go swimming and started a water volleyball game. The older folks, which was most of the guests, settled into some serious drinking and gossiping. Dr Bickers was not playing anything, but moved sociably around the room mumbling 'Mmmmm' at all the right places and thus impressing everyone with his intelligence. Mr Namamuri gravitated to the indoor pool and the water volleyball to watch the women's breasts bounce. Macavoy infiltrated the poker game and went broke.

Arlene Ecstein was playing her dicelife, varying her personality every fifteen minutes, exactly as her mentor Luke had done twenty years earlier. Her six personalities that day were grandmotherly society matron, secret mistress of Mr Battle, thoughtful intellectual, bank president, uninhibited nymphomaniac, and retarded bag lady who had once been Mr Battle's secret wife. When appropriate she would repair for a change of costume or wig from her huge bag stored in one of the guest bedrooms.

She carried all her roles off to perfection. She convinced Mr Sato that her bank – Eckle's Bank and Trust of Hempstead – was something his firm should look into. As society matron she made Honoria feel that perhaps her stunning off-the-shoulder red dress was a bit *de trop* for this particular gathering. As nymphomaniac she had Macavoy cornered in a large closet with his pants down when the fifteen minutes was up, and she became a thoughtful intellectual commenting on the severe psychological debility often experienced by men having a small penis.

Mr Battle, being a shrewd host, had urged all the bartenders to serve the stiffest drinks, consistent with people actually being able to down them, and soon a large minority of the guests were beginning to feel that this was one of the most wonderful afternoons of their lives. Friends who were normally utterly boring now seemed the soul of wit; a woman who had always seemed sexless now stirred fires in normally cold loins; business comments which could be summarized as stating that the market might go up and it might go down now appeared of uncanny wisdom.

But then the tragedy struck.

People began to gather around one area of the main living room and became so engrossed in something that others began to feel left out. Someone had brought in two copies of the afternoon edition of the *New York Post*. Its headline was the same, but now there were three articles about the raid on the dice communes. The third, a short one, said evidence was being gathered that linked the prestigious old-line Wall Street firm of Blair, Battle and Pike to the financing of Lukedom. The heart of the story was little more than that Larry Rhinehart had recently spent some time in Lukedom, that he was the son of Luke Rhinehart, and that he was a Vice President at Blair, Battle and Pike. A new page three headline read simply: 'WALL STREET FUNDS ORGIES?'.

There are two ways to respond to that question. First, one can be shocked. Second, one might comment that Wall Street has done a lot worse. In any case it was a provocative question, especially since the Wall Street firm in question was heavily represented at this party. Soon guests who had read the articles, or heard a few paragraphs from them, or who had overheard someone quote from a snippet from one, were happily circulating to commiserate with the employees of Blair, Battle and Pike and particularly, of course, with the unfortunate Larry Rhinehart.

The sizeable minority that was enjoying the liquor and the punch and the champagne found the whole subject of role-playing and random living and orgies rather amusing, but more sober guests were shocked and angry. Either angry at Larry and Blair, Battle and Pike for funding such abominations, or at the *Post* for having falsely accused them of doing so. The party became livelier.

Soon Larry found himself surrounded by a cluster of people asking him what Lukedom had been really like, attacking him for not practising safe sex, and commiserating with him for having been falsely accused of being at such a sick place and for having such a horrible father. He wasn't sure which attitude he hated most. But he no longer felt like a cool reliable hotshot. He could use a drink.

Arlene, whenever her diewatch signalled she play thoughtful intellectual, expounded the philosophy of diceliving to any and all, and when she was tossed by chance into desperate nymphomaniac she sometimes used the dice to try to get her prey loosened up. She began to pass out dice, a supply of which she apparently had in her large plastic bag. Since in one of her random incarnations she had told some guests she was the mistress of Mr Battle ('kept locked away most of the time'), and these guests, knowing a good conversational opener if they ever heard one, had repeated this information to any and all, it soon became common knowledge that the secret mistress of the host was handing out dice and advocating the dicelife.

This further polarized the party into those who were offended and those who felt that whatever a person as rich as Mr Battle thought was in must, by definition, be in. Some of the guests began to make decisions and play roles with the dice.

Larry, despite two double scotches, was still annoyed at whatever people said to him. They were all either assholes for believing the *Post* story or assholes for thinking he was funding the communes or assholes for thinking that Lukedom was an abomination or assholes even for attacking his father. Mr Sato was the straw that broke the back of Larry's restraint.

As translated by his aide, who stood so close to Mr Sato's right side that they were frequently mistaken for Siamese twins, Mr Sato said: 'I am so sorry your father has disgraced himself. American society is very sick to permit such chaos and lack of discipline. We are sure you and your firm have nothing whatsoever to do with this man and his theories.'

'Well, fuck you,' said Larry, having nothing personal against Mr Sato except that he was the guest who happened to be in front of him when he could no longer hold himself back. 'My father hasn't disgraced himself because, for one, he wasn't there, and for two, there was nothing happening at Lukedom to be ashamed of . . . '

The 'fuck you' opening to Larry's speech doubled the size of the crowd listening, and the doubling attracted further people. Mr Battle himself hurried over, hoping that Larry was distracting people from Lukedom by discussing pork belly futures.

'It so happens that my father founded Lukedom as a social experiment for freeing people from leading drab, repetitious, trapped lives,' Larry went on. 'Like most of the people in this room. The crazies I met in Lukedom were a lot happier than most of the crazies here.'

'What about the orgies?' asked a voice from the fringe.

'The orgies were terrific,' Larry found himself shooting back. 'So was the master–slave game. The only problem I had at Lukedom was rampant car-borrowing and the restaurant tabs.'

'Is it true your father has people scarifice themselves?' asked another voice.

Mr Battle began tugging desperately at his sleeve.

'Absolutely,' answered Larry. 'That's what my father's dicelife is all about: sacrificing yourself. If an individual isn't destroyed every day my father gets depressed.'

This elicited a fair amount of comment, not all of it favourable.

'Do you follow your father's philosophy?' someone else asked.

'Of course no – ' Mr Battle tried to get in.

'I use the dice all the time,' interjected Larry loudly. 'Especially in my trading for my clients.'

An awed silence greeted this remark, broken only by Mr Battle's long low moan.

'Why, without the dice I'd be just another investment adviser,' Larry went on. 'But with the Lord Chance working for me I double people's money in two years. How do you think I've been so successful?'

'Jeff, Jeff!' screamed Mr Battle desperately. 'Tell them Larry's lying!'

Jeff, standing at the edge of the gathering crowd with his newly-acquired serenity, moved in next to Larry and turned to Mr Battle with a gentle smile.

'Of course, we've been using dice,' he said serenely. 'Anything else would be blasphemous.'

A long sigh of awe rippled through the financial sections of the crowd. Akito's alert eyes narrowed in wonderment, and Mr Sato was listening so closely to his translating aide that his ear seemed glued to the man's mouth.

'No, no, no,' interrupted Mr Battle desperately. 'It's absolutely not – '

'What about the secret cadres infiltrating all of American life?' asked a fierce-faced lady at the fringe of the crowd.

'Absolutely,' said Larry. 'Why, who before now suspected me of being a secret diceperson? Or Mr Battle here? If Blair, Battle and Pike are working secretly to turn the world into Lukedom, how many others must there be?'

How many indeed. The listeners were awed by this prospect. Mr Battle a diceperson! That took some adjusting to. But then, of course, thought some, his poor mistress was one. And the man who had been his scheduled future son-in-law. And his daughter had been to Lukedom too, according to the latest rumour making the rounds. And that cousin – Kim something.

'This is preposterous,' tried Mr Battle. 'Why, I – '

'Is your father as nutty as he seems?' asked some fellow at the fringe.

'Of course,' said Larry, getting into the swing of things and downing another glass of champagne someone handed him. 'But it's all a fake. He's actually a deeply serious man intent on changing the world by blasting the chains of reason and consistency.'

'Where can we get some dice?' asked a young hotshot banker.

'I've got some, Sonny,' said Arlene from nearby.

The party from that point on proceeded to go in a direction neither intended nor expected by Mr Battle. First of all, many of those guests who were morally outraged began to leave, not even saying goodbye to the host, since he was apparently one of *them*.

But then, after Mr Battle had abandoned his fruitless sputtering against Larry and stood alone worrying about what people might be thinking, Mr Sato came up to him and gravely shook his hand. According to the translator Mr Sato then said: 'You are much shrewder man than we think, Mr Battle. We worry that you and your firm too stuck-in-the-muck to be good investment, but we see you have more arms up your sleeve than first appear.'

Mr Battle, who rarely spoke in less than six sentences, replied, after a pause: 'Uh, yes.'

Arlene Ecstein, playing a grandmotherly matron, came up to him and congratulated him on his party.

'Rarely,' she said in a distinctly New England twang, 'have I had such an interesting time.'

Mr Potter came up with his arm around a young girl.

'First good party you've ever thrown, Battle,' he said and, his ancient hand clawing the girl's buttocks, he staggered off.

'Uh, Mr Battle,' said Brad Burner, coming up to him pale and shaken. 'Anything I can do?' Brad was clearly appalled by all that was happening.

Mr Battle looked at him blankly for close to ten seconds, as he pondered the mystery of life. Was it possible that diceliving was a genetically inherited disease?

'Uh, yes, Brad,' he finally said in a subdued voice. 'Uh, perhaps you could . . . uh . . . send someone out to get more dice.'

But of course it didn't work out for Mr Battle that way either. The party really did get out of hand. When Kim saw what was happening she began introducing people to the emotional roulette she'd learned at Lukedom, and for half an hour about two dozen people got caught in a crying jag. After Arlene introduced a few people to a dice version of spin-the-bottle couples began to disappear into closets, bathrooms, guest rooms, patios, cellars, attics or, in one or two absolutely inexcusable cases, simply behind or up against the nearest piece of furniture. The water volleyball soon became topless waterball, then nude water volleyball and then nude volleying, and then simply nude balling.

Arlene and Kim encouraged the waiters and waitresses to abandon their narrow roles and join the party as guests or hosts. Guests were encouraged to become waiters and waitresses. One young man took his duties as bartender too seriously and added two dozen ecstasy pills to the supposedly non-alcoholic fruit punch. As a result, many of the more sober-minded guests at the party began to feel somewhat disoriented and laid-back and sensual and to find the abundance of naked flesh flashing in the hallways less objectionable than they'd first thought.

All this might have worked out well enough, and at first it did. Mr Namamuri cornered four of the bouncing breasts he'd been watching all afternoon and, with a little help from the thousand-dollar bills spilling from his suit jacket pocket, got all four breasts into the library, where he perused them at his leisure.

Mr Sato with his aide-translator tightly beside him introduced himself to a lovely woman and invited her to join him in the guest bedroom where he was staying and experience ancient Oriental lovemaking technique, and see why Japanese men were so 'big' in the world. Unable to resist such an idea, especially since her employer Shearson Lehman was also on the make for some of Sato's millions, the lovely young woman went with him. She had a pretty good time too, although it did make her slightly inhibited at first having the translator lying on the bed fully clothed, his mouth always at Mr Sato's ear.

But all good things must come to an end, and so too did Mr Battle's memorable 'Blast the Bastards' Party.

The dénouement began when Larry finally made up his mind – with the usual disastrous consequences.

He was standing a little drunkenly amid a group of guests who were looking upon him with awe when Honoria broke into the circle looking frazzled and frightened.

'Get me out of here,' she said. 'This is the worst thing that's ever happened to me.'

A bit sobered, Larry groped at her arms to steady her and then led her out of the circle of onlookers, though several followed.

'There's no place to go,' he said. 'This is your house.'

'This is hell!' she hissed. 'If I'm stupid enough to forgive you for causing this disaster, the least you can do is take me back to New York.'

'We can't escape this in New York,' he said, trying to guide her away from the several people who were persisting in following. 'I'm Larry Rhinehart – I'm carrying hell in my genes.'

Honoria came to a halt and pulled herself out of his grip.

'What are you saying?' she asked him.

'I mean that if you let me into your life then you have to accept chaos,' Larry said. 'I'm beginning to see I can't live without it.'

'I see,' she said, drawing herself up straighter. 'And does choas include Kim?'

'I'm afraid so,' he said.

Honoria glared at him for a long moment, biting her lower lip.

'Then I'll go alone,' she said, her voice almost cracking. 'This whole mess is your fault. I'll never understand why I had any hope you could escape your father's madness.'

'I'm beginning to feel that way myself,' said Larry, but Honoria had already wheeled and was striding away.

Seeing her leave, Larry felt a wave of sadness and wondered which fate was worse for her – with him or without him.

But otherwise everything was at last completely clear.

He went looking for Kim and soon found her happily teaching a group of five of Celeste's employees how the dicelife worked. He pulled her away.

'I've never seen people having so much fun in this house,' she said to him. 'Why, I think I even saw Hawkins smile.'

'My life is over,' said Larry.

'It is?' said Kim. 'That's wonderful!'

'You're all I have left in the world,' announced Larry. 'I want you to be my wife.'

'Oh you do?' she asked gaily as he began steering her out of the dining area and into a hall. 'Only when I'm the only one left do I get asked – some proposal!'

'That's not what I meant,' said Larry. 'I love you and want to marry you. Period.'

As the two of them passed Dr Bickers, he eyed Larry and nodded.

'At last,' he said, his most detailed comment of the entire party. Larry, oblivious, passed on.

'I'll tell you what,' said Kim. 'I think I'd like to marry you, but I'd like to know how some of the other dice-yous vote on this matter.'

'It's not a dice-me, it's me-me,' said Larry, leading her up the staircase towards the second floor.

'Maybe,' she said. 'Still I won't say yes until you've proposed to me on three consecutive Saturdays. How's that?'

'My love is eternal.'

'Yes, I know,' said Kim. 'But from what I've heard most marriages feel as if they last a lot longer than that.'

On the second floor Larry steered her down the hall and opened a door to a guest bedroom.

'What are we doing?' asked Kim.

'I'm sure we'll figure out something,' said Larry, and in they went.

Meanwhile, Arlene Ecstein noticed the demure wife of Mr Sato standing in sad dignity all by herself watching bright-eyed the astounding events around her. She went up to Mrs Sato and whispered in her ear. Mrs Sato shook her head: she didn't speak English. Arlene frowned and then pointed at Jeff who was weaving uncertainly but serenely in their general direction, and then poked a finger in and out of a circle she made with the fingers of her other hand, pumping her pelvis at the same time. Mrs Sato's eyes brightened further and she minutely bowed.

Arlene grabbed Jeff by the elbow and, as they passed Mrs Sato, she grabbed the Japanese woman's hand and the three of them weaved their way through the living room towards the hallway. When Jeff questioned their purpose, Arlene explained that it was the will of the Die and Jeff, relieved, walked serenely on. As they were passing Dr Bickers, the grave old philosopher eyed the three of them keenly and said, reverting to his usual succinctness: 'Mmmmm.'

When Arlene led them into a guest bedroom she was surprised to find it being used by Larry and Kim, but the bed was king-size and this particular Arlene was not high on the niceties of social decorum. Mrs Sato had never been to a party in the United States before, and since everything up to this moment had seemed somewhat past belief, Arlene's leading her and Jeff to a big bed already occupied by another couple, who were so busy at what they were doing they were oblivious, seemed right in the American style. Jeff, of course, never questioned the wisdom of the Gods.

The rest, of course, is history.

Mr Sato, having taught his new female friend from Shearson Lehman all he knew of ancient Oriental lovemaking technique (which, if truth be known, was the same as modern Western lovemaking technique) began looking for his wife. Mr Battle began looking for Larry. Several men were looking for Arlene.

When Hawkins was asked by Mr Battle if he knew where any of these people might be, he replied with an uncharacteristic giggle that he did, and led them up the stairs to a guest bedroom off the main hallway. Mr Battle, Mr Sato, his translator and several other hangers-on waited as Hawkins, having regained his dignity, gravely opened the door.

On the bed, sitting with his back up against the headboard, was a glassy-eyed and bare-chested Larry. To his left was a smiling and also bare-breasted Kim. To his right was Mrs Sato, giggling demurely, her small breasts jiggling in time to her laughs. Neither Arlene nor Jeff was anywhere in sight, although a toilet flushing could be heard from the guest bathroom.

For a long moment Mr Battle and Mr Sato and the other guests stared in silence at Larry, sprawled back against the headboard between the two women, and Larry and Kim stared back at them.

Then Mr Sato turned to leave. He was feeling a lot less enthusiasm for Larry's knack.

56

Most of the guests had an enjoyable and interesting time at the First Annual Battle 'We Beat Their Pants Off' Party, but on Monday morning they had to face the real world of Manhattan.

Mr Battle had to face the press. After an all-morning session with his public relations people and his partners, their strategy was in place: Larry Rhinehart was obviously a secret diceperson who had infiltrated Blair, Battle and Pike and even tried to seduce Mr Battle's daughter Honoria. Fortunately, he had been exposed by the courageous work of federal law enforcement officials and the *New York Post*. As soon as the story had broken Mr Rhinehart had been dismissed from the firm and expelled from the Battle household. In revenge he had put ecstasy and LSD in the drinks of the Battle house party honouring American war dead and encouraged the guests to run wild. He had even tried to rape the wife of a visiting Japanese businessman, but been halted by the timely intervention of wiser heads.

He also vigorously denied rumours of Honoria's wearing a diamond engagement ring and of scheduled February nuptials. She had broken off her engagement a month earlier, already suspicious of Larry Rhinehart's strange behaviour. To recover from the trauma of the party she was taking a three-week vacation in a weight-reduction spa in Puerto Vallarta.

Mr Sato, it turned out on Monday, appreciated that Blair, Battle and Pike had more arms up their sleeve than he'd thought, but didn't think he wanted to do business with an octopus. Although his senior Vice President Mr Akito seemed intrigued by Larry's 'knack' with dice, Mr Sato decidedly wasn't. He could put up with a great deal, but not the sight of his wife in bed with a vice president of the firm he was supposed to be investing in. Besides, he had discovered at the party that Shearson Lehman had an asset he'd been unaware of and he hoped, with any luck, to prolong negotiations with them for at least another week.

Jeff Cannister was promoted to Larry's post of Vice President and Chief Futures Trader. Rumours that he was a diceperson were categorically denied. People had only to look at his exemplary life of total dedication to the markets and his newfound serenity to know the rumours were false. It was said that Jeff had been a stabilizing influence on Larry and almost saved him from his just fate.

Dr Bickers crossed Larry off his list of patients and began treating Arlene Ecstein. She claimed she was afraid she was a multiple personality. 'Mmmmm,' said Dr Bickers.

As for Larry and Kim, they were on their way to find Luke.

From Luke's Journal

The purpose of society is to train human beings to take themselves and their roles seriously.

Our purpose is to free human beings from the training of society.

It is necessary to resign from the human race – with a forged signature, of course.

— 57 —

In the sky above the Pacific Ocean, in a first-class seat of a JAL Boeing 747, I sat staring out of the window, an unread copy of the *Wall Street Journal* on the empty seat beside me. I was surrounded mostly by Japanese businessmen, several of whom stared at me, then at their newspapers, then back at me, whispering to each other with various degrees of awe. For several days the *Post* had found the Battle party newsworthy.

As I sat there I wondered what had happened to my life. Only four months earlier I'd been well on the road to success, happily employed, happily engaged, confident and secure in all I did. Now I was on the road to failure, unemployed, unengaged, unconfident and insecure. All because of that horrible idea of finding my father. With that single act I had inadvertently set in motion events that seemed to have undone my life. Thank God.

Inadvertently. Accidentally. By chance. With the simple intention of just finding Luke I had somehow created a situation in which the tabloids were damning me and praising me as the 'evil offshoot' or 'worthy successor' to the very father I'd just months ago set out permanently to disown.

Where was the justice in the world? Where the reason? Where the logical, inevitable, rational unfolding of events that let a reasonable man get ahead in the world?

Kim came suddenly down the aisle and sat down happily beside me. I wasn't too sure how happy I was going to be as a failure, but though she'd been fired from her job with the health salons – her boss not taking kindly to her sudden open-ended trip to the Far East – Kim was as cheerful as ever. Since Mr Battle had now totally cut her off, and her lifetime savings consisted of less than eight hundred dollars, she couldn't really afford this trip, but I'd put our tickets on a BB&P credit expense card before my alleged attempt to rape the wife of the firm's most important client had got me cut off.

'I liked my old life,' I said when she had settled beside me.

'So that's why you spent all those hours with psychotherapists,' she commented.

'I liked my old life – even my complaining about my father,' I said.

'Now you've really got something to complain about.'

'I bet by the time I find out where my father is he'll be dead,' I said. 'At the last minute he'll disappear – just like he did when I was twelve.'

'He might have to,' said Kim.

'What's that mean?'

'That FBI agent we saw in Lukedom is in the back row of the plane, puking all over the place.'

'Really?'

'Really. You're still not the only one interested in finding dear old dicedaddy.'

At the Tokyo airport Larry and Kim cleared customs and found a cab to take them to the nearby train station to get into Tokyo. Putt and Macavoy, close behind, leapt into the very next cab and Putt leaned forward and shouted: 'Follow that cab!'

The Japanese cab driver nodded cheerfully, slammed down the meter and zoomed off. Putt, eyes gleaming, sat back in his seat and watched his cab quickly come up behind the one that contained Larry. He turned to smile at Macavoy.

But then his cab suddenly passed Larry's cab. Was this some clever Oriental method of tailing that the cabbie was using? Putt looked behind to see what was happening to Larry and saw the other cab make a right turn and move off in another direction.

'Hey!' shouted Putt. 'The other way! He went right!'

The Japanese smiled and nodded and went even faster as he tore up the ramp to get on the expressway to Tokyo.

'No, no, no!' shouted Putt. 'Other way! Reverse! Turn around!' He made circles with his hands, he pointed, he shouted, he raved, he collapsed. Through it all the cab driver merely smiled and nodded. The meter ticked on.

Ditonics was housed in a medium-sized skyscraper in the heart of downtown Tokyo. The architecture was magnificently modern, with long concrete curves, huge planes of glass, and several monumental modern sculptures. The building epitomized everything that Lukedom was not. When their cab from the train deposited them in front of this edifice, one look at it made both Larry and Kim feel that they must be on a wild goose chase. No element of chance could have created this building or the wealth necessary to pay for it. Their hearts sank.

The lobby was equally impressive, with the ceiling almost a hundred feet above the main part of the lobby and magnificent curved staircases soaring up to the various levels that led off this main lobby. Their hearts sank further.

But then there was the logo: a cubic design with the letters D and I in two of the three visible sides of the cube. Of course a cube didn't have to represent a die. But then again, why the name Ditonics? Was Ditonics a Japanese word? Could Luke really have had anything to do with this corporation?

One of the receptionists spoke flawless English. When they told her they were here to write a history of the corporation for a New York magazine she referred them to their Public Relations Director.

Mr Uro also spoke English, and after they had established their interest in the history of the corporation, Larry asked casually how the corporation had gotten its name. Mr Uro said he didn't know. Larry asked what the logo was supposed to mean. Mr Uro said he didn't know. Kim asked if an American named Luke Rhinehart had had anything to do with the creation of the corporation. Mr Uro said he didn't know.

However, he was clearly made uncomfortable by these questions. After having a woman bring them tea he asked to be excused for a short time.

Half an hour later he apologetically returned and said he had found someone who might perhaps better answer their questions.

Mr Mora was an elderly Japanese, dressed, as were all the men they met, in the standard business suit. He was a frail man with a mild twinkle in his eye who greeted them warmly in a large office on the thirty-ninth floor. He understood they were interested in the history of Ditonics and had mentioned an American named Luke Rhinehart.

'May I ask what your interest is in this American named Luke Rhinehart?' Mr Mora asked.

326

'I'm his son,' Larry said. 'I haven't seen him in fifteen years. I want to find him.'

'And why do you think he might be in Tokyo?' asked Mr Mora.

'Because Ditonics has been sending money to some enterprises that my father created many years ago and to his old friend Jake Ecstein,' answered Larry.

'Ah, is that so?' said Mr Mora, nodding and with his omnipresent soft smile. 'How interesting.'

'We thought so,' said Kim.

'You must know something about that funding,' said Larry, 'and therefore something about my father.'

'Is that so?' said Mr Mora, nodding and smiling. 'How interesting.'

'So would you mind sharing this knowledge with us?' suggested Kim.

'That would be interesting, too,' said Mr Mora. 'But first it is my duty to take you on a tour of Ditonics. I cannot explain the funding you speak of unless you know about our whole corporation. Will you, please?'

Mr Mora had risen from behind his desk and began to leave the room, bowing and beckoning Larry and Kim to follow. In the anteroom outside, a nervous-looking Mr Uro was waiting. Together the four of them began to take a look at Ditonics.

What struck Larry most strongly about the corporation and its operation was how closely it resembled what he had read about every other Japanese corporation. Everywhere they went everyone seemed to be working hard; everyone was dressed like everyone else; each office seemed similar to the one before. They saw a group of employees doing calisthenics before lunch, another group meditating. They saw massive armies of computers.

Mr Ura explained that Ditonics was a multifaceted company dealing primarily in creating computer software for design programs for other companies. For example, they had created many design programs that Toyota and Honda and other Japanese car companies used in designing their automobiles. Ditonics had created other programs for the Japanese fashion industry, which, he pointed out, was now one of the leaders in the world. Also design programs for leading architects, including the one that had designed the building they were in. They also created design

327

programs for Sony, Hitachi and other Japanese producers of video and sound equipment. They also created video games.

In addition to their computer software work, they invested in other enterprises throughout the world, usually on a small scale – as with Lukedom. They also funded studies about the effectiveness of some of these enterprises.

After an hour of peering at one roomful of hard-working Japanese men after another and the seemingly endless monologue of Mr Uro on the boring businesses of Ditonics, Larry and Kim were at a loss to see what all this had to do with Luke Rhinehart. Then Mr Mora invited them to lunch.

The three of them ate alone in the executive dining room.

'You ask earlier,' Mr Mora said, after they had eaten the main meal and were lingering over brandy, 'if Luke Rhinehart create Ditonics. Not so. Ditonics founded by Japanese computer expert, Iko Tarowu. However, something we not yet tell you throw a different light on Ditonics.'

He paused, took a sip of his brandy and, eyes twinkling, went on.

'Ditonics has succeeded because we have secret formula,' he said. 'Formula created by Iko Tarowu more than twelve years ago.' Again he paused. 'Mr Tarowu developed technique of introducing random elements into every piece of design software. He felt that as animal species have been improved over millions of years by chance mutations so too designs might be improved by chance mutation.'

Larry and Kim watched him, listening, knowing that this was leading them closer to Luke Rhinehart.

'In designing a car you feed in variables and design values and you push button and you get nice-looking car. A car that is nice-looking like other cars have been nice-looking. With random element introduced you get ugly cars, cars with flaws, cars with big noses or no ears, cars with one leg or pimples.' He smiled broadly for the first time. 'And, one time in ten thousand, you get beautiful car, a car beautiful and interesting in a way rational software never produce. You get a successful mutant.'

Larry and Kim simply waited for him to go on.

'Actually I say one in ten thousand,' Mr Mora went on after a brief frown. 'Not so. It more like one in ten million. We don't just introduce one random element into software, but have to introduce many different random elements in random combinations in order to create our beautiful mutants. But when we succeed we come up with something that no one else ever think of, something no one else's software ever possibly come up with, because everyone else following reason and cause and effect and purpose and these can only lead to slight modifications of things we already have and know. Ditonics alone produces mutants.'

He leaned back in his chair and looked pleased.

'Did Mr . . . Iko know Luke Rhinehart?' asked Kim softly.

'Mr Tarowu,' Mr Mora corrected. 'Yes, he did. Mr Tarowu was . . . what do you call it . . . hippie in London in early 1970s. He read your father's book. He conclude chance is important. He return to Japan and became Japanese again. He create Ditonics.' Mr Mora smiled.

'Does my father work here in Ditonics?' Larry asked.

'Not any more,' said Mr Mora without pause.

'Where is he?' asked Larry.

'Your father is in Zen monastery near Kyoto,' answered Mr Mora.

'Thank you,' said Larry.

'He is expecting you,' said Mr Mora.

— *58* —

When Larry warned Mr Mora that American FBI agents had followed them to Tokyo and that his father might be in danger of being arrested Mr Mora nodded as if this was old news and said simply: 'We are taking care of the matter.'

'May I ask how?' said Larry.

'We are preparing for them a grave,' said Mr Mora.

Both Larry and Kim had protested that this seemed to be carrying things unnecessarily far, but Mr Mora had simply nodded and assured them that everything would be taken care of.

On the train to Kyoto the two of them tried to figure out what the implications were of all they'd learned. Were the Japanese involved in Lukedom because of Luke's past association with the founder of DI, or because he still had influence in the company? But Mora had said Luke was retired. They agreed that it was DI's money that must have created the hidden complex in the Lukedom mountain and the sophisticated television prgramming. Was their money also behind the things that the FBI had claimed were going on in the IRS, other government agencies and some banks? Was DI systematically introducing random factors throughout the world? Was this good or bad? Did his father know what was happening or not?

When they'd exhausted their speculation Kim suddenly looked at Larry mischievously and announced that it was exactly one week since the Battle party and that the day was Saturday. It took several repetitions before he grasped the significance.

'Ah, yes,' he said. 'I proposed to you and you said – '

'Exactly!'

He casually took out a coin.

'Heads I pretend I don't know what you're talking about,' he said. 'Tails I ask you again to marry me.'

Larry flipped the coin in the air, grabbed it and opened his palm to look at the result.

'Will you marry me?' he asked.

'Ask me again next Saturday,' she said.

The monastery was in the hills on the outskirts of Kyoto, a lovely wooded area, seemingly remote but actually only a thirty-minute drive from the city.

A brown-robed monk greeted them as if they were expected. He led them from the gate through a lovely lush Japanese garden, then through a stone garden with seemingly randomly-placed boulders in the middle of raked pebbles, and finally into a wooden structure. They passed by the entrance to a meditation hall in which about thirty monks were walking about in a large circle chanting something in Japanese.

Their brown-robed monk passed them on to a second brown-robed monk, who smiled and nodded and seemed suspiciously like Mr Mora in disguise. In fact, in their discussions on the train Kim had raised the question as to whether this monastery might be a put-on, or Luke's presence here a one-day show. But a guidebook they'd picked up in Kyoto indicated that this was a well-known Japanese Zen monastery that had been in existence since before the Second World War.

The second monk led them out of the wooden structure and on to a dirty path that began to wind upwards towards a ridge. After they'd hiked about twenty minutes, the monk smiled and nodded and indicated they were to proceed further upwards on the path on their own.

So they hiked on upwards; twisted small pines and some sort of Asian shrubbery closed in the path except where occasional openings gave a vista of a small valley and stream below.

'My God,' Larry said after a while. 'You don't suppose my father's gotten religion, do you?'

'It looks that way.'

Finally they arrived at the top of the ridge and began to move along it. Ahead through the trees they soon saw a wooden roof. As they drew closer they saw it was simply a large roofed shelter.

Inside, seated cross-legged with a laptop computer, facing the open vista of the valley below, was a brown-robed monk.

They came to the edge of the shelter and paused. The monk, seen in profile, was Caucasian. His head slowly turned to look at them; Larry knew it was his father.

Luke Rhinehart had aged. He was greyer and had less hair, and was decidedly thinner than he'd been twenty years earlier. Without hesitation, he arose from his lotus position and approached. He stopped about five feet away and gazed at Larry. Larry was aware that, through the thick glasses his father wore, tears were forming in his eyes.

'What took you so long?' his father asked with a sudden smile that for some reason reminded Larry of Kim.

Larry was in a state of shock. If you've spent fifteen years visualizing a monster, and four months chasing a monster, an old man in monk's robes with tears in his eyes was definitely a shock. When Luke now came up and put his arms around him and embraced him, he could only stand stiff and frozen.

'But I'm glad you're finally here,' his father added. 'And I thank you for coming.' Then he released Larry and stepped back.

'Hi,' he said to Kim.

'I'm Kim Castelli,' she said, looking at this man in almost as much shock as Larry.

Luke nodded and looked back at his son. Then he suddenly broke into a big grin.

'Arlene told me about that house party last weekend,' he said, chuckling and shaking his head. 'Ah, those were the days.'

Larry was still too frozen to speak.

'She's been in touch with you?' asked Kim.

'Yes,' said Luke. 'And I told her she owes you two an apology.' He paused, then smiled. 'She told me she'd considered it, but the dice had said no.'

'What . . . are you doing here?' asked Kim. Larry was still standing like a zombie.

'As you see,' said Luke, 'I'm a monk.'

'You don't use the dice any more?' asked Kim.

'Oh, no,' he said. 'I stopped using the dice fifteen years ago.'

Kim looked at Larry, then back at Luke.

'What's your relationship to Ditonics?' she asked.

'I used to work for them. With Iko. He knew computers, I knew chance. We made a good team for a while.'

332

Larry recovered enough to look at Kim, then at the surrounding hills, finally at his father again.

'Why did you never get in touch with me?' he asked.

'I did,' said Luke. 'You told me to go to hell.'

'I mean before that,' Larry said angrily. 'Or after that.'

'I didn't do it before because you were doing fine with your mother,' he answered. 'I had nothing to offer you, and your mother did.'

'Then afterwards! It's been another ten years! You accepted one teenage "no" to last a lifetime?'

He sighed and moved away back into the shelter and over to the other side overlooking the valley.

'You were doing well,' he said, turning back to face Larry. 'You continued to do well. You are still doing well.'

'How could you know?'

'I knew,' he replied simply.

Larry strode past him to the overlook and then back into the centre of the shelter and then finally right up to him. He gazed at him and then slowly shook his head.

'You're a nobody,' he finally said.

Luke smiled.

'That's right.'

'For a few years twenty years ago you were a whirlwind wild man and now you're a nobody.'

Luke nodded, still smiling.

'If Ditonics is your legacy it's the most rigid society I've ever been in,' Larry went on. 'No matter how it spends its money. It's the exact opposite of Lukedom and everything you used to stand for.'

'Could be,' said Luke.

'You've sold out!'

'Ahh.'

'You've sold out!' Larry went on. 'You stood for something . . . interesting, challenging, even enlivening twenty years ago, and now . . . you're dead, a nobody, buried here on a mountaintop . . . '

'Nobody's perfect,' he said, with that disconcerting Kim-like smile.

Mouth open and eyes blazing, Larry was shaking his head.

'For twenty years I've been hating a man that no longer exists! You killed yourself off before I could get to you!'

Luke chuckled.

'Good point,' he said.

'You're a fraud. There are people all over the world who admire you as the great experimenter, the great risk-taker, the great son of Chance, and now all you are is a nobody monk in one of the oldest religions in the world.'

'You can't win 'em all,' he said.

Larry again shook his head.

'It's sad,' he said. 'Real sad. You've given up the dice.'

Luke shrugged.

'There's a time and place for everything,' he said.

Larry looked up at him and now tears came into his eyes.

'But still,' he said. 'You're my dad.' He came forward and for the second time the two men embraced, this time each hugging the other, both wet-eyed. As she watched, Kim was smiling.

Finally they awkwardly separated.

'Can you forgive me for deserting you?' Luke asked.

Larry nodded, wiping away the tears.

'I forgive you, Dad,' he said.

The three of them began to move out of the shelter and back down the path Kim and Larry had arrived on.

'At least I forgive you for deserting me,' Larry went on. 'But Dad! You've got to get out of this monastery! You've sunk into a horrible rut! You're stuck! Here you can only lead the most limited of lives! You've given up all the important truths you've discovered!'

He stopped on their downward trek and faced his father.

'I've come to rescue you from the cage you've trapped yourself in!' he announced joyfully.

Luke looked at him with a big grin.

'That's wonderful!' he said.

The father and son put their arms around each other's waists and continued on down the path, Kim trailing.

'What you've got to realize, Dad,' Larry went on earnestly, 'is that the personality tends to get stale and you have to discover something to wake it up and keep it alive! Particularly as you grow older.'

Kim was walking along behind them, feeling joy for Larry and joy for the father. As she walked, she saw a single green die abruptly appear in the path behind the two men and in front of her. She looked up quickly but couldn't tell where it had come from.

'Thank God I got here in time,' Larry said.

'Saved at the last moment,' said his father with a grin, and with a wink back at Kim, walked on.

Epilogue

It was raining hard in Tokyo that afternoon. In a graveyard in the outskirts of Tokyo, Agents Putt and Macavoy were trudging through the downpour, peering occasionally at a rain-blurred map Putt was carrying and then trudging on. They had neglected to bring raincoats to Tokyo and the single umbrella Macavoy tried to hold over them tended to funnel the water down each of their necks.

Finally, glancing once more at the map, Putt squinted through the rain off to his right and then slipped and slid in that direction. Finally the two men came to a halt and both stared through the rain at a gravestone. After a brief pause, Putt respectfully took off his hat. The rain poured down.

The gravestone was a simple slab three feet high. On it, etched in English, were these simple words:

LUKE RHINEHART 1932–1989
MAY CHANCE BE WITH HIM